BOOKS BY BRIAN MCNATT

Estranged

The "Legends of Heraldale" series
Legends of Heraldale
Legends of Heraldale II: Past Sins
Legends of Heraldale III: Warborn

Other books set in Heraldale
A Life Out There

LEGENDS OF HERALDALE II
PAST SINS

By Brian McNatt

Cover image by KY Dalley

Copyright © 2020 Brian McNatt
All Rights Reserved.
Second Edition
ISBN 978-1-7923-0399-9
www.authorbrianmcnatt.com

Table of Contents

PROLOGUE 1
CHAPTER ONE 11
CHAPTER TWO 35
CHAPTER THREE 61
CHAPTER FOUR 81
CHAPTER FIVE 115
CHAPTER SIX 149
CHAPTER SEVEN 173
CHAPTER EIGHT 193
CHAPTER NINE 215
CHAPTER TEN 255
CHAPTER ELEVEN 279
CHAPTER TWELVE 311
CHAPTER THIRTEEN 331
CHAPTER FOURTEEN 353
EPILOGUE 385

LEGENDS OF HERALDALE II

PAST SINS

PROLOGUE

"Once upon a time, the unicorns and gryphons of Heraldale shared peace and friendship between them. With our mighty wings and their mighty magic, we forged vast and powerful realms, committed wonders to the course of history. We drove out the savage Wolf-Lords from our lands, their venomous wyvern mounts eradicated. We forged the second Caliburn, and the shield Unangreifbar. The secrets of the Elementals became known to us. To the world, a new hippogryph was born. The lesser races paid tribute to our grand towers and steel helms, while those who should have known better stayed silent, content with this hard-earned yet unequal peace.

"Yet that which is unequal cannot last. Peace, love, and friendship turned inexorably to vanity, arrogance, and a lust for power beyond the proper. Paranoia leeched into the minds of ruler and common folk alike. And at the height of their power, when they might have made even the humans of the Old World tremble, madness and folly drove those ancient kings and queens to raid a dragon's lair. A second lair. A third. Drunk with their newfound prestige and treasure, the unicorns and gryphons of old brought their combined might to Kur, the Prime Dragon, known better as Snarl to the uneducated or disrespectful, and demanded even he bow to the alliance.

"To such hubris came a matching fall. Before the great crushing winds and flames of a million dragons, the armies scattered like so much summer brush. The cities of the great alliance burned and crumbled, save for lake-bound Gateway. From every field, town, and fortress rose the lamentations of the dying. For a year and a half, the sky turned dark from the smoke of ten million fires, the land black from the soot.

"Finally, when it became clear that total extinction of her people and the unicorns was all Kur sought, Quetzal, the Prime Gryphon, intervened. Though forever maimed by her millennia-ago battle with Toqeph, the Prime Unicorn, still did Quetzal fly to meet in battle her dragon counterpart to decide the fate of all Heraldale.

"The battle lasted three moons even in the shortest reckoning. Mountains crumbled. Rivers and lakes boiled away. The earth itself was rent apart! Yet at the last, Quetzal struck Kur down with Gungnir, the Oath Spear. And upon that spear she made him swear an oath of peace, an oath that dragonkind shall never again rise up in force against unicorns or gryphons, for any oath made upon Gungnir can never be broken.

"And so, Kur retreated back to the mountains we now call the Dragonbacks, falling into a sleep that has lasted across the centuries to this day. Harmless, his people our shield against the unicorn menace. Quetzal, meanwhile, gathered what gryphons still followed her lead and brought them south, past the Dragonback Mountains. Here... to the Floating Mountain, where we shine as a beacon of hope for all peoples."

"A beacon of hope for all peoples," echoed Bifrost, half-listening as the owl-gryphon storyteller paused for questions at a pair of jade statues depicting that fabled oath-swearing. Dooepiloguers and windows had been thrown open throughout the palace for summer's sake. Curtains of purple and blue fluttered in the rose-scented breeze. The gold-flecked marble floors sparkled brilliantly in the sunlight.

Bifrost found himself drawn from the group of gryphon children, through the nearest grand set of windows onto the ivy-bound veranda beyond. The young raven-gryphon propped himself over the veranda railing, basking in the sunlight and breeze as he looked to the city beyond. Clouds turned gold by mid-evening's sun drifted among floating mile-sized platforms of rock and dirt. Many of these isles in the sky had been hewn into buildings grand and humble, large and small. Other isles were gardens, groves of fruit-bearing trees and shrubs. Hummingbird-gryphons zipped along bearing packages or messages, chattering to all passing within earshot. Massive eagle-gryphons flew in organized flocks, armor and spears glinting as bright as the palace's gold floors. A thousand songs drifted from the gardens, cardinal-gryphons and nightingale-gryphons singing praises for Lady Quetzal and the city she'd provided.

Vogelstadt. The Floating Mountain. Home.

"Little boy," called the old storyteller, voice amused, "Are you quite finished, or should the Royal School continue its visit without you?"

Bifrost turned and hurried back to the group, hopping alongside the owl-gryphon leading them down the hallway. "What happened to Gungnir? Does Lady Quetzal still have it? Are all the dragons sleeping alongside Kur? Why didn't Lady Quetzal just kill Kur when she had the chance? Is this why the unicorns are still evil? Are we going to—"

A tug on his lion tail sent Bifrost stumbling back to the rest of the crowd. As the other children laughed, another raven-gryphon, his age but shorter and stouter, stalked up beside Bifrost and pinned him in place with a glare. "He would answer you if you took a moment to breathe, dummy!"

Bifrost flinched, reaching up to scratch at the back of his head as he bit back a retort. "Sorry, sis..."

Carina turned and tugged his tail again. "Not me, him!"

His cheeks flushing at the rapid-fire reprimands, Bifrost hurriedly bowed his head to the elder gryphon.

"Er, um... I'm sorry, sir. But... is Gungnir still around, somewhere?"

Humming in thought, the storyteller turned and motioned for them to follow. Down pillared halls he led the Royal School group, commenting on this mural or that statue as they ventured deeper into the palace. Bifrost kept his head on a swivel to see everything. Memorialized around them were the great heroes of gryphon history. Elsa, slayer of the hydra hordes. Sigurd, first king of Schwarz Angebot to the far north. Brunhild, who alone held the Featheren Valley pass for three days against a platoon of sphinx raiders. Judith, the first robin-gryphon to earn the title of knight alongside her faithful kitsune companion. Those two were Bifrost's favorites.

After a time, the group rounded a gilt-edged corner and stopped, the torch-lined hall before them killing all conversation. Holes filled the walls, Bifrost imagining arrows or crossbow bolts shooting from them at intruders. Above, the hooked heads of spears could just be seen glinting in the shadowed reaches of the high ceiling ready to drop. At the far end of the hall, 30 yards or so, stood a pair of onyx double-doors. Silver and gold flowed like air currents over its surface. Where the doors met at the center stood four peafowl-gryphons in armor as dazzling as their plumage, shields and spears at the ready.

"This," spoke the storyteller, sounding pleased at their awed silence, "is the Treasure Vault. Forged in likeness to those of the Wolf-Lord master smiths. Contained within is a host of dangerous and powerful artifacts from every corner of Heraldale. And if Gungnir is not the most dangerous weapon within... it is certainly close. Better to keep it safe and locked away."

"Who are they?" asked a dove-gryphon girl from Bifrost's left, nodding to the soldiers at the doors.

"They are the Children of Thunderbird, my most elite guards, dear children."

Her steps as she approached from behind had been as silent as snowfall, yet now that she had announced herself, a soothing warmth seemed to filter through Bifrost and the others, like a long-awaited embrace from a most cherished person. A soft glow emanated from behind them, dancing across the marble floor and walls in a kaleidoscope of colors. The sense of foreboding enveloping the area vanished.

Carina turned around first, Bifrost close behind her. The breath left him as he beheld the radiant form of Lady Quetzal, Prime Gryphon. The first gryphon made by God when the world was young, ordained to guide the skies and its creatures. She towered 30 feet over them, her lion coat ruby-red, her plumage a brilliant emerald, her eyes a startling white that was the perfect opposite of Bifrost's rainbow eyes. Mixed in among the feathers were subtle blues, yellows, and black. No gold adorned her, no silver or platinum, no precious gems, nothing more intricate than a simple bronze circlet upon her brow, feathers and magical aura royal adornment enough. Only the jagged scar from the left of her throat to the joint of her right front leg broke the illusion of perfect beauty.

All in the hall bowed to their holy leader. But Lady Quetzal laughed, beckoning with a talon for them to stand. "Please, don't bow. I cherish every visit from my Royal School. And my! It looks like we have a bumper crop this year. Wonderful! It's always my deepest pleasure to see young minds wishing to learn. Knowledge is a tool you can carry more reliably than any hammer, spade, or sword."

"More reliably than any hammer, spade, or sword," Bifrost repeated voicelessly to himself. At that moment, he swore to read every book and scroll in the Royal Library if it meant pleasing the Prime Gryphon.

As Bifrost made this silent vow, Lady Quetzal gestured to the Treasure Vault. "It is the highest of honors to stand guard here at the Vault. It takes years of dedication, training, and experience. I bestow the honor only to the bravest, the most loyal, the most honorable gryphons. For even if all of Vogelstadt falls around them, it is their duty to protect the items in the Vault to the very last, and NEVER to use them."

Carina, somehow possessing more courage than Bifrost felt he ever would, managed to raise a wing to show she had a question. At Lady Quetzal's nod, she blushed and shrunk down. "If... if the weapons and stuff in there are really so powerful... why don't the guards use them against the enemy? We... we could use Gungnir to stop the horrible unicorns, just like you did with the dragons!"

Excited chatter broke out among the children at this suggestion. It just as quickly died out as Lady Quetzal looked them all over, blind eyes solemn. When they rested on Bifrost he felt a bolt of lightning down the spine. As if those blind eyes were searching for something within him, delving into his heart for something, something dark...

Then her gaze moved on to the dove-gryphon and Bifrost could breathe again. Lady Quetzal kept silent until she had looked them all over. "Children, understand this. It is possible to win the fight, to banish the foe, to save whatever you set out to save, and yet still lose. Some paths to victory, you realize later on, should not be taken. Must NEVER be taken. No... even if Vogelstadt lies in ruin, the Children of Thunderbird know never to even consider the temptation of the Vault."

A few silent seconds to contemplate this, before Quetzal's voice grew lighter, raising them all up from the gloom like drawing curtains on a darkened room. "Perhaps there are such noble souls within this group? I perceive much potential before me. Who among you think you could stand proudly one day in these vaunted halls as a warrior of the Floating Mountain?"

"I do!" said Bifrost, ignoring Carina's flinch. As Lady Quetzal turned her full gaze on him once more Bifrost only stood taller, near-shivering with excitement. Brave, he hoped, for a child of 9. Hopefully not merely stupid. "I will be a great warrior! The greatest warrior to ever guard the Vault!"

"That means you'll have to be better than me," snarled Carina in a whisper. "That'll never happen."

This earned a round of snickers from the gryphons close enough to hear. Bifrost clenched his beak, trying his hardest not to snap at his sister right in front of the leader of all gryphonkind. Not for the first time he wondered why his sister couldn't let him have anything, even a moment's pride.

"Now, now," spoke Lady Quetzal, quieting all once more. "It is impossible to say what the future holds. Even the wisest of sphinx seers cannot foretell with perfect certainty." She turned her beak up in a gryphon smile. "In the face of such uncertainty, the best you can ever do is to hold your head high and go forth with full confidence. Be true to yourselves and stand strong against unicorn aggression. You will not fail, my sweet children."

Little more needed saying after that. Lady Quetzal bid her goodbyes and disappeared in a silver flash. The old storyteller spoke a little while more on the palace and its history as he shepherded the group back to the parents and caretakers waiting in the palace's courtyard. Along the way Bifrost's eyes caught again on the statues depicting Lady Quetzal's forcing of Kur to swear an oath of peace upon Gungnir. It was good to live there in Vogelstadt, he decided, smiling. Good to have the dragons as a shield between them and the war. Between them and the horrors.

CHAPTER ONE

Green. Forests of the richest green covered the world below Galaxy. The blue sky swelled with immensity, puffs of clouds like ocean foam. The sun was a gentle warmth upon her back and wings. Her heart light, Galaxy sang a wordless song into the bracing wind. She saw unicorns among the shadows of the trees, unicorns of every type and hue, laughing and whole and free.

A break in the forest revealed a winding river. Unicorns and gryphons lounged together along the banks. Owain and Brynjar caught Galaxy's eye, sitting together atop an outthrust rock, her dearest friend and eldest brother resting with necks entwined. Near the rock stood a unicorn mare, her coat white and her mane and tail gold. Bevin, an Imperial soldier no longer, entertaining children with piles of pebbles formed into wild shapes mid-air.

Galaxy left the river behind and flew on over the forest. There was more to see, more to feel, more to sing—

"Galaxy."

Galaxy looked left. A yard away flew Ida, Galaxy's adoptive golden eagle-gryphon mother, and past her the swan-gryphon twins Sascha and Siegfried, Galaxy's other brother and sister. The three smiled at Galaxy, yet something in the sight of them killed Galaxy's joy. "Mother?"

"You're going to get us all killed. You know that, right?"

Before Galaxy's eyes, the three gryphons began to break apart into flame and ash, laughing as they crumbled. Before Galaxy could do more than reach out, a gust of wind scattered them from her talons.

More laughter drew Galaxy's panicked attention down to half a dozen chains shooting up from the forest, wrapping around her limbs, her torso, her throat, squeezing until tears streamed from her eyes. She kicked and fought as they dragged her down, past the treetops, into a shallow, black-rocked gully dotted with muddy pools. The chains drew tight to the ground, holding Galaxy flat. Sharp rocks drew pinpricks of blood from her belly. However she struggled, the chains only drew tighter.

Fighting back panic, Galaxy closed her eyes, reaching deep for the magic to tear the chains apart. Yet determination turned to horror as she found none. No magic, not a drop. Only the dead lacked magic.

Hooves clacking on stone made Galaxy open her eyes with a sudden, fearful hope. Before her stood the unicorn that had visited upon her dreams since the Rotwald, towering above her, his snowy coat blinding in the gully's gloom, his storm-grey mane and tail lashing with lightning. His silver horn shone with might. Yet, then and there, his gaze struck Galaxy with the most horrible contempt. She choked on the loathing, shuddered, drew back from him as best she could.

"You don't even know where hippogryphs come from, do you?" The unicorn's muzzle split open into an impossible smile. The skin pulled back, back, back, tearing down the length of his neck, his chest and torso, dropping away, revealing a blood-smeared black coat beneath. Black tendrils whipped about, tearing away what flesh and hair remained. Before Galaxy's eyes now stood Lord Mordred of the Unicorn Empire, destroyer of Featheren Valley and haunter of her nightmares.

"Hehehahah. You don't even know where hippogryphs come from, do you?"

Even as he spoke, Lord Mordred convulsed. Cracks appeared in the black unicorn's body, glowing red, spreading. Flames licked the edges of the cracks, the skin and flesh crumbling away, leaving behind a scorched stench and blackened bones wreathed in fire.

The laughter returned now as screams, echoing all around Galaxy. She saw the forest beyond the gully aflame, tongues of fire lashing like angry serpents. The sound of crackling wood and bursting trees rang thick, but never louder than the screams. Then, she saw them. Burning unicorns and gryphons stumbled out of the forest to fall headfirst into the gully, staring at Galaxy the whole way down. Each CRACK of their bodies hitting the gully floor and shattering into cinders jolted her from head to hoof. Her eyes burned. She couldn't breathe.

Suddenly, vast flames hid all else from Galaxy. Before her HE stood, a unicorn stallion 40, 50, 60 feet tall, nothing but black bones and white fire that scorched Galaxy where she lay. The skull's eye sockets stared down at her, fire dancing within them. He spoke, voice like the grave.

"YOU DON'T EVEN KNOW WHERE HIPPOGRYPHS COME FROM, DO YOU?"

***

Galaxy woke up screaming. She rolled from her bedroll beside the air-yacht's mast, screaming and slapping at her body with wings and talons, still able to feel the flames burning her.

"Galaxy!"

Someone grabbed her by the shoulders. Galaxy punched the mystery assailant. At the feel of her clenched talons impacting hard beak the phantom fire left her, reality returning. She found herself halfway-standing and halfway on her side, Brynjar beside her, talons still gripping her shoulders, his eyes focused on hers. A few paces behind the golden eagle-gryphon stood Owain, the unicorn stallion's palomino coat blanched white, green eyes wide in panic. Behind him was the air-yacht's safety railing, and then only stars.

A split-second passed, and then Galaxy pushed her brother away from her for more space. It felt like her heart was going to stop. She still couldn't breathe. The world was closing in around her, squeezing, suffocating—

"Galaxy!" Brynjar reached for her again, expression nothing but brotherly concern. "Gal, calm down—"

She slapped his talons away with a wing and backed away several paces, barely managing to get out through her gasps for air "DON'T TOUCH ME!"

Brynjar obeyed, backing away with quiet hurt in his green eyes. Galaxy closed her own to keep from seeing it, focusing instead on her racing heart and shaking body. Every attack it became more of a struggle to regain control over herself. A minute passed as she fought... two minutes... three...

By the time the panic attack ran its course, Galaxy felt ready to collapse back into sleep. Instead she forced herself to stand and open her eyes. Brynjar and Owain were much as she'd left them, staring warily her way. She tried to work the corners of her beak up into a smile, hoping to blow the whole thing off. "I'm... okay. I... It was only a dream."

"Only a dream!?" rang Owain's voice, shrill in the late-night air, breath a burst of frost. "Sure, and I'm only mildly perturbed!"

Brynjar spared a glance at the unicorn. "Remind me later to ask what 'perturbed' means. For now..." He turned back to Galaxy. "It's been only a dream every night since we left Port Oil. Why lie?"

Galaxy shook her head, keeping up the false cheer as she moved to lie beside the mast again. Upon noticing the growing light along the eastern horizon ahead, she sighed and stayed sitting where she was. There was one escape from this conversation lost. "It really was only a dream. Doesn't matter. Just... fire. Lots of fire. You know me."

Owain, seemingly deciding it was safe to do so, trotted over to Galaxy's side and sat down, Galaxy instinctively by now laying a wing on his back. He accepted it without comment and stared at her. "Gal, listen, we're just worried is all." He paused for a yawn. "What friends are for. Plus, ehhh, you're a very... animated, dreamer."

"With a mean left hook," Brynjar added while rubbing his beak. Owain rolled his eyes. Galaxy chuckled.

A few minutes of companionable silence passed, before Galaxy looked over at Brynjar, yawning and leaning a concerning amount of his weight on the mast.

Frowning, she noticed dark circles under his eyes. "I uh... I didn't wake you two up."

Owain stiffened beside her. Brynjar started to say something, clacked his beak shut for several seconds, finally sighing and shaking his head. "Just bad dreams."

Galaxy stared. Brynjar did not meet her eyes. Nobody seemed willing or able to say anything after that, and slowly they broke apart. Brynjar yawned again as he padded back to the bow of the military air-yacht they had stolen from Port Oil, lying down and resting his head on the railing to stare ahead. South and eastward the dim horizon light had grown brighter, dawn nearing. Owain, after a short nuzzle of affection to Galaxy, slipped free from her wing and trotted back with all the speed of the sleeping dead to the quarterdeck, where the cluster of crystal control spires managing the air-yacht awaited his guidance. Though most airship's spell matrices could keep them functioning untended for hours at a time, someone close at hoof for emergencies was only practical.

Galaxy, for her part, went over to the north-facing side of the ship and lay down, draping her head and front legs through the railing to look down at the world below. To her immense, unspoken relief, no endless forest greeted her eyes, but stretches of farmland and rolling hills, clusters of cottages and groves of trees alongside wavering rivers, a keep or small hill-set fort every dozen miles, give or take. Snow adorned much of the land, thin scatterings that in the weeks ahead would only grow. Winter had come to this free-for-all country between Galaxy's northern homeland of Schwarz Angebot and the Dragonback Mountains to the south.

Unable to sleep, Galaxy turned her thoughts to well-worn territory. Two weeks and a day had passed since their leaving Port Oil, parting ways with friends and family for the dangers of the war-torn Midlands. Two weeks of curving their eastward path north and south, driving Imperial troops from every village and town they stopped in. Just three days before, they had skirted the lowest edges of the Rotwald, bringing to mind memories of that fateful encounter with the cockatrices, Galaxy and Brynjar saving Owain's life and setting this long adventure into motion.

Through those weeks, Galaxy had done her best to keep her condition from affecting them. She retreated somewhere private whenever she felt a panic attack coming to keep others from seeing their "hippogryph savior" so weak. She avoided anything she found triggered her attacks, as reasonably as she could. Yet, through it all, she had never considered that Brynjar or Owain might suffer the same...

Casting about for anything to distract from such morbid thoughts, Galaxy thought of where her mother,

Ida, and the rest of her family were since leaving Port Oil. Perhaps already in the sphinx city of Wedjet, safe and sound as they readied to travel to Vogelstadt. Galaxy could hope.

"You don't even know where hippogryphs come from, do you?"

Galaxy closed her eyes. Her view of the real world gone, she could see again that burning gully, the unicorn adorned in flames. Lord Mordred, who had chased her, Brynjar, and Owain from Featheren Valley to Port Oil, had nothing on that Beast. But what hurt the most, easily, was the truth. She didn't know where hippogryphs came from. There was no writing on it, no old stories passed down, nothing on why sometimes hippogryphs were born when ancient history was filled with unicorn and gryphon couplings. There was a secret here, by accident or design.

"If I could find some of Queen Grimhilt's... some of Mother's acquaintances... perhaps they would know." For that matter, perhaps they would know Galaxy's father. Seeing him nameless in her dreams only turned that mystery bitter...

The first branch of honest sunlight reached over the horizon, banishing any chance for further sleepy pondering. Galaxy huffed and left the railing for the mast once more. She dug out their maps from the satchels there and readied a self-inking quill. She'd just

caught sight of green along the horizon, and if Brynjar's map-reading lessons the past week had been any help...
"Brynjar, is that the Elderpine ahead?"

A moment's gazing and contemplation from the bow, before "Looks like it. Making good time today."

"Yeah." Galaxy frowned as she dragged a talon along the east- and slightly northward direction they needed to be going to reach the western edge of the Elderpine before noon. "Good time..."

The Elderpine Forest dominated the Heraldale Midlands, stretching on for nearly 100,000 square miles, four times the size of the Rotwald to the northwest. Stories said that half of all towns and cities within Heraldale contained lumber from the forest, carried wherever needed by the multitude of rivers feeding into and out of it. The name, as far as Galaxy knew, wasn't entirely accurate, the forest composed of hemlock, spruce, cedar, and more alongside the pine, but the latter certainly made for the best name.

Somewhere in that vast forest stood the fortress known only as Grimhilt's Folly, its original name forgotten. There, Grimhilt, last queen of Schwarz Angebot and Galaxy's blood mother, had made her last stand and perished. Galaxy didn't know what she would find there now after so long, but she wanted, needed, to go there and see it for herself all the same.

"Assuming we even can find the ruins..."

Hours passed. The land below, from Galaxy's occasional glances, changed from open fields and hills to increasingly dense woodlands, finally nothing but trees and snow as far as the eye could perceive. The noon meal, nuts and oats, and strips of jerky for Brynjar, came and went. Galaxy watched clouds gather, disperse, gather again. She used a talon to carve her name into the air-yacht's mast. At some point, barely realizing it, she drifted into a nap... broken by the achingly loud sound of Owain dragging a whetstone down the length of his sword. She groaned, peeling the map and quill from where she'd fallen asleep atop them and stuffing them back into their satchel. "I am bored. Bored. Boooorrred."

Brynjar yawned from where he'd taken Owain's place managing the air-yacht's course. "Should I throw stuff at you?"

"Mmmehhhh..." Practicing her reaction time with the shield spell didn't sound appealing, Galaxy having long reached the point where Brynjar and Owain together couldn't throw items fast enough to keep up with her spellwork.

"Or why not read more of that scroll of yours? Helped reach Port Oil."

The scroll, yes, the one they'd found among the supplies to escape Featheren Valley through the underground Wolf-Lord realm, Hollereich. The scroll of magic and spells. Useful, but... "I can't," said Galaxy, knowing she sounded like she was pouting. "I finished it back in Port Oil. Only for beginners, after all. You wouldn't expect it to be very long or have much to teach.

"And of course," she continued, letting her tone grow snippy as she rolled into a sitting position to glare at Owain, "Somebody had to knock the bag of books I'd gathered in Port Oil off the side of the air-yacht into that forest fire two days into our journey!"

"You're never going to let me live that down, are you?" Owain, lying on his left side with his back against the railing, didn't even look from his work. "It was an accident, I said I'm sorry, and we all agreed to fly the air-yacht higher to make catching dropped items easier. Why do you even need books? We're in the middle of an adventure. What's the point of reading about one?"

"Why do I...?" Galaxy stood and marched over to Owain, yanking the whetstone from his magic grip with her stronger magic and throwing it off the air-yacht. "There! Why do you need a whetstone when your sword's already sharp?"

Owain gaped up at her, blinking. Brynjar sighed from the helm. "You should go get that back."

Galaxy screeched her frustrations to the sky. "Morons! Illiterate hooligans! Ignorant barbarians! It's a wonder I'm not the only one here who can read! No, I'm sure at this rate, you two will erode whatever abilities of higher thinking I possess with your... your... not-smartness!"

Brynjar guffawed. Owain smirked. "Wh-what, not going to call our faces stupid?"

Galaxy entertained the brief fantasy of Owain's mane catching fire, before leaping over him and off the air-yacht. With wings tucked tight against her body, the amorphous green and white blob that was the Elderpine Forest below rapidly resolved into quite distinct trees. Galaxy focused on the glint of the whetstone tumbling a dozen feet below her, still well above the tops of the trees. Chuckling at discovering a new training exercise, Galaxy flapped her wings for a burst of speed and closed the distance, snatching the whetstone up in her talons. Whooping in exhilaration, she pulled out of her dive, close enough for her hooves to skim the tops of the pine trees. Then she was flying back up, whetstone clutched close to her chest and beak corners turned up in a smile. Were anyone to ask, the closeness of that catch had been entirely intentional.

Far above and away to the east, the air-yacht was just a slow dot against the blue sky. Squinting, Galaxy flapped her wings harder to catch up. "Of course they don't slow down even a little to wait on me. Brynjar knows how to slow the ship down. Getting back at me for yelling at them. Bad joke. I only just reached something resembling a healthy weight, surely they don't think I need the exer—"

"Help! Help me!"

"ROOOAAAARRRR!"

Galaxy snapped her gaze back down to the forest. Far below her the trees shook in a wide, roaming line as something massive smashed through them, heralded by the crash of breaking wood and thudding earth. Through breaks in the canopy Galaxy could just barely make out an Elk running at full gallop several yards ahead of the disturbance, yet even as Galaxy watched that distance slowly narrowed.

"Heeeeelllp!"

Galaxy gave no time to reflect on the bizarre familiarity of the scene. She dove, reaching the treetops in seconds. Limbs tucked tight, she spiraled through the narrow branches, only once using a pulse of magic to push aside a bramble of entwined boughs. Reaching the open space beneath, she spotted the Elk almost right ahead and below her. It was a young cow, coat auburn and antler-like horns split into four tines each, racing across the snow-dusted forest floor with ragged breath and foam-flaked flanks. Cuts and burns littered her body, her gate uneven with exhaustion. Galaxy adjusted her flight to catch up to the Elk, keeping a careful distance to the left and away from those deadly tines. "Hey there!" Galaxy shouted, causing the Elk to half-stumble, gaze snapping over. "I'm Galaxy, the hippogryph! You might've heard of me! I'm here to—"

The trees they sped past visibly shook with the force of the roar behind them, snow and pine needles raining down. Craning her neck to see what exactly they were fleeing, Galaxy's eyes widened, wings nearly freezing. Big as a house, smashing through trees like they were matchsticks, wings broad as a galleon's sails, scales a crypt's blackness, foot-long claws rending the earth, flames dancing among teeth the length of Galaxy's horn, red eyes gleaming with fury and hate.

Dragon.

"NOPE! Nope nope nope!" Galaxy grabbed the Elk with her magic and sloped her flight upward, sacrificing grace for speed as she smashed trees out of their way with a shield spell. Another roar from behind. On instinct, she cast another shield spell completely around her and the madly kicking and screaming Elk. Even through the shield she felt the heat of the dragonfire as they burst from the forest into the open sky. Flames erupted around them on all sides, accompanied by a cacophony of exploding trees and wood shrapnel whistling through the air.

Galaxy ignored everything and kept flying for sanity's sake, letting the updraft from the fire push her up, not slowing until the dragon's roars were far below and the air-yacht was close enough for her to make out the worried faces of Brynjar and Owain. By this point the Elk had calmed down enough to speak coherently and stop kicking around in a panic. Not that what the Elk had to say was all that much an improvement. "Oh, bless you! A thousand blessings for you and all your loved ones! I was almost dead, and the dragon, but then you, and fire, and bless you, hippogryph!"

The praise made Galaxy feel anxious and greasy, still unused to it even after Port Oil. Her mumbled "It was no problem" probably unheard over the rushing wind of their flight, she put on speed and quickly deposited the Elk onto the deck of the air-yacht. Landing, she slumped against the mast and worked to catch her breath. "I need... to work... out."

The air-yacht shuddered as Brynjar set it to hover, the golden eagle-gryphon flapping over to Galaxy and the newcomer. "What in Sheol happened back there? The fire, the roaring, the... what... who is this? WHAT is this?" He emphasized the question with a talon pointed at the Elk, who at the moment simply stood there and took in deep lungfuls of air.

"An Elk," spat Owain, coming over with a bowl of water. He glared dagger's the newcomer's way and dropped the bowl in front of Galaxy. She frowned at his venomous tone, too much like his tone back in Featheren Valley before they truly got to know one another, and found enough strength to step aside and grant the Elk the first drink.

"Honestly," continued Owain, turning that look on Galaxy. "You can't go anywhere without getting into trouble, can you? The Elk, mythic in their seclusion from anything and everything to do with the rest of Heraldale, and you meet one our first day over the Elderpine! Or is it something about forests? You just have to save someone from something any time you see a lot of trees together?"

Brynjar came to Galaxy's side with a water bowl of her own. Galaxy accepted it with a nod, ducking down for two deep drinks before meeting the unicorn's glare with a cool gaze. "Apologies. I didn't stop to consider if I'd reached my adventure quota before diving in to rescue her from the dragon. How thoughtless of me."

"What!?" Brynjar performed a remarkable impression of Ida's Heart Attack Face as he looked back and forth between Galaxy and the Elk, who had just finished emptying her water bowl. "Dragon? A real dragon? I mean... really!?"

The Elk radiated nervousness now that all attention was upon her and the water was finished. She cleared her throat, nodding and sidling rightward enough to be closer to Galaxy and Brynjar than to Owain, to Galaxy's resigned annoyance. "Yes, really. My name is, is Gwendolyn." She inclined her head until her antler-like horns touched the deck, before standing back up and looking back and forth between Galaxy and her friends. "And I have heard of all of you. The powerful Princess Galaxy! Savior of Port Oil! And of course, her brave and loyal gryphon and... unicorn... companions."

"Of course," said Brynjar dryly. "Let me say, impressed how you made 'unicorn' sound like 'stick-head' there. I should take notes."

"But Brynjar," said Owain, looking at the gryphon with a smirk, "That'd mean you'd have to learn how to write. Sure you're up to the task?"

"I'm up to any task to wipe that look off your muzzle."

Though she recognized this playful banter for what it was, Galaxy stepped forward to break it up before their guest could get the wrong idea. "Get a room, you two, gosh. It's an honor to meet you, Gwendolyn. What were you doing out in the forest like that? How'd you end up with a dragon of all things chasing you?"

The Elk sighed, turning away from them to look out over the forest below. "I was foraging through the woods for special medicinal herbs my people's healers are running low on, thanks to the dragon. I guess I somehow wandered near to the dragon's lair. None of us knew before where the beast lived..."

She looked down at herself, as if only just then noticing her bruised and scratched condition. "Oh...

now fixing me up might drain our stores completely. I, I messed up so badly here..."

"Don't worry about that," said Galaxy, sensing here a chance to engender some goodwill between her horned friends. "Owain here is a master of healing magic, and we have plenty of medicinal supplies down below to share. Don't we, Owain?" It was difficult, but Galaxy believed she managed to say "Agree or I will shove your horn somewhere horns don't belong" in nothing but tone. Owain seemed to catch her meaning, at any rate.

"Wait," said Brynjar. "Pretend for a moment I'm a fool and... Gal, stop giggling. What in Sheol's an Elk? Just some kind of... talking deer, or something?"

"Basically," said Owain, making no move to do as asked.

"Inasmuch as unicorns are basically horses with horns," replied Gwendolyn, matching Owain's frosty tone.

The unicorn bristled. Galaxy hurriedly moved between the two, holding her talons up both to placate and to guard. "Oookay, let's just be calm, everyone. We're all friends here. Or, no Empire supporters, anyway."

To Brynjar, she said "Unicorns and the Elk have a long history of animosity, going back even to the old world. They're like... cousins to unicorn-kind, you might say. Antler-like horns are composed of alicorn, just like unicorn horns, so they channel magic the same. Let me think... There's an old, old tale about their start..."

Yet it was not Galaxy to speak it aloud for the group, but Gwendolyn herself, voice soft and clear.

"In distant ages and ancient woods there dwelt an elk named Erentil.
His many-pronged antlers arcing high proved him true the battle-king.
Grey was his coat, as the oaks of his realm, where oft he roamed in grim mood.
Of many he sired, all sons silver-coated, their prongs the ire of hunting men.
And daughters too he duly delivered, gold as the sun and glad of their goodness.
Unicorns too lived in that wood, who stood and delivered onto Erentil scorn.
'Horns over antlers,' they'd answer his call, and for a horn he would trade all.
Pure does not promise good, the wise ones wrote, of which the elk could
Truly attest. East and west Erentil trod, to find and ease to his troubled thoughts.
The unicorn beauty he loved, though in truth a lowly elk was he. But lo,
At western edge of the wood one morn, he met a woman by travel worn.

For food she begged, and drink, and freedom from an unnamed fear.

Daring Erentil could not answer no, and so led her to secluded dale.

A feast on gathered fruit he fed her, and water too from snow-fed river,

'til at last the lady bowed down low and thanked him for his grace.

Then like a veil lifted from his eyes, the elk beheld no beggar-woman, but

Fearsome and fiery Morgan the Fae, wielder of magic both wicked and fair.

Before her he bowed, knees buckling, his better by far.

'Good elk,' she spoke, words like the wind, 'What is your wish?'

Then Erentil told her of his travels and troubles, his hope for a horn.

'For kindness a reward, oh lord of my realm.' Morgan reached out

Her hand to the hart, resting upon the brow of the old battle-king.

And Erentil felt a light flood into him, magic and might to master the True.

Taller Erentil stood, his antlers felt strange, more solid now yet light.

Thus born were the Elkish, beloved of Morgan, her bairns thereafter."

Gwendolyn finished, the silence of the sky returning once more for a moment. Brynjar turned to Owain. "Morgan the Fae... as in... the Knights Le Fay? Your sword, Mordred, all of that?"

Owain nodded. "That's right. The Elk left Avalon at the Empire's founding, opposing it every way through the knights until Lord Mordred betrayed them. Young fillies and colts are taught to... despise..."

A look of disgust passed across the unicorn's features. Swallowing, he looked at the silent Gwendolyn. "I apologize for my earlier rudeness. I... have only been coming to my senses on certain matters recently, and only thanks to these two. Old beliefs die hard, but I'm trying. If you would permit me, I would..." He gestured with his horn to the Elk's various hurts.

Seemingly also embarrassed at her behavior, Gwendolyn nodded. Owain moved to her side, horn shining green as he started the healing spell. Several seconds passed, and then before their eyes the Elk's cuts began knitting themselves back together, slow but noticeable as the blood drained away.

As Owain's magic worked over her, Gwendolyn looked to Galaxy. "Again, my deepest appreciation for rescuing me. I can't ever thank you enough. Now I truly believe the tales my people have been hearing of you."

Galaxy barely held back her grimace. "Stories about Port Oil already. Well, I'd have gotten nowhere without these two. Discovering the Empire was experimenting with cockatrices and Elementals and had accidentally created a nigh-invulnerable monster of pure magic was a... team effort."

There passed a moment of quiet contemplation by them all at the strangeness just stated, Galaxy wondering if all hippogryphs had led such lives. Eventually, Gwendolyn continued. "Right... but anyway, if it pleases you, I humbly request you return with me to my people. My father, ever since he heard of you, has been anxious to meet the first hippogryph since the Days of Dragon Rage."

Galaxy perked at hearing this. "We would be honored! My friends and I actually came to the Elderpine Forest in search of something, and if your people call the forest home, perhaps we can help each other out?"

"Hold there a moment," said Owain as he began wrapping bandages around one of Gwendolyn's legs, near the knee. "Sorry, burns are extremely difficult injuries to heal, and I've no practical experience with Elk anatomy. Why would your father specifically be interested in meeting Gal like that? Is he someone important among your people?"

Gwendolyn tested the bandaged leg with a few careful steps before answering. "Were you not listening to the poem? My father is Erentil, High King of the Elk."

CHAPTER TWO

Clouds rolled in from the southwest, turning what had been a cool but sunny day biting and grey. Galaxy felt the coming snow, lurking among the clouds.

At Gwendolyn's guidance, their path turned from straight east to southeast, toward the heart of the Elderpine Forest. There was no directly flying the air-yacht to the Elk kingdom, she explained as they went. Her home lay hidden, protected both by layers of misdirecting illusion spells and the natural thickness of the forest.

"There is a small clearing but a mile hence from the edges of the clearing. Meant for groups of trustworthy gryphons. I... think this craft will fit."

"What's your father like?" asked Owain from where he managed the air-yacht's guidance spires. "Must be wise, to keep your people safe all these years."

"He is," replied Gwendolyn as she paced the length of the ship. Though her frostiness had lessened with Owain's honest contrition, she remained far from friendly with the unicorn. "Calm, stern, and fair. But the forest itself helps as well. We are far from the edges of the woods where most go for lumber, and few even know we are here, so none visit us save the most trusted of Lady Quetzal's gryphons and a lone trader. Armies from all sides either circle around the forest or fly over. Until the dragon showed up, life was perfect. Secluded, but safe."

"How long has the dragon been here?" asked Brynjar.

"Only a week and a half. It hasn't killed anyone yet, but there's been much damage and injury."

Galaxy stood at the bow of the air-yacht, talons worrying the wood of the railing as she scanned the forest below them. Lord Mordred was the closest she had come to meeting royalty before. There'd be no getting around her own royal lineage here. The thought tasted foul on her tongue.

Brynjar joined her. "Hey. Is this a good idea?"

Galaxy shrugged, not looking over. "I don't know. Has anywhere we've gone been a good idea? The Rotwald, Hollereich, Port Oil..."

"Good point."

A moment of silence. Galaxy could picture her oldest brother glancing back toward Gwendolyn's pacing. His next few words were quieter, almost indiscernible over the wind. "Suppose again that I'm a fool. Why can't the Elk deal with the dragon themselves? One could be helpless, but a whole group of soldiers? I don't trust it."

Galaxy frowned and turned to her brother, grabbing his shoulder. "First off, you are not a fool. You aren't. As to your question, my studies taught that the Elk are capable mostly in the softer magics, illusions and nature. I suppose that's not all that helpful against creatures that breathe fire."

"Illusions?"

She nodded, letting go and looking back to the forest. "Making things look like they're there when they actually aren't and vice-versa, changing one's perceptions, actions of that nature. Dragons possess a natural resistance to such magic. And as for nature..." She gestured to the all-too-flammable trees below. "Fire. Plants. No good. Fire bad."

His glare was all the response needed.

Time seemed to pass them at a crawl, told only in the building cloud cover. By Galaxy's reckoning it took two hours for them to find the clearing Gwendolyn had promised them at the speed she asked them to go, an oblong space covered over in dead leaves and fallen pine needles. There arose an awful racket as Owain brought the air-yacht in for a landing, the outstretched limbs of the surrounding trees scratching their sides, but once past this barrier there proved enough room. Until it came time to leave, at least.

Galaxy led the way off the ship, followed by Brynjar and Owain, Gwendolyn hobbling down the plank at the rear. Galaxy had barely hopped to the ground, leaves and needles giving a satisfying crunch beneath her, when a trio of armored Elk materialized out of thin air from the edge of the clearing. They stood shorter than the unicorn soldiers Galaxy was used to, ignoring their branching horns, their build lighter and spryer of hoof. Leather and iron armor in cool shades of white and grey covered head, chest, back, and sides, blending them in with the surrounding trees.

"Halt," commanded the lead Elk, rank distinguished by a strip of gold down his chest. "You walk uninvited in the lands of King Erentil. Hippogryph, are you not Princess Galaxy?"

"She is!" Gwendolyn slid her way to the front of the group, making her presence known. The three Elk soldiers straightened in her presence, a rustling from the surrounding trees telling Galaxy that more soldiers remained hidden. "Captain Hywel, it is true. She is Princess Galaxy, daughter of Queen Grimhilt and savior of Port Oil. She saved me from the dragon! Take us to my father at once."

If there was any hesitation, any slowness to obey, it was for but a moment as the Elk identified as Captain Hywel glanced Owain's way. Before Galaxy could comment on it the hesitation passed, the captain bowing to Gwendolyn. "Of course, your highness. If you will follow me."

Two sharp whistles sent the other two Elk soldiers disappearing, quite literally, into the surrounding foliage. Captain Hywel motioned with his head for the group to follow him, turned, and started down a path Galaxy was sure had not been there moments before. It took them through clusters of trees thick and sparse, across trickling streams barely worth skipping over and frothing brooks over which were laid stout logs. At unpredictable moments Hywel curved their path right, left, once in what Galaxy was certain was a loop, until Galaxy was sure she'd never find her way back to the air-yacht without help.

On top of this were the illusion spells they encountered on the path, subtle layers of magic portraying false trees or hiding stumbling roots that only faded from vision at Hywel's approach. Galaxy could feel the remnants of the spells as the group passed, ready to return afterward. The sensation reminded her of walking into a spider web, invisible to the eye and difficult to shake off.

"Princess Gwendolyn, how do you keep the illusion spells in place over long periods of time? Surely you don't have Elk go through the forest multiple times a day just to re-weave them."

"It's thanks to another spell, actually. We can't use the natural magic of the Elderpine, but we can, for lack of a better term, 'piggyback' through the natural ley lines to influence even the most remote sections of our holds without leaving the central valley. Energy-intensive, but worth it in time saved."

"Ley lines?"

"For magic, Bryn." Owain let off a sparkle of magic from his horn. "Think of it like blood veins in a person, but for magic."

"Huh. Nature can bleed."

"That's, that's not... Yeah, sure."

Around them the trees began to grow taller and thicker, the ground sloping subtly downward. Among the trees Galaxy began seeing stone and wood structures, walls and high archways, bridges leading to platforms built into and out from trees. Elsewhere lower branches were woven together, forming high roofs beneath which Elk in twos and threes lounged, watching the group in shameless curiosity. Or in Owain's case, angry wariness. Many stood and followed, a crowd soon forming behind them.

Suddenly Hywel stopped, prompting Galaxy and the rest to do the same. Galaxy looked past him and gasped. Ahead of them the woods opened into a wide, shallow valley untouched by winter. There was thick green grass, springy beneath their hooves, flowering trees and shrubbery, many fruit-bearing, nourished by a thin river weaving among several long stone buildings. The closest of these was also the largest, three stories tall and connecting to several of the other buildings via broad wood archways. A paneled-glass dome covered the roof.

Dozens of Elk with silver and gold coats stood in the clearing, but Galaxy only had eyes for the one Elk in the entrance to the primary building. He stood as tall as Lord Mordred, chest broad and legs solid with muscle, his coat grey like the trees of the Elderpine, his horns broad and many-tined. His eyes were the night sky. He wore no armor, no crown, yet all the same radiated power and authority. Galaxy could almost see the magic flowing off him.

Silent, Gwendolyn crossed the open space to King Erentil's side. Sharing a look, Galaxy, Brynjar, and Owain followed, stopping a yard off and bowing.

"Rise, travelers."

His voice rang rough, rigid. They did as commanded, Galaxy struck quiet by the sadness within Erentil's black eyes. A sadness of centuries, millennia. She swallowed, almost crying until he spoke again. "Brave souls, at last we meet. Glorious Princess Galaxy, hippogryph and Shieldqueen. Brynjar, loyal and strong. Owain, the Decent."

"I am strong," said Brynjar with a grin, while Galaxy had to bite back a laugh at Owain mouthing back his moniker in disbelief.

"Your exploits are well-known even here, of course, but important than any of that, you have my deepest thanks for saving my daughter from the dragon. That alone is something for which I can never repay you."

Galaxy bowed again, taking the moment to remember what little etiquette she had learned in her lessons with Ida. "Your words are too kind, fair king. The honor of this meeting is ours."

"Nay, Princess Galaxy, Brynjar, Owain. The honor of this meeting is mine. I foresee you each have a long journey ahead of you, and to meet you so early upon it is surely a good blessing." King Erentil bowed, then stood and looked around at the crowd gathered around them, swelled now into the hundreds. "A feast, then, so I declare, to celebrate this miraculous meeting! Bring food, music, and stories for all! Let us forget for a little while the dragon and the troubles of the world beyond our borders!"

Only then did the watching crowd give voice and form to the jubilation Galaxy had felt building up. While those farther out turned and galloped off to spread their king's word, those closest rushed the three, shouting questions and greetings, praises and blessings. Owain only managed to not be shoved away with the rush by Brynjar's protective wing across his back. Galaxy froze up at the sudden countless strangers swarming her, heart thudding a panic attack, wings screaming to spread and fly her far away from there. Clenching her beak into a grimace of a smile to keep the nausea away, Galaxy foresaw a long, long day.

***

The anxiety stayed with Galaxy to the start of the festivities later that evening, despite her silent assertions that this was all okay. It was a feast, the valley lit by a dozen bonfires that Galaxy made sure to stay clear of, warming against the approaching winter night. The scent of roasting oats and apples drenched in cinnamon wafted thick through the air, accompanied by the laughter of Elk children frolicking around or plying her and Brynjar with endless questions. Some tried doing the same with Owain, most too afraid or unwilling, the rest warned away by their watchful parents. Other Elk were annoyingly touchy, fascinated by her and Brynjar's avian features. It only took one snarl of "You can't just touch a gryphon's wings!" from Brynjar to get most of that stopped, though, at least for a while.

But there were so many Elk around them, so many strangers, as much of Erentil's kingdom as could make it by that evening. It was a minute-by-minute battle for Galaxy not to curl up into a ball and sob the night away. Had she, Brynjar, and Owain been outside among the general celebrations for long, she would have lost the battle. As it was, the three of them dined with Princess Gwendolyn, King Erentil, and the rest of the royal house within the domed building. No doors fully separated them from the crowds outside, a symbolic gesture on Erentil's part, but there were walls, and Brynjar and Owain at her sides which was enough. Well behind them, blessedly out of Galaxy's sight, burned the largest of the fires in a grand fire pit, illuminating a feast made beautiful by the weeks of travel and careful meal management. Apples and carrots, grown there in the forest. Rice, millet, and quinoa from the southern fields of Wedjet, corn from Gateway to the far southeast. Warm ciders in heavy wood bowls, heady glogg, nameless berries from the forest that glistened red and tasted fiercely sweet. Breadfruit, salted and dried sunflower seeds, sweet potatoes boiled and mashed, or sliced and fried, or cubed and coated in heavy layers of sugar, and the sweetest, most heavenly-scented lemon tarts Galaxy had ever tasted.

In this strange meeting of inward unease and outward cheer, Galaxy recounted the tale of her travels with Brynjar and Owain's help. She told of her fateful trip to the Rotwald with her siblings that had started the whole mess. She told of saving Owain from the cockatrices. She told of her capture by and escape from Lord Mordred and his soldiers, a deathly hush falling over the small crowd of listeners at the destruction of Featheren Valley.

King Erentil asked many questions concerning Lord Mordred, how the unicorn spoke, how he acted. Galaxy told as best she could of the horror Mordred exuded, bloodcurdling and stomach-churning. She told of the dark journey through the subterranean tomb of Hollereich, the wyvern swarm attack bringing gasps from the crowd. She told of Port Oil, of the mysterious nighttime petrifications, the determined Commander Bevin, the revelation of Spell Virus and the Unicorn Empire's experiments to harness the power of the cockatrice. The defeat of Spell Virus, destruction of Lord Mordred's warship, and reuniting of Galaxy's scattered family spurred a long and deafening drumming of hooves on stone as the Elk applauded. All but Erentil, Galaxy noted, who for another moment bore a look of utter sorrow. It disappeared just as quickly as the discussion turned to what Galaxy hoped to do next.

"The long-term goal is, of course, to end the Unicorn Empire's war against the world and bring back true peace and fellowship, however long that takes. More in the here and now, though..." Galaxy frowned, rolling one of the red berries between two talons as she thought over how to explain herself. "We came to the Elderpine Forest to find Grimhilt's Folly. I feel... compelled... to see the place of my blood mother's final stand."

Another pause, then she lifted her beak in a smile toward Erentil and Gwendolyn beside him. "It's a good thing I felt such too, or else we'd have never found your daughter, and..."

"Indeed," said Erentil, that sadness in his voice now. But then the light of the great fire behind them dimmed and he seemed to find cheer as an Elk with a rose-gold coat stepped into the open circle before them. "Let that wait a little longer. Now it is time for our stories. An oral tradition Elk and unicorns share. Or shared, before the time of the Empire."

Galaxy breathed, relieved. Retelling her adventures had been a pleasure, but an exhausting one, and she was content now to be the listener.

For a moment, there was only the crackling of the bonfires, the creaking of the wind-driven trees, the subdued sounds of revelry from out in the valley beyond. At some unseen signal, thin streamers of silver magic flowed from the tips of the Elk performer's horns, forming figures and landscapes above the royal crowd. She wove the stories before them, flowing them together like one continuous narrative. The Unicorn Princess and the Three Gryphon Bandits. The Minotaur in Yellow. The Dark Out There. The Roaming Throne. The Sphinx Prince and the Witch. Many of the stories Galaxy had read before, but to hear them recounted so expertly here gave them all a new flavor. Galaxy felt a magic in the air quite apart from the conjured imagery.

The sky was all stars when the storyteller paused. The food remnants were removed, the young ones sitting at the inner edges of the listening crowd ushered off to bed by family. Seeing this, Galaxy missed Ida's warm hold, Sascha and Siegfried's gentle jokes.

The storyteller looked solemnly upon the waiting audience, no more light streaming from her horns to paint pictures in the air. "I present now the last story of the evening. This comes to us from the United Zakarian Confederacy living in the Golden Plains to the east, dating at least as far back as their tribal days. Extraordinary in subject matter, yet perhaps relevant to our times."

Galaxy perked at hearing this. There had been no stories or scrolls from the lizard-folk in Ida's library.

"Once, many generations ago," the storyteller began, "we Great Hunters lived beyond these plains, in all areas of the world. We climbed the cold mountains. We ran beneath the red-leaved trees. We felt the salt seas on our scales. Our tails dragged the desert sands. We built great cities like the newcomers from Earth now do. We hunted every beast that lived under the sun, and it was good.

"But then, with no warning from our prophets, the Monsters rose from the seas in their orbs of stingers and flesh. Numberless Monsters, with fingers webbed and teeth serrated. Our bravest warriors fought for every inch of soil, drenched the land in red blood and blue, but they were too few and their enemies too horrid.

"Our cities fell. We fell back. Away from the hostile seas, over the mountains, through the burning forests, all the while pursued by the Monsters. No rest, no respite, no hope of victory. No help from the other peoples. No salvation from our gods.

"But then, once we found our last refuge in these plains, once there was nowhere else to flee and doom settled upon us, the Monsters ceased attacking. They fell back, back across the lands to the waters from whence they had come. Yet here we have stayed, no longer trusting in seas and safety. Never again will a Great Hunter build a city or man a fortress, especially near to the ocean, for fear it was such pride that led to the coming of the Monsters.

"In all these years since, there have been no more Monsters from the water. And yet... the newcomers from Earth, the gryphons and unicorns and hosts more, they build many cities. They sit their fortresses beside the ocean. We Great Hunters will wait in our plains, and see what happens."

The Elk storyteller fell silent and, with a bow of the head toward King Erentil and Galaxy, backed out of the circle. Silence sat heavy over all. The returning firelight did not bring back the feast's previous joviality.

"Well," said Brynjar, breaking the silence, "I'll have great nightmares tonight."

The ripples of laughter this sent through the hall dispelled much of the lingering nervousness. Elk began to disperse, going off to food and fun out in the valley or heading to other buildings to rest. Galaxy watched them leave until only she, Brynjar, Owain, Captain Hywel, Princess Gwendolyn, and King Erentil remained in the hall, discounting those tending the fire. Galaxy's anxiety drained with each departing Elk. She sighed once the last had left and turned to the ancient king. "Your majesty, uh, was there any truth to all that, you think? It's so morbid."

King Erentil bowed his head in thought. "It is difficult to say. You are young, and still with much learning ahead of you. So young, to be so important… so wanted by so many… no matter. To your question, I doubt it. Never once in over 2,000 years since Heraldale's establishment has anything like the creatures in the story been encountered. And the zakarians, with their confederacy, certainly haven't kept to the promises of the tale. I believe this is a fable meant to warn against becoming too proud in your strength. Hubris is a fatal flaw as old as time. Or, perhaps it was meant for us newcomers to hear, as a cautionary tale against becoming so focused on fighting each other we become blind to other threats. It is the hidden threat that takes us in the end, as they say. The unexpected foe. Like Spell Virus, back in Port Oil."

"Or the dragon out in the forest," said Owain.

King Erentil nodded. "Like the dragon. For too long now has it harassed us, burning our crops and waylaying soldier and innocent alike. My people are ill-prepared to fight such a fiery foe, yet many want to do so anyway."

Closing his eyes, the elder Elk's voice aged with the weight of untold memory. "War and bloodshed... safe within the Elderpine Forest, these are strangers to my people. They cannot imagine... the damage war does to the mind. To the heart. To the soul. War... on the right or wrong side, good intentions or ill, we all become monsters in the end. You need only look at Empress Nova and Lord Mordred for that truth to become apparent."

Galaxy frowned at that phrasing "Your majesty, do you... I mean, did you... know Mordred and Nova?"

Eyes still closed, Erentil nodded again. "Live as long as I have, you get to know everyone important to some measure. Mordred, in the days before his betrayal of the Knights Le Fay, was a brave and honorable unicorn. He lived and fought with honor and integrity. The only unicorns more loyal to the northern gryphons and their Queen Grimhilt were Knight-Commander Arthur,

Mordred's foster-father, and the dazzling Sir Lancelot. His betrayal hurt many."

Owain fidgeted where he lay. "And Empress Nova?"

By now, even much of the revelry outside was winding down. King Erentil stood after another lingering moment of silence. "I will not speak of her. The hour grows late and tomorrow is a new day, so I suggest we all retire. Captain Hywel will show you to the bedding prepared for you. Tomorrow we may discuss Grimhilt's Folly and what help we might provide you, though know now that you are all welcome to stay as long as you wish. The longer the better, even."

"Wait," said Brynjar, drawing all eyes. "What about the dragon? We still need to help with it."

Galaxy felt a gear slip loose in her thinking parts, as if Brynjar had grown a second head that happened to speak perfect Wolf-Lord. At her expression he shrugged. "After wyverns, cockatrices, Spell Virus, and Lord Mordred, what's a lone dragon?"

"Well, er, right." Galaxy struggled to find language again. "It's only, well, selfless, some might say senseless, acts of kindness are generally my thing and talking sense is yours."

King Erentil looked equally surprised. "I wouldn't ask of you that which I am unwilling to do myself. But... my daughter is only with us thanks to your help once. I would be lying if I said I don't wholeheartedly welcome your assistance. Rid us of this dragon and I shall lead you to Grimhilt's Folly myself."

"And I shall lead you to the dragon's lair," said Gwendolyn, standing with an uncertain sway. "I couldn't forget the way there if I tried."

"Your highness—"

"I'll be fine, Hywel. I won't direct them into danger without being in it myself."

"If she's going with us," said Owain, standing as well, Galaxy following his lead, "then I suggest waiting a day or two. I'm not experienced at healing Elk anatomy as I am gryphon and unicorn, so I'd like to make sure everything's working fine before any long treks."

"Whatever is necessary," King Erentil agreed. He looked to Galaxy. "You will help us, then?"

Galaxy nodded, a glance to her sides showing her companions doing the same. "However we can."

***

Markhaven rested among several tall hills 35 miles southwest of the Elderpine Forest. It was a well-sized village, as such things go, 800 people working as permanents, the town oft seeing half that many again staying for short whiles as laborers, mercenaries, and traders. Along the town's southern edge ran Quicksilk River, one of many feeding from that land into what eventually became the Sandwine River marking the border between the Heraldale Midlands and Wedjet.

This status as a key trading town had made it a prime focus for Imperial occupation, to the suffering of the native gryphons.

It was night when a unicorn mare trooped into one of many waterfront taverns. Weariness had long worn away any embarrassment over her dirty white coat and ill-kept gold mane and tail, her regular soldier's poise and strength leaving her unbothered during the long walk for the table near the tavern's hearth. Still, she felt the eyes of the tavern following her.

A minotaur from the bar soon stomped over to her on his bowed legs, his body a patchwork of scars and one horn broken clean off, a pencil and notepad in his hands. "What ya want?"

"Revenge," growled the unicorn as she levitated her satchels off her sides. "I want my enemy writhing in pain before me, begging for forgiveness and mercy, feeling an ounce of the hurt I felt at his betrayal before I take his head from his neck."

The minotaur blinked, pencil scratching something onto the pad. "We don't... serve that."

"   oh. Cider and oats, is what I meant."

"One-horn usual, right. Any name for this order?"

"Bevin. Name's Bevin. A room for the night, too. Any room with a roof will do."

The minotaur nodded. "Bevin, then. Fine. Back soon with Bevin's needs. Won't be long."

He stomped away. Bevin scanned the tavern, eyeing the other patrons. Gryphons clustered at tables, clutching drinks tight. A scattering of unicorns both civilian and soldier in low, hushed conversations. In the rafters, a zakarian hunter slept, grey scales blending her in well against the ceiling. None SEEMED to pay Bevin any mind. She was just another traveler on the road. Nobody's problem.

Feeling somewhat safe, Bevin rested her head and neck on the table. The long weeks settled into her bones, drawing out a sigh. She closed her eyes, thinking she might rest them as she listened to the tavern...

Shadows. Smoke. Screams. A unicorn filly, barely older than a foal, trembling in a doorway. Smoke stung her eyes, tearful at the room before her.

A mare, shaking as gryphons crept around her, stepping over the body of a unicorn stallion, his throat slashed open. The mare's begging filled the air, begging for mercy, met with laughter and jeers.

No, not a mare. Another gryphon, queenly,

Talons flashed, fighting. The begging turned to gurgling, blood arcing through the air to splatter the walls. The filly stayed silent, eyes wide, watching the gryphons stab and kick the two corpses on the floor. Stay quiet. Stay quiet.

The gryphons stopped, many dead on the floor. A blur, the scene growing hazy and scream-filled once more. The sudden heat of fire everywhere. Flames licked at the corpses, cooked the bloodstains from the walls. Smoke clogged the filly's throat now. Couldn't breathe. Couldn't breathe. Fire everywhere, the sound of cracking wood and a baby's crying as a walking shadow loomed into sight, something wailing—

Bevin jerked awake. Looking around, nobody in the tavern seemed to have noticed the lapse of attention or sudden return to wakefulness. Nobody except the palomino unicorn stallion now sitting across the table from her. "Commander Bevin? Are you alright? That seemed a nasty dream you were having."

"Governor Urien... surprising to see you." The minotaur arriving with food and drink let Bevin ignore the newcomer's observation. She dove in the moment the bowls were on the table, gulping down half the cider before shaking her head, relishing the burning in her throat. "Should be on a short leash. Never noticing the hippogryph under your governorship. Your own son turning traitor. Being anywhere involved in Port Oil..."

"Yes, well..." The stallion's voice was heavy with exhaustion. In fact, watching him, Bevin thought him almost indistinguishable from sufferers of Horror Sickness. "A short leash would be most accurate in these circumstances you've so far outlined, but oddly enough a short leash often left unattended on the other end. Lord Mordred has been secluding himself more and more since Port Oil, his gaze turned ever to the south. To the dragons, and beyond. When he is not overseeing the renewed military campaign against Gryphonbough, at least. One such preoccupation took him to the garrison some dozen miles upriver two days ago, and I have found Markhaven a more than adequate place to while away the lonely, miserable hours."

Well. Being a pariah hadn't hampered Urien's frustrating verbosity. Bevin sighed and began on her food. "It's a complete coincidence then how you find me here like this. Mordred hasn't the faintest idea where I am at this very moment."

"Disbelieve me if you wish, but you are actually correct in that regard. In all truth, as far as I can tell, Lord Mordred believes that you perished back in Port Oil."

Bevin paused at that. She signaled to the counter for another drink with a spark from her horn, a hoof idly tipping the mostly-empty bowl around as she fixed Urien with a stare. "Dead? You don't say?"

Urien nodded, waiting for the bowl to be delivered before saying more. "That is the distinct impression I have gathered from the limited interactions I have had with Lord Mordred and from general rumor among the soldiers under his new command, the warship *Behemoth*. As far as I can tell, you not returning to him once all was said and done in Port Oil, inasmuch as your possible participation in the destruction of the rogue and accidental monster Spell Virus, indicates a distinct lack of life on your part, here in light of previous years of perfect, loyal service."

Three weeks before, Urien's inability to say anything quickly would have frustrated Bevin beyond all measure. But three weeks before, she hadn't been abandoned to die at Mordred's own hoof, hadn't found common ground with Princess Galaxy the Hippogryph, and hadn't had her rose-colored view of the Unicorn Empire thoroughly shattered by Owain. And so, she ground her teeth as a different anger filled her, a searing rage at her former lord. She grasped that rage, cherished it, let it burn away the lingering impulses toward respect and obedience.

"I might have returned to him... if he had not... so easily left me to die. Just left me to die with the rest of that city, discarded like... like some rusted sword or spear you can't be bothered to care for! A decade and a half of my loyal devotion and he..." Bevin could not say it, did not have the words for the bubbling rage inside. All she could do was stamp a hoof on the table and wonder dimly if this was even a fraction of the emotion Princess Galaxy had felt after the destruction of Featheren Valley.

"It appears then that the two of us share a common foe."

Bevin snapped her head back up to Urien, eyes narrowing. "What are you getting at?"

Before he answered, the elder unicorn dragged her cider over to him with magic and dove his head down, emptying the bowl faster than Bevin had ever seen anyone drink before. She let this go. He clearly needed it more than she did.

"What I mean," Urien said once he finished and had dried his muzzle, "is that my son is in danger. Not from the hippogryph or her brother, but from Lord Mordred. He plans to kill Owain or worse, I can feel it. If not through intentional murder, then through utter disregard for his wellbeing. He tells me otherwise, promises me otherwise, but I swear I am not as foolish as some might sometimes think I am. Lord Mordred cannot fool me on this."

Bevin nodded, honestly impressed. Urien was more than likely correct. Brave, too. Slander and libel against leaders was treason within the Unicorn Empire. "Maybe so. What do you want to do about this?"

Urien answered by levitating a package from the floor onto the table. It was long, at least two and a half feet, vaguely crucifix-shaped, tightly wrapped in expensive purple silks. Urien unwrapped the package to reveal a longsword, its glimmering blade engraved with runes of the old unicorn tongue and a white rose above the crossguard.

"A Ley Fay knight's sword," he explained at Bevin's questioning look. "My wife's, before she... left. The blade is pure silver, forged and infused with magic to have the strength of true steel. With this, and ONLY with this, can you kill Lord Mordred. Spear him through the heart, gut him, behead him... your choice."

Frowning, Bevin picked the sword up, testing the weight and balance, checking for flaws in the blade and writing. She found nothing. It was perfect. Mordred would approve.

"If you agree, I can get you close to him," Urien continued. "Soft illusions for your mane and tail, some armor, and you will look precisely the same as any other soldier. Tomorrow night I bring one with me, you take her place when we return to the *Behemoth*, and nobody knows the difference. What do you say?"

Slowly, to keep herself calm, Bevin set the longsword back down and rewrapped it, being sure every tie was tight and not an inch of silver showed. From there she grabbed the package with her magic and strapped it to the rest of her bags, before standing and signaling to the minotaur to lead her to her room for the night. "Until tomorrow, Urien."

CHAPTER THREE

The days passed quickly as they waited for Gwendolyn to be well enough for travel. Much work remained to do even at that late time of year, work Galaxy was happy to take the Elk princess's place in where she could. Foraging far abroad through the forest for suitable firewood, for more of the year-round roots and herbs that made of most of their medicines, frost-proof mushrooms the head healer explained could keep an Elk on their hooves and marching through a blizzard for hours without issue. Elsewhere there were gardens to carefully tend, outposts to carry messages to and fro, repairs on buildings to be made, food to be prepared; all that it was, somehow, absolutely vital to have the visiting hippogryph or her gryphon brother help with.

When not busy with all that, Galaxy enjoyed herself marching the pathways of the hidden kingdom with Gwendolyn, discussing the basics of Elk-brand magic and how it differed from the unicorn-brand magic Galaxy was accustomed to. Owain rarely walked with them, kept busy as he was by Elk who had apparently decided that, if they had to tolerate a unicorn among them, would at least take him and his healing spell for all they were worth.

Brynjar, meanwhile, struck a fast friendship with Captain Hywel and the rest of the Elk guard. By the end of their first full day there, as she and Owain joined Gwendolyn and King Erentil once more for dinner, she found her brother sitting and laughing alongside Hywel and another soldier, the trio laughing as Brynjar regaled them with what like a sensationalized recounting of an encounter against several Imperial soldiers a week back. She would've found Owain's jealous aggravation adorable, if Brynjar did not draw so much attention to the moment in the fight when she'd gotten her horn stuck in a tree. Again.

Through it all, there was only a minor, yet persistent, worry about the dragon. A bitter aftertaste to every task, every conversation, every glance out into the forest surrounding the valley. No Elk traveled alone, and the children were kept herded together with several adult watchers.

"It is fear," said King Erentil on their third night there, his back to the firepit. "Fear can be good. It sharpens the mind and readies the body. But to live in fear, to become old acquaintances with it, is to not live at all."

***

Galaxy bolted up from where she'd been sleeping, spine protesting the sudden movement, barely strangling the scream trying to escape until it was but a weak gasp. She sat there until her heart stopped hammering, until her panicked breathing stopped tearing her throat, until her body stopped shaking with the phantom flames burning her. It took minutes longer once the panic had passed to orient herself. She was in the small, glass-roofed structure King Erentil had set aside for them. She sat closest to the door. To her left slumbered Owain, seeming peaceful as a foal. Across from him, near their personal bags—

"Hey."

Galaxy flinched away from Brynjar's distant, haunted gaze piercing at her from the shadows of the building's far corner. The golden eagle-gryphon sat like a statue against the wall, turning one of his crossbow bolts over between his talons as if seeking comfort in the repetitive motion.

Brother and sister sat there regarding each other for the longest time, Galaxy wondering what sorts of nightmares or twisted memories had driven Brynjar from his sleep and wishing dearly she had the selfishness to share hers. But then Owain mumbled something between them and rolled over, a rear leg feebly kicking. Galaxy stood, looking between the two males before turning for the door, just managing a muttered "Need... air..." she doubted Brynjar even heard.

Outside, the pair of Elk warriors standing guard stopped talking and stood at attention, the one with the silver stripe down his chest armor clearing his throat. "Princess Galaxy. Are the arrangements not to your liking?"

Galaxy looked around, trying to enjoy the beautiful trees that so skillfully wove their way among and through the glass and stone structures the Elk kept for important storage. Even with magic, it must have taken the most careful planning to achieve this kind of close symmetry she saw all around her.

"Princess?"

She wondered where the Elk had gotten the stone for the buildings. Glass might have been heated, blown, and shaped easily enough in the glades and valleys she had seen, but she hadn't seen a single pathway straight or wide enough to efficiently transport the amount of stone she saw around her. And the Elk didn't seem the sort for mining, either, with their tall and broad horns. Gryphons could have air-delivered it, she supposed...

"Princess Galaxy?"

She blinked, shaking her head before looking back at the Elk warrior. "I'm... sorry, my mind was just... what were you saying?"

The Elk shared a look with his comrade. "We were only worried that your accommodations weren't—"

"No, no," said Galaxy, turning away again, to the darker woods surrounding them. "I just need air, I'm... going for a walk."

"Would you like one of us to accompany you? The enchantments can make these woods a maze to the unaware."

"No. I'm... good..." Galaxy, already turned away, started down the closest path at talon. The woods were silent as she walked, the slightest sound subdued under those shadowed boughs. Now and then through the minutes she saw Elk walking hidden paths, the sparse moonlight glinting off armor or blade, but they didn't bother her and she didn't bother them. The silence felt too sweet to spoil.

As Galaxy went, she wondered where the dragon came from. In all her reading, no dragons had left the Dragonback Mountains in decades, not since the Unicorn Empire had driven them from the north. Lacking gold and gems, the Elk seemed a poor target for dragon attack. Trade towns like the nearby Markhaven would be better targets. After cockatrices in the Rotwald and Spell Virus in Port Oil, Imperial involvement was obvious.

Spell Virus... Port... Port Oil... Spell Virus...

The imperial garrison at the center of Port Oil, tall and multi-turreted block of metal and stone—

Steel corridors, hooves clanking, black-coated unicorns trotting past rows of crystal containers holding twisting Elementals—

"Progress continued as foreseen, Lord Mordred—"

Different corridor, different unicorn, rows of cages filled with blindfolded cockatrices—

A filly crying in front of a burning cottage, a wall of shadow advancing on her—

"Isolated the petrification pulse, Lord Mordred—"

Group of unicorns in a darkened room gathered around one such cylinder, metal cables leading from it to a cage-held cockatrice, more cables leading to a pedestal, on which rested a crystal orb—

"The Empress demands... faster... invasion—"

The filly watching through a cracked door as gryphons slash mother and father to pieces, blood pooling, advancing on the door—

Galaxy found herself on her side, talons clenching her head, eyes wet. Breathing deep, she wiped the tears away with the tip of a wing and forced herself to stand before anyone found her like that. Taking another deep breath, she looked around in search of whatever had brought her up from the sudden gush of rancid memory, quickly recognizing the sound of splashing water. Curious, seeking anything to spare herself another attack, Galaxy took to the trees in flight and followed the sound northward, soon finding a wide, starlit clearing.

Galaxy perched atop a high, thick branch and looked down into the clearing. A pond took up most of it, sitting there in the dark like a fallen piece of night sky. At the pond's edge, to Galaxy's surprise, sat a raven-gryphon, probably no older than Brynjar, dipping his beak in to scoop sips of water. Occasionally he would pull back and reach in with his talons, groping for something. He sat tall, slim of build, body taut with a warrior's grace that matched the long-bladed spear beside him. He wore unfamiliar armor, heavy plate that might have been silver in the daylight, the joints and seams accented with blue. Seeing a long blue scarf wound around the raven-gryphon's neck to finish off the ensemble, Galaxy amended her previous thoughts. HER armor bore blue accents.

Curious, Galaxy dared a half-step forward for a better look and heard her branch creak. The raven-gryphon's head snapped up, but Galaxy had already managed to put the tree between them. Even then, she feared her heart's pounding might give her away.

"Hello? Is someone there?" The raven-gryphon's voice was low and scratchy, nervous. "Captain Hywel?"

Swallowing, Galaxy peeked around the tree trunk. The gryphon stood on two legs and faced in her general direction, wings flared and that spear of hers clenched in her talons. Galaxy couldn't help but ogle the stranger's eyes, glowing with a rainbow of colors there in the dark. The way those rainbow eyes shifted left and right to scan the area, Galaxy didn't think she'd spotted her yet.

"Please, away with your weapon," Galaxy called out, only loud enough to be heard. "I mean you no harm. I'm only a traveler through here, friend."

The raven-gryphon did not lower her spear, though her wings somewhat relaxed and her voice carried less hostility. "That's not all that helpful. Oft a hidden friend is worse than an open foe."

Galaxy perked at that last bit, smiling as she leaned out further around the tree. "I know that quote! The Tragedy of Sascha. A famed gryphon general ages past collapsed a narrow pass to slow a human army's march, unaware that minotaur forces were hidden there to ambush the enemy. Relations between our peoples were strained for decades afterward.

"Although," she continued, watching the gryphon stranger relax a measure, "your use of it here seems rather flawed. Aren't I the tragically-killed minotaurs in this scenario, and you the careless gryphon general? And who're the humans we both must worry about?"

Silence for a long moment, before the stranger's body shook with a laugh. The raven-gryphon set her spear back down, using her now-free talons to give a light clap. "I guess you've got me there. Imagine. The most well-learned warrior of Vogelstadt, bested by a strange voice in the Elderpine Forest."

Galaxy's breath hitched. She couldn't help the excitement in her voice as she leaned still farther out from behind the tree. "You're from Vogelstadt? The Floating Mountain? Oh, oh, do you know Lady Quetzal?"

"Somewhat. I... travel at her command." The raven-gryphon turned to nearly where Galaxy hid, making her duck back behind the tree. When next the gryphon spoke, there was a touch of amusement in her voice. "My name is Bifrost. Would you permit me to put name and face to so lovely a voice?"

Galaxy rolled her eyes and giggled. At a rustle of movement, she flew behind another tree as Bifrost flew her way, barely managing to stay out of her sight. Peaking back around, Galaxy giggled again at Bifrost's show of scanning the surrounding woods for her. "You ch-charmer. Would you mind if I asked what you were doing, down at the pond? You seemed to be searching for something."

A pause, a silence heavy with contemplation before Bifrost spoke again. "I travel long miles for Lady Quetzal, and forage resources where I can. I know from experience that winter ponds like these often contain eisrosen."

Galaxy nodded, her mind canvassing all she had read for that familiar term. "Eisrosen? That usually only grows in more permanently cold climes farther north... oh! The water, it keeps a steadier temperature than the surrounding environment, slower to change, so... the plant takes hold more easily there."

The silence this time was surprised. Galaxy, chancing another peak, saw Bifrost rapidly blinking. "That's... that's right! What's eisrosen good for?"

"Easy," said Galaxy, grinning and giddy. "Grind the leaves down into a powder and mix into a paste for a powerful coagulant. Useful for getting wounds to start healing faster. Although, you need to be extremely careful with it. Too much of the paste will cause the blood at the wound to harden to nearly crystal sharpness, while inhaling the powder form in too large doses—"

"Can cause the lungs to become gel-like and solid," Bifrost continued, her own voice light with excitement as she alighted on a branch opposite the side of the tree Galaxy clung to. She made no move to circle around, while Galaxy made no move to flee. "The victim can't take in oxygen and quickly suffocates. However—"

"A quick dose of powdered dragonleaf in the right dosage can eliminate these symptoms." Galaxy's heart beat a strange rhythm in her chest, cheeks hurting from the smile turning the edges of her beak up. Moving to rest against the tree and stare up at the moon from her branch, she wondered when she had ever had the chance for a conversation like this. Had she ever had the chance? She couldn't remember. "You need to be sure it's dragonleaf, though. Mixing powdered eisrosen with nightshade and ash from the fire of a dragon produces a powerful incendiary mixture. A talonful could blow up this entire clearing."

"Aye..." A pause, then, "I owe you an apology. From your accent and excitement over Lady Quetzal I knew you for a northern gryphon, Gryphonbough probably, and assumed a... lesser, education."

Galaxy thought back to the strict education laws the Empire had forced upon Featheren Valley, laws Ida had gleefully ignored, and found herself caught between a sigh and a laugh. "In most cases, you'd be right. I was lucky. My mother was both brave and had the resources for that to mean anything."

A sharp gust got the branches all around them creaking. A sense of movement from behind as Bifrost ruffled her feathers, the faint sound of talons digging into wood. "Cold night. I'd hate to not be a gryphon right now."

At that, Galaxy did laugh. "It's a dangerous night, too. There's a dragon loose in the Elderpine. I'm helping the Elk deal with it tomorrow."

"A dragon? This far out from the Dragonbacks? And bothering the Elk of all people? That's... strange."

"That's exactly what I was thinking about before I met you!"

"Well, great minds think alike—"

"But fools seldom differ."

"Hah! Aye... I suppose. Hm..." The sound of Bifrost's branch creaking again, then "Perhaps I should be on my way."

To her surprise, Galaxy felt a twinge of sadness at this, the reality of the ephemeral situation hitting her. "You don't need to leave just yet. The clearing's been safe enough so far, and I'm sure the two of us together could handle the dragon if it roamed here. No harm in staying a moment and... talking. What's Lady Quetzal like? Have you served her long? What's Vogelstadt like? What are you doing so far from there?"

A sigh carried around the tree, Bifrost's branch creaking a third time as she settled down. "The Lady Quetzal is... magnificent. The most beautiful gryphon you will ever lay your eyes on. Kind and wise, she has led us justly from atop the Floating Mountain since the beginning. She is especially kind to orphans, like myself and my sister, taking us into her school and providing for us. Such generosity, how could I not repay it the moment I came of age?"

A chuckle echoed around next. "For so long my sister and I trained together, tested ourselves against the other to prove ourselves. Now she remains in Vogelstadt while I fly out here, delivering messages and searching for... searching for something I don't even know I can find."

Galaxy turned, looking around the tree trunk at her companion. The raven-gryphon seemed not to notice, her eyes turned up to the night sky. Up close like this, Galaxy could almost get lost in those rainbow eyes of hers. "What do you search for?"

Bifrost took a long while to answer. "Glory, I suppose. Glory in battle against the foes of justice and virtue, like the heroes of old. Something to make me... worthwhile, in the world's eyes. My sort of folk are... tolerated, but... little more than that. Ugh, sometimes I want to grab the people who look at me, grab them and shout that this is me, this is truly who I am, not something I can only ever struggle to be."

These words struck a chord within Galaxy. She pulled back, turning to the moon as she pondered. "I think... I know that struggle too,"

"And how's that, if I might ask?"

Galaxy remembered stones thrown at her head on morning outings, overripe fruits and vegetables sold to Ida at premium prices by sneering unicorn and gryphon vendors, Brynjar's childhood indifference, windows broken in the dead of night, hushed words and sneers when all she could do was grin and bear it. Then, a shift in her life. Galaxy remembered her destroyed valley home, her scattered family, the long journey to the Elderpine just to see her blood mother's final resting place, and the hopes the Elk put in her to solve their dragon problem. The numberless host of unspoken, unformed anxieties around these thoughts every day squirming in her gut. "The Empire, I guess. I want... I... don't even know how to say this. Sometimes it just feels like there is so much... waiting for me. So many expectations. Enough to crush me. I don't know if I'm worthy of it all."

"I see..." A rustle of wings as Bifrost turned her way, but again did not try to circle the tree. "I don't know you well, but... if the Elk trust you enough to help with the dragon, then surely you already have a better grasp of who you are than most. We all have the power to make the world a better place, if we have but the courage."

"If we have but the courage..." Galaxy felt her spirits lift with the phrase. "You think so?"

"I do. Trust me."

"I do. Thank you."

Another long stretch of silence passed, before finally Bifrost stood and fluttered her wings. "As much a pleasure as this has been, my lady, duty calls elsewhere.

And though I will respect it if you still wish otherwise, I would cherish greatly to know you, if I could?"

Galaxy's smile dropped. She had enjoyed talking to someone without the baggage of being a hippogryph. And yet, the raven-gryphon had bared more of her soul to Galaxy than could have been asked for, and it felt almost dirty to leave what would probably be their one and only encounter so steeped in such one-sided secrecy...

"The pond. Go back down to it."

Bifrost obeyed without hesitance or complaint. Galaxy followed her like a shadow, flying as she flew, landing as she landed, standing still as the raven-gryphon turned around. The widening eyes were nothing new, nor the bowing head. "My princess—"

Galaxy held her talons up. "Wait, please. I don't know what you've heard of me, but I'm merely Galaxy. I'm from Featheren Valley up to the northwest. I'm adopted. I'm traveling with my oldest brother and a close unicorn friend. I'm terrified of fire. My unicorn half can't properly process it, so eating meat makes me physically ill. The princess... issue, shouldn't matter as much as it does. This is me. Who I truly am."

Bifrost stood, respect shining in her eyes. Without a word, she turned and strode to her pack beside the pond, retrieving something she playfully kept from

Galaxy's sight. When she returned, she held out a clear orb of crystal, glowing bright with an inner yellow light.

Galaxy heard the crackle of the blue lightning building up below her. She struggled to climb the mast, felt her legs burning and her talons ready to rip free of her digits, and instead reached out with her magic to the crystal battery high atop its pedestal—

"This," said Bifrost, snapping Galaxy back to the now, "Is a frozen spell, gifted to me due to the distance and dangers of my travels. Few unicorns of notable magical skill dwell in Vogelstadt, so these are incredibly difficult to come by, but well worth the trouble. One only needs to crack the crystal to finish casting the spell, so handle with care. One use only, obviously."

Galaxy took the offering with only the slightest hesitation, looking it over with fascination before glancing back up at Bifrost. "What's the spell? Lightning? A fireball?"

Bifrost raised an eyebrow. "Violent, aren't you? But no, it's a humble teleport spell." She turned again and went to strap her packs on, nestling them between her wings, her spear at her side. "Casting that will take you and anyone touching you straight to Lady Quetzal's court. I don't know your planned path, but in a worst-case scenario..." She shrugged, smiling Galaxy's way. "You'll want to meet her at some point, anyway."

There was a point to what the raven-gryphon said. Their plan was to turn back around to join up with family in Wedjet after another week of traversing the Heraldale Midlands, but going straight to the Floating Mountain via teleport and going from there to Wedjet was undeniably safer. Smiling for the precious gift, Galaxy stepped back to give Bifrost room to lift off. "Many thanks for this, Bifrost of the Floating Mountain. Perhaps luck will have us meet again someday."

"Perhaps," Bifrost agreed, flashing Galaxy another gryphon smile. "I fly northeast to meet Queen Vigdis of Gateway, who leads an army to lift the Imperial siege against King Gundahar of Gryphonbough. If we share the same crusade, to end this war and herald justice, I believe we will meet again."

"The same crusade..." Galaxy thought that phrase over, liking it. "Until that day comes, fly with swift winds, friend."

"And you the same." Bifrost beat her wings to rise into a hover, staring at Galaxy a moment longer before flying off with an impressive speed for one so heavily armored. It was not long before sight of the raven-gryphon was lost to the night.

Seconds passed as Galaxy stared up at where Bifrost had disappeared, before a clearing throat made her eep and whirl around. King Erentil stood near the clearing's edge, an amused gleam to his starry eyes as he looked Galaxy over. "Make a new friend, young princess?"

"I, uh..." Galaxy glanced from the Elk king to the night sky and back again, cheeks warm from her blush. "I've never met a gryphon from Vogelstadt before. She seems nice."

King Erentil joined her beside the pond, gaze turned to its mirrored surface. "Oh, Bifrost is certainly that. Confused in the head, but he's a dependable messenger and fierce warrior, at least, to have such a dangerous job so young. It is good to keep in contact with old friends and allies. Let them know of you. More, it is fascinating how lives so apart can for a moment brush against one another before continuing on their way. People come and go, living their own lives, their own stories. Fascinating."

"I suppose," said Galaxy, letting the Elk's dig at the departed Bifrost go unremarked upon as she looked at her reflection in the water. The hippogryph staring back at her looked fuller, surer, if a little more worn for wear than she remembered. The month and some change of travel and battle since Featheren Valley showed itself in numerous little scratches and scars across her front and sides, a look in Galaxy's eyes that might have frightened her if she'd seen it in anyone else's eyes. "I've met so many people on this journey. Mordred. Bevin. Rocky the rockodile. Blackbird. Zita." She glanced at

Erentil, seeing again that sad gaze. "You and your people. And for that matter, tomorrow brings with it a dragon of all things!"

"As I said," spoke Erentil, a touch of humor to his voice, "fascinating."

At this they fell into a companionable silence for a minute, the air frosty and the pond alight with the night's stars, before Galaxy's curiosity got the better of her. "Why do you look so sad? Is there anything I can do?"

He looked at her with distant eyes and said nothing for long enough that Galaxy worried she had offended him with the blunt question. But then the sadness came over him again and did not flee. "I could ask the same of you, young princess. My warriors told me of your strange distance earlier, how you seemed hardly to know where you were. And though you might have fooled most of those there, I recognized your tension during the feast."

Galaxy hurriedly looked back to the pond. She swallowed, struggling for the right words, not wanting to discuss her problem with anyone but knowing full well there was little getting out of it with the ancient being beside her. "Horror Sickness, the books I've read call it. Fighters suffer it, survivors of tragedies, of abuse. Nightmares and fear and anger and... and..." She swallowed again, refusing the tears that wanted to fall now that she had started. "I think my brother has it as well, and maybe Owain. I'm not sure. It's... it's pathetic, really. Broken by my first great act against the Empire. I should be stronger than this. I'm a hippogryph, I shouldn't..."

"Be so cowardly?"

Galaxy jerked as if struck, looking up at Erentil's understanding gaze. "Galaxy, my young princess, Lady Quetzal is a Prime Being, the only one present and capable of action remaining in the known lands of Heraldale. And yet, she remains secluded in her Floating Mountain. For all her power and unbroken mind, she does nothing. It is you, and your companions, who are out here fighting the war, facing monsters, and saving my daughter. And so, think what you like, but I do not see a coward standing before me."

A smile then, a gleam in those starry eyes that reminded Galaxy strangely enough of her playful twin siblings. "And neither, I think, did Sir Bifrost."

Galaxy's blush returned, warmer than ever. Yet her heart felt lighter than it had in many a night as she and the Elk king began the trek back the way they had come, hope for a peaceful sleep in her thoughts and Bifrost's gift of the frozen teleport spell tucked beneath a wing. Tomorrow would bring dragons.

CHAPTER FOUR

"—and then after that, she flew off into the night. Surprisingly fast, for someone wearing so much armor."

"And then, innocent little Galaxy felt her heart blossom with her first adventurer's crush."

"Owain! I don't even experience infatuations!"

"Not sure I like you seeing strange gryphons at night, Gal. Although... how long was this Bifrost's spear again?"

"Aaugh. Appetite gone. Let's go, maybe the dragon will be kind enough to burn me to ash and away from this nagging."

"Might be bad idea bringing you, Gal. Dragon might ask for top flight speed of unladen swallow-gryphons. Then we'd really be in trouble."

"AAUGH!"

Galaxy sat back from the circle, weathering a few more minutes of teasing from her family and bemused stares from the few Elk rising early enough to break fast with them before, finally, it was time to depart. They left early, their path going in a generally northwestern direction and more difficult than Galaxy expected. From above, the forest looked flat, but ground level told a different story. They came upon dells, deep brooks, fallen trees and loose groupings of rocks and pitfalls hidden by the fallen leaves and snow. The latter had been falling since they awoke. Without Gwendolyn guiding them, there was no telling how much slower progress would have been.

Yet, time passed. Nearly a full hour since they passed the last regular Elk patrol, the land grew flatter, many trees smashed apart and knocked down in a wide, staggered corridor. Much of the wood looked burnt.

"Is this where the dragon chased us yesterday?"

"That is right," said Gwendolyn, springing over a fallen tree. "At least we always hear it coming. Don't expect this destruction to last, though. The nature magic of the Elderpine Forest is strong. It grows faster here than anywhere else in the world, I have heard. In a week and a half, it will not look like a dragon had ever been through here.

"But come, it is not much farther now to where I found the dragon, so we need to be careful. I hadn't been fleeing for long before you rescued me, Princess Galaxy."

"Just Gal, please. It's what my friends call me." Fluttering above the others, Galaxy tried to remember everything she knew about dragons. Their long lives, though not quite as ageless as unicorns. Their size-changing magic. Their hunger for gold and jewels alongside meat. Their fire-proof bodies. Their superior magical reserves. Nothing encouraging.

"So... princess," said Owain, looking ahead of them at Gwen. "How's that work when your king is immortal? Or, is the forest divided into principalities beneath a High King?"

The Elk shook her head, Brynjar having to swerve to avoid losing an eye to her horns. "No, it's not like that. For us Elk, the prince or princess is a... safety measure. There is always meant to be a line descended from King Erentil in case tragedy strikes, for our king is safe from dying of age and disease, not injury. If the royal line ever dies out, he chooses an Elk and sires a new line. Like me."

Gwen walked with her head high and her steps light, looking like the woods were her queendom and her remaining bandages royal robes. "If Father ever dies, leadership of the Elk people will pass to me. It is a duty I hope never to assume."

"I see..." Galaxy thought she heard a touch of bitterness in Owain's voice. "I hope the same for you. You know, my father is... I mean, was... a governor for the Unicorn Empire. Planned for me to follow in his hoofsteps, had me tutored by the best from the moment I could string together a full sentence."

Gwen glanced his way. "It was not something you wanted?"

Owain chuckled and shook his head, coming within a hair's breadth of gutting Galaxy as he did. "I admit, growing up I bought into the Imperial thinking like anyone else. I loved telling people what to do, lording my 'natural unicorn superiority' over the gryphons of the valley." Here he gave an apologetic look to Galaxy and Brynjar. "But truthfully, at night, I would wonder how much more... exciting, another path might be. Maybe the kind of path my mother took when she disappeared."

A hedge of thorny brambles crossed their path. Without needing to be asked, Galaxy lifted Gwen over the obstacle with her magic, while Brynjar flew over with Owain. "What path was that?" asked the golden eagle-gryphon once he set the unicorn down and they started forward again.

"I'm not sure. I have my suspicions, though. Just... something I hope for. Better than thinking she just up and left one day."

"I see." Gwen looked up at Galaxy next. "And what of you, Gal? I already know Brynjar's father here was the brave and knightly Kurt, of the Queensguard, but what is there to say of your father?"

That brought Galaxy up short, a brief sting hitting her heart. Seeing Brynjar about to speak up for her, she cut him off. "I don't know. All I ever really gathered from Ida was that he was already dead for some time by the time of Grimhilt's death, but..." She hesitated, debating whether she should mention her dreams, the visions of the white unicorn who SEEMED like her father... but with the way the dreams had turned into nightmares lately...

Seeming to sense the unease with this line of thinking, Gwen changed tracks. "It seems weird to me, not knowing. Grimhilt was the last of her house after her sister's death during the war, but just imagine if you had relatives on your father's side. Oh! What if you had brothers or sisters from your father's side?"

Galaxy laughed at that, thinking of Brynjar and the Twins, Sascha and Siegfried. "Oh, goodness. I wouldn't know what to do with more siblings."

The conversation continued as such, hushed but comfortable, friends getting to know one another better, all the while the ground gently sloping up. Caught up in Owain once more teasing about Bifrost, Galaxy didn't notice the trees opening up into a clearing ahead of them until Gwen called for them to stop. Galaxy landed beside the Elk and peered around. Aside from most of the clearing being made up of churned mud and snow, a broad hill set in the center, nothing jumped out at her as particularly foreboding. "Is this it? Where's the dragon?"

"You can't see it from here," said Gwen, "but on the other side of that low hill there is a cave. I think it's a hidden entrance to a Wolf-Lord structure below the forest."

Galaxy groaned. She remembered well the last time they'd ventured into one of those underground cities.

"Maybe..." Owain coughed. "Maybe the dragon killed or scared off anything that was already in there?"

"Or maybe it's breeding with them, creating half-dragon, half-wyvern monsters!"

Owain looked at Brynjar oddly. "Wygons? Draverns? Or, wait, can dragons crossbreed with other races in the first place?"

"I mean, unicorns and gryphons can clearly—"

"And that's a conversation I don't want rattling around in my head. Gwen?"

"Nope. Follow me."

They followed Gwen across the several yards of brown, mushy snow, Brynjar still flying above to keep a lookout, while Galaxy elected to struggle along on the ground. Gwen walked a wide circle around the hill until there, opposite the side they'd started from, was the cave. Galaxy thought it uncomfortably resembled an open wound in the earth, stretching three yards horizontally and two yards vertically, solid stone visible just beneath a crusting of dirt at its edges. The edges were burnt and scratched, leaving little doubt that the dragon at least frequented there.

"That looks fun." Brynjar's voice possessed a manically happy tone to it. "Who wants to go down into the pitch-black cave of a fire-breathing monster first?"

"You should," quipped Owain with a toss of his mane. "You might get stuck and have your front half roasted off by dragonfire."

"No, you should," replied Brynjar, smirking back at the unicorn. "You might trip down that incline with those clumsy hooves and snap your neck."

Owain smirked back up at Brynjar, eyes half-lidded. "You go, you might bring the ceiling down with one flex of your wings."

"You go, you might wedge your horn against the ceiling and break your skull."

"Once again, get a room, you two, gosh." Galaxy shook her head, marveling at the hypocrisy for them to needle her regarding flirting. "I'll go first. I'm the smallest and... probably, won't suffer all that horrible stuff. You three stay and wait for my signal to follow, okay?"

"Is there any point in me saying how much I don't like this?"

"Also," said Owain, scuffing a hoof against the crevice edge, "what exactly would your signal be?"

Galaxy paused halfway into the crevice, pulling back out to stare at them. It was such an old line, she hadn't actually thought to come up with anything beyond it. "Uh... well, I'm sure you'll know it when you hear it."

"AUGH."

Chuckling at her brother, Galaxy turned away and slipped down through the crevice before another word could be said. The rough-hewn tunnel she found beyond went four yards down at a slant, quickly hiding Brynjar and the rest from her sight. Beyond that point, she could see it sheering off into a straight downward fall.

Galaxy paused at that sudden fall and lit up her horn. Her magic shone bright, but failed to illuminate the black rock of the vertical tunnel past a few feet. She eyed the dark depths warily. Despite her flippancy moments before, in the light of day, she found the thought of venturing into such dark unknowns like this... daunting. There could be anything down there, now that she let herself think about it. Old and forgotten Wolf-Lord traps. Wyverns. Ghouls. The dragon itself. And with dragons there came fire...

"It is you, and your companions, out are out here fighting the war, facing monsters, and saving my daughter. And so, think what you like, but I do not see a coward standing before me."

Galaxy took a deep breath, stilling her quivering wings. She turned and slowly backed over the edge of the drop-off, waiting until she was hanging by her talons, the rest of her body swaying in a weak draft, before spreading her wings and letting go. She hovered slowly down into the deep shadows of the tunnel, eyes wide and scanning around for any hint of movement.

Yet all she saw as she descended foot after foot was darkness, or else the craggy rock walls of the tunnel, glimmering in her magic's red light.

Five feet...

Ten feet...

Fifteen feet...

At twenty-five feet down the tunnel opened into a larger space, its walls, ceiling, and floor a glassy black in the red light. An antechamber of some kind, Galaxy guessed. At the far end she could see a large pair of doors similar in style to those she'd seen in Hollereich, ponderous slabs of stone inlaid with metal. The doors stood open a crack, flickering orange light seeping through. A rumble echoed from beyond.

Galaxy looked back the way she had come and considered her options. This seemed like a good area to regroup and assess the situation. She could shout and the others would hear her and come down. There was room for all of them to move around without getting in each other's way and thick stone to slow the dragon if it attacked. More, if she didn't let them all know that she was fine soon, Brynjar was liable to start having a panic attack. It would be a shame if he flew in at a random moment and ruined Galaxy's sneaking about.

"And yet..."

Galaxy turned away from the exit and marched to the cracked doors. They pushed open easily despite their weight and age, perfectly silent. Enchanted, perhaps. The next room was at least double the size of the antechamber, conjuring further unpleasant memories. Towering statues of armored Wolf-Lords, ten feet tall each, lined the walls down the length of the hall, ten to a wall. Between each statue sat a bronze bowl atop a pedestal, in each of which burned orange fires.

Galaxy took a moment to look over the statues of the Wolf-Lords, unsettled. Most of the races of Heraldale were quadrupeds, or at least bipedal and possessing heavy tails or slouched postures to keep them balanced. And though these statues depicted them as indeed having wolf tails, that seemed all they had in common with the other peoples. The Wolf-Lords stood tall and straight-backed, arms hanging at their sides, axe in one gauntleted fist and shield in the other. Their gazes turned straight ahead and muzzles open in panting smiles, Galaxy wondered what sorts of beings would make such statues. No writings of theirs remained after their exodus from Heraldale, no art other than their architectural marvels and scattered murals in Gateway. No Wolf-Lords remained in Heraldale to question, to ask about their lives and worldview. They were gone.

"Ahem."

Galaxy jumped, nearly screaming, whirling around to see Brynjar, Owain, and Gwen marching up the hall toward her, an annoyingly knowing look on Brynjar's face. "I, er, who?"

"Yeah, not even giving you chance for stupid hero stuff this time," said Brynjar. "I don't like this place. Dark and creepy. Let's make this quick. Before these statues come alive and attack us."

"What!?" Owain let out a frightened whinny and spun toward Brynjar. "Why!? Why would you even say something like that!? Haven't you realized yet that the universe is actively LISTENING for ideas on how to make life miserable for us all by this point!?"

Brynjar shrugged. "What? Seems likely after everything else we've seen."

"But you don't have to make it easier!"

Intentional or not, Galaxy's fear withered from the familiar back-and-forth. Seeing Gwen's nervous expression, Galaxy fluttered over and patted the Elk's back with a wing. "It's really not as bad as they're making it out to be. I'm sure if these Wolf-Lord statues could actually come alive and attack intruders, they would've attacked the dragon by now."

Gwen nodded, not looking all that reassured. "Yeah, sure. Let's just do this and go, like Brynjar said."

Galaxy nodded and turned back, reaching out to push the second set of doors open with her magic.

"Actually," said Owain, Galaxy pausing at his tone, "it suddenly occurs to me that we don't... actually...

have any idea what we are going to do with the dragon. Unless someone came up with a plan but didn't tell me?"

Seconds passed as they looked at each other in silence, before Brynjar walked over to the nearest of the statues and started banging his head against its leg. "Verdammt. Verdammt. Verdammt!"

"Wow," said Galaxy, cheeks burning. "We are really bad at this, aren't we?"

Gwen looked around at them all. "You must be joking. No plan? At all?"

Brynjar stopped giving himself a concussion long enough to say "Usually everything goes to Sheol before we have time to think up a plan," before resuming banging his head against the statue.

"Yeah," continued Owain, looking appraisingly at the next-closest statue leg. "Things happen so fast, plans are usually just spur of the moment. Has worked surprisingly well, actually. Guess we're sticking with what's not broken today."

"Okay. Okay." The unease in Gwen's voice was slowly being replaced by annoyance. "But you are going to get rid of the dragon, aren't you? That is why we came here. Come up with something."

Finally, Brynjar stopped battering his head and staggered back over to the group. "Don't worry, I... I got this. Gal, we'll watch exit. Go in and do your best

Commander Bevin im... impress... collapse the room on the beast. That'll do it."

"I like that plan," said Owain. "It's the best plan. My favorite part is not having to do anything."

Galaxy looked between the three of them, an unexpected knot forming in the pit of her stomach. The idea of striking first, of violence not in plain self-defense... "You sure I can't just go in and try... try talking first?"

"Gal..." Owain's tone rang frustratingly calm. "Dragons debate with fire breath. I think you'd rather skip that."

"Yeah, but..." Galaxy looked toward the door again, that knot growing and bubbling up into her chest. She sat and folded her front legs across her chest, trying not to look angry or pouting. "Catching the dragon unaware, it wouldn't even know what happened. Just snuffed out, just like that. I've never... never done that before. With pre-planning, at least."

Owain blinked. "That can't be right. What about when you rescued me from the cockatrices?"

"Brynjar killed them. I just kept them from you."

Brynjar stepped closer. "The wyverns?"

"You two killed them. I just held the door closed with my magic."

"Spell Virus?"

"Eh... Already dead from the magical accident that created him. What we fought was his body's physical matter transformed into its equivalent in magical energy and driven by echoes of his and a cockatrice's will all melded together. And anyway, Brynjar loosed the crossbow bolt that took him down."

Brynjar groaned. "Destroying the *Titan*, then! Come on, Gal!"

Galaxy glared at her brother, talons digging into the floor, horn flaring with magic, anger suddenly filling her. "That was do or die, and you know it! And I didn't know their city-destroying barrage would reflect right back at them, and we saw unicorns escaping in troop carriers as it went down, and, and I'm not talking about moments of self-defense here, I'm..." She swallowed, anger roiling inside her, articulating these thoughts a struggle. Why couldn't they grasp what she meant?

Gwen stepped closer, a pleading look about her. "If not killing, then what? What else could you possibly do to stop the dragon as you swore to? Talk to it?"

Galaxy glared in silence at the far wall. Brynjar groaned. "Oh Gal... who next, the Empress?"

"Gal," said Owain, "that is a terrible idea. Truly, simply your worst idea. This isn't some angry unicorn or something, it's a dragon! They're just... violent! Down to their core."

"Oh, stuff that!" Galaxy stood, wings beating into a hover, talons clenching, angry and embarrassed and resolute in the face of their judgment. "Guess that's just the same as how all unicorns are power-mad to the core, huh? Or gryphons are mentally inferior to the core, yeah!?"

"Gal!" Brynjar's voice was a hoarse whisper, as if terrified to go louder. "Calm down! You're going to give us away!"

Galaxy kept her glare focused on a shrinking-back Owain as she hovered backward to the door. "That's my gottverdammt point! Let's just all stop acting like we have any idea what anything's like, any people are like, or who can be relied on, because I don't know if you've noticed, but we're always proven wrong! So don't tell me I simply have to kill this or that without at least the common decency of finding out for sure first! It's not about killing, it's about murder!"

She turned, horn glowing brighter as she shifted her focus into telekinesis to throw the doors open. "So let's just MAKE SURE before I murder what probably is a big... ferocious... gryphon-eating... dragon. Huh."

The grand hall before them seemed carved from a natural cavern beneath the Elderpine Forest. The ceiling ranged anywhere from 10 to 30 feet high, the main area stretching on for half a mile and branching off into smaller caverns and corridors. An underground lake sat at the bottom of a slope toward the right. To the left sat tall piles of ash. Directly ahead of them, two dozen feet away and sprawled across a raised platform, rested the dragon.

Or, thought Galaxy, perhaps snoozed like a content cat would be a more accurate description, the dragon's wings and tail and limbs and long neck all askew, limp as wet noodles. The dragon's scales, strangely, were not the black that Galaxy remembered, but a vibrant pink, and at eight feet from head to tail it was far smaller than it had seemed that first encounter

"That's not the dragon!" Gwen hissed as she backed away from the entrance to the hall, looking around in a panic. "That's not the same dragon! It's too small, and it's not the right c-color! Oh God, there are more than one of these monsters! We need to go, get out of here and warn my people while we can!"

"Forget that," said Owain, also backing toward the exit. "Let's bring the roof down as planned, and THEN warn your people!"

"No, wait," said Galaxy, pulling the panicking unicorn and Elk back over with her magic. She made a shushing motion before gesturing to the sleeping dragon. "That's definitely the same dragon that's been attacking your people, Gwen."

Brynjar, hunkered down behind a fallen chunk of ceiling near the door, crossbow readied, turned to stare wide-eyed at her. "What. What!?"

"It makes sense," Galaxy insisted. "The crevice we came through is too small for the dragon we saw. Sheol, I bet Gwen had trouble, with her antlers. Yet really powerful or old dragons possess the magic to change their size to a limited extent. A really young dragon, like this one here, might be able to push herself to 30 feet long.

"And then look," she continued, pointing first to the piles of ash and then the underground lake. "She covers herself in ash to appear more fearsome, washing it off when she's done. Because, honestly, dark grey is far scarier than pink."

Owain looked between the dragon and Galaxy, eyes narrowing, not looking quite as ready to bolt for the exit as he had a moment before. "Maybe a stupid question, but... how do you know it's a girl dragon?"

Galaxy rolled her eyes and hovered closer to the sleeping dragon, close enough to draw promptly-ignored gasps from the others. "One day, perhaps, it will register that I am quite well-read. Also, it's not too different from how unicorn stallions have curved horns and mares have straight horns. Look here, see the way her two horns are toward the back of her head and curve backward? Male dragons of this species have horns closer to the brow and that curve forward. A male dragon also has a horn-like protrusion at the end of his snout, mostly decorative."

She gestured to the other end of the dragon, voice rising with excitement. "And see here, the tail is long and slender, tipped by a blade for whipping instead of a male's stubbier, clubbed tail. And look back up here, at her eyes! They're oval like a cat's—"

Galaxy realized what she'd said just as a roar shook the cavern, followed by a blur of pink knocking her to the ground. She found her front legs pinned by grasping hands, the dragon looming above her, oval eyes staring down at her, nostrils wide as they blew scorching air into her face. Scaled lips pulled back, showing off a mouthful of fangs, each as big as one of Galaxy's talons.

Yet seconds passed and no fiery doom came, the dragon seeming content for the moment to sniff the hippogryph over, bare her fangs, and growl. At this, Galaxy felt more hope than was probably warranted. Not much hope, when her heart felt moments away from stopping and she had to put conscious effort into not wetting herself from sheer terror, but it was something. Oh... that maw looked big enough to take her head off in two bites.

"Gal!" rang two voices in the cavern, snapping Galaxy from the moment. She saw Brynjar and Owain charging from the left, crossbow aimed and sword raised. Her eyes widened.

"Wait, don't attack!" Her shout made the dragon flinch back, while the two "rescuers" skidded to a halt. "Please, just stay right there! I can handle this!"

"ARE YOU MAD!?" Brynjar's voice rang shrill, the golden eagle-gryphon landing only to smash a fist into the stone floor. The dragon's growl and Galaxy's hiss went ignored. "How can you... how... the dragon's right there! Holding you! Fangs bared and tail raised and looming and, and—"

"And she still hasn't really hurt me yet," Galaxy said, cutting him off. Not entirely true. The dragon's grip felt ready to snap her front legs like twigs. "Please trust me here... just stay..."

Hoping the others obeyed, Galaxy refocused all her attention on the dragon above her and wracked her memories for the one thing that had a chance of resolving this all peacefully. ~Ssstop... hurting... am friend.~

The dragon reared her head back, eyes suddenly wide, grip loosening on Galaxy's front legs. ~Ssspeak dragon?~

Galaxy started to nod, just remembering that was a sign of aggression in dragons in time to stop herself. ~Ssspeak dragon... not... well. No harm... you... friend.~

"Gal? Sister? Are you... talking to the dragon?"

"Probably badly," Galaxy replied, continuing to stare at the dragon and remaining perfectly still. "Mom wanted to teach me a second language. I thought dragon would be fun. Really hard, never had occasion to practice. Kinda wishing I hadn't gotten so lax with it..."

~No!~ growled the dragon suddenly, grip tightening again, eyes flicking from Galaxy to Brynjar. ~What wasss that? No tricksss! No hurt me! No hurt!~

These last few words were screamed. Galaxy flinched from the force of the hot breath. ~No, no hurt. Talk truth! Talk friendsss!~ Galaxy cursed her limited vocabulary as she struggled for the right wording. ~How... be? What... what do... Unicorn... foresssst!~

"Aaaugh!"

Galaxy's voice broke into a cry, for at the word "unicorn", the same as Elk in dragonic, the dragon snarled and clenched Galaxy's front legs tight. Then, just as suddenly, the dragon let go, eyes remaining trained their way as she backed off, back onto the raised platform. It was during this movement, in the light of the torches lining the walls, that Galaxy finally noticed the burns. Black burns and splotches of dead-looking skin and scale ran in lines over the dragon's body, crisscrossing down the sides and over her belly and back, running up and down her legs and streaking across her neck. Half-healed holes perforated the membranes of the dragon's wings, explaining why she had not flown after Galaxy and Gwen the day before.

"Oh God," said the Elk in question. Little fear remained in Gwen's voice now, to Galaxy's relief. "What could have done that? What kind of fire burns a dragon?"

"I can make a guess." Hobbling closer again to the dragon on her still-aching legs, Galaxy pointed to the most prominent corrosion lines along the dragon's right side. ~Zzzakariansss?~

The dragon flinched, letting out a series of hisses that Galaxy could not fully interpret. The most she got were the words "hurt", "steal", "make change", and "unicorns".

"Gal," said Owain with forced calm, "mind filling in those of us who can't speak lizard? All I got out of that was what you said, zakarians."

Galaxy sighed and took a tiny step closer to the dragon, who hissed and inched back, but did not attack. Galaxy continued. "Fire isn't all that burns. The acid spit of a zakarian warrior, if properly concentrated, could melt through dragon scale and — and flesh." Her thoughts darkened, a tightness coming to her heart that she tried to keep from her eyes. "The pain must have been horrible."

The dragon roared as Galaxy took another step closer. ~No ssspeak alone! Ssspeak me! No hurt, hurt unicornsss! Make change... eye... gem! Alone!~

Galaxy held her talons up in a placating gesture, speaking slowly to avoid any mistake in pronunciation. ~No hurt... no bad... truth... friendsss here, how... how pain? You... age? Where from you? Other... other dragonsss?~

With each word, the aggressive front the dragon had managed up to this point crumbled. She huffed and shuffled back, away from Galaxy's reaching talons. Her hisses and growls were a strain to filter into anything meaningful. ~No other dragonsss dead dead dead changesss failed! No ssstone ssscale head talk make changesss only fail! Not make think right! Unicornsss hurt pain burning. Ssstorm essscape! No hurt thought, no hurt!~

The dragon loosed a pathetic mewl as she stopped retreating and huddled down, hands moving to cover her eyes and tail wrapping tightly about. ~Misss Mother!~

Galaxy froze, talons hovering an inch from the dragon's side. She thought over the possibilities of that one whimpered plea and trembled with horror. ~How... old? I... gryphon 15, almossst 16. You?~

The dragon peeked out between two fingers, looking up at Galaxy with one watery eye. ~163. Pain ssstart half age. No hurt please.~

Galaxy swallowed, forcing herself to stay calm as she closed the distance and rested her talons on the dragon's side. She could feel ribs through too-thin skin and too-brittle scales. Starving, then. Starving, but even then, never resorting to eating any Elk. Galaxy smiled, though she knew it to be a bitter smile. ~All okay now. Keep you sssafe.~

"Gal?" Brynjar had wandered a few steps closer. "We have any problems?"

"That's an understatement." Galaxy looked away from the dragon to her companions, only then allowing the absolute RAGE to show in her eyes, the urge to burn and break and crush and HURT on the dragon's behalf. "No problems here, not from... not from here. Some of it I couldn't understand, but I got enough... She was one of many dragons captured by the Empire and experimented on, some decades ago. I'm... guessing the experiments failed in some way, but before they could kill her like the rest, there was a storm. She escaped. Hid in the first cave she found, perhaps. Too scared and hurt to go far."

"There was a storm a few days before the dragon first appeared," said Gwendolyn, little fear in her voice now. "And there is an Imperial fortress many miles south of the forest, near to a village called Markhaven."

"Good Toqeph..." Owain's eyes were wet. Galaxy could feel the guilt radiating from him as Brynjar fluttered over and rested a comforting wing over his back.

Galaxy took a deep breath for this next part. She needed another, heart aching, wanting to punch the floor until her bones broke. "She's also... young. God above is she young. Hardly, if I remember my lessons... hardly more than 12, in dragon years. Half that when first captured."

The dragon shrank from the shouts of dismay, shock, and rage that echoed through the cavern. Galaxy sighed again, gently stroking the child's side, mindful of the worst hurts. ~I ssso sssorry. Ssso sssorry...~

***

Run. Run. Need to run, fly, flee. Lungs burning, smoke stinging eyes. Pain. Blood, blood. Blood from wound. Chest hurting. Magic bolts sizzling through night sk—close call, almost hit, run, run. Can't breathe, can't see, can't, need to flee, flee, dead, dea—

TRENCH.

Bifrost fell into the cratered earth, dragging one mangled leg as she clawed for room beneath the twisted roots of a half-fallen tree. Worms and spiders coiled in the bloody muck with her. No time for thinking, only escaping and hiding and the shallow gash in her side from a unicorn horn slipping under her armor. Blood poured out from between talons pressed desperately over the wound as she wished she'd never given that teleport spell away.

Above, behind, all around Bifrost came the screams of the dying, the flash of bolts flying, smoke giving all a dreamlike vagueness. With the screams were the heavy beating of hooves. Yards off, Bifrost beheld a minotaur crushed beneath a dozen trampling unicorns, paying him not a moment's heed as they chased after a broken-winged gryphon. Bifrost couldn't look away as five horns pierced the helpless sparrow-gryphon's side, his scream choking out in a gurgle of blood. Above this chaos flew crystal drones, clusters of sharpened crystal spires glistening with blood in the firelight as they slashed and skewered any gryphons trying to keep to the skies.

Bifrost didn't know how it all happened. The battle seemed theirs at first. Queen Vigdis's relief forces, 1,500-strong, had attacked the 2,000-strong Imperial force guarding the southern paths to the Gryphonbough Forest under cover of night, hitting the resting air-yachts and warships with explosive fire-bombs and lead weights, destroying them all before a single one could rise, taking the Imperial general, Bors, with them. At the same moment, sphinx and minotaur mercenaries struck from the southwest with volleys of heavy cannon fire, throwing the whole encampment into disarray. It should have been a massacre, Queen Vigdis of Gateway leading the flocks of gryphons in from the sky to rake through the confused enemy like... like hawks taking mice in the plains, relieving the siege King Gundahar of Gryphonbough had been suffering.

But then the second Imperial force had appeared, materializing from a black thundercloud and rushing the battlefield from the west. Those on the ground, gryphon and sphinx and minotaur alike, fell beneath the rain of thousands of trampling hooves and stabbing horns, while those gryphons dominating the skies found themselves swarmed by more of the crystal drones than Bifrost had thought possible. And not only drones, but troop carriers, warships with their magic batteries blazing, and worst of all... the wyverns. Hundreds of them, moving in perfect sync under the direction of a winged unicorn black as oil. Queen Vigdis had gone down screaming, the condor-gryphon disappearing beneath dozens of leathery wings and snapping jaws. No hope for victory after that, no chance for even an organized retreat. Death, death all around them, pain, fire, blood, screaming and shrieking and the blast of—

Bifrost's increasingly panicked thoughts scattered from a heavy THUD just outside her hiding place. Trembling, the raven-gryphon looked and saw in the mud a stone minotaur statue, hands gripping a massive war hammer. His face was twisted into a look of terror.

More bodies began to fall, more statues, gryphons shattering to pieces when they hit ground. Bifrost crawled farther out from the tangle of roots to look up. She beheld the obelisk-like warship leading the Imperial forces firing a lightning-like blast of magic from its bow at the remaining airborne gryphon forces, turning to stone all struck by the new weapon. Her heart quailed as she recalled the stories of Port Oil, of the magical beast Galaxy had bested.

An eagle's screech of defiance made Bifrost look away from the falling statues, in time to see some of the few gryphons left in the air engulf a troop carrier in flames with their fire bombs, all of them caught in the point-blank blast. Horrified, she watched the flame-riddled box of metal and crystal tumble in circles from the sky, crashing and exploding in a blinding fireball some dozen yards from where she hid.

"God help us..."

Even from that distance, the heat scorched Bifrost's feathers. She ignored that, crawling out of the crevice and dragging herself talon over talon toward the flaming wreck. Her limbs were growing numb, exhaustion and blood loss demanding she stop moving, to just lie there and rest regardless of the consequences. Bifrost couldn't, though. Through blurring vision, she saw hope in the fire, faint as it was.

A spear lay discarded near the wreck. Bifrost grabbed it before rolling into a kneeling position, the wound in her side tearing wider from the movement, making her scream. Panting, inching as close to the fire as she dared, she stuck the blade of the spear into the flames, shivering and looking all about. Nobody was in sight, the raging warzone slowly dying down.

Bifrost pulled the spear back out of the fire when the blade blazed a cherry red. Her talons trembled as she undid the clasps for her chest armor on the right side to open it, allowing her to bring the heated metal close to the wound. The blood shone in the light. She just had the presence of mind to bite down on the tattered end of her scarf. Before the blood-freezing terror could stop her, she pressed the fiery blade against—

PAIN.

Bifrost screamed around the scarf, limbs thrashing as she collapsed onto her back. She screamed until her throat tore, until stars whirled before her eyes, until the stench of burning feathers and fur and flesh finally forced her to pull the spear back from her cauterized wound and toss it away. Bifrost barely noticed the scarf slipping from her cracked beak, letting her scream her agony to the burning apocalypse around her unhindered.

The thunderous fall of approaching hooves answered her. Sobbing for air, Bifrost rolled onto her uninjured side, forcing herself to stand and grasp half-blind for the discarded spear. Yet her limbs had lost all strength. She barely managed to lift the weapon from the churned earth before the first of the unicorns was upon her. The blinding flash of a steel-shod hoof flying at her head—

***

Consciousness returned slow, in fitful bursts. Bifrost still hurt, hurt all over, but not as much as before through the throbbing in her head. Everything felt sluggish, little strength left to the raven-gryphon's limbs as she struggled to recall anything that had happened. A battle... a wound... fire and pain...

Nearby hooves and a pained grunt made Bifrost open her eyes. She found herself clustered together with dozens of other gryphons, more being herded their way by unicorn soldiers. The battle was over, the blasted-out plain around them fallen eerily silent save the crackle of still-burning fires and the shouted orders of Imperial commanders. Her wings were strapped down to her back, her talons tied tight together in chains. Through the slowly lifting fog in her head, the cauterized wound in her side demanded attention.

A roar sounded from above, drawing all eyes up. Bifrost gaped as a half-dozen emaciated wyverns landed

10 feet ahead, moving with unnatural symmetry as they formed into two rows of three facing each other, yellow eyes glazed over and lifeless. Next the winged unicorn that had led the wyvern swarm landed on the far side of the rows, glowering at the gryphons gathered together. He marched their way between the wyverns, a stomach-churning sound of flesh tearing and bones breaking sounding out as the wings withdrew into the unicorn's back. Some gryphons in the crowd around Bifrost emptied their stomachs, others looking ready to bolt and face death at the hooves of the surrounding troops. Bifrost, well-learned, kept herself as still and unremarkable as possible.

Lord Mordred came to a stop before the gathered prisoners of war, an unreadable expression adorning him as he looked them over. To Bifrost, those yellow eyes looked more tired than angry, unsatisfied at the victory.

After a moment, Lord Mordred turned to the nearest soldier. "Are these all your troops found, lieutenant?"

"Almost, my lord," responded the mare, drawing a green crystal from her armor and seeming to consult it. "11 were found in critical condition and deemed unlikely to survive unless treated immediately. These are those deemed fit to remain. Further, we are still searching the outer reaches of the battlefield for any that tried fleeing but were too hurt or exhausted to make it far."

Bifrost felt sickened upon hearing this. The armies of Queen Vigdis had numbered in the thousands. There could not be more than three or four dozen gryphons around Bifrost, alongside a scattering of minotaurs and sphinxes.

Lord Mordred looked far more pleased by the response. Turning back to the gathered prisoners, the unicorn stallion stepped closer, pacing leisurely from one end of the crowd to the other and back to the center. "Gryphons. Minotaurs. Sphinxes. You... lesser creatures. The day is the Avalon Empire's. Your armies are crushed, your leaders killed, your hopes shattered. Your nations, cultures, and... physiologies, have been found thoroughly lesser than ours. Someday, perhaps, you will be found fit to stand alongside unicorns as properly civilized people, but that is not today. No. Today you will be sent to various secure fortresses throughout Heraldale. You will be questioned. Interrogated. We have ways of getting the answers we want—"

"TORTURE!" bellowed a minotaur somewhere far right of Difrost. By the time she turned her head to look, he was already being restrained flat to the ground by a number of chains conjured from the horns of surrounding soldiers.

Lord Mordred went on without missing a beat. "Torture is such a dirty word. The word we use in Avalon is interrogation. It's a subtle difference, and I wouldn't expect creatures like you to see it. Don't worry. You will have the rest of your lives to become intimately familiar with that careful distinction. For all your sakes, I would strongly recommend willing cooperation. There is no hope otherwise. Your nations are doomed, your lives forfeit, your people ripe for destruction. Your God cannot save you. Your Prime Gryphon does not want to save you. NOBODY is saving you. There is no hope, so just—"

"There is hope!"

All eyes turned to Bifrost, standing now, wobbling on her shackled legs but staring defiantly at Lord Mordred all the same. From the corners of her eyes she saw several unicorns turn and charge their horns to restrain her as they had the minotaur, but at a Look from Lord Mordred, all of them stopped and bowed their heads, able to feel the punctuation. The Empire's Lord of War looked at Bifrost then, an alarmingly appraising gleam in his eyes as he stepped closer. "Is that so, scarf-wearer?"

Bifrost knew she had made a mistake standing, a mistake speaking, but she hadn't been able to stop herself. Unable to go back, she swallowed and steeled herself to forge ahead. "There is hope. Princess Galaxy, daughter of Queen Grimhilt and hippogryph of

Featheren Valley! She defeated you in Port Oil, and she'll keep defeating you until the Empire is finished!"

Whispers broke out among Bifrost's fellow prisoners, some standing as well. Lord Mordred's gaze darkened, losing all humor as he stomped with a heavy trod toward Bifrost. The raven-gryphon stood firm, chalking the trembling in her limbs to exhaustion and nothing else as the second-most powerful unicorn in the world shoved gryphons aside with bursts of magic to reach her.

It was harder to ignore the armor-wetting terror as razor-thin tendrils grew out from Lord Mordred's back. Before Bifrost could react, they had whipped forward, encircling her neck and tightening, lifting her choking and kicking into the air to let Mordred look her in the eyes. Bifrost, struggling for breath, found her gaze trapped by the unicorn lord's eyes, the yellow sickly and faintly glowing, strangely ragged, the pupils narrow pits of black. Bifrost felt that fog of before encroaching once more, something more now than oxygen deprivation, something clawing and biting its way into her head—

The yellow eyes moved, Bifrost able to somewhat breathe again as Lord Mordred looked down from her eyes to the ragged, blood-stained blue scarf around her neck, then down to the chest plate still hanging halfway off her body. The eyes widened, something approximating a smile spreading across his muzzle, something filled with too-sharp teeth, too-many teeth. "I never realized they had your sort in Vogelstadt..."

Brynjar's eyes widened. Before she could say anything, Lord Mordred turned, tendrils throwing Bifrost to the hooves of the nearby Imperial soldiers. A scream of pain as her hastily-cauterized wound ripped open tore from her beak. "Take him somewhere secure. Make sure he doesn't die. I will want to question him myself."

"Yes, Sir."

Shaking her head to fight the encroaching darkness, Bifrost forced herself to sit up and turn to where she guessed the retreating form of Lord Mordred to be, only to once more be met by a steel-clad hoof.

CHAPTER FIVE

"What is that beast doing here!?"

"Someone summon the soldiers, quickly!"

"We trusted you to kill the dragon, not befriend it!"

"The animal!"

"Child or not, it's still a dragon—"

"What is wrong with you!?"

Galaxy jerked awake, immediately regretting the sudden movement. She groaned and slumped back onto her side, remembering a moment later that the stone floor of the Wolf-Lord hall wasn't that much better. Two yards off slumbered the dragon on her dais, peaceful in the sparse torchlight. Brynjar and the others were not to be seen, Gwen remaining with her people and Brynjar and Owain staying with the air-yacht now hovering over the cavern entrance's clearing.

From a certain stillness in the air, the humidity, Galaxy guessed it early morning, the sun probably just starting over the horizon. The fifth such sunrise since befriending the dragon and losing most Elk goodwill. Despite Brynjar's insistence otherwise, Galaxy had slept down in the forgotten Wolf-Lord hideaway with the dragon and continued communicating as best she could.

Reacquainting the poor girl with friendly company is the best way to help her right now. Just trust me, please."

"Of course I trust you." Brynjar brushed an errant feather back into place on Galaxy's head and tried to smile. *"It's everything else I don't trust."*

That lack of trust, to Galaxy's distress, had proven warranted when they tried bringing the dragon back with them to the Elk. Those that had not fled as if their lives depended on it at the first sight of the dragon had stayed only for cruelty's sake, demanding the dragon's head or else lamenting Galaxy's foolishness. Even King Erentil had been all too hesitant to quell this uproar, doing little more than insuring she and her friends could leave unhindered. Ever since, Galaxy had mostly left Elk matters to Brynjar, Owain, and Gwen. There were others in greater need of her time and attention.

At that thought, with the fear of the nightmare well faded, Galaxy yawned and rolled to all fours, taking her time stretching her legs, wings, and back. Yawning again, she trotted around the slumbering dragon to the underground lake, dunking her whole head in and pulling it back out after several seconds, wet and gasping. All thoughts of sleep fled from the icy water. "Euugh! Guh!"

~Friend?~

Loose pebbles danced on the cavern floor as the dragon joined Galaxy beside the lake. And if the dragon was awake, it really was time to start the day.

~Good... morning... friend,~ Galaxy said as she set about preening her feathers with the help of the reflective water. ~Sssleep good?~

The dragon hissed something Galaxy couldn't quite decipher and dunked her head into the water just as Galaxy had moments before. Like Galaxy, she surfaced sputtering and far more alert. Huffing, the dragon blew breath hot enough to send steam rising from the lake's surface, quickly dunking her head in again. Galaxy watched the dragon do this for a moment, before shrugging and backing up a step. With a shout she dove forward into the lake, flaring her wings at the last moment to send water splashing to the left and right.

SPLOOSH.

"RAAARGGGHHHH!"

Galaxy bobbed back up to the surface, blinking water from her eyes to find the dragon fallen onto her back. Seeing the pink-scaled beast flailing her arms and legs in the air in a struggle to right herself, Galaxy clamped her talons over her beak to stifle a laugh. ~Sssorry... friend... no harm...~ She struggled for the best way to say this through her limited vocabulary. ~No harm not-mean?~

The dragon finally managed to roll back onto her feet, fixing Galaxy in place with an unamused stare. Before Galaxy could react, the dragon loosed a thin stream of flames that sent the water's temperature skyrocketing.

"OUCH!"

Galaxy leapt out of the water, swearing as she flew around to dry off. The dragon's deep-throated laughter echoed through the chamber. ~No harm not-mean!~ she roared out between laughs, a fist slamming the ground. ~No harm not-mean!~

~Okay, no not-mean now,~ said Galaxy, landing eventually and smiling too. She gave a final shake before heading for the hideaway's entrance, jerking her head for the dragon to follow. ~Food time!~

***

The early morning sunlight shone through the royal meeting hall's dome, soft as the hoof-falls of the watching Elk. Ignoring their wary stares, Owain slowly unwound the last of Gwen's leg bandages with his magic to show the cut beneath had fully healed, leaving little more than a thin white scar. Owain breathed his relief. "And there you go, your highness. As good as new, with a little refinement besides."

Gwen tested her weight on the healed leg. When it was clear the limb could support her without issue, she placed a soft doe's kiss beside Owain's horn before stepping back and assuming a more royal posture and tone. "I believe this settles it for all of us when I say that Princess Galaxy was not the only fortuitous meeting a week ago." She paused for the reluctant murmurs of agreement to run through the crowd, few and far between as they were. "As the daughter of King Erentil and representative of all Elk here, I thank you and your healing magic, Owain."

Owain could only hope he wasn't blushing too hard as he bowed to the princess. For once, finally, all the time his father had spent drilling proper etiquette into his head could pay off. "The honor and pleasure are all mine, your highness. As with Galaxy, in the name of friendship between our peoples, I remain at your service."

Gwen nodded, before sighing and motioning out the doorway with a tilt of her horns. "Gwen is fine among friends. Please, come, walk with me. In the name of friendship, I... don't think it would be good to have Brynjar hurt himself preparing for your departure on his own."

Gathering what they needed did not take long, eager as the rest of the Elk seemed to be to see the unicorn amongst them gone. Soon enough, he and Gwen were walking a more direct route from the Elk haven to where the air-yacht waited above the dragon's den, pace quick but comfortable. Each carried heavy packs filled with food and spare tools set aside by King Erentil for their use.

"It's a shame you must leave so soon," said Gwen as they crossed a bridge over a deceptively-deep stream, the surrounding trees casting strange shadows and reflections in the slow water below. "And as a fresh snow approaches! You can only imagine the beauty when the pine needles turn to little ice crystals in the cold, the sound of hooves crunching through snow, the chill of the night air beneath the moon and stars."

"You paint a lovely picture," said Owain, gaze shifting skyward. Clouds were moving in, the kind heavy with snow and ice. "And yet, it's probably for the best. To put your people at ease."

"I start to think my people are fools," said Gwen with a scoff. The scorn in her tone surprised Owain, as did the regret in her eyes. "I know that I was, at our first meeting. I realize I haven't really apologized yet for my hostility toward you, based only on you being a unicorn. It was... childish, of me."

"You're not apologizing for anything I'm not guilty of myself," Owain said, looking at her. "To your kind and so many others. It's been wonderful getting to know you and your people. So different from how I grew up in the Empire, but you live a good life here."

Gwen nodded to this, plucking a red berry from a bush they passed. "As different, I imagine, as life was for Galaxy and Brynjar. It must've been difficult, but you have good friends. If there's one lesson my father has taught me above all others, it is to always value your friends, big and small."

Owain made a noise of agreement. As they circled a particularly large tree, his thoughts turned to Brynjar without his direction. Handsome Brynjar, unlearned but insightful, kind despite everything, feathers like rich oak and fine-spun gold, dark eyes that dove deep into Owain, a rough voice to send chills down his spine, big—

"Owain, you there? You're blushing."

Owain coughed, tossing his mane and looking around to check where they were. "—wings. Big wings. Um, so listen, something Gal and I have been thinking about. She and Brynjar can fly for hours at a time, so it wouldn't be too crowded even with the dragon coming with us... and I mean, surely King Erentil would approve of experiencing the wider world... would you like to come with us when we leave?"

Gwen paused, eyes wide, a prey animal surprised. "You would... I... all but the oldest of my people have lived their whole lives in the Elderpine Forest. I... I wouldn't even know what to do out in open fields, or big cities, or towering mountains."

Owain laid a gentle hoof on one of hers, marveling quietly at the size difference. "I imagine the same as the rest of our group does. Try putting on a brace face for the innocent masses while stumbling from one life-threatening encounter to the next, coming up with hare-brained plans just in time to not die."

Gwen's laugh was strained, tearful, oh-so-needed. Owain took it as a yes and started again for the clearing and the air-yacht, hearing from the crack of pine needles Gwen following close behind.

***

Looking over the new map gifted to him by King Erentil, Brynjar thought he had their next step figured out. Leaving the Elderpine Forest, they would turn southwest for the village of Markhaven, situated along a river feeding from eastern Heraldale into the southern Sandwine River. Making a show there, battering around whatever Imperial troops they found, would keep it looking like they were heading for Gateway. Their actual destination would be entirely unexpected. And from there, Vogelstadt and the rest of their family.

A twig snapped somewhere behind Brynjar. He turned to look off the air-yacht's side and froze. At the edge of the dragon's clearing sat the biggest wolf he had ever seen. It was at least as big as him, its coat a stark black against the white snow, its eyes shining yellow. It sat there like it owned the forest, regarding Brynjar with too-intelligent eyes.

"Scheisse," Brynjar muttered, glancing to where his crossbow and quiver sat several lengths away, beside the controls for the air-yacht. Too far to reach if the wolf decided to charge and jump. Owain's sword was even more useless, away with the unicorn in question. The living weapon he called his sister was who-knew-where with the dragon.

Refocusing on the wolf, Brynjar found that it had stood up and advanced several steps into the clearing, ears perked and eyes focused on him. Brynjar thought maybe he could fight the wolf in close quarters with beak and talon, but... that'd be a close one. Not the worst odds he'd ever faced, but probably the worst he'd ever faced alone.

The wolf took another step toward the ship—

"Brynjar, we have returned!"

Startled, Brynjar turned to look over the other side of the air-yacht, where he could see Owain and Gwendolyn emerging into the clearing. When he looked back he saw the wolf was gone, no sign of its having been there at all beyond a few pawprints in the snow and mud. "What?"

"You say something?" Owain trotted up the wood ramp onto the ship, setting his pack beside the mast before huffing and shaking his mane. "I think that's the last trip we need to make. Good thing, too. My hooves are killing me. I will simply never get used to all this physical labor."

Coming up the ramp behind him, Gwen rolled her eyes. "Oh, this was hard labor? I hadn't noticed. My mind was on all the plowing through frozen ground to do in the coming months, the clearing away of ice and snow, the gathering of literal tons of firewood to keep us warm and alive. Please, do go on about how carrying a few packs has been the utmost toil for you, oh precious unicorn sir."

"Well," continued Owain, to Brynjar's amusement, either not noticing the sarcasm or electing to ignore it, "about halfway here I caught my tail in some thorny brambles, and I think I've got an aching... never mind. Where's Galaxy? She knows how to treat me."

Brynjar turned from where he'd last seen the wolf, shuffling it from his mind as he set to work sorting through all that the unicorn and Elk had brought. "She left half an hour ago to find food. Took dragon with her."

Gwen trotted over, setting her own packs down to be sorted. "That should take a while. We need to discuss certain issues here. There is still the matter of the dragon to resolve."

Brynjar nodded, having been expecting this to come up sooner or later. At least it happened while Galaxy was away. He knew she wouldn't like certain opinions of his on the matter. "Your people will be safe. Gal and I will take the dragon with us."

"So I've heard." Gwen nodded toward Owain. "Mostly I was curious where you're taking the dragon. If Galaxy was right about her age, she's but a child of her kind. It would be irresponsible of you to take her along into whatever dangers you face."

A sound of hysterical distress emanated from Owain, who quickly shot to his hooves from where he'd been sorting their food stores and trotted away to fiddle with the air-yacht's control crystals. Brynjar huffed at the dramatics, turning to address Gwen's quizzical stare. "Owain still afraid of dragons. At least, adult dragons. Doesn't matter. We're going to Markhaven to show off, before making straight shot for Dragonback Mountains to return dragon to her people."

"And there are no other places you could take her? Gateway perhaps, or Wedjet?"

Brynjar lifted his wings in a shrug. "Owain and Gal say the Dragonbacks are only place in Heraldale dragons live. Best chance of finding any family left. Besides, as I keep telling Owain, taking lost, hurt dragon back home will be great for Gal's friendship with dragons."

Gwen frowned, visibly put off by the reasoning. "That seems a cold-hearted way to treat the situation."

"Pragmatic," called Owain from the controls. "The word you're looking for is pragmatic. Not that Galaxy cares."

"It doesn't matter if she cares or not," said Brynjar, returning most of his focus again to the supplies. "As far as anyone else should know, it's her kindness, plain and simple."

Gwen looked like she wanted to say more, but just then, movement from the surrounding woods made them all perk up. The Elk princess turned back the way she and Owain had come minutes before. "Father!"

Brynjar stood, seeing indeed King Erentil entering the clearing, a dozen Elk guards with him. "Your majesty."

"Greetings, my daughter. Apologies for not coming with you. I had to make some... last-minute arrangements."

To Brynjar, he said "Are you certain that you wish to leave so soon? For your help with the dragon I would have welcomed you into my house for the entire winter, if you had asked. That's the... least, I could do."

"There's no helping it," said Brynjar, glancing at Owain to see the unicorn studiously paying them little heed. "Even if your people accepted the dragon, Galaxy needs to be out there fighting the fight. It's who she is."

The Elk king nodded, frowned, glanced around the area. For what, Brynjar couldn't say. "Very well, then. However, once she returns from her hunting with the dragon, there is one last boon I hope to offer you all."

***

Luck was with them. 20 minutes into their search, the forest brought them the den of a black bear bedded down for the winter. One blast of fire breath made it a meal fit for a growing dragon. Galaxy left that alone, preferring instead a satchel of the sweet red berries gifted to her by Gwen.

As she perched in a tree and ate, Galaxy watched the dragon, at the moment shrunken down to about the same size as Galaxy. Almost, save the unhealthily lanky build and spindly limbs. Galaxy watched and thought. She had the dragon's trust, for the most part. She was allowed to sleep reasonably close by, they walked together through the woods, and the dragon had even offered Galaxy a leg from the bear, though wasted no time insisting when the hippogryph declined. Yet, Galaxy wasn't satisfied. Whatever the unicorns had been doing to the dragon, she knew, was likely still being done somewhere in Heraldale. The experiments on this dragon had failed, like the experiments in Port Oil. But what might a successful experiment result in...

Tweeting drew Galaxy's gaze from the feasting dragon below to the crossing branches above. A pair of birds flitted among the tree limbs, dark against the grey sky.

~Flying?~

Galaxy looked down and saw the dragon staring past her, watching the birds with naked envy. Her tattered wings twitched on her back.

~Hey,~ hissed Galaxy, drawing the dragon's attention. ~You... want fly?~

The dragon nodded, her eyes wide as she shifted in place, at the moment looking more like a puppy wanting to play than anything else. Galaxy dropped down to the dragon, casting her gaze around in an overly theatrical manner and circling about. With limited language to get her meaning across, she needed to add as much subtle dragon body language as she could. ~Take journey... reach mountain, good fly. Go home. Heal... pain, make fly again. Dangerousss... journey... many enemiesss. Ssstill come?~

~YESSS!~ Galaxy stumbled back from the dragon's roar. A few tongues of flame flickered from her mouth, making Galaxy flinch. ~Go home family misss ssso much! Take journey, will help! Help friend heal fly!~

~Okay,~ said Galaxy, forcing her fear of fire down. ~I do that. Heal friend. Fly bessst... promissse.~

A sudden burst of song made Galaxy look back at the two birds, cardinals, dancing among the limbs of the trees in their flight. She watched how the two kept so close together. Looking back to the dragon still sitting there, tail wagging as she continued watching in expectation, Galaxy let a giggle slip from her beak as she had an idea. ~Hey.~

~Hey,~ the dragon hissed back. ~What now?~

~I... have... idea,~ Galaxy snarled, stepping closer. ~You go on journey... trussst me? Think friend?~

The dragon hesitated for a moment, before nodding. ~Yesss. Bird friend. Bird'sss friendsss, friendsss. I trusssst.~

~Thank you,~ said Galaxy. ~I... I gift you. Fear at firssst, I promissse you love. Promissse no ssstruggle?~

A shadow of doubt passed through the dragon's eyes, but again she nodded after only a moment's hesitation. ~Promissse. What gift?~

~Fly,~ Galaxy answered with purposeful mystery, smiling as she reached out with her magic and wrapped it gently around the dragon's mid-section. The dragon stiffened, eyes growing wide and fearful. Galaxy paused, recognizing immediately the sort of fear and panic that bubbled ever beneath her thoughts, ready to breach with the slightest provocation. ~It good. I ssstop if you want. Jussst sssay ssso.~

The dragon shifted her weight, digging her claws into the dirt. Finally, she shook her head, tail smacking the ground. ~No, keep going, can do.~

Galaxy nodded, allowing another moment for the dragon to keep calm before continuing. She made her magical grip around the dragon's mid-section thicker and more evenly distributed so as not to put too much pressure on any one spot. The dragon was still dangerously thin, after all, and Galaxy didn't want to break a rib or bruise an organ through poor support.

~Remember, keep ssstil,~ Galaxy hissed, before rearing back and with several flaps of her wings rising up into the air. Seven feet up her magic tugged on the dragon, making her squawk as she was lifted up into the air following Galaxy. The hippogryph kept her pace slow for the dragon's sake, taking half a minute to rise above the forest canopy into the open air beyond, speeding up only gradually once there as they rose higher and higher. They did not reach anything approaching fast until the Elderpine Forest became only a mass of green and white and the sky opened up for miles and miles around in every direction, up to the clouds. The dragon panted and shuddered in near-panic, limbs clawing and tail whipping, right up until Galaxy pulled a barrel roll and gave her a sweeping look all around.

~Look! Dragon, you fly!~

Silence for a moment, before the dragon released a joyous roar and spread her wings out wide, the tattered membranes shining translucent in the sun, her bladed tail whipping behind her as she basked in the wind against her scaly face. ~FLY! I FLY!~

The sight of such happiness after such misery sparked a wish to feed it within Galaxy, spurring her on to fly faster, the pair barreling through the sky. The forest passed as a distant blur beneath them, the clouds above a stormy grey. Galaxy spun once, twice, slow spins that let the dragon see without getting dizzy as they flew within feet of each other. It was difficult, dangerous keeping them that close with those spikes and that tail, but Galaxy thought it worth it for such a clear look at the joy in the dragon's eyes.

~Higher! Faster!~

Obeying, Galaxy stopped the spinning and flipped so that she and the dragon shot upward toward a towering bank of clouds. The dragon roared her approval, wings beating in time to Galaxy's own. The green of the forest and fields disappeared below. The world turned blue and white as Galaxy raced through the clouds, putting magical and flight dexterity to the test as they moved in synch, first Galaxy above and ahead, the next moment the dragon ahead, another moment flying side by side, the farthest tip of Galaxy's right wing touching the farthest tip of the dragon's left wing. The water of the clouds swirled at their passing, somewhere lightning cracking and thunder rolling.

For the first time in the longest while, Galaxy allowed herself the pure joy of flight, up there where there was no Empire to constrain her, no Spell Virus to threaten her, no anxiety to strangle her thoughts, only the wind and frost and light. The clouds her stage, the dragon her partner, the flight her dance of spins and dips, tumbles and pirouettes, their laughter the song of their play.

Another roll and flip saw them bursting out of the clouds, the whole world opening up like never before. Above, blue dipping into black stretched out into infinity, the sun blazing as it beat upon their backs and warmed their wings. Below, a sea of foamy white dominated, broken few and far apart to show a dark world of pains and sorrows. Galaxy could see her breath leave her thicker than the depths of winter, their height pushing even her gryphon endurance to the limit.

For long minutes the pair simply hovered there, soaking it all in. Galaxy had only ever ventured so high once before, and for the dragon it must have been the first time, so silent had she fallen. Galaxy looked left to where her magic held the dragon and saw tears frosting at the edges of those oval eyes. The dragon was crying, filling Galaxy at once with guilt. ~No! Sssorry, friend! I no mean sssadnesss...~

~Ashe...~ The dragon dragged one clawed hand across her face, wiping away the icy tears. She looked over at Galaxy, the corners of her mouth curling up into a smile. No pain or sadness lingered in that smile. Galaxy, heart beating like a war drum for reasons she couldn't name, could almost forget the acid scars littering the dragon's body. ~Name Ashe. Thank... friend.~

The two hovered there above the clouds, spying stars along the distant horizon, their new bond unspoken but, Galaxy hoped, unbreakable. Only when the thin air began to bother even her through her inherited gryphon capabilities did Galaxy finally begin to slowly coast the pair of them down.

~Time to go... lassst goodbyesss before journey.~

***

Owain stood at the air-yacht's helm as Brynjar circled the craft for a final maintenance check. Ashe curled slumbering around the air-yacht's mast, pink scales shining in the light glinting off the metallic sails. Gwen stood at the starboard sails, stowing away her own supplies. Aside from her, only a few other Elk warriors, such as Captain Hywel, had come out to see them off, the rest readying for a coming snowstorm. Or so Galaxy had been told, at least.

Deep in the feelings of anxiety and excitement that accompanied the nearing departure, Galaxy took a moment to notice King Erentil approaching her on the lowered boarding ramp. She quickly ducked into a bow that he was gracious enough to return. "The safety of my family and my people is of utmost importance to me. You have helped both. Now, I believe the time has come for me to hold up my end of the bargain we made, concerning Grimhilt's Folly."

Galaxy stiffened, looking first to her companions, then to the Elk soldiers scattered across the clearing to monitor the proceedings. "I'm sorry, I had assumed from the... unhappy, response your people gave to my sparing the dragon..."

"A promise is a promise," said Erentil, giving those same soldiers a look that had them ducking their heads. "And a good Elk keeps their promises. A good leader, doubly so. It's how you build trust."

Galaxy grinned, bowing once more to Erentil. "I'll try to keep that lesson in mind. Very well, then. Lead on, my king."

"Gal, do you want—"

"No, no," said Galaxy, smiling and waving Brynjar back to the safety ropes he'd just been securing to the air-yacht's railing. "You keep getting things ready here. I'll be fine."

A strange look passed through Brynjar's expression then, a frown that was there and gone before Galaxy could get a firm look at it. Then the golden eagle-gryphon had turned away and back to work, leaving her no room to ask what was wrong before Erentil descended the boarding ramp. Caught between the pair, Galaxy swallowed her unease at the situation and followed the king eastward. There would be time to talk to her brother later. Now was the chance to answer a question haunting her dreams for untold time.

A soft snow fell, had been falling for the last hour, covering the land beneath a white, downy robe. Time passed in tense quiet as they walked, the loudest sounds to be heard their hooves crunching the snow. Galaxy tried to engage Erentil in conversation at the start, and though he seemed happy enough to speak with her, he also seemed remarkably ill-used to it.

"Did you know my mother?"

"Not as well as I should have. Queen Grimhilt was fierce in defense of her people, slow in acceptance or forgiveness to those who wronged them or her, but not one to hold grudges once forgiveness had been granted. I remember her grimness, especially toward the end of the war, as well as her weariness. Cardinal-gryphons are not built for war, and I believe it took much out of her even before battles started to go badly. Why, perhaps, she gave up so much to prevent war between unicorns and gryphons from breaking out in the first place. Has Sir Ida never told you of this?"

"Not in such detail. I guess it hurts too much. She always got so sad when I asked, but... I never knew Grimhilt. I wish I had. Then... then maybe I could feel sad too."

Erentil frowned and looked away, and that was the end of that conversation. Time passed. It seemed to grow colder and colder with every step, the silence of the Elderpine deepening. Galaxy followed where Erentil led her with increasing trepidation, gaze sweeping around and finding no other Elk in sight. Even on that night of her meeting Bifrost, there had been others wandering the woods.

"There might be a way to help with your Horror Sickness, you should know."

Galaxy snapped her gaze back to the Elk king, surprised after the long silence. Not looking down to meet her gaze, he continued. "It's a dangerous magical technique, to be performed by two who absolutely trust each other. The participants must sit together, calm and collected, and reach out each to the other's mind with their own magic, at once, not missing a beat. A mistake could leave both with their minds permanently mixed together, impossible to tell where one ends and the other begins, but done properly... it could allow you and the other person to objectively perceive whatever memories haunt you, gain closure with them, and heal."

Galaxy stared up at him, wondering why he had brought it up. "Well, if I ever have the chance to settle down in peace for a while again, like I have here..."

Erentil nodded, finally glancing down at her with a brief smile. "Something to consider, at least."

With that, the silence returned, not so hard to stomach now as Galaxy had the hope of healing to ponder. Erentil had spoken of both participants reaching out with magic, but perhaps there was a version to include gryphons. If she could help Brynjar get his rest and peace...

Their trek nearing the hour mark, the trees ended more abruptly than Galaxy thought possible. She staggered to a stop, barely avoiding running into Erentil from behind. He glanced back at her with a touch of amusement, before sidestepping to allow her an unhindered view ahead. "I am sorry I could not show you sooner, but it has taken all this time to remove the numberless magical defenses and hiding illusions keeping it safe."

Before them a great gorge opened in the earth, north and south almost to the edge of vision and half a mile wide at the widest point to be seen. The bottom of the gorge was hidden from them by a deep, swirling fog, but Galaxy could just make out the sound of rushing water echoing up from the deep. Across the gorge from the pair, half-hidden from sight in the falling snow, stood the remains of a magnificent fortress. It dwarfed Governor Urien's Featheren Valley castle, a layered rectangle upon rectangle of stone and wood and iron, all shaded in whites and greys. Three towers rose from it, two narrow and toward the front, the third toward the back and large enough to almost seem a second fort fused to the first. Holes pockmarked the outer walls, and much of the fortress was cracked and covered in dead, withered husks of clinging ivy. Numerous trees grew around and into the stone carcass, nature well on its way to reclaiming the space.

"Mein Gott..."

"Behold, Grimhilt's Folly," said Erentil, walking the edge of the gorge. Galaxy followed, spying a white stone bridge some yards ahead, still miraculously connecting their side of the gorge to the fortress. "Built in cooperation between the Knights Le Fay and Queen Grimhilt during the war as a secret stronghold. This was before my people lived so far this direction. We were unable to lend aid in time when Lord Mordred attacked."

A chill altogether unconnected with the weather crept up Gal's back, a talon tracing over some of her burn scars from Mordred's lightning. If the journey so far had been quiet, it was now silent as a church as the pair began across the bridge. Nothing but the tap-tap-tap of hooves and talons on cracked stone, a nervous shifting as dislodged rubble tumbled out of sight down the gorge. Before she knew it, Galaxy's heart pounded with terror. Somewhere, an unseen crow cawed. The path stretched on and on ahead of them, straight and narrow, littered even to that day by fragments of bone and armor.

"After Mordred was done here, did he... did he come after your people?"

"At first, yes. I soon put a stop to it."

At the moment, Mordred was the last of Galaxy's fears. She began to imagine the ghosts of those long-fallen on this bridge appearing around them, crawling up over the sides of it to block their way forward, cut off their escape, start crowding in with gaping wounds and hungering beaks and empty, eyeless skulls filled with the darkness of Sheol itself, hungry, grasping Sheol. The geists danced on the edges of her vision, whispering just beyond her hearing, their cold a stab in the gut...

They reached the other side of the bridge. Galaxy collapsed against the fortress wall, shaking, breathing heavy. "What... what was that?"

"The dead, and other things." Erentil, expression a picture of pain, conjured an orb of white light between the prongs of his horns. "There aren't so many inside. Keeping your thoughts focused on a singular something, a scrap of poetry or fond memory, can help."

Once Galaxy had managed to regain control of herself, they ventured into the ruins. Moving slow, they strode through long halls and gaping entrances where grand doorways had once stood. Rotting, tattered remains of banners lined some walls, fluttering in an unseen breeze. The weight of the pervasive darkness reminded Galaxy of Hollereich. It was a knowing sort of darkness. A WATCHING sort of darkness.

"Aside from Sir Ida and a scant few others who had fled, there were no survivors of the battle that took this fortress. Lord Mordred slew every unicorn, every gryphon, every Elk and minotaur and sphinx that defended these walls. Those were strange days, following his betrayal of Queen Grimhilt. He seemed... half-mad, and the spirits of his victims were oft caught in that mad aura and made to linger. Spirit... stuck among flesh and material things, the jaws of Sheol ever gnawing at them... torturous."

A door creaked to their left, but when Galaxy looked she saw only a jumble of wood shards and shattered stone. Somewhere else there was almost a scream. Behind them echoed a lingering sigh. Hooves clattered among piles of bones and dust, rusting weapons and armor left where their wielders and wearers had fallen. Galaxy's throat burned from an acrid stench. She moved closer to Erentil and started to wish she had not followed him. "There's only death here."

Far their path took them into the fortress, past a throne room, up flights of stairs teetering and crumbling, through rooms clothed in cobwebs. Up into the highest of the towers. Yet Erentil still moved with a purpose, as if there were one place or sight in particular he wanted to show her. Galaxy, feeling herself caught in a cobweb of curiosity, fear, and simple forward momentum, could only follow.

The answer to Galaxy's unasked question came at the far end of what must have been the highest room in the fortress, behind what was surely the last door still standing in those ruins. The stone was inlaid with metal Wolf-Lord runes, and unlike everything else she'd seen, stood clean, obsidian-black.

Erentil pushed the door open with his magic before stepping back and nodding to Galaxy. She hesitated before stepping through, gathering her courage under the guise of examining the runes. The room beyond was immaculate as the door, no dust or cobwebs, no cracks or mold, no rusting weapons, no aging skeletons. Lit candles sat on benches lining the circular room, tall and glowing with a welcoming orange warmth. Galaxy could almost taste the magic preserving the room. Stepping deeper inside, Galaxy noticed a painted mural covering the walls just above her head level, a candle beneath each scene. A sensation in every way at odds with the rest of the ruin filled the sanctum, heavy and light, welcoming and forbidding, holy in a way Galaxy had never encountered before. "What is this?"

There came the sound of Erentil shutting the door behind them before answering. "Your past, in a manner of speaking. All structures associated with the Knights Le Fay contain similar chapels. Here is shown the story of where hippogryphs come from. The scenes to the left and right are the same, both leading to the final scene in the center, opposite the door."

Galaxy swallowed, her heart thumping in her chest as she approached the leftmost edge of the mural. "I've wondered for so long…"

The first scene depicted a gryphon and a unicorn facing each other, weapons and armor cast down around them. The next scene showed the unicorn and gryphon alone, bodies curved together to form the romantic image of a heart. Love, Galaxy took this to mean. The next image in the mural portrayed the two standing together before a group of taller unicorns armed with spears, behind them a broad and flat bowl. The unicorn and gryphon couple were kneeling in supplication, or perhaps worship.

The final image, directly across from the door they'd entered through, showed the gryphon and the unicorn on opposite sides of the broad basin. Their heads were lowered, the gryphon's talons clasped together in prayer. Wavy lines, a sign for water, rose from the basin. Above the lines arose a hippogryph, wings spread and horn surrounded by an aura of light.

Galaxy looked at this final image for a long while, before turning to Erentil. "I'm… not sure I understand. It reminds me of… something… but the thought escapes me."

Erentil nodded and moved to Galaxy's side. "There is a legend, a hidden truth, going back to the earliest days of creation. God entrusted a trio of powerful artifacts to the Heralds of three of the realms of material life. To the gryphons, the Aetherial Chalice, lost long ago after war with mankind. To the dragons, the Flames Eternal, housed to this day in the gullet of the Prime Dragon Kur, known among lesser folk as Snarl. And to the unicorns went this," he nodded to the basin, "the Waters of Life. The key to... many things."

Galaxy placed her talons against the central image of the basin. Even within that room, sheltered from the wind and snow outside and warmed by the many candles, that spot was cool to the touch. "The Waters of Life..."

"Yes. Guarded for untold millennia by the highest of unicorn priests, and then by the Knights Le Fay after them. Their more commonly-known use was the healing of wounds. Any wound bathed in the Waters is healed, completely and fully, no matter how deadly, no matter if the injured is on Death's door. Less known than this is that the waters react in strange and wonderful ways to love."

"Love?"

Galaxy must have sounded more incredulous than she'd intended, from Erentil's chuckle. "Yes, truly. Love is a force terribly underestimated in these days, something far grander and more terrible than any magic. It drives people to the heights of heroism and... and to the depths of villainy. And when true and pure love is brought into the presence of the Waters of Life, miracles can happen. Between a unicorn and a gryphon, the Waters can bridge that physical gap and gift to them—"

"Me." Galaxy could finally say it as she looked the mural over again. Tears blurred her vision, chest aching. "Unicorns and gryphons are too different to produce a child, but the Waters of Life..."

"Remember, Galaxy." Erentil's voice went low and solemn. "In order for it to happen, for YOU to happen, Queen Grimhilt and your father must have felt true, pure love for each other. And for you. Something regrettably few can say with certainty in this sad, broken world of ours."

Galaxy let the tears fall. She ran her talons over the mural, over the images of unicorn and gryphon and basin and hippogryph, and felt a weight leave her. Here was the answer to the question plaguing her nightmares. Another piece of her past revealed at last.

"I've said it before, but... I don't know how to feel about them. I never knew them, never grew a connection, never... I wish I could have known them." The words hurt, Galaxy's heart clenching as guilt now mixed into the sadness. "That is, I... I love Ida with all my heart. She took me in, raised me, made me who I am today. She's my mother in every way that matters, and nothing will change that. But I... Grimhilt was a queen and a hero! How can I ever live up to that? And my father... I don't even know his name, or what he looked like, or what brought them together, or... or..."

A shudder rolled through Galaxy, a sob barely choked back as she began wiping hastily at her eyes. "It's, it's ridiculous, I know. I have a family. The best family. But there's still an... an ache, not knowing if they... if Grimhilt... would be proud of me. It hurts like losing Featheren Valley hurt."

". . . I am certain," said Erentil eventually, "that Grimhilt would be unbelievably proud of everything you have accomplished. From what I've seen of you and what I've heard, you are kind, loyal, smart, and so, so brave. You, and only you, are who Heraldale needs."

Galaxy had seen it from the corner of her eye as Erentil spoke, his voice growing darker with every word, his gaze sadder, the same kind of sadness she'd seen so many times before. But this time, it came with guilt. She turned halfway to look at him, frowning as the Elk king avoided eye contact. "What's wrong?"

Erentil stood tall and proud, but that pride didn't reach his eyes. "I mentioned before your mother's fierceness in defense of her people, but... something a wise king or queen must learn, something I kept trying to tell her, is that sometimes the best defense of that which you care for is to NOT fight."

Worry turned to alarm. Galaxy faced the king fully. "Your Majesty?"

"You must understand that I truly believe in your cause and the Empire's evil. But... more than a king, I am a father, and a parent must always take any measure to protect their children. You must understand, Galaxy."

Alarm turned to horror. The whole feel of the room changed, the outer world's cold seeping in. Galaxy, wings half-flared, glanced from Erentil to the door and began edging around toward it. "What have you done?"

"What I have always done. Protected my people. Of course the Empire didn't know the precise location of this fortress. They would have burned the whole forest down and Elk-kind with it if I hadn't done something."

The horror crept up from Galaxy's gut to clench her heart. Abandoning all pretense of normality, she rushed for the door past Erentil, throwing it open with a thrust of magic and flying through—

The world disappeared behind blinding white. The blast of lightning slammed Galaxy into the cracked and pitted wall beside the door. There was a sound. Perhaps her screams. She fell to the floor, wheezing, smoke curling from her scorched coat. Through pain-blurred eyes she watched a black unicorn emerge from the shadows of the fortress chapel's outer chamber, flanked by a trio of desiccated wyverns.

"Hello, dear Galaxy." Lord Mordred's lips spread, showing off wolfish fangs. His yellow eyes gleamed in the dark. "Long time, no see."

CHAPTER SIX

"You traitor." Galaxy struggled to stand, terror and rage driving her talons into the stone. "You bloody trait—"

Another bolt of lightning sent her back to the floor, writhing as her nerves were fried, voiceless screams tearing through her throat. "My my," said Mordred, voice a taunt. "What a foul child. I blame the parents, personally. You told your cute little story to her, good, hehe, fair Duke Tree Branch?"

Galaxy dimly heard the clack of hooves as Erentil joined them in the outer chamber, felt him move around her toward Mordred and, past him, the stairwell. Had the foul unicorn not been there, she would have leveled the king with hate to shatter mountains. As it was, it took all her willpower to simply look in the traitorous Elk's direction. "Why? After everything I've done for you, after everything he's done! Why!?"

Erentil ignored her, continuing to stare at Mordred and his wyverns while edging for the stairs. "You'll not hurt her any more than needed, as you swore? And you'll never threaten the Elderpine or my people within again? You are done with us?"

Mordred glanced his way, grin spreading up his muzzle in a horribly unnatural way. "Dearest Baron Bramble-head, do you not trust an old friend like me?"

Erentil snorted and stomped a hoof. "You mock me, but not so brave to do it muzzle to muzzle."

"Of course not." Mordred looked back down at Galaxy, winking as if sharing a joke just with her. "Getting that close, an errant sneeze and you'd take one of my eyes out. I imagine it will be easy going back to your people, telling them whatever fanciful lie you come up with regarding what happened here. The flighty fools will eat up whatever their ancient leader says."

"At least I have a people to return to."

Those few words were as confusing to Galaxy as they seemed to be enraging to Mordred. The stallion snarled and whirled to the Elk king once more, the wyvern puppets around them hissing and drawing closer. Yet just as soon as Galaxy thought the two about to come to blows and grant her an avenue of escape, Mordred let out a humorless bark of a laugh, horn glimmering red. From the darkness of the outer chamber materialized a red crystal crackling with contained magic, Mordred presenting it to Erentil as if it were a fine treat. "To deal with that pesky dragon you told me of. Strike it with this to teleport the beast to my personal fortress, Hiraeth Arian. The dragon, like the Empire, will no longer trouble you, old friend."

"I'm not your friend," said Erentil, taking the frozen teleport spell with his magic all the same. "My stomach churns from merely standing so close, let alone the foul deed I've committed for you. May I never have to lay eyes on your evil again."

Galaxy couldn't believe what she was hearing. She laughed as she struggled back to all fours, this time no blast of lightning stopping her. "Then may you never look in glass or mirror or reflective pool again, Betrayer! Those fine words you spoke to me before should've caught in your throat and killed you!"

Erentil paused at the stairs and spared Galaxy one last look. "Could you speak such were the roles reversed? You refused to go quietly with Lord Mordred and he destroyed Featheren Valley, your own family spared only by a stroke of luck and mercy. We can't all take that chance."

And then it was just Galaxy and Lord Mordred at the top of that tower, Erentil's hoofsteps quickly disappearing down the stairs. Mordred looked at her and she looked at him, rage shifting easily as she figured the ruin her mother had died in a fitting enough place for revenge after everything the Empire had done.

"So come on," said Galaxy, wings battering the air. "I think we both know this won't go half as easily for you as our last encounter did."

The wyvern puppets began circling Galaxy, Mordred himself staying comfortably away. "Do we need more violence, though? Maybe this time we can just... talk. After everything you've been through, after ol' Prince Splinter-horn's quaint history lesson, you've got to be just BURNING with questions. Heh, burning. Who was your father? What exactly does Empress Nova want from you? What's with all these experiments you keep galloping into? Why, I'm not ignorant of others' thoughts, so how about this. What in Sheol even am I?"

Galaxy eyed the Brynjar-sized wyverns trying to encircle her, horn flaring with magic as she backed up a step to keep them all in sight. In truth, she had wondered all these questions and many more. More recently, why the dragon Ashe had been tortured so. Yet... "I'm no fool. I'd never believe a word you said."

"That really is too bad." Mordred looked away a moment, seemingly in thought. "You have begun to dream of a white unicorn stallion, tinged perhaps with a feeling of fire. Your father was once a brave knight of the Knights Le Fay, and not killing him is, in my opinion, one of my greatest failures. Empress Nova's planning a terrible fate for Heraldale, something that makes my destruction of your Featheren Valley look like a joke. The experiments you've come upon are but small keys to this plan. And you, dear, sweet princess... could be the key to either fruition or ruination of that plan."

Galaxy's heart fell with each truth, Mordred's words a doom growing over her. She backed up further, keeping the wyverns in sight as she thought for a way to disregard his claims. Yet somehow he knew of her dreams, and those were truth enough. "It can't be."

"It can be, though. I just said it, you just heard it, and we have the endless dead around us as solemn witnesses." Mordred's voice dripped like poisoned honey as he moved to keep even with her. "Come with me. Let me answer all your questions. Leave your companions behind here, with the Elk. Safe, as you've always wanted."

Had Galaxy been a dumber person, or more hurt by the lightning, or more worn by the long road, she might have given the offer truly serious thought, more than a scoff and stomp of her hoof. But she was smart, she was happy to say, and she could see at once the weakness of the trap. Erentil had betrayed Grimhilt for protection, and her, and there was nothing stopping him from betraying Brynjar and Owain if he needed to. There was only one response to that.

"Go die in a flaming pigsty, you motherless concubine."

The wyverns lunged, claws outstretched. Acting faster, Galaxy projected a shield spell straight down through the time-weakened floor, blowing through the stone and dropping her to the room below. She did this again just as fast, again, again, the wyverns' shrieks and Mordred's raging screams chasing her as she bashed her way down the castle tower at blinding speed.

Through another shattered floor, Galaxy found herself out of the tower, emptied into what might once have been a grand hall or throne room, its tall ceiling supported by numerous broad pillars, many narrow windows filled with cracked, half-missing stained glass turning the light of the room into strange splotches of red and blue and gold.

A screech echoed from far behind her, growing nearer. Galaxy flared her wings to break her descent, spun to face the hole she'd blasted, fired broken timber and stone back through with her magic. Red blossomed in the darkness above. One of the wyverns fell from the hole, narrowly missing Galaxy as she dove aside. The body hit the floor with a bone-breaking crunch, writhing there as the black tendrils within struggled in vain to move their broken puppet.

Two more wyverns crawled from the broken ceiling, snarling as they spread their wings and lunged again at Galaxy. She dove out of their way once, twice. The third time, the wyvern to her right swung its tail as Galaxy moved, her breath smacked from her as she flew into a far wall.

"Augh!"

The room spun. She somehow managed to land on all fours. Shaking her head, Galaxy eeped and ducked beneath a sudden snap of jaws, projecting a shield spell to shove the offending beast away for a few seconds' breathing room.

"You are powerful," came Mordred's voice suddenly, echoing from all directions. "Powerful, intelligent, and surprisingly inventive. But you lack the simple combat experience to win this battle. First off, always know where your enemy is. Secondly, don't ever let your foe's talking distract you!"

A hiss, all the warning Galaxy got before a wyvern dropped onto her, clawing away at her sides and back with its hind claws, biting at her neck. Galaxy screamed, panic and pain sending a bone-breaking shield spell every direction. Pillars around her splintered, the wyvern flopping away.

Silence, but for Galaxy's labored breathing. She struggled to organize her thoughts through the pain in her back, sides, neck, hips, breath throat-searing. Eyes roamed the hall for any sign of life. Inside, animal panic, fighting to stop her body's shaking, blood dribbling from the deep gashes crisscrossing her body. The panic bubbled out, spiking as she realized what was happening. "N-no... p-puh-please, no-not now..."

"Now, if I recall, you were just now refusing my offer of MERCY!"

Before Galaxy could process what had happened, bolts of lightning shot from Mordred's horn and slammed into her. She screamed, pain worse than any she'd felt before coursing all through her as she flew off her hooves and slammed into the wall above the doorway. Something audibly cracked in her side and Galaxy screamed as yet more pain flared.

Galaxy fell onto her rear, wings shielding her as she fought not to let her breathing get away from her. She clenched her head in her talons, digging in until skin broke. "N-no, no, no, nnnn—"

"Run! Fly! WYVERNS!"

Sheer animal panic arose at this last word. The three travelers fled for their lives, as behind them a nightmare erupted from the eternal night beneath the mountain. Galaxy chanced a glance behind and saw hundreds of black-scaled monstrosities twisting through the air, slithering against each other on leathery wings, screeching like talons on glass. The bastard cousins to dragon-kind swarmed after the fleeing trio, burning with hunger and hate.

"So," came Mordred's voice again, dragging Galaxy back to the surface of her thoughts. "So, so, so. The little hippogryph princess suffers Horror Sickness... so WEAK!"

Caught mid-attack, Galaxy could do nothing as bolts of lightning struck around her, sending her reeling from the dust and rubble stinging at her wounds. The next lightning bolt tore through her hastily-cast shield spell, sending Galaxy tumbling.

The final wyvern waited for her. It smacked her with a wing the size of Galaxy's body, sending her flying into one of the few pillars still standing. Somehow, the weakened stone cracked rather than her bones. As she fell to the floor, a shudder and groan ran through the fortress from the parapets to the foundations. Dust and chunks of masonry fell from the ceiling.

Moments later, Lord Mordred dropped into the hall, landing in a crouch and looking at Galaxy with yellow eyes ablaze. "We've all had our fun," he said, standing and advancing on her with the remaining wyvern once more at his side. "But as impressive as your showing has been, I'm afraid beating you down has grown boring. Give up. Don't make me destroy you."

Galaxy almost laughed. Grabbing at the pillar for support, she hauled herself back to standing, a cough rattling her body and dotting the floor before her with red. Upon turning to face Mordred, she felt no fear, none of the panic of moments before, only a kind of resignation. "It's like I said before. This won't be half as easy for you as last time."

"So you did." Mordred tossed his mane, eyes glittering with mirth. "Very well then, if you really—"

Galaxy didn't let him finish. With thoughts of Brynjar and Owain, she dove deep into the second magic deep within her, the magic of the Waters of Life that had let her shield all of Port Oil weeks before. Screaming, she let the magic explode from her in one overpowering burst. Out and out from Galaxy the shield spell grew, knocking Mordred to the ground, breaking every remaining pillar in the hall, shattering the remaining stained-glass windows and surrounding brickwork. The fortress released a death wail and buckled inward.

Through the red tint of the secondary shield spell she'd cast around herself, Galaxy saw Mordred stagger to his hooves, laughing as rubble fell around him. Laughing until a slab of broken stonework as big as a rockodile crushed the mad unicorn. A similar fate befell the remaining wyvern puppet as it tried to flee for the nearest window, leaving Galaxy alone as the fortress collapsed over her. Debris bounced off her shield and the head-filling rumble grew to an ear-shattering roar. Galaxy closed her eyes, friends and family imagined before her as she put the full of her focus on her spell.

***

Brynjar paused halfway down the air-yacht ramp, conversation with Captain Hywel on the efficiency of crossbows over longbows forgotten as a sudden terror speared his heart. A moment after came a deafening roar. The world shook as a shockwave of air and lingering magic passed through the trees, blasting away the snow and knocking all present to the ground, the air-yacht nearly tipping onto its side. Even once the initial earth-shaking tremor passed, the sound of breaking branches continued on.

Brynjar regained his footing, the terror fading to a dull pain as he and those around them looked in the direction the shockwave had come from. Far off could be seen a mountainous plume of smoke and dust, joining with the storm clouds still loosing snow.

"Brynjar," said Owain, lurching to the golden eagle-gryphon's side. "That's... that's where Gal and the king went."

"I know." Brynjar's throat felt dry. Dizzy, heart stuttering, unable to breathe, a hundred nightmare scenarios rampaging through his head. As if of their own volition, his legs were already taking him back up the ramp onto the air-yacht. "We need... we need to go. Now."

***

The sound of shifting stone broke the cold winter silence. A bulge formed in the ruins near the bridge, a blue light shining through from beneath. The swell of rubble grew, grew, then burst, scattering its debris far and wide. Her magic sputtering out, Galaxy dragged herself out of the hole left behind, feeling every bit like a building had dropped on her. Blood trickled down the right side of her head, blinding one eye. For a split-second toward the end, her magic had given out and her shield collapsed beneath the weight of the fortress. She'd barely managed to cast a new shield in time to save her head.

As the silence fell once more over the forest, the gorge, the fields of rubble where once a fortress stood, Galaxy looked around with her good eye to take it all in. The towers had fallen to the wayside, the broad halls and barracks sundered to the root, the once-mighty defensive walls tossed down to the depths of the gorge, swallowed by the eternal fog. The bridge alone still stood, barely. The ghosts, too, still lingered.

"It's over," she said aloud, needing to hear the words to believe them. Tears fell from her seeing eye. Shudders wracked her body. "I did... I did it."

Talons reached out, grasping for any firm purchase among the rubble. Galaxy made for the bridge where she might rest more comfortably. That collapse must have been heard. Help must have been on its way.

"You're okay... you're okay... everything's... going to be..."

Galaxy had partially staggered, partially dragged herself halfway to the bridge before the sound of more shifting stone reached her. Fear rose up her throat into a cry as she looked back. Three yards behind her, a cracked and bloody hoof had forced its way to the surface. A black leg followed the hoof, then another hoof and leg, then the head, neck, shoulders of Lord Mordred. Skin hung off him in flaps, jagged edges of bone stuck out from knees and chest, but still his eyes burned with infernal life.

"God above," groaned Galaxy, "what's it take to kill you!?"

A wolfish growl rising from his throat, Mordred planted both front hooves against the ground and heaved himself forward. Galaxy flinched, gagged at a meaty tearing sound, only the beast's front half escaping the rubble and dragging itself toward her. Blood and black tendrils dragged in his wake and bloody froth spilled from Mordred's mouth. Seeing this, Galaxy turned and started crawling for the bridge with a strength born of utter terror, no thought but to flee. The jagged stone beneath pricked her palms and scratched her belly, flickers of pain driving her on like a whip to her torn back.

Then, two feet from the bridge, a seemingly stable slab of wall broke, sending Galaxy tumbling the rest of the way. She bit back a scream as she landed badly on one wing, a crack of snapping bone ringing out. A moment passed as she fought just to breathe before, pushing the pain aside, she stood and hobbled as fast as her battered body could manage over the cracked and uneven bridge.

Seconds later came the thud of flesh on stone. Galaxy glanced back knowing it would cost her, knowing Mordred was already too close. Still she froze at the impossible sight. "What?"

Even as he dragged himself toward her, Mordred's body changed. Broken hooves bulged with every grasp and lunge, splitting with gut-churning cracks into clawed hands. Skin knotted back together, muscle and bone beneath shifting to new structures. His head and neck shortened, muzzle narrowing, unicorn coat growing longer and shaggier, horn thinning. The tendrils dragging behind lengthened, stitched together into bone and muscle and skin.

"Impossible." Galaxy backed away, panting as she struggled to summon a scrap of magic for defense. "You can't... What are you?" She asked this, already knowing. She had seen creatures like this before. Or at least, statues of them.

"Kheheheheh..." Yellow eyes bored into her blue as Mordred pulled himself upright with the bridge's stone railing. "Oh, you know what I am. You know the tale, khehehehe." He swept an arm out over their surroundings, the lingering spirits wailing. His tail, bushy now, beat the air behind him in childish glee.

"Upon the souls of the numberless dead, thou shalt know revenge by more dread!"

"Wolf-Lord." The title came out in a whisper, breathless, heralding a new kind of fear. "All this time, you've been a Wolf-Lord."

"The last in Heraldale," said Mordred, ducking down into a bow. Looking up again, his wolf muzzle split, row upon terrible row of teeth revealing themselves, lips gushing red. "Empress Nova's dream... her Harmonized world... better than any revenge my General Nero could've dreamed of. And right now, hippogryph, YOU'RE STANDING IN THE WAY!"

Galaxy backed away, stumbling on rubble and nearly falling, eyes locked on the giggling beast as he dragged his claws along the bridge railing. "But no, wait, the unicorns helped drive your people from Heraldale! Why would you do an-an-any of this? Wu-why—"

It happened in a blink, and yet so slowly. With a howl, Mordred lunged at Galaxy, fangs and claws bared. Galaxy screamed, horn flickering with a failed shield spell. She raised her talons to defend herself—

SWISH.

"AAAAUUUGGHH!"

Galaxy gaped as Mordred's severed right hand tumbled past her, the Wolf-Lord backing away and clutching his arm to his chest. The wrist blazed as if aflame, cinders breaking off from it to dance away in the wind. She didn't notice the silver sword until it floated past her, held aloft in a golden glow of magic. She followed it behind her and saw a unicorn soldier striding up the bridge toward them, horn glowing gold as she brought the sword back to her. Thoughts sluggish as they were, Galaxy didn't recognize her savior until the mare threw off her helmet and gave her golden mane a toss. "Bevin!"

Nodding in greeting, Bevin paused as she passed Galaxy to look her over. "You look like Sheol. Was dropping a building on yourself really necessary?"

Galaxy laughed once, winced at a pain in her chest, and decided not to try again until Owain could fix her up. "Probably not, but... it felt really satisfying."

"A sentiment I can get behind. Speaking of..." Bevin turned back to Mordred. The wolf creature had dropped to one knee, panting as he glared at them. The stump of his right hand had burned down to the elbow now. Snorting, Bevin readied her sword, her voice containing all the tension of barbed wire coiled tight. "You. You left me to die in Port Oil. Did it gladly, even."

Despite his pain, Mordred laughed and rolled his eyes, Galaxy watching with disgust as the eyes rolled all the way back into his head to show their whites, coming back around a totally different way than they should've to focus again on the pair. "Oh, the reasons you could want revenge against me, kheheheh. Precious. Galaxy and Bevin, reunited once more. Not to, heh, monologue, but you can't possibly think this absolves you of... ANYTHING you did at my command? The blood... staining your hooves. The stench of terror... BAKED into you. The sobs of the innocent ECHOING through your head at night. Kheheheheh. Stupid, stupid Bevin, crying out for some greater purpose—"

Bevin swung her sword again, slashing Mordred's muzzle along the right of the lips and leaving the Wolf-Lord howling in pain. "Don't! Don't, you bastardly monster! Just tell me why! Why after everything, why... I was your soldier!" And here the barbed wire snapped, Bevin's voice breaking. "Yours! Saved by you, raised by you, trained by you! Why, dog, WHY!?"

For several seconds there came no answer as Mordred knelt there, groaning as the cheek Bevin had slashed crumbled to cinders, bared muscles twitching to roll their eye in its socket. Then he fought his way to his feet again and looked at them. The whole side of his muzzle curled into a grin. He backed away a step, then another, glancing between the pair. "The reason... heh... the reason... you'll DIE wondering!"

Faster than either of them could react, Mordred flung himself backward over the bridge's railing, chased by Bevin's scream of rage. The unicorn galloped to the spot her quarry had fallen from, skidding to a stop as a wyvern rose into view. Mordred was connected to the beast by countless tendrils. He looked back at them as he flew away, ruined but terrible. "KHEHEHEHEHE!"

"No! Get back here! GET BACK HERE, COWARD! AAARRGH!"

Turning, Bevin glared at Galaxy. Already knowing what she was about to command, Galaxy hurriedly shook her head, instantly regretting it for the sudden hammer beating away at her brain. "I-I cu-can't, my wing, see, it's... b-broken..."

She saw Bevin's eyes flick to the wing in question, the soldier's gaze softening by a degree. They both looked back to the fleeing Mordred, the Wolf-Lord and his wyvern mount little more than a speck in the distance already. Bevin's whole body slumped in defeat then, a sound halfway between a growl and a sob leaving her. The sword clattered to the bridge, forgotten in the snow. "I was so close... I was so close..."

"I'm sorry," said Galaxy, trying to step toward her rescuer. Immediately pain shot up her leg. She fell to her side with a grunt, thankfully not on the broken wing. "Nnngh!"

In an instant Bevin was kneeling beside Galaxy, horn glowing and the ever-unfamiliar sensation of healing magic suffusing her injured leg. Used to Owain's calm, minty magic, Galaxy barely kept from panicking at the sheer craggy unease that was Bevin. "Um, th-thank you..."

"Don't mention it," said Bevin, voice terse, the vulnerability of moments before gone. "Ever. It's not a favor, and we don't owe each other anything."

"If we don't owe each other anything... then..." Galaxy tried to smile, the blood loss and exhaustion from the last however-long starting to catch up to her. "Then you're just... doing this out of kindness, yeah?"

Bevin didn't pause in her work, but as she switched from healing Galaxy's leg to the worst of her cuts the unicorn glared, drawing a real chuckle from Galaxy. Then Bevin's gaze moved past Galaxy. She looked over her shoulder and tensed. King Erentil, emerging from the trees on the far side of the bridge to stare in bewilderment at them. "Traitor..."

"Seem to be a lot of those nowadays." Bevin's voice was unflinching. "I'm right here and I have a sword. I might as well enact SOMEONE'S vengeance today."

Galaxy laughed despite the shudder in her chest. Coughing, she slowly shook her head. "N-no, don't bother. He has the rest of his life to think about what he's done."

"But... King Erentil is immortal."

"Yeah. He is." Galaxy smiled, vicious, feeling Bevin look at her with a new appreciation. Before either could say more, Galaxy noticed a growing speck over the Elderpine, soon resolving into an air-yacht barreling their way. "My friends are coming."

At this, Bevin stood and stepped away, leaving Galaxy to watch in worry as she retrieved her dropped sword. Galaxy didn't know what exactly the unicorn mare planned, but she had an idea, and she didn't like it. "Bevin, please, don't go. Come with us."

Bevin wiped the blade of her sword against her leg to clean it of ash and snow before sliding it into a sheath hanging from her side. "And what? Fight my own people at your side? After everything I've done, every way I've hurt you?"

Galaxy knew those words from Mordred's taunting. Fighting to all fours, she shook her head. "Not after everything you've done. Before everything you're going to do."

Bevin stared at her for several long seconds then, no clue in her expression to the internal debate that must have been raging. Galaxy waited, glancing once to the nearing air-yacht to find it close enough for her to see Ashe the dragon looking out from the bow. Galaxy found herself able to smile and wave.

"I suppose staying with you is my best chance for another shot at Mordred," said Bevin at last, moving to stand in front of Galaxy and stare her down. "He won't allow you or your friends far from his grasp, now that you know his secret. He will come for you again."

Galaxy nodded, having already guessed that much. "If that's the case, we'll just have to come for him first."

That, at last, made the soldier smirk, before she lifted her gaze to the air-yacht. Galaxy followed her, wishing at that moment, more than anything else after all that had happened that day, for a long, dreamless sleep. Something she doubted she'd get any time soon.

"GAL!"

Galaxy braced herself, uncertain if her battered and bloody body could take the full-body hug she saw Brynjar flying her way with, a look of panic on his face. He blessedly restrained himself at the last second, instead coming to a staggering stop on the bridge and kneeling before Galaxy to pat her over in a way more befitting a mother than a brother. "Oh God, oh God, what the Sheol happened!? You're hurt, the castle, the, Erentil—"

"Brynjar, stop, just..." Galaxy sighed, permitting him to continue checking her over as she searched for the right words. "It's... it's a long story... Erentil betrayed us. He sold me out to Mordred."

That gave him pause. Talons on her shoulders, he took in the fresh scars marking her just-healed hurts, Bevin at attention nearby, the collapsed fortress, King Erentil watching from the tree line, the blood still staining the ground from Mordred dragging himself after Galaxy, eventually seeming to grasp the basics of the battle well enough. "Right. Right. Rest on the air-yacht while we fly. Get away from here."

That sounded like the best idea Galaxy had ever heard. She yawned, blinking as the air-yacht drifted down to float parallel with the bridge, then relaxed as her far, far larger brother effortlessly scooped her up in his front legs and fluttered onto the ship. Taking the weight off her limbs felt good enough to hurt. Not saying it aloud, Galaxy knew she'd have probably let Brynjar carry her even if Bevin had healed her wing enough to fly.

"Oh my goodness, Gal!"

Galaxy startled. She pulled from Brynjar's hold, stumbling as she hit the deck on all fours. She saw Owain piloting the air-yacht, and the dragon Ashe looking on in fear from the bow, but trotting over with a look of pure worry was Gwendolyn. A fire roared to life in Galaxy's gut at the sight of the Elk, an ugly fire, a fire she relished. "YOU."

Gwendolyn paused a half-yard away, worry twisting into confusion. The Elk jumped slightly as Bevin leapt onto the ship, Ashe also tensing up. After a moment, Gwendolyn tried taking another step toward Galaxy. "Gal, what happened here? Where's my father?"

"What..." Galaxy barely restrained a snarl, swallowing as she fought to not explode on her seeming friend. "Gwen, I need to know. Did you know why your father brought me here?"

"Did I..." The Elk princess looked past Galaxy, mouth opening the slightest bit at, Galaxy guessed, the sight of her father lurking near the edge of the bridge. "Gal, what happened?"

Galaxy stared, talons digging into the deck, heart aching to trust... but she couldn't be certain. She couldn't be certain. That lone thought reverberated, steeling her as she called upon the second magic within her. "It doesn't matter. Not going to happen again. I can't risk it."

Gwen let out a startled squeal as an aura of ice-blue magic grabbed her, lifting her from the deck of the airyacht and slowly levitating her over to the bridge. She looked to Galaxy rotating to watch her, eyes tearing. "Gal!" Gwen thrashed in the few seconds neither the airyacht nor the bridge was beneath her, only the swirling fogs of the canyon far below, Galaxy grimacing at the inner struggle not to drop her. "Gal, please! What happened?"

Galaxy ignored the cries, legging go of Gwen the moment the Elk was safely above the bridge. She watched with a small, bitter pleasure as Gwen fell wrong, twisting an ankle on a misplaced stone. The quick cry of pain from this stoked the ugly fire inside her. "If you want to know, ask your father. Ask him, and hope I never see any of your traitorous kind ever again."

Ignoring the Elk's further pained cries for her to stop, for her to come back, Galaxy turned away. She glanced to Bevin and Brynjar at her sides, then to Owain staring in mild terror from the controls. "Let's go. I'm tired of this place."

CHAPTER SEVEN

Galaxy didn't know how long they flew. Once the moment had passed and the adrenaline faded, time crept by in a sickly haze of exhaustion and pain. She remembered telling the others of her journey with King Erentil, the secrets of the hippogryph explained to her there, and the whole battle between her and Mordred. She remembered Owain and Bevin both sitting beside her, horns aglow in the dim storm light as they tended her wounds, Brynjar piloting. Galaxy's back had been the worst of it, their magic aggravatingly slow and methodical to heal the muscles just right, or else risk her ability to even fly.

There had been little objection to bringing Bevin along with them. Brynjar kept a wary eye on the unicorn, clearly not forgetting her assault on Ida and encounters with them in Port Oil. Owain came on far more welcoming, speaking to Bevin as if to an old friend. Ashe kept quiet and watchful.

Once the healing was finished as completely as possible given the circumstances, Galaxy settled in against Ashe's side, the dragon's natural warmth a blessed relief to Galaxy's lingering aches. Resting such, she half-listened to Bevin's tale of her doings since Port Oil. "I left the same night you did, working my way eastward following news of your sightings. Luck brought the former Governor Urien to me in Markhaven, and through him, a chance to kill Lord Mordred."

"You've met my father? He's alive, and okay?"

"Alive, yes, and deeply missing you. Don't know about okay. Mordred probably won't think I needed help to attack him as I did... but if he does, Urien will certainly be his first suspect. Hope that your father can keep a low profile."

From there, conversation turned to what to do next. As Brynjar, Owain, and Bevin discussed this in uncertain tones, Galaxy found herself struggling to care. She lay near the bow of the air-yacht with Ashe, watching the Elderpine Forest below. A wing stroked down the length of Ashe's neck as the dragon curled up around Galaxy. It was fascinating to watch the snowflakes land on those scales and immediately melt away, without any effort on Ashe's part. Galaxy would have thought such proximity to an inner fire like that would frighten her in the same way other fires did, and yet...

"Gal? Galaxy!"

Galaxy shifted at her name, glancing over her should to look at Brynjar before looking back down at the forest. "Yeah?"

"I uh... I was asking if you're okay. Owain and Bevin said they couldn't heal it all fully in one sitting, and you're tired..."

"I'm fine."

"You sure?"

"Yes."

". . . please, Galaxy."

Galaxy slammed her fist against the air-yacht's railing. "I said I'm fine, you idiot! Be quiet!"

Silence. Galaxy took a deep breath, slowly relaxing again where she lay as she heard her brother shuffle where he stood. A tinge of guilt wormed its way into Galaxy's thoughts at the wary way Ashe was looking down at her. She scrambled for a change of topic. "Bevin! How many people know that Mordred's actually a Wolf-Lord?"

The quiet lingered a moment longer, then hoof-falls on wood as the mare in question paced. "It's... hard to say. Empress Nova, for certain. The other Lords of the Empire, or at least Lords Thoth and Beauty. Members of Mordred's staff at his personal fortress, probably. As for outside of the Empire... King Erentil, obviously. Any surviving members of the Knights Le Fay and their confidantes, if any such remain."

The silence returned. The forest below remained ever-present. Lightning flashed far northward, followed by leisurely thunder. When Bevin said no more, Galaxy frowned. "That's not many. Do... do you think it would change anything if we spread word of Mordred's secret?"

The clomp of Bevin's pacing stopped. "I doubt it. Those remaining nations opposing the Empire don't need anything else to rally around, while the Empress keeps too tight a leash on information for such news to cause a disturbance in the Empire. It would be immediately derided by all authorities as false, lies, propaganda. Perhaps in the territories once known as Schwarz Angebot..."

"What about Mordred, though?" came Brynjar's voice. He sounded like Galaxy had never shouted at him, to her unspoken relief. "We need to be ready for him. How do we kill a Wolf-Lord?"

"That's simple enough," said Galaxy, twisting around to face the others. Owain stood at the controls far to the rear, Bevin near the mast, while Brynjar lingered somewhat nearer, antsy, wanting closer. Galaxy ignored that, hoping her participating in the conversation enough of a peace offering. "The legends say that Wolf-Lords are immune to the ravages of aging and diseases, capable of healing in seconds from any wound inflicted upon them by a normal weapon. Minutes, at most. Silver is the only surefire way to deal a wound that will stick, and even then... Mordred will probably, eventually, regrow that half an arm Bevin cut off, for example. Aside from silver... there's the legendary alloy, Lunar Steel, that could harm them, but only Wolf-Lords knew how to make it."

"And magic?"

"Debatable." Bevin resumed her pacing. "Extremes of temperature, like fire and ice, allegedly can weaken a Wolf-Lord's healing powers enough for more conventional weapons to work." When next her pacing had her facing toward Galaxy, her smirk was vicious. "Fortuitous our travels bring us a dragon. Once we get her wings healed enough to fly with her own power…"

Conversation continued on in such a manner, but Galaxy decided to stop paying attention and turned away again, mumbling a summary of what Bevin had said in response to a questioning growl from Ashe. Galaxy rested her head on her folded talons, voicing no objection as Ashe curled in tighter around her. The warmth shielded perfectly from the wider world. Galaxy felt her thoughts drifting, eyes aching to close. Sleep… sounded good…

***

Mordred tumbled through the tides of consciousness, kept from the peace of true sleep by the erratic flight of his wyvern puppet north, north, ever north. Between flashes of darkness, of long-past screams and the squelch of blade passing through flesh, he caught the forest disappearing below, the snow stopping, new and darker clouds, fields turning into hills turning into bare-faced mountains disappearing into torrential rain. Mordred clutched his maimed arm tighter to his chest and shivered in the cold tearing through him.

A CRACKLE-BOOM of nearby thunder jerked Mordred into something approaching full consciousness, the ache of his body telling him of the hours passed flying. Evening was falling among the mountains barring Schwarz Angebot from the rest of Heraldale, Mordred fearing for one irrational moment their jagged peaks spearing up to tear his mount's belly. Then a darker structure emerged from the gloom of the rain and the remaining half of his muzzle pulled back in a grin. The black fortress rose tall among the mountain peaks, almost one of them itself but too angular, too straight-lined, a layered pyramid measuring 2,300 by 2,300 feet, 1,000 feet high. Four towers half that height connected to the corners, while broad landing platforms for troop carriers and wyverns had been retroactively built three-quarters of the way up the pyramid's sides at the cardinal points.

Hiraeth Arian. Once the headquarters of the Knights Le Fay, now his. All his.

With a thought, Mordred guided his wyvern through the crystal drones kept in constant guard around the fortress and up to the nearest landing platform and the party of unicorn soldiers awaiting him there, alerted by the drones and monitoring spells cast on the surrounding peaks. Not in the mood for pleasantries, Mordred landed his wyvern right in the middle of the group, loosing a bark of laughter as they were forced to scatter. The laugh quickly devolved into a pained gargle as his burnt-away face flared in agony. "Augh!"

"My Lord Mordred! Your unicorn form—"

Mordred ignored the attendant's blathering, detaching and sliding free of the wyvern's back, stumbling as he landed hard on the platform's rain-slicked metal. A snarl sent those approaching away, Mordred forcing himself to stand upright and start striding for the thrown-open doors leading from the platform into the fortress proper. "Prepare a meal for my quarters. Meat and marrow, fresh and bloody. Then call upon my steel smiths. There is armor to be readied."

"My lord," spoke the attendant again, trotting along beside Mordred toward the escape from the ever-present rains. "The steel smiths have already been summoned and your meal is being—"

Mordred stopped, looking down at the simpering stallion with all the anger he could muster. He could guess well enough how and why everything was already being prepared for him. This was the last thing he needed. "WHY."

The unicorn swallowed, glancing aside to the platform's edge as if it might be preferable to answering the question. "My lord... Lord Thoth awaits you in your quarters at Empress Nova's bidding."

The growl came unbidden, freezing the attendant in place. Mordred reached out with his right arm at first, remembered in his pain and anger that it was naught but a stump at the elbow now, and quickly turned to grab the stallion's throat with his left hand instead. He relished the look of resigned despair in those watery eyes for a moment before squeezing and pulling.

***

Mordred licked his claws dry of blood as he stalked through Hiraeth Arian, unbothered now by attendants or guards. In contrast to the forbidding walls of black stone outside, the innards of the fortress were decorated richly in light tones of white and rose marble, hallways brightly lit by incandescent crystals housed in brass holsters. Though doors were solid steel further reinforced by ancient unicorn and Wolf-Lord runes, the frames were decorated in eye-catching lavender jade. The enchanted security mirrors lining walls and set high up in corners were lined with white pearls. All save the mirror guarding the door to Mordred's personal quarters, decorated by gold pearls gifted to him by Lord Beauty himself.

The doors opened on their own. The room beyond was long and wide, two stories tall, walls of iron and onyx lined with weapons and armor originating from all cultures and points of history. A life-size statue of a Wolf-Lord occupied the left corner closest the door, a falchion in each hand and a snarl curling its muzzle. Mordred paused in his stride long enough to grab the red cloak left hanging from one of those swords and throw it on himself, before joining the tawny sphinx awaiting him at the roaring fireplace taking up the entirety of the far wall.

For long minutes the pair stood side by side, silent. Mordred watched the reds and oranges of the fire dance through the black of the marble floor, not needing to look to know his fellow Lord of the Empire to be staring serenely, even smugly, into the flames. Lord Thoth. Lord of Secrets, of the Empire's intelligence network, its spies, its killers. Worst of all, an utter—

"You seem to have lost some weight, my Lord Mordred."

His remaining hand clenched into a fist, claws digging in. The drip-drip of his blood pattering on the marble echoed through the room.

"Empress Nova and I thought you could HANDle the hippogryph situation better than this, to be honest."

Mordred thought his teeth might break, so tightly was he clenching his jaws now.

"Ah, but troubled times as these, it's important to put on a brave face."

Mordred closed his eyes, counting to ten and breathing deep through the flaring pain of his burnt-open face. "I've always hated you, Thoth. Can't even say I've ever respected you. But even I never thought you so despicable to attempt murder by bad comedy."

The sphinx snorted, laughed, looked up at Mordred with a wide smile and green eyes gleaming with mischief. "Me? Murder a fine Wolf-Lord like you after all these years of loyal service to Empress Nova? Why ever would I do that? Yours is the iron fist of the Empire!"

If Mordred could take solace in only one thing, it was that Empress Nova was bound to her castle in Avalon and could not be there in person to witness him being reduced to a joke. But then, he mused as he turned to face the sphinx, if the Empress were there he'd only have to suffer a charred smear on the floor rather than actual lingering agony. "I will kill you someday, cat. Until that day comes, tell me. If your psychic powers let you know what was happening to me, why not simply come to my aid in the Elderpine in the first place?"

The sphinx rolled his eyes, sitting back on his rear and combing some locks of hair from his disgustingly human face with a wave of a paw. "I have my reasons, all of which were satisfactory to the Empress. The real question you should be asking is how will you ever come back from this? Three failures to capture the hippogryph child in a row, oof. As competent as you are in your capacity as Lord of War, we are all starting to wonder if this task requires more... finesse. Perhaps I would be better suited to it?"

The fire and stone around it tinged a deeper, bloodier red. Mordred stepped forward, jabbing a claw at Thoth's face. "You dare—"

"But of course," Thoth continued, batting the claw away with a swipe of a paw, "I argued strongly against the Empress's first impulse to turn you into a, as you so elegantly thought, charred smear on the floor. After all, there's that lovely prisoner of yours from Vogelstadt."

Mordred jerked back, feeling as if physically struck by that too-knowing comment and its accompanying smirk. Gritting his teeth, he let a low growl roll from his throat as he glanced around for time, forcing down the flickers of paranoia for safer thoughts on what was taking his meal so long to arrive. "You can't... I have the entire floor his cell's in specially warded against sphinx scrying and mind-reading. You dare install your spies in my domain?"

A matching growl rose from Thoth, though all the humor remained in his eyes. With another toss of his mane he turned and began to stroll the length of the fireplace, tail swishing behind him. "I dare because it is my job, wolf. Don't forget your place. The Empress has been lenient in your failures so far, but it shall be I who performs the interrogation of your prisoner. Object and, well..."

He stopped and turned to regard Mordred. Smiling as if they had only just met in passing on the street, the sphinx dragged the extended claws of one paw across the surface of an onyx table, four unwavering lines of white in the black surface, perfection marred. Mordred ignored it, fist clenching as, away from them both, the doors opened once more to admit several unicorns levitating platters of meat to his specifications. Mordred did not fear the physical threat. The threat of Nova's wrath behind it, however...

"Tomorrow, or the day after," Mordred spat, hackles rising at the triumph flashing in the sphinx's eyes. "I shall have time to recuperate from this debacle and to deal with certain... loose ends. Then, you can have your interrogation."

"Excellent." Thoth abandoned the table as the unicorn attendants began setting the platters down there, padding past Mordred for the exit. "I shall make my quarters here in the meantime, then, make sure all is to Empress Nova's liking."

"Yes." Mordred turned to watch the sphinx go. "You do that."

But of course, Mordred realized in hindsight, it couldn't have been that easy, as Thoth paused halfway across the room and looked back at Mordred with a fresh twinkle in his eyes. "Oh, on a minor note, before I go. I'm sure you stopped thinking about it during your long years living among us quadrupeds, and I certainly can't object to my eye-level view, but for the sake of official business, might I suggest adding... pants, to your ensemble?"

Mordred pulled his cloak tighter around his body, his roar sending the unicorns scattering for the nearest exit, eyes bulging and hooves clattering. "GET. OUT."

***

The sound of hooves on stone made Galaxy open her eyes. There before her stood the unicorn from her dreams, taller and more regal than ever before, his snowy coat blinding in the gloom of their surroundings, his storm-grey mane and tail veritably crackling with lightning. His silver horn glowed with magic. "F-father?"

His gaze turned to her, striking Galaxy with the most horrible contempt. He stepped her way and she chocked on the loathing, shuddered, drew back from him as best she could.

"Fear us." With those words, the unicorn's muzzle split open into a terrible smile, an impossible smile. The skin pulled back... back... tearing down the length of his neck, his chest and torso, dropping away, revealing a blood-smeared black coat beneath. Black tendrils whipped about, tearing away what flesh and hair remained. Before Galaxy's eyes now stood Lord Mordred,

destroyer of Featheren Valley and haunter of her nightmares.

"Hehahahah… fear us!"

Even as he spoke, Lord Mordred convulsed. Cracks appeared in the black unicorn's body, glowing red, spreading. Flames licked the edges of the cracks, the skin and flesh crumbling away, leaving behind a scorched stench and blackened bones wreathed in fire.

The laughter returned now as screams, echoing all around Galaxy. She saw the forest beyond the gully aflame, tongues of fire lashing like angry serpents. The sound of crackling wood and bursting trees rang thick, but never louder than the screams. Then, she saw them. Burning unicorns and gryphons stumbled out of the forest to fall headfirst into the gully, staring at Galaxy the whole way down. Each CRACK of their bodies hitting the gully floor and shattering into cinders jolted her from head to hoof. Her eyes burned. She couldn't breathe.

Suddenly, vast flames hid all else from Galaxy. Before her HE stood, a unicorn stallion 40, 50, 60 feet tall, nothing but black bones and white fire that scorched Galaxy where she lay. The skull's eye sockets stared down at her, fire dancing within them. He spoke, voice like the grave.

"FEAR US!"

Galaxy snapped awake to the darkness of late-evening. The air-yacht had been landed while she slept, the trees of the Elderpine Forest still around them in all directions, to Galaxy's disappointment. "Still here, then..."

"Yeah," said Brynjar beside her, making Galaxy jump. He raised an eyebrow, but left the reaction without comment, to her relief. "Big forest. Bevin says we have two more days at least before we're free."

Galaxy nodded, slowly climbed to all fours and, after a stretch that had her back audibly cracking, looked around. The others were gone, though the warm light of a campfire flickering from beside the craft gave her an idea of where to look for them.

Before Galaxy could make a move for it, Brynjar had placed a gentle but firm talon on her shoulder. "Hey. I'm sorry for before. I shouldn't have pushed. I... don't know what you're going through."

Galaxy looked at him, her heart softening at the sincerity in his eyes. Swallowing the sudden lump in her throat, she reached out and patted his leg. "It's okay. I shouldn't have yelled. I really don't know what came over me."

"Sure you do," said Brynjar, the three words like a slap to the beak. "But, it's fine. We're all... hurting. At least we can hurt together, right?"

Hurt together. Yeah. That sounded right to Galaxy. She nodded and tried to work up a smile, eventually dropping her talons and turning away. Her wings still felt like lead. Her sides, back, and flanks, healed by Owain and Bevin but still sporting more than a talonful of scars from the wyvern's clasping claws, twinged in discomfort when she tried spreading her wings. Instead she staggered down the air-yacht's boarding ramp. Several logs had been found and arranged as makeshift benches around the campfire, where she saw Owain tending to a pot of something thick and heavily scented. Ashe lay on the side of the campfire opposite Owain, watching the unicorn carefully, her tail thumping the snowy ground. Bevin was nowhere to be seen.

"Has anybody noticed any Elk near us?" asked Galaxy as she joined Ashe, snarling the same question in dragonic. "I don't want to see Elk again for... for a long time."

~Haven't sssmelled any since landing.~ Ashe yawned. ~Foul sssmell.~

"I haven't seen any," said Owain, magically levitating a pouch over the cooking stew and sprinkling in a pinch of some red powder. "Bevin left a few minutes ago to encircle the camp with motion detection spells. Just in case anyone is out there."

"Speaking of..." Brynjar sat down beside Galaxy, ramrod figure a contrast to her relaxing against Ashe's side. "Can we trust her?"

"Ugh. Brynjar..."

"Don't 'Brynjar' me!" His wings beat nervously. Galaxy actually sat up at the agitation worrying his voice. "The timing! Getting there just in time to save you? How'd she even get there at all? Why just cut his arm off? Why no killing blow?"

Owain snorted and stomped a hoof. "Come off it, Brynjar. There's nothing to gain in betraying Gal now. She's a frien... okay, probably not a friend, but she's an ally! You weren't there when I finally convinced her that Mordred and the Empire were in the wrong. I don't think she could ever return to him."

"And you weren't there when she confronted Mordred," added Galaxy, wincing even as she said it. She had been the one insisting to go alone with King Erentil, after all. "The venom in her voice. The fury in her eyes. Owain's right."

Brynjar's features twisted in the brief silence that followed, hurt and passing anger as he looked between Galaxy and Owain. His wings quit their beating, the golden eagle-gryphon visibly steeling himself. "Then what about after her revenge? She could still return to the Empire then."

"Your brother is right. Listen to him."

Galaxy jumped once more that night, back shrieking protest as her wings half-opened for flight. She grimaced as Bevin marched out of the darkness of the surrounding woods to her side of the campfire. The unicorn moved sluggishly, exhausted, but still exuded satisfaction as she levitated a wild boar carcass alongside her, its neck cleanly broken. Galaxy's stomach churned seeing those dead, rolling eyes. "Um..."

Bevin dropped the carcass in front of Ashe, the dragon's eyes widening in surprise, tongue sliding out to lick her lips. At Galaxy's questioning look, the unicorn tossed her mane in a shrug and marched back to Owain's side of the fire. "The dragon needs to eat to heal, and needs to heal to fly, and despite everything I just said, your brother's still right. Once Mordred's dead, Empress Nova will want a new Lord of War. The unicorn to kill him, perhaps. For the Unicorn Empire's enemy number one, you possess a shocking lack of instinct for self-preservation."

"That's what I keep saying!"

"I can preserve myself just fine," said Galaxy, ignoring her brother. "You helped in Port Oil. You helped here. I know I can trust you."

Bevin snorted as she levitated a bowl up to scoop from the stew pot, ignoring Owain's glare. "The same way you knew you could trust King Erentil, I assume? Fine ideas, if this were a children's tale. It's not." She ducked her head down, taking a large mouthful from the bowl. "It's life, and life is—"

The arrogance of moments before vanished as Bevin paused. Galaxy blinked, then almost laughed at the sour grimace passing across the soldier's features. Struggling, Bevin eventually swallowed the mouthful before looking at Owain. "Needs more salt. Try counter-stirs once every three regular stirs."

Snorting, Owain chanced eyes with Brynjar for a moment. "Next you'll be telling me that stews and soups work best when containing water."

The first laugh broke from Galaxy's beak like a cross between a belch and a hiccup, and from there, it was impossible to stop. Brynjar slumped onto his belly beside her, one fist beating the ground with his full-bodied guffaws. Ashe, though Galaxy doubted she had been able to follow a lick of the conversation, let out a snarling sort of chuckle that, if anything, made Galaxy laugh all the harder. It was a good laugh, the kind that worked its way up from the gut, teetering just on the right edge of breathless. Through tears she could see Owain fallen on his rear, head back, adding his own whinnying laugh to the mix.

Sometime later, once Galaxy had finally gotten herself under control and Owain announced that now, yes, the food was done, she found Bevin still sitting there across the fire from her, stone-faced, blue eyes shining bright in the dancing fire. Galaxy felt herself caught by that stare, those familiar eyes, a chill racing down her spine. But then the spell ended. Galaxy shook her head and stood, walking a wide berth around the fire to get Owain's bowl of stew prepared for her. As she walked back around to Ashe—

"You're not ready, hippogryph. You're going to get us all killed."

Galaxy stumbled. She didn't let the chill of hearing that nightmare phrase show on her features as she sat again with Ashe and looked at Bevin across the flames. She tried to smile, not certain it worked. "Not if you have anything to say about it. If it's so important to you, teach me how to fight. In return, when you do finally get your next chance to kill Mordred, you'll have it with a hippogryph at your side."

Slowly, as if the very act pained her, Bevin smirked. "I like those odds."

CHAPTER EIGHT

They rose with the sun. Or at least, Bevin rose with the sun and Galaxy allowed the soldier to think she had done the same. In truth, Galaxy had already been awake for some time, nightmares be thanked. It was bad enough that Brynjar and Owain knew about the nightly terrors. Galaxy didn't even question trying to keep her enemy-turned-teacher out of the loop for as long as possible. She didn't want that kind of questioning, not when just standing up still hurt.

Brynjar was rousing from sleep as the pair left camp, an apple sufficing for breakfast. Galaxy let the unicorn lead the way, content to lose herself in the nature surrounding them. Fresh snow had fallen during the night, though that morning the clouds remained empty and still, both sky and earth in deep white. Galaxy wanted to lose herself in that snow. It was all so simple and clean.

"So, what's the deal with the dragon?"

Galaxy shot a look Bevin's way as they crossed a fallen log. "She's Ashe. She escaped from a nearby Imperial fortress some weeks ago, and had been terrorizing the Elk. We... we helped them put a stop to that, though they weren't really thrilled with me doing so non-violently. Now I've promised to help get her back to the Dragonback Mountains where she came from. She's only a child. It's not safe or right to take her into danger."

"Hmm..."

Galaxy frowned, letting the anger smolder. "What, you disagree? Think we should make the CHILD fight?"

"You're still a child," Bevin said back with a glare of her own, Galaxy stumbling at THAT being something the soldier cared to remember when she, somehow, had honestly forgotten. When Bevin looked back forward, her voice was softer. "I only... didn't know dragons came in pink."

"That... was one of my first thoughts too."

Soon, Bevin brought them to a stop beside an ice-choked river, thin and winding into several stagnant pools, most frozen over. Moving to the edge of the river, Galaxy saw herself for the first time since her fight against Mordred. Deep bruises circled both eyes. Patches of fur and feathers across her neck, chest, and belly were thinned by mostly-healed burn scars. Most eye-catching, thin but jagged scars from wyvern claws trailed along her sides and flanks, up her back between her wings. At least, with a second healing session with Owain and Bevin the night before, the pain keeping her from flying was gone.

"You're starting to look like a real gryphon warrior," commented Bevin, the soldier standing at the edge of one of the stagnant pools and looking Galaxy over. "If I'm to teach you anything, I need to know what I'm working with. Tell me what you can do."

That sounded a sensible place to start to Galaxy. "Well, besides magical telekinesis, I can also perform the shield spell and the magic transference spell."

Bevin nodded again... then stood still and stared. Galaxy, not sure what she was wanting, stared back. A minute passed as they stared at each other, a cold breeze ruffling Galaxy's feathers and sending Bevin's mane whipping. Eventually, the unicorn narrowed her eyes. "You... you're not saying anything else. That's really all you can do after all this time."

Another spark of anger lit within Galaxy, quickly consumed by embarrassment. Coughing, she looked away from Bevin. "I'm... really good with the shield spell..."

Without warning, without even a command of "Show me," Bevin ripped a boulder twice again as big as her head from the stream and threw it at Galaxy. On instinct, Galaxy cast a shield spell, the boulder reflecting off it and crashing straight through the trunk of a nearby tree with all the force of a cannonball. In the time it took for the tree to completely topple to the forest floor, Bevin threw five more rocks of varying sizes at Galaxy, forcing her to keep casting the shield spell and reflecting them away.

As the last echoes of the fallen tree faded, Bevin motioned for Galaxy to drop her shield. Galaxy did so with full gratitude, immediately sitting down to catch her breath. "You're right, mostly," said the unicorn, staying standing. "You are better with the shield spell than I see most Imperial soldiers bother getting. Tell me, are you consciously making striking forces reflect so powerfully off your shields, or is that an unconscious act?"

Galaxy gaped up at her, surprised at the suggestion that it even could be one or the other. "Uh, unconscious, I guess. It took me completely by surprise when the *Titan*'s city-destroying blast reflected back at it over Port Oil. I had assumed it was something the scroll I learned from didn't mention—"

Bevin fired off a flurry of magic bolts at Galaxy, forcing her to cast another shield spell. "H-hey! I was talking there!"

The magic bolt barrage cut off, to be replaced by a rapid-fire onslaught of pebbles from the riverbed. Galaxy growled and kept her shield up, straining as Bevin slowly advanced on her. The unicorn's stride was steady, even relaxed, as if this were a calm stroll through the woods. "Of course you were talking. That's the best time to strike. You should know this already."

Galaxy, shield still up, looked around for some kind of advantage. Her eyes found the fallen tree. Looking back at Bevin, she smiled as she reached out with her magic for the treecausing the shield spell to falter. "Oh cr—"

Two minutes later, the pair sat at the edge of the river, Bevin going over Galaxy's newfound bruises. The hippogryph tried looking anywhere other than at her teacher. "The, uh, the weather sure is nice today... doesn't look like we'll be needing to worry about snow for a while, maybe even all... day. Was nice that no Elk showed up... you'd think they'd be drawn to the sounds of... crashing, and uh... cursing..."

Bevin said nothing, merely knitting up a cut over Galaxy's left eye. Sighing, Galaxy slumped where she sat. "That would have worked, if I hadn't dropped my shield..."

"Good." Bevin pulled away and stood back to her full height. The look Galaxy found cast her way was stern, but not unkind. "You've figured out what you need to do next on your own. That's a good sign."

"A sign that I'm smart?"

"That you don't have a concussion."

Stifling a chuckle, Galaxy stood as well and looked from Bevin to the fallen tree still several feet off. "I need to learn how to manage multiple spells at once?"

"It's the most useful skill any soldier of the Empire develops." Bevin added weight to her statement by first casting a shield spell of her own, then levitating a number of rocks from the river. No strain appeared in her features from the feat. "Any half-intelligent enemy isn't going to wait around for you to switch back and forth between offense and defense. Mordred is more than half-intelligent. You want my help killing him, not just surviving him? Don't just try to overpower him."

When no further comment came, Galaxy sighed and squared herself. Breathing deep, she cast again the familiar shield spell. Then again, breathing in and out, she reached with her magic to the fallen tree, slowly this time, far slower than she would in actual combat. Immediately she felt a strange sort of strain, not painful so much as disorienting, like a sudden blow to the stomach, but to her head. With a grunt, the magic to the shield cut off, the resulting backlash both staggering her and shattering the tree in her grasp.

"Hmm," sounded Bevin from somewhere nearby, Galaxy preoccupied with blinking the sudden stars from her eyes. "That was a sad attempt. Glad to know crushing an enemy is always an option for you, at least."

Galaxy shook her head to clear the last of the haziness, frowning as she looked back at Bevin. The unicorn seemed to have either forgotten or gotten over the brief moment in Port Oil where Galaxy had very nearly crushed her to death in such a manner, driven to near-madness with grief. Not something Galaxy expected to ever forget. It was the closest she had ever come to consciously trying to kill someone. But, if the unicorn wasn't going to mention it... "What did I do wrong?"

Bevin bit her lip as she looked the shattered remains of the tree over, tail flicking behind her, a hoof digging at the frosty ground. Behind, the river murmured. Above, branches cracked and creaked with ice. "If I had to guess... you tried for something too big for your first attempt. The amount of magic put into the telekinesis was disproportionate to the amount in the shield spell and completely unbalanced you. Like trying to carry a load when one end of the stick is far heavier than the other.

"What you need to remember," Bevin continued, looking back at Galaxy, "is that magic is not just some tool to get a job done. Magic is as much a part of you as any limb or organ. When it's unbalanced, YOU'RE unbalanced. You must always be mindful of your power, in and outside of battle."

Galaxy raised an eyebrow. "Huh. No offense, but... that's a lot more, well, philosophical than I'd expect from you."

Surprisingly, Bevin looked almost amused by the observation as she lifted a pair of rocks from the river and idly floated them around. "Well, for all his faults, Mordred was as fine a teacher as any, I suppose. All the better to eventually kill him. Here, close your eyes and focus solely on the magic. Feel it all around you, but focus on mine to see how it's done."

Galaxy did as commanded, breath catching as the darkness exploded into light all around her, startling with its vibrancy in comparison to the seemingly dead winter landscape. She beheld in the earth beneath them a deep, roiling sort of green, whatever magic the Elderpine Forest possessed to make it so rich and bountiful, sprouting up in countless winding paths through the trees surrounding them. She beheld the cool blueness of the river, lazy but persistent as it went its way. And there, so close—

Wait. Galaxy frowned, casting her inner sight for magic toward the anomaly in her vision, more startled by the second as she came upon... her own magic. Or not quite her own, not quite as soft or warm or cherry-red, and carrying a strange feeling of earthiness. But even with all that, the resemblance was—

"Hippogryph, are you paying attention?"

Galaxy opened her eyes and found herself staring at Bevin, who glared back with blue eyes now startlingly familiar.

Swallowing in sudden nervousness, Galaxy wracked her brain for any plausible excuse for her spacing out, anything other than the actual questions burning to be asked. "I'm sorry, I was just caught off-guard by your... your..."

"My Elemental."

It wasn't a question, giving Galaxy an idea this came up often with others. Well, if she was going to jump to conclusions... "Sorry, I've just never felt someone in possession of an Elemental. Spell Virus probably doesn't count. It kind of reminds me of my second magic."

Bevin's glare dissipated, the unicorn nodding. "The Waters of Life King Erentil told you about."

"Yeah, that." Galaxy coughed and scratched the side of her neck with a talon, looking around for anything else, any excuse to move on. Nothing jumped out at her, and before she could stop herself, "How did you end up with an Elemental, anyway?" Then, at seeing her companion's expression darkening once more, "Or never mind! Sorry, I shouldn't have asked, sensitive topic, I was just—"

"Blathering," said Bevin, features carefully neutral as she moved away from the riverside to sit in a relatively dry patch of ice-free grass. "You're blathering. Stop. With how much trouble I've caused you with my power, it's a fair enough question. And comfort's a luxury anyway."

She paused, staring off into the distance. Galaxy moved to sit some paces from her, wings twitching with a mix of unease and excitement for this unexpected chance to learn more about her once-foe.

When Bevin starting talking again, her voice was solemn and surprisingly soft, an emotion Galaxy couldn't quite identify simmering below the surface. "I was just about your age, maybe a little younger. It was my second year training for the Imperial Army, enlisted early by Mordred for reasons I... can only guess at. I'd been at it long enough for the other, older recruits to realize my exceptionalism, but not long enough for them to accept it. Guess I should have seen trouble coming, but when you know you're being groomed by Lord Mordred himself as his own personal troop commander, you tend to get... proud.

"It was a simple combat exercise, in theory. A series of 12 rooms, 12 arenas representing any and every possible environment we could expect to find ourselves in, from freezing tundra to a sprawling urban. The goal for each room, finding and securing the key for the next room while evading a gryphon captive, starved and... and..." She paused, brow furrowing as if she'd only just realized the depravity of her admission. Galaxy, though sickened, could not find it in herself to blame the child Bevin for just trying to survive.

"Anyway," Bevin said, cleanly sidestepping the issue, to Galaxy's relief, "there'd be a different gryphon for each room, chosen at random. I was, I remember, the third of my group to go through. It went well at first. I got through the urban, forest, and desert arenas well enough. It... it was... the storming marsh area where it happened. There should only have been one gryphon, but there were more, there... a raven-gryphon and a vulture-gryphon, a-and a sparrow, and, and—"

Galaxy stood at the pain and fear that suddenly passed through Bevin's eyes. Before she could say that this was fine, that she'd heard enough, that Bevin could stop, the unicorn shook her head and cleared her throat, forcing a look of uncaring that even to Galaxy was dead on arrival. "By the time Mordred reached me, I was in more pieces than I care to think about. I watched, dying, as my adoptive father tore my tormentors apart with his lightning. First the gryphons, then the unicorns. Then darkness came, and by the time I woke again... I was whole, and scared, and able to feel every speck of rock and stone around me."

A deep breath, Bevin closing her eyes and grinding a hoof against the ground. From where she sat, Galaxy blinked back unshed tears at the feeling of a small flicker of magic, seemingly from the earth itself.

"I learned two lessons that day," continued Bevin after a long minute of silence, snapping Galaxy's attention back to her. "The weak will always, always resent the strong, whether they've done anything to deserve it or not, whether they even know they're the powerful or not."

Galaxy swallowed, reaching a wing out to rest its tip on the unicorn's shoulder. "And the second lesson?"

Bevin opened her eyes, turning those icy orbs on the wing for a moment before shrugging it off and turning to march back to the stream. "Trust always has limits. Come on, the day's wasting. Back to work."

Galaxy remained standing there a moment, watching Bevin stalk off. Those words whirled through her head. She didn't want the moment to end on such a dispiriting note. "Hey! Thanks!"

Bevin stopped on the riverbank, looking back in confusion. Galaxy flapped her wings, scratching at the hard soil with a talon. "You said trust has limits, so... thank you. For trusting me with that story."

For a second, even half a second, something like a smile graced Bevin's muzzle, the hate lifting from her eyes and the weariness from her shoulders, her tail giving an almost happy flick. But then a cloud passed across the sun and the look was gone, replaced by the far more familiar glower. "I just knew you wouldn't stop asking. Now don't make me repeat myself again. Back to practice!"

The memory of that smile burning bright in her mind's eye, Galaxy did so with pleasure. Like Bevin had said, the day was wasting away, and there was still a ways to go ahead of them.

***

Galaxy lay slumped against Ashe's side, eyes closed as she basked in the dragon's natural warmth. Ashe, for her part, seemed mostly amused as she devoured the brace of rabbits Bevin had brought for her. Galaxy didn't care. She had never guessed she could feel so thoroughly thrashed outside of a life-or-death battle. That somehow, after a whole day of training, she still could not multicast, made the pain worse. Bevin's comments that it wasn't something that even could be accomplished in a single day did little to keep the food tasting of ash and broken dreams.

Dinner that evening was another helping of Owain's stew, not half so appetizing looking or smelling the second night on. The repetition was offset somewhat by several bags worth of the sickeningly sweet berries Galaxy and Bevin had noticed during their slow, aching march back to camp.

"Noticed isn't the right word," interrupted Bevin from her place by the fire as Galaxy tried relating the day's events to the others in the group, leaving out the story of Bevin's trauma for the unicorn's benefit. "This sad sack of bruises and exhaustion tripped on a root, rolled down a hill, and fell literally beak-first into a bush of the berries. It was the funniest thing I've ever seen in my life."

"Not bad," said Brynjar once he'd finished slapping Owain's back to help dislodge the chunk of potato he had started choking on in the middle of a laughing fit. "But I've seen better. Somedays I don't know how Gal survived long enough to bother you unicorns."

Galaxy's stomach dropped at the look of interest on Bevin's muzzle. "Ohhh no," she said, heaving herself up into something approaching a respectable sitting position. "You are not bonding over tales of my most embarrassing moments. That's just sick."

"I concur," said Owain, immediately gaining Galaxy's wariness. Though his voice still rasped from his brush with death moments earlier, it didn't diminish the tone of mischief she heard. "And besides, is it even really possible to embarrass someone whose go-to insult is calling your face a freak?"

Brynjar made a noise that quickly transitioned into coughing as Galaxy glared his way. Before she could give her say on the matter, a matching noise escaped Bevin, immediately stopping Galaxy in her mental tracks. It was the closest thing to a genuine laugh she'd heard from the unicorn. She couldn't help but stare as Bevin shook her head. "Good Toqeph, I'd completely forgotten... when she and I were fighting in Port Oil, she called my face a... what was it? Right, a 'freak.' And before that, she called Mordred's face a childish fool... has she done this a lot?"

Brynjar and Owain shared a look. Galaxy felt like sinking down into the ground and away from the stallion's smirk as he said "She called my face a useless freak once, when we met by happenstance as children. I imagine it was a far better insult in the days when your age is in the single digits."

Galaxy didn't need to lay against Ashe to flush with heat, her cheeks feeling ready to burst into flame from embarrassment. She covered her eyes behind her wingtips, groaning at again hearing that noise from Bevin. "I don't need this. I did nothing to deserve this. You are all awful people and I hate you. You should all go die in a fire."

~What'sss going on?~ asked Ashe, shifting around behind Galaxy. ~Isss all okay?~

~All isss okay~ replied Galaxy, lowering her talons to find the dragon craning her long neck over to stare at Galaxy upside-down. The sight brought a weak grin to her beak. ~The othersss... jussst mean, being... fun... with me. No real... hurt.~

~Oh.~ Ashe blinked, looking up at the others nearer the campfire before looking back down at Galaxy. ~Tell about time I ssset water boiling. Good fun.~

"Oh God, not you too!"

The others laughed, even Ashe seeming to get enough of what Galaxy had said to join in. Galaxy sighed and leaned back again, gaze turning up to the night sky, to the multitude of stars reaching through the treetops. They were faint in the light of the fire Galaxy kept her distance from, but still visible past the shimmering air. Slowly, she relaxed again, struck by an inexplicable bout of nostalgia. She remembered late nights spent stargazing with the whole family in Featheren Valley, Sascha and Siegfried keeping it from ever getting too quiet with their steady line of jokes and "witty" insights punctuating Ida's stories of the constellations and their folklore. Neither her mom nor the Twins were there with them that night, the trio away south in relative safety, but if Galaxy closed her eyes and imagined the campfire as the burning hearth, ready with roasted corn...

"It's like home."

Galaxy looked down to find Brynjar's gaze turned up, eyes alight, half with the campfire and half with the stars. A wing rested comfortably on Owain's back, the unicorn's gaze similarly starlit. Bevin had retreated half a pace, expression returned to careful neutrality, relaxed posture betraying her current contentment. Even Ashe had looked up, a rumble of satisfaction echoing up from her slowly rising and falling belly, moving Galaxy with it.

Nodding to herself, Galaxy relaxed back and let the night sky command her sight, as was its wont.

Eventually, after what could have been hours, whole days beneath those stars, someone spoke. To Galaxy's surprise, it was Owain, voice miles and years distant. "I remember family trips out to the smaller islands north of the Avalon capitol, where the skies were clearest and air the freshest. My mom would tell the most amazing stories about the stars and their constellations, where they came from, what they meant. My father always treated them for the points of light that they are, I don't think he has it in him to treat them any other way, but my mom… she could make the stars sing. She could make them dance. She could make them live."

Galaxy looked down again to see tears falling freely from Owain's cheeks, glints of amber in the firelight. To Galaxy's surprise, Bevin also watched him, the silver sword she'd wounded Mordred with unsheathed and held in a loose magical grip before her. Galaxy kept quiet, wary how this might go as the soldier stood and circled the campfire to where Brynjar and Owain sat together, the clop of Bevin's hooves drawing her fellow unicorn's eye as she knelt before him.

"Owain, I want… to trade silver swords. Your father gave me this to kill Lord Mordred with. He told me it was his wife's sword. Your mother's. I think it best if you wield it."

Fear and heartbreak danced in Owain's wide, watery eyes. Slowly, the magical glow around the sword's grip turned from gold to green as the hold changed from Bevin to Owain. The stallion held the blade up in the firelight, gaze raking across it hungrily, body trembling. Galaxy could see the moment his eyes found the symbol of the Knights Le Fay, his whole body jerking as if struck, composure breaking as the tears fell heavier down his cheeks. "She... she really was a knight, then. So, when she left..."

"It must have been done to protect you," said Bevin, voice like stone as she took Owain's former sword in turn. "Cherish the thought. Not all can say the same."

Owain nodded, lowering his mother's sword to sheath it as Bevin returned to her original spot by the fire. Galaxy found her thoughts returning again and again to the rose, the symbol of the Knights Le Fay emblazoned on each sword. Even as they all sat there, the night still felt incomplete to Galaxy. She could see the same feeling in the eyes of all her companions. There was something more to be done, the fire, the forest, the stars above trembling their anticipation.

"Well, I am royalty, aren't I? I've absolutely got the authority."

The eyes of all present turned to her at Galaxy's murmured remark. Feeling their weight, she sighed and stood, looking to Bevin, the closest aside from Ashe. "If I could have your sword for a moment... is it just commander, or sir as well?"

An understanding light sparked within the soldier's gaze. Standing, she unsheathed the silver sword once more, several long seconds of uncertainty as she contemplated the weapon until, finally, she sighed and knelt, the sword turned to Galaxy hilt-first. "Just commander, your highness. The Empire doesn't put much thought to knighthood anymore."

Galaxy nodded, having expected as much. Moving to stand before the kneeling unicorn, she grabbed the sword, not with her magic but with her talons, sparing a moment to marvel at the surprising lightness of the weapon. She glanced to Owain and Brynjar watching from across the fire, both understanding the magnitude of that night, her brother solemn, Owain almost frightened, the tears still fresh in his eyes. Behind Galaxy, Ashe fidgeted where she lay but kept her peace.

"By my authority as Princess Galaxy, daughter of Queen Grimhilt of Featheren Valley and the fallen Schwarz Angebot..." She didn't know where the words came from, only that this felt right, that this felt important. She followed them more than spoke them, touching the tip of the sword first to Bevin's right shoulder, then her left. "Beneath God and the three Primes, I pronounce you Sir Bevin. Champion."

Bevin closed her eyes, a hoof stamping, a sudden tremor in her chest. "It is... my honor."

Looking away again, Galaxy saw Brynjar and Owain now kneeling, looking at her with green eyes that left a sudden doom upon the hippogryph's thoughts.

Tightening her grip on the sword, Galaxy circled around the fire to them now, repeating the joyless motions from before.

"Beneath God and the three Primes, I pronounce you Sir Brynjar. Guardian... Beneath God and the three Primes, I pronounce you Sir Owain. Counselor..."

The deed was done. Galaxy passed the sword back to Bevin, then looked around at her companions. The soldier sat and stared into the fire. Brynjar and Owain sat together again, the golden eagle-gryphon looking off into the surrounding woods, the unicorn studiously examining his mother's blade. There was a new feeling over the whole camp, the lot of them bound together now in ways Galaxy couldn't begin to understand, not yet.

"Mother would be proud of you," Brynjar said suddenly, Galaxy starting and looking at him. He remained looking out to the woods. "She'd be real proud. Grimhilt too, I hope. Just... don't wait for me to start calling you queen or something."

Galaxy snorted at that terrible thought, though her heart remained warmed all the same by her brother's words. Pride. A warm smile in the morning, a hug after a long day apart, a glimmering shout and laugh after a job well done. She didn't know if she could ever feel proud of herself, but if others could be...

~Galaxy,~ rumbled Ashe, breaking the hippogryph from her thoughts. The dragon sounded pensive, voice soft as her claws kneaded the ground before her. ~I recognize knighting. Recognize word mother. Tell of mother. Pleassse.~

And Galaxy did so, happily, talking in Dragon and Gryphon and Common deep into the night, recounting all she knew and had ever been told of her mother. The campfire flickered and the starts turned on their paths above as the story of Queen Grimhilt of Schwarz Angebot, at least as far as Galaxy knew it, unfurled among them.

CHAPTER NINE

For the next four days, from dawn to noon, Bevin would lead Galaxy off on their own to train, Owain sometimes tagging along to watch. At noon they would return for lunch, flying south on the air-yacht until mid-evening. The time spent training slowed their travel more than Galaxy was used to from the weeks before reaching the Elderpine Forest, but feeling each use of the shield spell become less exhausting, each casting become faster and more instinctive as Bevin trained her, made it time well spent.

The training did not stop once on the air-yacht. Because, with Brynjar's usual eloquence, "You keep throwing yourself into stupid danger. At least throw yourself into smart danger."

With pieces magically sculpted from rocks from that first river, they tried Galaxy's talon at strategy games of every sort. Avalon's native Chess, the Go practiced by the reclusive Tengu of the far western islands. Sphinx senet, dragon liubo, gryphon tafl. It was here, far more than the physical training, where Galaxy almost longed for the days when Bevin was an enemy, not a teacher, as Galaxy failed again... and again... and again. Even Owain, they found, could put up a more respectable fight against Bevin on the board. Even BRYNJAR, they found, could put up a more respectable fight against Bevin on the board.

"Don't worry," said the unicorn late into their fourth day of travel, resetting the board after an eight-game Chess marathon. "Some people simply don't have the mind for it. Nobody is good at everything, so specialists work in tandem to achieve objectives. That's the military way, at least."

"Sounds pretty," said Galaxy, slumped against the mast and dancing a marble across her talons. "Still doesn't keep all this from burning like—"

"DOWN!" shouted Brynjar suddenly, flying from where he'd been keeping watch at the bow, past Galaxy and Bevin, past Ashe, landing hard beside Owain working his turn at the air-yacht's controls. "Ship down, now! Crystal drones ahead!"

No more needed saying. Owain pushed the air-yacht into a steep dive toward the protective cover of the trees. Once landed, Bevin set to work with a feat of magic that never failed to amaze Galaxy. Horn blazing gold, Bevin raised the forest floor around them with a mental heave, lifting earth and rock and the trees lodged within up and over the craft into a false hill. There they waited, hidden, listening with bated breath as the seconds passed. Soon enough, Galaxy perked at the sound of distant chimes. She listened as two... five...

twelve crystal drones passed overhead, heading straight back the way her group had come from.

"That's the third patrol we've seen today," said Owain, whispering so as not to risk notice by any of the sensitive detection spells enchanted into the drones' crystal framework. "What's up with that? They can't possibly be searching that hard for just us."

"I concur," said Bevin, as another wave of drones could suddenly be heard. "Before Mordred came to the Elderpine for the hippogryph, there was a battle to the northeast. A force from Gateway trying to relieve the siege on Gryphonbough was routed, almost totally destroyed, the gryphon kingdom falling not long after. Any survivors that weren't captured at the battle would have fled to the Elderpine."

Galaxy wilted upon hearing Bevin's explanation, guilt and the memory of a raven-gryphon with rainbow eyes bringing tears that she hastily scrubbed away. "Oh God, Gryphonbough's gone? Like Schwarz Angebot?"

Bevin nodded, barely perceptible in the dim light permitted beneath the false hill. Galaxy groaned and raked her talons over her face and down the back of her neck. "That just leaves the Dragonback Mountains, Wedjet, Vogelstadt, and Gateway itself... and if their forces were routed, they're not long for this war either..."

Brynjar cursed beneath his breath. Bevin spoke over him, breath a sad sigh. "This war's been going on for decades now, with a lull for a few years here and there to catch a breath. ALL the nations must be running low on strength and resources by now."

Another drone passed overhead. Galaxy could just make out Brynjar looking at Bevin in surprise. "Even the Empire? You've always seemed... all-powerful."

To that, Bevin tossed her mane. "Especially the Unicorn Empire. Not that the propaganda would ever let you know. We're undoubtedly the most powerful, magically and technologically, but... there are only so many unicorns compared to the hordes of gryphons, dragons, sphinxes, and minotaurs lumped together, and we take longer both to give birth and grow to full physical maturity than gryphons, so the years have been harder on us. It's why we rely so heavily on our air-yachts and crystal drones. A unicorn who's lost a leg in battle can still, with proper training, operate a drone fine. But even then..."

Silence. Galaxy watched as Bevin seemed to wrestle with saying something. Before she could, Ashe growled from where she'd moved near the railing, head lifted high. ~I hear no more.~

Galaxy looked up to the layers of earth and trees above them after relaying the dragon's comment, straining to catch any sound. For a moment, she thought they were in the clear and it was safe to start moving again. But then Owain hissed, gaze down as he wandered over from the controls. "Look at the marbles..."

They looked, saw the Go pieces vibrating along the air-yacht's deck. "Warship," growled Bevin. "Same kind as the *Titan*, straight over us. They wouldn't use that to search for survivors. A prisoner transport, maybe, or renewed guerrilla fighting in the Gryphonbough Forest..."

But there was another possibility. Galaxy knew it, could barely think about it, much less voice it to the others. Vogelstadt, Gateway, the Dragonback Mountains, and Wedjet weren't the only nations left for the Unicorn Empire to attack, as they'd said minutes before. There were the Elk, too. The Elk, who King Erentil had only been able to protect by promising Galaxy to Lord Mordred...

The confused, hurting look on Gwendolyn's face appeared in Galaxy's mind. She shook it away, looking down to find the Go pieces had stopped vibrating. The sky above was, most likely, free of danger once more. For the moment. She stood from where she'd crouched, starting to ask Bevin to get rid of the artificial hill when she noticed the unicorn staring at her. "What?"

Bevin stood there, staring at Galaxy a moment more, before huffing and glancing away. "Nothing, just a thought. Pass me the water bowl near the bags, won't you? A drink before we move on."

Galaxy blinked, sharing a look with Brynjar and Owain, who to her relief looked equally confused by the odd request. Shrugging, she reached for the bowl in question with her magic, pouring a measure of water from the bags into it before turning to pass it to Bevin.

Halfway around, Galaxy caught the gleam of a sword slicing through the air for her neck, stopped at the last second on a hastily-cast shield spell. Heart thudding from the close brush with death, Galaxy used the shield to shove the sword away, before growling and stepping toward a frustratingly smug-looking Bevin, Brynjar and Owain already armed at Galaxy's sides and Ashe somewhere behind her. "And what in Sheol was that for!?"

"Just checking," answered Bevin, sheathing her sword and sitting back down. "Wanted to prove something. Now then, my water, please? I really am thirsty."

Once more, Galaxy blinked. Owain's excited whinny from her right just barely managed to beat her turning her head to see the bowl of water still held aloft by her magical telekinesis, not a drop spilled as far as she could see. "Oh. Oh, I... I did it."

"Yes, you did." The touch of pride in Bevin's voice was unfamiliar, but painfully satisfying. "Now it's time for the training to start getting hard."

***

The hard slam of her body against the unyielding floor jarred Bifrost back to full consciousness, a pained gasp slipping from her cracked beak as she landed bad on her right arm. For several seconds she just lay there on the floor, listening to the retreating hoofsteps of her unicorn guards and relishing simply in being afforded the opportunity to lay as she was.

A minute passed. Bifrost could not remember the last time she had been able to rest for so long. Trying to think, she found her memory a hazy patchwork of pain, her beaten body an ever-aching reminder of the needles, the hot irons, the soaked rags draped across her face, choking, drowning—

"Don't focus on the suffering so much. You will learn to miss it, for it was only physical."

Bifrost jerked at the sudden, soft voice from somewhere else in the room, the first hint that she hadn't been left alone. Limbs too weak to lift her up alone, she crawled to a nearby table of ebony and soft-wrought gold, grunting as she pulled herself up into a half-sitting position. She looked around the room in wary awe, taking in first the complete map of Heraldale inlaid into the surface of the table, then the walls mounted with weapons and armor, and then at last the hearth taking up the entire far wall, and the strange pair standing in front of the roaring flames.

The one on the left, Bifrost knew to be Lord Thoth, the Empire's Lord of Secrets, the only sphinx to join the Empire. The one on the right, Bifrost recognized at once as a Wolf-Lord, the yellow eyes and tooth-crammed smile that still haunted her nightmares confirming in one blazing moment all the darkest rumors she had heard concerning the Empire's dreaded Lord Mordred. He stood at attention in simple grey robes, a black floor-length cape thrown almost lazily over the left shoulder. The wolf beast's right arm, to Bifrost's shock, was missing below the elbow. And there was something else, something wrong with his face...

"You really must teach your soldiers greater efficiency, Mordred," remarked Lord Thoth, the softness of his voice alerting Bifrost to the identity of the earlier speaker. "Depositing him on the floor way over there. Look at the miserable creature, trembling so as he struggles just to keep standing. As if he could make it all the way over to us, dog."

"Well then," responded Lord Mordred, voice strangely wet and guttural, "Why don't you help him over, cat?"

Bifrost had a moment to ponder the sheer scorn passing back and forth between the pair, before an unseen force seized her body and yanked her through the air to their side of the room. She screamed in fear and pain as she was squeezed with enough force to get her already-bruised bones creaking, before landing in another undignified heap at their feet.

"There, dog. I helped him over. Happy now?"

"Hmm... no. It would have been hilarious if I'd sidestepped and the bird had kept flying right into the fire. It's all I'm going to be able to think about now whenever I see this guy, just him flying right into the fire, screaming his beak off."

"You know, total honesty, when he was halfway across the room I had that exact thought, just stepping a foot to the right and letting him sail past... blast it, now that's all I'M going to be able to think about!"

"Oh, poor Lord of Lies and Intelligence, struck down by his own intelligence!"

"Oh, poor Lord of War, losing us this cussing war!"

Bifrost struggled back up into a sitting position, limbs protesting louder than the pair argued, one back leg almost giving out when she tried putting weight on it. Panting from the pain, she kept her gaze down on the floor as she contemplated the ridiculousness of the moment. The idea of valiantly resisting torture for the sake of her country carried so much less weight when it got treated like a joke by her captors. She could've expected this attitude from Mordred, the apparent Wolf-Lord had literally named himself "More dread", but—

Lord Thoth broke out into sudden laughter, snapping Bifrost from her thoughts and silencing

Mordred mid-rant. The sphinx's high-pitched laughter was almost nauseating in the echoes, accompanied by the thump of one paw slapping the floor. "Oh, oh that's too, just too..."

"What is so funny," growled Lord Mordred, the plain venom in his tone raising the feathers along Bifrost's back.

The laughter began to die down, flared back up briefly as the sphinx seemed to glance over at Lord Mordred, eventually turned muffled as Lord Thoth got himself under control. "I just caught... a thought from our bird here... and now I can't st-stop imagining you wa-waking up one day and deciding for yourself 'I SHALL BE MORE DREAD LIKE THAT SONG, BLARGLE RAWR'!"

Bifrost clamped her talons over her beak, body shaking as she willed the laugh bubbling up her throat to stay down, to not make this situation any worse. Somewhere, she could feel the raw, unadulterated rage seething within Lord Mordred, hear the ruinous clack of bones and teeth against each other. It was close, so close, too close—

"Oh, you think THAT'S FUNNY, DO YOU!?"

Bifrost flinched from the shout, head snapping up on instinct, eyes going wide and breath hitching in her throat at the sight of *Lord Mordred's face right there, inches from her own.* It was a horror that took all humor into a back room and gutted it. The left side seemed fine, a normal black-furred wolf head marred only by an infernal yellow eye glaring, but the right side... from just past the edge of the nose, past the eye to the bottom of the ear and down over most of the jaw, the skin and flesh were just gone, burned away, the edges of the remaining skin black and charred. Bifrost could see every twitch of a muscle fiber that tightened the Wolf-Lord's snarl or sent his exposed eye rolling within its socket.

The scream came late, Bifrost's throat closing after it, choking her. She stumbled back, sat, talons reaching up as she forced a rattling breath in and out. The beast before her smiled as he backed away, a smile too wide, possessed of too many teeth. In Mordred's place Thoth stepped in, almost a relief, voice barely to be heard over the rapid pounding of Bifrost's heart from that scare. "You'll have to forgive my compatriot here. He clings fiercely to every scrap of self-worth he can find, and doesn't take well to any... infringes on it. A sick mind, yes?"

Bifrost, getting her breathing back under control, said nothing. She focused on earlier, when the pair had talked among themselves, insisting on identifying her by her body rather than by her heart—

"Sad, confused little bird." Thoth's smile was softer than Mordred's, and all the deadlier for it in Bifrost's mind as he stepped forward, forcing her to step back. "But that's not why we're all here today." A paw idly combed through his mane. "We're here because the tortures have been done, and now is the time for questions..."

For nearly a minute, the two merely looked at each other, Bifrost clenching her talons, Thoth batting his tail against the ground. Breathing steady, Bifrost kept her thoughts low and sparse as she'd been trained to do when dealing with an unfamiliar sphinx. She ran small, meaningless ideas through her head, thoughts of her favorite fruits, favorite gemstones, what made spring the best season of the year. The minutes ticked on and she thought of the known medicinal qualities of every root and leaf native to Gryphonbough, of that time she met a zakarian—

"Do you have any family in Vogelstadt, Bifrost?"

Bifrost conjured up memories of flying high, watching the storm-driven waves of the Southern Sea crash against Vogelstadt's southern shores, the terrible roar and crash of two worlds so much bigger than her clashing together.

In front of her, Thoth's smile grew brittle. "I asked, do you have any family in Vogelstadt, Bifrost? A mother? A father? Brother? Sister?"

Bifrost's wings twitched on her back at a growing pressure inside her head. She dredged up every lay, song, and poem she could remember, feeling the minutes turn to an hour as she recounted them to herself in full, intimately, feverishly. The tale of Sir Judith and her kitsune companion, Sir Tiberius, was her favorite, the morality of friendship overcoming prejudi—

Thoth's smile disappeared completely. Snarling, he lunged forward, Bifrost squawking as the sphinx gripped the sides of her head, claws digging into her temple. Unable to look elsewhere, unable to close her eyes, Bifrost starred helplessly into the depths of Thoth's cold gaze. The pressure inside Bifrost's head peaked to actual, physical pain, alerting her to the wet sense of blood oozing from one nostril. "DO YOU HAVE FAMILY IN VOGELSTADT!?"

Bifrost's talons cracked against the marble floor. She jerked and thrashed, panting and heedless of the blood dribbling from Thoth's claws digging in. Desperate, she drew on life's pains and pleasures for defense. Her first broken bone in training, an elbow when she failed to properly block a sword strike. Her first heartbreak, learning a sparrow-gryphon she'd been courting was being shipped off to fight in Gateway. Joy, receiving the all-important job of courier between Vogelstadt and Gryphonbough. Intrigue, blossoming into hope upon meeting—

"Enough."

The lion claws digging into Bifrost's head disappeared, allowing her to slump to the floor. Panting from the ordeal, quivering in relief as the pressure in her head faded, she looked up to see Thoth backed away a step, staring resentfully at an alarmingly thoughtful-looking Mordred. "I am the Empire's Lord of Secrets, Mordred. You do not give orders to me lightly. Especially not in my own realm of authority."

The Wolf-Lord huffed, waving the sphinx off with his remaining hand. "I listened to your command not to rain vengeance on the Elk, for the Grand Harmony's sake, so just... relax. The bird's just not ready for you yet. He needs a little more softening, physical and..." And there a new wickedness came to Mordred's mind, Bifrost able to see it gleaming within those sickly yellow eyes. "Emotional."

Thoth himself seemed perturbed by the look in his compatriot's eyes, glancing from him to Bifrost and back. "If you think I've done all I can this session... do what you will, then send him back to the 'caring watch' of your Markhaven soldiers."

But Mordred had already begun to move before Thoth even finished talking, squatting down right next to Bifrost and tilting his head in a lazy, curious smile, to her immediate discomfort. She had seen that particular look before in her courier duties, from blunt allies and ignorant friends and mocking better-than-yous alike. The feeling grew worse as Mordred drew from the depths of his cape Bifrost's blue scarf, torn and singed and stained with blood and mud and soot, but hers all the same. And when he spoke, idly turning the scarf over in the fingers of his remaining hand, it was honey-laced poison. "It's interesting, really. I didn't think there were any of your sort from Vogelstadt. For some reason, the use of blue scarves like your Gateway brethren surprises me."

Bifrost said nothing, content to glare at her tormentor. Wounding the scarf messily around his neck, Mordred continued. "But you know, it must hurt you something fierce to see me. Wolf-Lords never had to wear scarves, or badges, or anything else to let the world know what we really were inside. Not when, hehehe, we could do thi-isss!"

The last word was punctuated by a grunt, almost a moan. Bifrost flinched, then stared, transfixed with pain, as Mordred changed. A subtle softening of brow and snout. The fur on the top and back of his head lengthening, a shaggy mane reaching down to shoulders that were suddenly slimmer. Redistributed body mass spread back over the burnt ruin of the Wolf-Lord's face. Each change accompanied by a stomach-churning ripple of flesh and clenching muscle, a huff and painful squeal.

When Lord Mordred spoke again, that nightmare voice of reverbs and layered snarls reigned back into something low, guttural, almost feminine. "Tonight, you're going back to your cell, back to your tortures, knowing that this is something your pretty little scarves will never give you."

Bifrost didn't hear the soldiers return, barely feeling the metal collar snap around her neck. A sharp tug, almost neck-breaking, sent her reeling to her back, where the soldiers began dragging her back across the room to the doors. Through it all she looked back at the grinning Lord Mordred, standing back to her new full height, infernal yellow eyes and cluttered teeth soon veiled in tears.

***

It was sometime early into the fifth afternoon since Galaxy and Bevin began their training sessions when they finally, to Galaxy's unending relief, reached the southern edge of the Elderpine Forest. She stood at the air-yacht's bow, gaze ahead as she took in the new lands opening up before them, thick with hills and strewn with winding rivers and lakes covered over in snow and ice. Villages were closer together, lone homes and homesteads less common as the waterways formed natural connective tissues between specks of civilization. Onto the scene drifted snow from heavy cloud cover, gentle at the moment, lending an air of remoteness and calm that Galaxy wished she could feel all the time.

"What beautiful land," said Owain, coming up beside Galaxy. "It reminds me of the northernmost isle of Avalon, Cairn. It's almost always snowing there, and the snow that falls lingers nearly all year. Erf. It's freezing up here!"

Galaxy nodded, assuming Owain was right. "Well, I'd lay a wing over you, but I don't feel like spraining my back overstretching."

"Eh, Brynjar might get jealous if you did that anyway."

Galaxy rolled her eyes and smiled. "Get a room, you two."

The land continued passing below them, the minor streams and ponds spreading out, winding southward into a longer, greater river than any Galaxy had seen yet. It lumbered northeast to southwest, almost completely free of ice from its sheer size, cutting the flatlands in half. The villages along its banks were larger, refined into full-scaled towns.

"The Smaragd Fluss," called out Bevin from the air-yacht's rear. "Farther south it will join with rivers running out of the Dragonback Mountains to become the Sandwine, Wedjet's northern border. Upstream a ways from where we are is Markhaven, the village Urien found me in. If he's still free and able, he'll surely try to contact me there."

"Too much danger for all of us to go," said Brynjar, working the air-yacht's control spires. "Let's set down for evening, plan for tomorrow."

The clomp of hooves heralded Bevin's joining Galaxy and Owain at the bow, gaze scanning the land below. The stallion looked over Galaxy's back at his fellow unicorn, a nervous stamp to his hooves. "Do you think he's safe? If Mordred or the Empire ever figure out he helped you..."

"I'm sure your father is fine," said Bevin, not even looking in Owain's direction, to Galaxy's appalled frustration. Before she could call the soldier out on it, however, Bevin snorted and lowered her head over the railing to point at a grove of trees running along the Smaragd Fluss with her horn. "There, that woodland. I passed through there on my way to Markhaven, not more than an hour's walk on hoof. It should fit the air-yacht."

"Right," came Brynjar's voice, Galaxy looking up as the mast and sails creaked, the air-yacht adjusting its course. "Bevin's Grove it is."

Looking back ahead, Galaxy sighed but said nothing. All the talk of Markhaven had gotten her looking forward to a real bed and a real inn's roof overhead, to gossip and fighting and more substantial food than what they could eat on the metaphorical road. Yet, it looked like it'd be at least one more night with nothing but a thin blanket between her and the air-yacht's deck.

Watching Owain and Bevin trot away, Galaxy noticed Ashe keeping her gaze up the river and trembling faintly. ~Sssomething... trouble... you?~

Ashe rumbled, shifting where she lay and curling her tail tighter. ~Clossse now unicornsss... hurt me. Up water.~

Galaxy dug her talons into the wood railing. As their view of the surrounding lands disappeared behind the rising treetops of their chosen clearing, she strode to starboard side and rested a wing on Ashe's back, relieved when the dragon didn't flinch. ~I ssswear, I will... bring unicornsss to jussstice. Sssolemn vow.~

Ashe growled her appreciation, excitement fluttering her mostly-healed wings. Galaxy wished she could have shared that excitement, knowing that any such justice would have to wait, something Brynjar made sure to let everyone know as the air-yacht settled down and the ramp was lowered. Now it was time for camp and its monotonous chores, something Galaxy threw herself into with all the fervor she could manage. A training session with Bevin that evening was just what she wanted.

***

Brynjar sat on the campsite-side of the air-yacht, wings lifted over his head to shield from the drifting snow as he whittled the hours away with a stick and his talons. Boredom circled the corners of his mind as a predator circled the light of a campfire. Not that Brynjar minded being bored. Boredom meant nothing trying to kill him, no hard tasks to set his mind to, and no troubles to dwell uselessly on. Boredom could be good. Yes.

A shout of excitement echoed from where Galaxy and Bevin had left to an hour before. Brynjar glanced that way, an entirely unwelcome moment of jealousy tugging at his heart, before he returned his focus to the dwindling piece of wood in his talons. He paused for a moment and puzzled over what it was he had even carved. "It, uh... a wolf... or a squat table... or..."

A flicker of multicolored light through the trees, followed by another happy shout, this time Galaxy's voice for sure. Brynjar sighed and let the figure fall from his talons to the snowy forest floor some yards below, feet from where the dragon slept. "Curse it all, Gal. Why do you have to do this to me?"

Brynjar didn't enjoy this jealousy, this resentment. He knew that Galaxy enjoying the new, greater role magic played in her life, the new unicorn and Elk friends she had made (as briefly as the latter had lasted), was more than deserved after all she had accomplished. And if that meant less room for a gryphon who had grown up neglecting her, well, that seemed fair. She deserved to have Bevin back in her life.

It was only...

"Years and years of hating you
Well past your due
Now with everything we come across that's new,
I fear our mended ways are through...
"Look at you, out there, fighting the good fight!
Being better than I could ever be!
Learning what you need to set things right,
But Gal, oh, can't you see,
"See that there's more than magic?
Must you neglect your gryphon side?
I can't make our past less tragic
But please let me try to be a guide!
"Then we can show the world there's more,
More than magic in life
Then we can end this war,
Forge ahead and forget our strife
"Just please...
"Don't you forget there's more than magic...
I promise that I'm so sorry...
Don't you forget there's more than magic...
Let me in as your big brother... again."

The magic left and Brynjar felt no more urge to sing as his kind did. He sighed and rubbed at his eyes. He didn't know when he had become so sentimental, but if anyone ever realized it—

"If it makes you feel any better, I think you're pretty great."

Brynjar did not scream. He did not jump and nearly fall off the air-yacht. He did not throw the closest thing at talon, a satchel of coins, in the direction of the sudden voice. What he did, despite anyone else's claims to the contrary, was look down from where he sat to Owain below him, gathering back up the fresh firewood that had most certainly not been knocked from his magical hold by any ballistic sacks of coin. "If you breathe a word of this to another living soil..."

"Understood, wait until we meet a ghost to start blabbering, got it." Owain set the last branch near the campfire and turned to meet Brynjar's gaze. "More importantly, I don't think you need to worry about Gal resenting you or anything like that. I don't think she has a mean-spirited bone in her body. If she does, you can wager money that all its focus is on Lord Mordred. Eh, maybe the Elk, too."

Brynjar wanted to agree, remembering well the coldness with which Galaxy had removed Princess Gwendolyn from their group. But... "She still should resent me. And ever since Bevin saved her from Mordred, she's seemed... distant. I feel so, so..."

"Superfluous?"

Ignoring Owain's fancy word, Brynjar looked up at the grey sky, relishing the pinpricks of cold from the falling snow. The sight of the sky provided a change in topic he could live with. "The day grows late. I don't feel like wasting time while Gal and Bevin beat each other up to ready for beating Mordred up. Should do something."

"Well," said Owain, sounding nervous and excited and sneaky in equal measure, catching Brynjar's interest at once, "Everything seems in order around here and Gal's likely to be training for hours still. Surely it wouldn't hurt any to see what we can find out in Markhaven, right?"

Brynjar raised an eyebrow, before jumping to join the best unicorn he'd ever met down on the ground. "Just us? No hippogryph to draw unwanted looks? Just another unicorn and another gryphon roaming Heraldale? Sounds almost... safe."

Owain nodded, eyes shining. "Spying. Just catching whatever big news we can and seeing which way the wind's blowing. Who knows what's been happening while we were traveling."

Brynjar nodded back, starting to smile himself as he took in what the unicorn was saying. Everything made just enough sense to be excused. "Yeah, it'll be... useful."

Owain glanced behind them at Ashe, who had lifted her head to stare at them as they talked. "Er, I'm sure the dragon will be fine, but do you have anything we could leave a note to Gal with in case she and Bevin get back before we do? I think I prefer not worrying someone who can juggle the air-yacht with her magic."

"I—" Brynjar paused, frowning as he turned from the dragon to look at a badly-hiding-his-amusement Owain. "You know I wouldn't be able to write or read any such note, right?"

"Nooo," said Owain, failing to stifle a chuckle as he tossed his mane. "Don't be absurd..."

Brynjar rolled his eyes. "Forget it. Will just tell the dragon we're leaving."

He could almost feel Owain's confusion as a physical presence. "Uh, did Gal teach you how to speak dragon while I wasn't looking?"

"No," said Brynjar, walking over to the still-watching dragon. Stopping three paces away, he took a moment to both size his intended audience up and stretch his wings and limbs, stiff from the time spent sitting in the cold. Then, as best as his larger body could manage, he set about mimicking the sort of body language he had seen Galaxy make use of while talking to the dragon, wide stances and undulating backs. "I've heard Galaxy talk, though. I think I can do it."

"That really doesn't seem like something you can just pick up on," said Owain, this time Brynjar noticing his voice coming from substantially farther away. "Also, you look ridiculous."

Ashe hissed in seeming agreement, tail slapping the ground behind her. Brynjar ignored it, wings twitching on his back in aggravation. "I need to learn something to be more useful. Now quiet, I'm going to try..."

A deep breath, a shake of the head to dispel his doubts, then, ~Ducksss drill... half a lime... from beefcake the sssun...~

The dragon stared at him for several seconds, completely motionless save her slow blinking, making Brynjar cough and shift his footing as the time dragged on. Then a ripple ran down her body, from head to tail, followed by her lips pulling up into a toothy smile. Brynjar was alarmed by the sight of tears in her eyes, but the series of rapid hisses leaving her didn't sound sad or distressed. He glanced back at Owain, finding the unicorn standing several yards away and well clear of any fire breathing that might have come from the wrong phrase. Looking back at the dragon, Brynjar chuckled and began backing up to Owain, waving with a wing. "I don't know what you said, but I feel mocked right now. I'll just... be on my way."

The dragon returned his waving with a wing, before settling her head back on her folded front legs, still loosing those short, breathless hisses. Swallowing from what felt like a close call, Brynjar turned and hurried to Owain. Markhaven awaited.

**

"Remember, hippogryph. Concentrate. Feel the properties of the stone before you. Weight, density, coarseness, the individual materials that went together into it. Feel the nature magic there, though you cannot touch it or use it yourself, feel how it binds the properties together into the stone, making the stone BE stone. Feel it, but ignore it. It is Heraldale magic, and incompatible with yours without an Elemental to bridge the way. Instead, extend your magic into the stone, infusing it with your power and focus. Concentrate."

More easily said than done, thought Galaxy, noting the exasperation creeping into Bevin's voice. Once more taking a deep breath and holding it for five seconds, as her teacher had recommended, Galaxy at once inhaled and reached her magic out to the cart-sized boulder before her. With her eyes closed, she relied only on her magical sensitivity for guidance, feeling the difference as her magic moved from cold air to dense stone.

"That's it... keep going... keep your pace STEADY, hippogryph..."

Galaxy breathed in and out again, feeling sweat bead on her flanks as she kept her flow of magic slow. Two minutes passed before the magical saturation in the rock was satisfactory to Bevin, though try as she might, Galaxy couldn't discern whatever clued the soldier in.

"Good. Now, stop, but don't let go. Keep rooted to the magic suffusing the boulder. Keep every property at the forefront of your mind. You have that, now... concentrate now, begin mentally changing those properties. ONLY ONE AT A TIME. Make a specific property of the stone as you imagine it... and speak the spell."

Galaxy breathed, focusing on the property of the rock that most stuck out to her, its hardness. She licked the edge of her beak, summoning to mind the honey taffy they would serve at festival time in Featheren Valley, the fun of stretching the sickeningly-sweet confection between her talons, working a square of it around in her beak with her tongue until it dissolved, watching as Siegfried and Sascha held their squares over the house hearth until the taffy oozed and dripped from its own weight. The rock was like that, she told herself. The rock as not hard and unyielding. The rock was weak, soft...

"Moligi!"

For a moment there followed only silence, no sign of the spell at work reaching Galaxy. But then, "Very good, hippogryph. Hardness is the best property to start with."

Cheeks heating from Bevin's rare praise, Galaxy opened her eyes to see her talonwork. She saw the boulder sitting there, slumping down into a tar-like puddle from its own weight, just as she—

As she did this, the black-eyed unicorns began to, for lack of a better term on her part, deflate. Their skin folded in, legs buckling, empty eye sockets staring madly out at nothing, teeth showing in dumb, mindless grins.

"Gal?" She'd never heard Brynjar so scared. "What's going on?"

Mordred stomped his heavy hoof and the table flew away, slamming into the far wall and shattering, and Galaxy gasped. Black tendrils, slimy and writhing, connected each of the deflating unicorn soldiers by the belly to Lord Mordred. As she watched, the needle-like ends of the tendrils withdrew from the formless lumps of flesh that remained on the stone floor, slithering—

Then Galaxy was back in the woods, fallen and panting for breath. Bevin hovered nearby, snorting and pacing, a hoof digging at the ground. "Horror Sickness... the attack has passed?"

Galaxy ignored the question, her body tired as she worked to get back to all fours. Bevin stepped toward her and Galaxy backed away, breath hitching again as she struggled with the urge to spread her wings and fly. "Stop! No closer!"

Bevin did as commanded, even taking a step back. "Okay, okay, still happening. That's fine. You can do this."

"I can't d-d-do this, I can't—"

"You can. You're strong. Deep breaths. Slow breaths."

Galaxy struggled, talons digging into the dirt and a rear hoof kicking a snow bank as she fought back to the breathing for the spell. She couldn't focus, little terrors creeping in at the edges of her vision, peeking out from behind trees that felt like they were closing in, branches reaching down to grip and grasp and strangle. Her heart hammered away inside her chest, faster than her breathing could compete with, blood pounding through her temples until her head felt like bursting.

"You can do it, Galaxy... you can do it..."

Just remember the breathing exercises, that was all she needed to do. Deep breath in for five seconds... hold for five seconds... release for five seconds... deep breath in for five... hold for five... release for five... deep breath... hold... release...

Slowly, impossibly, Galaxy's heart slowed to its normal pace, the tremors faded, the woods retreated back to their normal space, her headache numbed to a mere dull throbbing, lessening by the second. Sitting up, Galaxy swept her talons up her beak and past her horn, down the back of her neck, managing a choking sort of laugh. Her eyes felt wet. "I-I thought, after so lo-long sss-since my last, somehow... b-but no, of course..." Of course. Even she knew Horror Sickness rarely ever just went away, no matter how long a reprieve she might be granted. And oh, how that thought made the tears quicken down her cheeks. "I'm sorry. I'm sorry. I'm sorry, I'm sorry—"

"What are you sorry for?" Bevin broke in, gaze pitying, frustratingly so.

Galaxy glanced at the still-softened puddle of rock, hurriedly looking away before the panic could set in again. "It's my fault. It's all my fault, all of it, I couldn't... I couldn't stop any of it. I couldn't, I can't, I just..."

She felt a hoof touch her shoulder and jerked away from it. Bevin backed away again. The unicorn regarded her in silence for a long moment, heedless of her glare, blue eyes possessed of a look reminding Galaxy uncomfortably of her mother, Ida. Galaxy considered speaking again, brushing the entire breakdown away and getting back to spell practice, or camp, or anything other than that horrid conversation, that knowing look.

But just as Galaxy opened her beak to speak, Bevin beat her to it. "I'm not a sphinx or a mind healer, I don't know if I can really help you, and I don't know how... comfortable, I'd feel, touching your mind again after our brief joining through Spell Virus in Port Oil. However, I have been where you stand. Normally, the Empire just Harmonizes soldiers suffering from Horror Sickness, but there are other methods of dealing with it."

She paused there, snorting, the urge to start pacing visible even through Galaxy's distress. "There are certain things that are your fault... and certain things that aren't. It was I who wounded your mother and dragged you to Mordred—"

"I should have fought harder, escaped."

"I stood by as Mordred sentenced Featheren Valley to destruction, too assured in the Empire and my surrogate father to truly object."

"I should have gone with you all from the start, never angered him, never given him a chance to destroy my home."

"If you had down that, nobody would have been there to save Port Oil from Spell Virus."

Galaxy started to retort, only to clack her beak shut when nothing came to her. Bevin huffed, tossing her mane. "You are not responsible for the atrocities of others, only your own. Each person must accept responsibility for their failings... their sins... and NOBODY ELSE'S. It is unjust to do otherwise. I trust you don't lay the blame of my attacking your mother on Owain, do you? And you trust me not to blame you for my parents' deaths, yes? And so, we are just."

It took a moment for Galaxy to absorb all that had been said, regarding Bevin with fresh awe. This was easily the most that Bevin had ever said to her in one go, and a part of Galaxy felt relieved, even honored, that the soldier felt so secure in opening up to her. "I... Thank you. I want you to know... I forgive you for everything."

For a moment, something like relief flashed through Bevin's gaze, too fast for Galaxy to be totally sure. But then the unicorn shook her head as if bothered by a fly and backed away, horn glowing as she turned to hide the softened boulder beneath dirt and snow. "I've said before, beware that trust. Now, unless you would prefer stopping, let's return to actual spellcraft."

"Empress Nova's dream... her Harmonized world... better than any revenge my General Nero could've dreamed of. And right now, hippogryph, YOU'RE STANDING IN THE WAY!"

"Actually," said Galaxy, thoughts catching on that bit of phrasing she'd heard before, "could you tell me what you mean by 'Harmonized'? I remember Mordred saying something similar."

Bevin's expression became unreadable. After a moment, she began to pace from one end of the small clearing they worked in to the other, tail flicking in agitation. "It is a... it's... Harmonization is Empress Nova's special tool, how it's said she first ascended to power and formed the Unicorn Empire. It's a spell, but don't ask me how it works. Just know that it only worked on unicorns. Perhaps unicorn-like creatures as well."

"Okay," said Galaxy, following her mentor's aggravated pacing. "But what does the spell DO? The way Mordred described it, it must be awful."

"I don't know about that, but—" Bevin stopped, frowned, turned back to Galaxy. "What if you could feel nothing except happiness for the rest of your life? No fear, no sadness, little anger, just joy in whatever you're doing? That's the Harmony spell. A life free of all negativity, a life of absolute joy and purpose in the Empress and her Empire. Forever."

Galaxy stared, cold and lonely. Almost immediately into the explanation, horror had swelled to life in Galaxy's gut, bubbling up to her heart, her mind, her wings telling her to take flight, horror that had only grown as Bevin continued. The wretched half-life of a creature afflicted by such a spell, Galaxy felt like vomiting. "But... without hurt, without sadness and fear, how does the good MEAN anything?"

To that, Bevin seemed to have no answer, looking away. Galaxy looked down, closing her eyes and dragging her talons down her head and neck. She no longer wondered what sort of monster Lord Mordred was, not now at knowing the sort of monster that must sit upon the Empire's throne. "God help us all..."

***

Brynjar liked Markhaven. Of all the towns and villages he and the rest had visited on their long journey from home, Brynjar could say with certainty that he liked Markhaven the most. Here was another true gryphon town, controlled by the Empire or not, its shops open-roofed for customers to fly in, its air thick with song and the scent of roasting meats and holiday treats. Lanterns were strung up crisscross over roadways, while at every corner stood carts brimming with puppet shows and traditional knick-knacks.

"I can't believe it," he said, pausing to look over a roasted chestnut cart set up in front of the local temple. "Kalt Nacht already. Time flies."

"What's that?" asked Owain, walking close beside Brynjar. The unicorn's eyes were wide with a wonder only slightly dampened by the cold, mane whipping about as he continuously craned his neck every which way to take in everything around them. Combined with the way he was clearly trying to hold back his shivering, Brynjar thought it undeniably cute. "Sounds... and looks... fun."

"It is fun." Brynjar stopped them at another cart, just long enough to trade a silver coin for a heavy woolen scarf he thought matched Owain's eyes well. He quickly wrapped it around the unicorn's neck and shoulders, making a point of ignoring the cart's owl-gryphon vendor's scandalized look as he led the way on down the street. "The festival celebrates Lady Quetzal's saving of the gryphon people from Prime Dragon Snarl's wrath. Lasts through the three days before Winter Solstice to three days after. The slow end to long nights."

"Avalon doesn't have anything like this," said Owain, not surprising Brynjar at all, "though Quetzal saved us as well. Six days of this left..."

They walked the festival. As they walked, they talked. Of the prevalence of greens and yellows and reds in reflection of Lady Quetzal's plumage. Of the traditional boiled and unsweetened mulberry wine first drunk in the harshest times of their war against Ancient Mankind. Of the puppet shows retelling myths and folktales any good gryphon child would know by heart. They talked of ghost stories and mythic romances and glories long past.

The sun had sunk beneath the horizon and the snowfall finally found its end when Brynjar admitted to himself that this was no spying mission. He and Owain found their way to the river's edge, away from the main roadway and its festival. Here they stopped to catch a breath, basking in the relative silence after the previous hustle and bustle. No others strode the boardwalk, the loudest sounds to bother the gryphon and the unicorn some raucous singing from a nearby inn.

Brynjar glanced at Owain beside him, the unicorn admiring the changing reflections in the river, and with a smile finally allowed himself to look at his companion, his... friend, without deceit or excuse. The stallion had grown at some point during their journey, his body no longer lanky and groomed and refined, but harder, made solid by the miles walked and battles fought. There was a feeling of readiness about him that Brynjar did not see before, those many weeks and months back in the Rotwald, saving him and Galaxy from the cockatrices. Brynjar had thought the unicorn pitiable then, a forever-child. Now Owain seemed handsome, and befitting of the older tales from before the war between their peoples began, the tales of unicorn and gryphon knights fighting and living side by side.

All of a sudden, a feeling of loneliness came upon Brynjar, out there beside the river, away from home and family. Slowly, chest aching with his heart's pounding, Brynjar lifted his left wing and let it settle over Owain's back. The unicorn started at the touch, but made no move to pull away, in fact sidling half a hoof closer after a moment. Another moment, he looked up to meet Brynjar's eyes, Brynjar recognizing a familiar fear in the stallion's green eyes. Something about this brought a chuckle out from his throat.

At once, Owain's brow creased. "What's funny?"

"Nothing," said Brynjar, swallowing, still smiling even though it was true, nothing was funny, and this might have been the most terrified he'd ever been. "It's only... I don't know how, but your green eyes... I never noticed the green before. They're the same as mine."

Owain stood there, blinking, eyes straight on at Brynjar's, studying him with an intensity that made Brynjar nervous. Then a ripple of laughter passed through Owain as he seemed to recognize the same inconsequential detail. The laugh turned into a sob halfway through as he clenched his eyes shut. "You're a gryphon."

Brynjar's heart seized, those three words like crossbow bolts striking in rapid succession. He swallowed again, nodding rapidly, fighting to keep his voice steady. "You're a unicorn."

The sounds of the nearby inn fell away, as did the river lapping against the boardwalk, the creak and thump of moored boats hitting and rebounding, the crunch of hooves on snow, the light of the stars whirling above, the world abandoning the pair in a moment of black anticipation. Owain opened his eyes, glimmering and beautiful with tears, Brynjar's breath hitching. "I don't care."

Brynjar shuddered, breath leaving him in a sobbing chuckle. He wiped at his eyes with his free wing, then pulled Owain closer against him, leaning down to nuzzle his beak against the other's cheek—

"Oi, birdie!"

Jerked away as if from a dream, Brynjar looked behind them to the source of the shout, spotting a trio of unicorns, the lead mare's horn alight as—

CRACK.

"Aaugh! Brynjar staggered, wing slipping off Owain's back, stumbling over his own legs and shards of glass. Pain, pain and blindness, blood and wine choking out his left eye. Helpless but to flare his wings to ward off further blows. Somewhere he heard voices shouting, one he knew, the others unknowing and cruel.

"What in Sheol's wrong with you stick-heads!? That gryphon's my friend!"

"Calm down! He, he had his wing over you! He was leaning down to bite your throat out or something!"

"It's cold, he was keeping me—"

"What kind of unicorn makes friends with gryphons? Don't you know any proper sorts to be around?"

"Teehee, maybe this little palomino's a feather chaser!"

"O-Owain..." Brynjar tried turning in the direction of the voices, body lurching beneath him. A groan left him. His head throbbed. The ground swayed. Reaching up, he hissed in pain at a wide gash crossing his brow. By now he could hear a crowd gathering around the scene, mutterings full of gryphon and unicorn accents, many angry, many disgusted, some calling for the soldiers. Above, wings beat the air. "Owain..."

"I'm here," said a vague figure moving in front of Brynjar, who in the next moment felt the warm touch of magic gently pulling his talons away from the gash. "Careful, there's glass in the wound."

"What's he doing with that stick-head, Mommy?"

"Hey, did he say Owain?"

"Filthy!"

"Gryphons not good enough for—"

"—and in public, too, disgusting little—"

"Shut up," came Owain's voice, distressingly feeble. "It, it's not..."

Another throb from Brynjar's head, another lurch of the ground beneath him. Brynjar had to sit down, body starting to shake. The sound of wings above them drew louder, and behind his blood-clouded vision, a nightmare thought began to untold to Brynjar. A thought of gryphons swooping down, grabbing Owain by the ends of the scarf and dragging him kicking and choking into the air, Brynjar unable to reach him as the crowd turned mob and swarmed in, horns stabbing and talons rending and eyes ablaze in nightmare yellow in wolf eyes in blood and screams—

"O-Owain, we, we need to gu-go..."

"I know," said the figure before him. Brynjar felt a hoof rest on his shoulder. "Hold on, please."

Somewhere nearby, another thrown bottle smashed the ground, voices rising to shouts. A blinding flash, Brynjar doing his best not to faint as the gut-squeezing sensation of the teleport spell washed over him.

CHAPTER TEN

~GALAXY!~

The roar of her name froze Galaxy where she stood, primed and ready to cast a perfect magic bolt. She took to the air, flying fast as her wings could drive her back through the woods to the campsite. Nightmares galloped through mind, dreadful imaginings of what could have possibly driven Ashe to loose such a roar, heedless of whether or not Bevin followed behind her.

Soon alighting in the clearing, Galaxy immediately spotted Owain, Ashe pacing nervously near to the unicorn as he tended to a bleeding and swaying—

"BRYNJAR!"

Galaxy ignored Bevin's nearing hoofsteps, flying across camp to land beside her brother. She gasped at the ragged gash across his brow, heart-stoppingly close to his left eye. Bits and pieces of some kind of dark brown glass stuck out along and inside it. Owain breathed hard, horn shimmering as he carefully extracted each piece, discarding them into a bucket beside him. Fear, pain, blood boiling, Galaxy fought for words. "What happened here!? Who—"

"It's... it's okay, Gal," Brynjar mumbled, reaching trembling talons out toward her. "It's nuh-nothing to worry about—"

Galaxy turned to Owain, putting steel to her voice this time. "What. Happened. To. My. Brother?"

Owain tried avoiding her gaze, failing miserably. The last of the glass removed and discarded, the glow of his horn turned a brighter green as he began the healing spell. "We only... it was my idea, my fault. You were busy with training, so we, we went to Markhaven to spy. Just us, less attention-grabbing than a hippogryph or dragon, right?"

He looked at her as if expecting her to actually respond to this. Galaxy, seeing red and wondering from how high she could drop the stallion without killing him, said nothing. He swallowed, continuing. "Well, there was a festival... we started enjoying ourselves. We had a... a moment, then... then some unicorns thought Brynjar was attacking me—"

"Wait." Bevin prowled the edge of the conversation, eyes glinting with a rage alike to Galaxy's. "You idiots went to Markhaven without even telling us... Were these unicorns soldiers, or civilians? What made them think the gryphon was attacking you?"

Owain's cheeks flushed with shame. His eyes, however, matched her glare with a spark of unfamiliar defiance. "Just civilians. It was cold, snowing. Brynjar offered me his wing for warmth. We did nothing worth violence."

"Nothing worth vvvviolence," mumbled Brynjar as Owain's magic knit the skin across his head back together. "Not that... Empire cares..."

"Disgusting," said Bevin, stopping her pacing. Galaxy, working to keep her own temper under control for her brother's sake, couldn't tell who or what the soldier was referring to.

"It's fine," said Brynjar after another moment, trying to stand from where he lay before Owain's gentle hoof pushed him back down. "Don't... we can't worry about—"

"Don't," spat Galaxy, jabbing a talon at her brother's chest. Her wings flapped at her sides, ready to take her to the sky, ready to fly her to Markhaven and hurt those who had dared hurt her most precious people. "Don't you dare say not to worry about it, or get worked up over it, or anything like that! Not after our childhoods, not after every murderous rage you fly into when I get hurt!"

"That, that's not the same." Again, Brynjar tried to stand. Again, Owain cautioned him. "You don't understand."

"It's plenty the same to me!" Galaxy turned, paced to the far end of the air-yacht and back, feeling on fire, feeling burning, feeling boiling in her veins and guts and eyes hurting from the spark and crackle of magic leaping uncontrolled from her horn. "Those stupid, selfish, arrogant stick-heads hurt you! Hurt my brother! Break them, let me break them, let me fly and shatter and tear—"

This time, Brynjar managed to stand, a wing brushing Owain aside. "You can't!"

"Why not!?"

"BECAUSE YOU CAN!"

Galaxy staggered back from the force and heat of the shout, anger fleeing for instead a wrenching flare of terror. "What?"

The heat of the moment given pause, Brynjar swayed, Owain hurrying forward to support him. Brynjar sagged against the unicorn, seeming suddenly to all present 20, 30, 40 years older. His gaze drifted down, away to the fire smoldering in its circle of rocks. "Because growing up there were days when I, or Sascha, or Siegfried, came home bruised with hoofmarks, with... sh-shouted words that made Mom cry when we repeated th-them... years of rocks and rotten fruit thrown at you, at us, s-su-slurs on our walls about you, returning from the market... and n-n-nobody Mother could go to for help without bruises for her tro... trou... so she just learned to live with it.

"But you..." He looked back at her, Galaxy marveling in horror that she could remember none of this, not until she saw the Horror Sickness in her brother's eyes. "But you can get blood for every pain...

destroy cities like an Imperial warship... and th-that terrifies me."

Silence fell over the camp, an ugly, angry silence that gnawed at Galaxy's nerves. Her power frightened her brother. SHE frightened her brother. She had only wanted to help...

Before anything could be said to start fixing the growing rift in the camp, Bevin let out a theatrical sigh, reminding Galaxy that the other unicorn was still there, that a world existed beyond the argument. The soldier stepped past Galaxy and the others to dig around in the packs beside the air-yacht, seeming to purposely make as busy a ruckus as possible. "Gryphon drama queens... If nobody is going to get along here, I'm off to do something useful and see how badly these two...friends, ruined things for us in Markhaven."

Strapping on her sword and a satchel of coins to a belt around her barrel, she stepped back and glared at them all. "Don't expect me back before morning. Don't hurt yourselves."

They stayed where they were until the crunch of Bevin's hooves in the snow faded into the night. Then Brynjar, with Owain's help, shuffled over to lay down next to the campfire, his back to Galaxy the entire way. Galaxy did not watch them go, waiting for the sounds of them getting comfortable on their sleeping blankets to quiet before rushing up the air-yacht's landing plank to her usual spot near the mast. She threw herself down onto her blanket, allowing herself a single dry, soundless sob. A mistake, another sob slipping out after it, then another, each less dry and soundless than the last. She hated this. She hated the journey. She hated unicorns and gryphons. She hated the world for the hurt it caused them.

"What g-good is the world, anyway…"

As lost in her thoughts as she was, Galaxy still heard the creak of wood, felt the sudden warmth of Ashe settling down in a long semicircle around her. ~Everything good, friend. Brother good. Tomorrow good.~

But Galaxy didn't believe that. She was tired, so tired, and the world was dimming, and she couldn't believe…

There were no endless fields and forests this time, no gryphons and unicorns frolicking in harmony with one another, no family bursting into flame and ash, no chains ensnaring her, no dark gully. There was only Galaxy, the Void, and the Unicorn.

It was impossible to take in the totality of the Unicorn. The being stood as tall as the tallest mountain, skin blackened and constantly breaking into cinders that reformed from the fires writhing within. And oh, the Fire. It poured from his mouth and gaping eye sockets, white and blinding as the Sun. Galaxy, floating there in the

Void before the Unicorn's head, was but a mote of dust in the light of those flames.

The Unicorn, and the Fire, GLARED at Galaxy, forcing speech from her. "Who... who are you?"

Slowly, with the overbearing momentum of continental plates shifting, the Unicorn smiled. "I AM THE BURNING KING."

The rush of supernova breath washed over Galaxy, burning away feathers and fur and skin in the time it took to scream. Shuddering and bared down to muscle and bone, Galaxy gasped out "Why!?"

The Burning King opened his jaws to answer again, jaws opening and opening, spreading forth above and below Galaxy to swallow her whole. "YOU'RE GOING TO GET THEM ALL KILLED, YOU KNOW THAT, RIGHT?"

Galaxy screamed as Fire and Void smashed together—

Galaxy jerked up into a sitting position, nearly smacking her horn into the air-yacht's mast. She clamped her talons tight around her beak to stifle the scream tearing her throat to shreds in its efforts to escape.

~Friend?~ hissed Ashe, loosing a toothy yawn from around Galaxy. ~What'sss the matter?~

Not answering at first, Galaxy closed her eyes and imagined the snow falling upon the heights of the mountains surrounding Featheren Valley, sent fluttering every which way by the lightest breeze, the pleasures of rolling around in the deep powder, legs kicking and wings flexing. Over the course of minutes, she felt her heart slow, her breathing die down to its normal rhythms, the panic attack passing at its own leisurely pace. The dream, already fading, became little more than a memory of terror.

Eventually she released her beak, coughing at the soreness of her throat, the flat of a talon wiping away the lingering wetness around her eyes. Giving Ashe a reassuring pat with a wing, Galaxy looked up to the night sky past the treetops. The clouds had passed for now, the stars twinkling up there as normal, distant and beautiful. With a twinge of jealousy, Galaxy imagined they never had to deal with the struggles of the living.

"I... I don't know where I went wrong,
I don't know how to be strong,
I thought I could at least trust me...
But... what else do I not..."

"Gal?"

Galaxy flinched, turning reluctantly to the air-yacht's boarding ramp. Brynjar stood there, wings half-spread, one front leg raised as if caught mid-step. "O-oh, Brynjar." Galaxy rubbed at her eyes, trying to dispel the tears from her nightmare. Ashe loosed a low, barely-audible snarl at Brynjar from her place around Galaxy. "I didn't, that is, sorry if I woke—"

"You didn't," said Brynjar, stepping forward, hesitating, and then taking another step. "I was already awake, watching the sky. I heard Ashe grumble and it made me worry."

Galaxy smiled at that, quickly dropping her head down to look at the air-yacht's deck. A touch of gryphon magic sparked to life within her, so that when she looked back up at her brother she dropped her smile. "Brynjar..."

"I'm sorry."

"I'm sorry."

They stared at each other, caught off-guard by both saying it at once. After a moment, Galaxy found her voice again, that spark of gryphon magic growing stronger.

"There are fears I just can't name,
Burdens and duties too impossible to bare.
I thought it'd be too horrible to share,
Never imagined you could feel the same...
I guess I can only take the blame..."

Brynjar hurriedly shook his head, stepping forward again, close enough now to reach out and touch her if he wanted.

"I could never blame you your fear
Just look at all we've seen,
Just look at the horrors obscene
And I'll tell you it's pretty clear
All the dangers we've been near."

"Brynjar, please..." Galaxy swallowed, brushing more tears away.

"I know I made an awful mistake
Something I can never hope to undo
Something to bare until my life is through
But I was just filled with so much anger and hate—"

"Yet you think I can't relate?"

Galaxy stopped short, staring at her brother. Brynjar stared back, beak lowered in a sad and tired smile. It was a smile she found herself sharing after a moment. And when next the magic urged them to sing they did so together, voices as one.

"Sometimes you don't need to name your fears
Your regret can be enough,
Your will to help can be enough,
And you don't need to hide your tears

Because I'll be with you through the years…
"And the fear can go… away…"

The magic died down and they fell silent, a more comfortable silence than the one before. Her heart lightened, Galaxy closed that remaining step separating them and wrapped her front legs around Brynjar's neck in a tearful hug, those gargantuan golden eagle-gryphon wings quickly closing around her to return the embrace.

"I love you," said Galaxy.

"I love you," said Brynjar.

"I love a good night's sleep!" shouted Owain from below. "For Toqeph's sake, save your singing for the morning!"

Brother and sister shared a look. Galaxy held her beak to keep the giggles in, hurriedly looking away as Brynjar made no effort to contain his laughter. Oh, how time had changed them all.

Sometime later, after Brynjar's laughter had run its course and the siblings had settled beside each other against Ashe, gazes turned together to the stars, Galaxy heard him clear his throat. Looking, she found him staring instead at the air-yacht's deck, flexing his talons as if his joints ached. The look in his eyes alarmed her, reminding Galaxy of how he had been only shortly after the destruction of Featheren Valley, before they'd made their plan to journey south. Lost, hurting, a gryphon uncertain of what to do with himself. "Brynjar?"

He looked at her, looked away, gave his throat another clearing as a frown creased his brow. "My father died at Grimhilt's Folly. Same battle your mother did. Sir Kurt. Not remembered like your mother."

At once, Galaxy realized her fault. All the time heading to the Elderpine Forest and staying with the Elk, she had thought only of herself, what it would mean to her to visit the site of her mother's last stand. Not a moment had been spent considering it as also the place Brynjar, Sascha, and Siegfried had all lost their father, where Ida had lost her husband. Even King Erentil and Princess Gwendolyn had done it, focusing only on her.

"And you made that last attempt to go with me," she said, groaning and hiding her face behind her talons. If only there were a deep hole to crawl into and die. "I told you to stay with the air-yacht... I didn't even..."

"I guess it all worked out in the end," mumbled Brynjar, not sounding like he felt it had all worked out at all. "If I'd gone with, maybe Mordred or Erentil would've killed me."

Galaxy let her talons drop, frowning as she looked at her brother. "Brynjar—"

A deafening CRACK and flash of light from a teleport spell burst from over the side of the ship, followed by Bevin shouting with a panic Galaxy had never heard from her before. "EVERYONE TO ME NOW!"

Galaxy spared only the briefest moment for a shared look with Brynjar before getting to all fours, a flap of her wings sending her racing to the ground below. From somewhere above came the distant buzz of crystal drones, sending Galaxy's worry into double-time as she joined her brother and Owain at Bevin's side, followed a moment later by Ashe. Above them could be seen moving pinpricks of light, mistakable for stars save for their erratic movements. Not half as unnerving as the deep roar of a warship somewhere out of sight, just now becoming noticeable, rapidly growing louder, nearer.

"Bevin!" shouted Owain, hunkering up between Galaxy and Brynjar, "what in Sheol happened in Markhaven!? How'd they follow you out—"

Owain's voice was drowned out by the crackling blast of Bevin's horn igniting with magic, Galaxy having to look away from the eye-searing light. She startled as mound of earth rose over them, waves of dirt and stone blocking off sight of the night sky and surrounding woods. Galaxy's alarm grew as Bevin kept going, the soldier panting with effort as she depressed the ground beneath them, sinking them even as she piled more and more over them, raising pillars of stone to support the lurching, heaving ceiling over their heads. Galaxy shut her eyes and forced herself to breathe steady, scampering away from thoughts of those tight, claustrophobic tunnels that had led them to Hollereich.

"Bevin!" shouted Brynjar, barely heard over the roar of the churning rock, "what in Quetzal's name are you doing!? What—"

A sudden earthquake struck from above, sending Bevin reeling and silencing Brynjar. Galaxy opened her eyes as the quakes continued. Terror seized her heart as a crack appeared in the stone ceiling, fire and smoke pouring through. "Bevin!"

"Grrraaarrrr!" Bevin's horn reignited, another pillar rising to reinforce the damaged stone. The minutes passed. Galaxy stood at the ready to cast a shield spell, thoughts focused there and not, despite their best efforts, on the myriad questions still waiting on her tongue. Surely the Imperial forces would not keep up their bombardment of the area for long.

"What happened, Bevin?" asked Owain after some minutes had passed, Galaxy looking to where he crouched between her and Brynjar, watching the trembling walls around them with wide eyes. "Did they recognize you? Are there wanted posters? Did you see my father?"

For a moment Bevin said nothing, all her attention on maintaining their protective shell. Eventually she glanced down at Owain, Galaxy recognizing the regret in her eyes without her saying a word.

Eventually, the quakes stopped. The buzz of crystal drones and air-yachts faded into the distance. Bevin raised them back to the surface, the soldier wheezing with exhaustion, her horn sputtering and foam gathering on her flanks. The scene they found topside was utter ruin. The small woodlands had been completely demolished by the bombardment, the snow melted away to steam, earth and trees and animal life in all directions reduced to cinders. Looking to where the air-yacht had been before the attack began, Galaxy allowed herself a sigh of relief at seeing it emerging from a cave similar to what Bevin had made for them.

"Makes no sense." Brynjar took wing, hovering a few paces away and up to take in the devastation from a higher vantage point. "Can't just be because of me and Owain. What happened, Bevin?"

Bevin gave no immediate answer, managing a few stumbling steps toward the air-yacht before collapsing into a half-sitting, half-lying position, tremors wracking her body and sparks still weakly sputtering from the tip of her horn. Galaxy stared for only a moment before taking flight, worry gnawing at her gut as she flew to the water bags atop the air-yacht. She filled a bowl with water and raced back to Bevin, the soldier panting as Owain ran a horn glowing with healing magic over her. Brynjar and Ashe stayed off to the side, watching on with helpless concern.

The moment Galaxy set the bowl of water down within reach, Bevin lurched forward and dunked her muzzle into it, chugging the water down for half a minute, pulling back just long enough to take a ragged breath before diving back in. Galaxy sat and watched with all the patience she could muster, wringing her talons and batting the ground with her tail.

Only once the bowl was empty did Bevin look back up at them all, finally starting to somewhat look like her usual collected self once more. "It was," she started, pausing to cough deep from her chest before trying again. "It was... not... what I'd been expecting. Gossip ran rampant about the, the giant gryphon and his... feather chasing... friend," and at that term Galaxy saw from the corner of her eye Owain snort and duck his head away, "but no, no names or anything, no speculation, just complaining."

Galaxy wanted to ask so many questions, but at a querying growl from Ashe she bit them back, instead turning with a sigh to fill the dragon in. As she did, keeping her voice low, she heard a flapping of wings as Brynjar hovered closer. "Then what happened?"

The unicorn soldier took two tries before managing to stand to her hooves, swaying alarmingly at first but managing to grow steadier as she began pacing. "I went to the tavern I'd encountered Urien in, my first visit to Markhaven. Seemed the safest bet, but after several hours of waiting and subtle questionings, I had nothing. I'd just been ready to call it quits when a fresh round of soldiers came in from the Empire's upriver fortress. From the way they bellowed and bragged, I figure they were already more drunk than Imperial troops should have been. For good reason, as they made sure to let the entire tavern know."

"How so?"

Bevin started to answer before pausing, allowing Galaxy a moment to repeat the gist of what'd been said to Ashe before continuing. "They were part of a contingent of soldiers from Lord Mordred's fortress, Hiraeth Arian, assigned from the Lord of War's own forces to transport and guard a special prisoner. A gryphon from Vogelstadt, captured during the fighting for Gryphonbough."

The ground dropped out from beneath Galaxy, heart leaping up into her throat as she tumbled into a memory—

"Perhaps," Bifrost agreed, flashing Galaxy another gryphon smile. "I fly northeast to meet Queen Vigdis of Gateway, who leads an army to lift the Imperial siege

against King Gundahar of Gryphonbough. If we share the same crusade, to end this war and herald justice, I believe we will meet again."

"I know this gryphon," said Galaxy, drawing all eyes to her. At Bevin's look of confusion, Galaxy elaborated. "The first night of our stay in the Elderpine Forest, I went walking for a moment of... peace. I ran into a Vogelstadt warrior there, journeying north to join Queen Vigdis. Her name was Bifrost. She was... well-learned."

"She means attractive," said Owain, completely unhelpfully.

"You met—" Bevin shook her head and stepped closer to Galaxy. "Does she have family in Vogelstadt? Parents, siblings, cousins?"

Galaxy nodded, heart dropping from throat to gullet as she caught on to what Bevin meant. "A sister."

Owain swore, Bevin turning and kicking a pile of cinders apart. Noticing now Brynjar's confused look, Galaxy sighed. "Remember our explanation for how teleportation spells work, Brynjar. Connecting to another point where your magic is and appearing there. Magic between family members is close enough alike for it to work too. If we had a general idea of where they were right now, we could use you to teleport right to Mom and the twins."

"Oh... oh God." Brynjar looked between Galaxy and Bevin, brow furrowing as the obvious implications and even more obvious follow-up question seemed to come to him. "But wait, if the Empire's had this warrior since Gryphonbough, why haven't they invaded the Floating Mountain yet?"

Bevin, pacing once more, shook her head again and lashed her tail. "Several possible reasons. Haven't been able to confirm if she has any family to connect to. Haven't forced her consent to use the magic. More torture either way. And then, a visit from a Lord of the Empire... an opportunity."

~. . . more torture... a visssit from a Lord...~ Galaxy growled, shaking her head and turning back to the others. "We can't let this happen. It doesn't matter if we get Ashe back to the Dragonback Mountains or rejoin with Mom and the others in Wedjet. If the Empire manages to use Bifrost to teleport an entire invasion force past the dragon defenders to Vogelstadt, this war's over. There'll be no way for Wedjet or Gateway to rally, and like Sheol would I be able to turn the tide. We need to rescue Bifrost now, before it's too late."

Past Brynjar and Owain nodding their agreement, an honest smile in her brother's eyes, Galaxy saw Bevin whirl around near the edge of their former clearing, nostrils wide and eyes glaring daggers. Snorting, the soldier marched back over. "Too late—are you insane!? This is it! This is our best chance to find and kill Lord Mordred! This gryphon is a prisoner of war, meaning it will be Mordred's duty to keep guard of her and oversee every interrogation! What we NEED to do is set up reconnaissance of the fortress she's imprisoned in and ready ourselves to strike the moment that damned Wolf-Lord shows himself!"

Galaxy held her ground in the face of Bevin's snarling, helped by the emboldening presence of Ashe behind her, familiar warmth a comfort. "I can't do that, Bevin. You know that. Even ignoring how you're suggesting we just leave someone to torture and pain, there's something bigger at stake here than you and Lord Mordred. This is the entire war at stake, the entire world—"

"Damn the world!" The ground shook, Owain whinnying in fright as he struggled to stay standing, Ashe yipping as she stumbled and fell onto her back, Brynjar cursing as he took to the air. Galaxy backed off a step from Bevin, the unicorn's horn once more sparking with her gold magic. "I'm not in this for your war, princess, and I'm not in this for you! I'm in this for my revenge. You promised me you would stand beside me if I trained you, which I have. Don't make a liar of yourself, hippogryph."

"I'm not lying! I never lied!" Galaxy squinted her eyes against the light of Bevin's horn, desperate to make the soldier understand, make her SEE the desperation Galaxy felt, the desperation that had quietly built toward insanity day after day, conjuring into monsters from myth in her nightmares. "I just... I can't abandon Bifrost to her fate. I'm her princess, her friend! I can't abandon her like Mordred abandoned you to Port Oil!"

For a moment, Galaxy thought the soldier might strike her. But then Bevin's posture grew slack, her magic fading, taking the tremors with it and leaving blue eyes alone clashing. "Tell me... please... that you at least have a rescue plan."

Galaxy let out the breath she'd been holding, ending with a near-hysterical laugh. Sitting down, she raked her talons up her head and down the back of her neck as they moved on to the next problem. "I do have a plan, actually... but... you're probably not going to like it."

CHAPTER ELEVEN

"I hate this plan. I hate this plan. I hate every part of this plan. It is the worst plan. Ever. Of all—"

"Quiet," snapped Bevin from Brynjar's left, causing the babbling Owain at Brynjar's right to snap his mouth shut. "It's definitely not going to work if you don't keep calm. Just let me do the talking."

"But—"

"I hate saying this," said Brynjar, glancing Owain's way and finding it hard to see him past the white and silver Imperial armor, "but Bevin's right. Just... please, let her do the talking."

Owain made a noise of distress, but otherwise remained as quiet as the surrounding snowfall. Brynjar sighed in relief and glanced Bevin's way. The soldier was looking at him oddly, bright blue eyes peering from within her helmet. "Um, what?"

"Nothing," said Bevin, quickly looking away to scan the snow-bound fields to their left and ice-churned river to their right, as if to dispel the moment with seeming alertness. "I simply think... that might have been the closest thing to a compliment you've ever said to me."

"Oh." Brynjar looked ahead to the Imperial fortress looming ahead of them, stone and metal arching over the river to perch on both sides like a beast ready to pounce. It wasn't the most impressive structure he had seen in his travels, not even close, but it was large, he could give it that. "Well, we don't talk much."

"No, I suppose we don't."

"You keep busy training Gal. Good work there, by the way. She's seemed happier since that started. I'm glad she has you."

"Hm, another compliment. And she's a good student."

The three kept walking, the two unicorns dressed in armor found stored away in the air-yacht. Brynjar walked between them down the pocked road, chains loosely binding his wings to his body, loosely enough to slip off with just the right twitch. More chains Bevin had conjured kept his four legs connected, easily dispelled with a thought from the mare. Overhead, far overhead, Brynjar knew Galaxy and Ashe followed in the air-yacht, keeping hidden in the low clouds in case anything went wrong. Which shouldn't, considering how simple the plan was.

Galaxy's plan. The two unicorns, disguised as soldiers, would escort Brynjar into the fortress with the excuse of taking a "suspected sympathizer" to the dungeons. With the way Bevin had described the soldiers she'd listened in on, it seemed a good bet that nobody would ask too many questions about unfamiliar soldiers. Once inside, Bevin would disable the fortress's security spells while Brynjar and Owain broke Bifrost and anyone else they found out of the dungeons, before sneaking out together through the fortress's river-bound escape tunnels. Simple. Easy.

"The biggest problem," said Bevin as she outfitted herself in the armor, "will be if Lord Mordred's there. I make no promises that I won't abandon the plan if I get the chance to kill the Wolf-Lord once and for all."

"No arguments here," said Brynjar, helping Owain secure the straps for his unfamiliar plating. "Good distraction from our prison break."

Bevin rolled her eyes, coming over to assist with the armor. "We should strive for it not to come to that. If Lord Mordred's not there, slipping out unnoticed through the cellars will be good enough. UNNOTICED. Let someone hit an alarm spell, those escape tunnels close."

Brynjar was snapped from his thoughts by Bevin and Owain slowing their strides. He saw they had reached the fortress, its tall and stout tower walls looming over them as they passed unharried through the raised gate into the outer courtyard. The area teemed with dozens of unicorns rushing about in half-controlled panic, shouting orders for more plate to be requisitioned from Markhaven's smiths, for more foraging parties to be organized, for weapons to be sharpened, for someone to do something about the stench of charred meat from the last escape attempt.

Some unicorns far to the north wall stood before several dozen zakarians in strange armor and carrying unfamiliar weapons.

"Soldiers of fortune," muttered Bevin with some disgust. "Never seen so many used together before. Risky."

In the other direction, along the south side of the courtyard, stood a dozen unicorns out of armor, all white- or black-coated, humming to themselves as they, to Brynjar's surprise, tended a garden somehow free of the ice and snow enveloping the rest of the area. Their eyes were vacant, their muzzles stretched open in what a charitable soul might have called smiles. Brynjar couldn't stop staring, something in his deepest guts revolted by the sight.

"Harmonized soldiers," answered Bevin, following his gaze. "Unicorns subjected to Empress Nova's Harmonization spell. No anger, no hate, no sadness, no fear. Only happiness."

Brynjar finally found the strength to look away. "Must make for awful warriors."

Bevin nodded, a frown crossing her features. "To see them this far from the Avalon Islands, the untouched center of the Unicorn Empire, emphasizes how low we are getting in martial strength. Kingdoms have fallen, but unless the Empire takes drastic measures, you gryphons might still win out through simple attrition."

Brynjar, remembering the horrors of Spell Virus, had a good idea what sorts of drastic measures the Empire was already taking.

They reached the fortress's inner gates without issue. Passing through those, Brynjar almost bumped into Owain as Bevin veered leftward through an open rampway. They ducked into a corner that hid them from the sight of those in the courtyard, Bevin indicating with her horn first the ramp down, then the ramp upward. "That way to the storage rooms first, where we'll find the discreet entrance to the closest escape tunnel, and then farther down the dungeons and hopefully this Bifrost character. Up that way for the fortress's communications hub, at the top of the tallest tower. There are going to be unicorns monitoring heat and motion detection spells for the tunnels, but I can deal with them no problem. And if we don't get through those tunnels within five minutes, backup time-lock spells will—"

"Hey! What's going on here?"

Bevin, bless her, remained steady as she stepped to the side to look past Brynjar at a unicorn in the doorway to the ramps. "Nothing, sir. Just giving this prisoner one last chance to play nice before throwing the feather-brain to the dungeons."

The unicorn, a chestnut mare with a silver lieutenant stripe up her chest plate, hmmphed and tossed her black mane, stomping forward to yank the end of Brynjar's chain from Bevin. "Never mind niceties, soldier. Checking prisoners in requires a commanding officer's signature. Go have the comm operators know we have another gryphon."

A flare of panic at this unforeseen strike at their plan, Bevin and Owain exchanging looks, the lieutenant raising an eyebrow as the silence stretched on, Brynjar readying himself to tackle the soldier, a crushing clamp of his beak on her throat, knowing they'd never take her down before the commotion drew more soldiers from the yard—

"Of course, sir," Bevin suddenly managed, backing a step away and toward the up ramp as if to obey the command. Her gaze swiveled to Owain, an impressively embarrassed, what-can-you-do sort of smile on her features. "A moment, though, if it's no trouble. I'm not sure of the policy here on this, but my cousin, well, he was hoping he could see the unusual bird you have caged here already? If it's no trouble?"

The lieutenant's gaze switched between Bevin, Owain, and Brynjar for several seconds, expression worrisomely neutral. Brynjar was just on the verge of tensing for his leap at her when she finally nodded, clearing her throat and nodding toward the ramps. "No, no trouble at all. On your way, soldier. Come along, bird."

Unable to shake the dread in his gut, Brynjar watched Bevin march up the ramp and out of sight, before a tug on his chains had him stumbling along after the lieutenant down the second ramp, Owain trudging beside him. With every step down toward the dungeons, Brynjar hoped to himself that at least Galaxy was keeping calm through all this.

***

"This was an awful idea. I hate this idea. I hate it so much. Why in blazes did I ever even think to think this blasted idea up!?"

Ashe grumbled, letting out a puff of smoke from where she lay near to the air-yacht's starboard side. ~You already thought it... jussst be patient... or why no go down yoursssself?~

Galaxy stopped her pacing along the port side of the air-yacht and looked across to Ashe. She pondered the suggestion for a moment, then sighed and shook her head. ~I ssstick out like... like... sssore claw. Mussst trussst... friendsss.~

Ashe growled and stood, full wings stretching as she joined Galaxy port-side. ~Then trusset friendsss... yesss? Good plan.~

Galaxy sighed again, looking back down at the Imperial fortress far, far below them, hundreds of feet down where even the lowest-hanging clouds were between them and it. ~Right... trussst them...~

Of course she needed to trust them. Galaxy raked her talons down her head and neck. She knew that. And it had been her idea in the first place, to send Brynjar, Owain, and Bevin straight into danger while she and Ashe hung back just in case, so at some level she knew she trusted them. But feeling trust and acting upon it...

~I... guesss I... cannot believe they t-trussst... me ssso much.~

Ashe said nothing to that, only laying down and looking at the distant fortress. ~Can you really sssee anything down there? Unicornsss like antsss to me.~

~I can, if I... concentrate.~ Galaxy smiled despite her nervousness, accepting the change in topic for what it was. ~Gryphon eyesssight... friend. Er, um...~ Smile turned to frown, her next word not having an equivalent in Dragon. "Literally," cough, ~asss sssharp as a... a hawk'sss visssion. Hard not ssseeing thingsss.~

That seemed to satisfy the dragon's curiosity. Relieved, Galaxy kept her peace as well. The minutes swept by in that half-tense silence, Galaxy just remembering to look up and around them in case of any errant crystal drones. She saw none, as expected. The only drones to be seen were all far below them, closer to the ground. "Perhaps they can only go so high before the cold starts negatively affecting them."

~Hm?~

~Nothing,~ said Galaxy, refocusing on the task at hand. "Nothing. Just thinking."

Another minute, then Galaxy glanced to the inch-long spike of glass-clear crystal set next to the railing. There had been a baker's dozen of the personal communication crystals stowed aboard the air-yacht. Both Owain and Bevin had taken one for their uniform disguises, with thorough instructions to both Galaxy and Brynjar on how to operate them in case of emergency. If something serious were to happen down there, surely at least one of them would be able to contact her about it. Silence was only a good thing in this situation. Silence, and patience.

***

The first thing to catch Owain's attention as he followed Brynjar and the lieutenant through the solid steel doors to the central dungeon was the stench of scorched meat and fur, just as he'd heard a soldier in the courtyard complaining about. It sent him into a brief but intense sneezing fit, his stomach objecting to the powerful odor that seemed to drench the area in thoughts of pain and death.

The second thing he noticed, almost immediately after the stench, was the large scorch mark marring the otherwise-pristine white room, a large, dark splotch that looked as if someone had recently tried and failed to clean it away. In the thin light emitting from glowing crystals set in alcoves along the walls, it looked grotesque, ghastly.

"An escape attempt," the lieutenant growled, seeming to read Owain's mind. "A unicorn went insane. Lord Mordred kept it from succeeding."

The third detail Owain noticed as the door slid shut behind him and Brynjar with a mechanical hiss, was how empty the entire dungeon was. To the right, only one gryphon watched them from beyond the cell bars, a ragged and half-starved raven-gryphon, rainbow eyes alight with a wary surprise toward Owain that at once set him on edge. He almost didn't notice Brynjar and the lieutenant stopping, nor the unicorn soldier trotting over from the guard station to the left. Or, no, more like hobbling over, now that Owain watched him.

"Greetings, Lieutenant Lamorak," said the soldier in a high-pitched, wheezy voice, Brynjar beside Owain flinching in shock. It went uncomfortably naturally with the glassy eyes and vacant smile that betrayed the stallion's Harmonized nature. "Another awful gryphon to keep this one company? I suppose everyone deserves some company. Perhaps keeping company would make gryphons less mean and—"

"Actually," spoke Lamorak," half-turning to look at Owain, a new and dangerous gleam in her hazel eyes and a magenta glow to her horn, "seeing as our current prisoner being from Vogelstadt is a strictly kept secret, might I ask were you heard it from?"

Owain resisted the urge to glance at Brynjar, a hoof stamping nervously at the ground. "Oh, you know… the grapevine. Just came in this morning, got a big ear for gossip. Somewhere in Markhaven—"

"Markhaven, yes," spoke Lamorak again, turning to face them fully. "There was trouble there last night. Nearly a riot. Some sick, sad little stallion parading around town with a swan-gryphon—"

"Golden eagle-gryphon," Owain corrected, unable to stop himself, unable to not hear Brynjar's groan or look away from the lieutenant's victorious grin. "I… I mean…"

"Owain," spoke Lamorak, the glow of magic around her horn turning brighter, a double-headed axe materializing beside her. "As brave, it seems, or perhaps as stupid, as your father."

***

Bevin had read enough intelligence reports in her time serving Lord Mordred to know how deeply feared Imperial communication hubs were by gryphon warriors, how much of a nightmare they were to assault. Even ignoring the fortress built around them, half a dozen unicorn soldiers would guard each hall into the hub, with another dozen stationed inside the circular room itself, plus the half-dozen technical mages and crystal tenders working the long-distance communication spells. Gryphon prisoners of war called it suicide to try assailing one without a full tactical team at your side.

Bevin passed the guards, marched through a wide-arched doorway into the central hub to take everything in at a practiced glance. Pillars of clear crystal shot through with rivulets of pulsing color stood from floor to ceiling along the walls of the 20-by-20 room, each pillar emitting a low hum as it was tended to by a plain-garbed unicorn. At the center of the room stood a similar pillar of crystal, this one twice the thickness of the others and tended to by three dedicated mages.

Walking farther into the room, Bevin changed focus to the guards. Two unicorns in heavy armor stood at each doorway, counting the one she'd come through, with a doorway at each of the hub's cardinal points. Another four soldiers paced the circumference of the room, two clockwise and two counterclockwise. Twelve guards in all. Not close to the worst odds she'd ever been faced with.

"Excuse me, sir," said one of the pacing soldiers, coming her way from the right. "I need to see some identification, or for you to explain what you're doing here. This is a highly secure area and we are in the midst of serious preparations. The slightest risk can't—"

"Of course, of course." Bevin nodded to the soldier, then turned to the rest of the room. Clearing her throat, she gave her horn a flick and twist, casting a spell to enhance her voice's loudness without the effort of shouting. "Attention, all communication hub attendants! May I have your attention please for official business from Lord Mordred!"

As expected, every unicorn in the room immediately stopped what they were doing and looked her way. Bevin nodded in appreciation at the swift professionalism on display. As she spoke again, she reached out with her Elemental to the stone ceiling. "Thank you, all of you. I just want to say—"

A slight twist and pull with her magic, and in perfect synchronization, chunks of ceiling dropped onto each soldier and mage head. The chorus of thuds ringing out as nearly two dozen unicorns hit the floor was oddly, intensely, satisfying.

"—sorry for the headaches in a few hours."

Hopping over one of the technical mages, Bevin strode to the local pillar designated for that fortress itself and, after a moment of feeling it out with her magic, shut it off. Then she turned back to the unicorns littering the floor, one or two groaning, none quite ready yet to move. She allowed herself a moment of regret. If she had managed to kill Mordred back at Grimhilt's Folly...

Then she forced Soldier Mode back on, drawing up her own magic rather than that of her Elemental. With a whisper of "Soften" the stone floor beneath each unconscious unicorn did as commanded, the equine bodies slowly sinking into the stone like rocks into pudding. Pacing, Bevin adjusted each unicorn with her magic so that the heads and necks stuck free, canceling the spell once all had been secured.

With that done, Bevin drew her personal communication crystal from its pouch at her side. Yet, just as she began to key in for Owain's personal magic—

***

Owain and Brynjar stared at Lieutenant Lamorak and the pair of dungeon guards. The three unicorns stared back. In the long silence of their standoff, Owain had a moment's desperate thought. It had worked with Bevin... "So... I don't suppose you're open to having a calm debate regarding the evils of the Empire?"

"Sure," answered Lamorak, giving her axe a playful twirl before pointing toward the cells behind Owain. "After you're behind those bars and Lord Mordred's on her way."

Ignoring that strange slip of the tongue regarding Mordred, Owain sighed and shared a look with an equally annoyed Brynjar. "Yeah, we were afraid you were going to say that."

At this signal, faster than Owain could even follow, Brynjar flared his wings to break Bevin's chains and lunged forward, slamming Lamorak past the Harmonized guards and into the far wall.

CRACK.

Brynjar leapt back as magic bolts lashed out from the guards' horns, blasting apart the wall as their officer dropped bonelessly to the floor. Before they could turn to fire on Brynjar again Owain charged forward with a whinny, reared back to slam his forehooves into the head of one of them, the mare stumbling back in a daze. Owain dropped and sidestepped as Brynjar flew in at the opening, Owain watching in awe as the golden eagle-gryphon grabbed her around the barrel and lifted her over his head with a roar of effort. Flapping his wings for extra force, Brynjar spun and flung the mare kicking and screaming past Owain, BAM into the second guard moving in for a sneak attack, both mare and stallion colliding against the cell bars to the whooping and clapping of the watching Bifrost. Before either could regain their senses, the raven-gryphon reached through the bars, grabbed each by the horn, and slammed their heads together with a CRACK, and that was that.

The sound of shifting stone and unsteady hooves made Owain look back with Brynjar to where Lamorak was regaining her stance, scuffed and panting and with a trickle of blood running down from the curls of her mane. She looked back and forth between Owain and Brynjar, a spark of terror even in her dazed eyes. Owain stepped forward, an offer of peaceful surrender for the soldier on his lips when, suddenly, she turned and tapped her horn against a seemingly-random stone in the wall next to her. Owain had a moment to think perhaps the head injury had gotten to her, before feeling a pulse of magic sweep through the room from the tapped stone, followed by an ear-piercing wail.

***

Bevin's stomach dropped at the tell-tale wail of the fortress's alarm spell. She turned from where she'd been dismantling the communication pillar for Avalon to find the soldiers and tech mages she'd neutralized only minutes before jerking back to consciousness, their shouts adding to the cacophony as they struggled to free themselves from their stone restraints.

"Son of a snail-brain—" Bevin knocked out the closest three unicorns with concussive spells, before realigning her communication crystal for their eyes up in the clouds. "Galaxy, do you hear me? Everything is FINE down here! Understand?"

"What!? Are you insane!? I can hear that wailing from here! What happened?"

"Nothing you need to worry about." Bevin circled the central pillar, eyes narrowing at the shadows of soldiers appearing in the nearest doorway. "The fortress's alarm spell was tripped, but we're already on our way out. Just stay where you are and don't pan—"

A magic bolt blasted the crystal from Bevin's telekinetic grip, the shards clattering against the floor. She snarled and spun, raising a shield of stone from the floor to block the next flurry of bolts, throwing it next at the oncoming soldiers. Behind it she charged, the battle joined.

***

Once Lamorak had been downed for good and Owain set to work trying to shut off the blaring alarm spell, Brynjar grabbed the keyring from one of the guards and hurried to the cells. The raven-gryphon waited for him there on the opposite side, knuckles white as she gripped the bars, feathers raised in elation and alarm. "I'm Bifrost, of Vogelstadt. You must be Brynjar, son of Ida. And the unicorn there, Owain, son of Ur... Urien. You've come, you've really come, but how—"

"Questions for later," snapped Brynjar, throwing the cell door open after finally finding the right key. He paused a moment at the familiar cuts and burn marks scattered across the raven-gryphon's body, angry and raw rather than Ashe's mostly-healed hurts. Shaking his head, he stepped back and aside. "Right now, we need to leave. Can you fight?"

"I c-can, I think, but..." Bifrost looked between Brynjar and Owain, who had moved from dispelling the alarm spell to foraging through the contraband chests tucked into a far corner. "Where's Galaxy? Is she safe? I heard rumors, Elk betrayal—"

The dungeon doors slid open with a crash, a trio of unicorn soldiers in heavy armor and caparisons charging in with horns lowered and crackling with spells. "Halt at once! Return to your—"

Brynjar flew forward with a single flap of his wings and body-checked the two unicorns in front, halting their gallop dead. With talons gripping their horns tightly, another beat of his wings and he slammed them back into the wall next to the doorway, then cracked their heads together. As they crumpled to the floor he turned to meet the third unicorn's charge, pride flaring in his chest as Owain skid in to knock the foe's horn aside with his own, before spinning and sending the soldier to the ground with a kick from both rear legs.

The exchange over, Brynjar knelt down to draw a bastard sword from the sheath of one of the soldiers, turning to toss the weapon to a staring Bifrost. To the raven-gryphon's credit, she caught the weapon mid-air without battling an eye-lash, assuring Brynjar that, whatever else, she could probably hold her own in the coming fight. "Gal's guarding our backup exit. We've got another good unicorn here, Bevin, throws rocks a lot.

Probably already waiting for us." Without breaking eye contact, Brynjar caught the solid iron war hammer tossed his way by Owain, gripping the haft tight in his talons. "We should get going."

Rainbow eyes flicked from Brynjar to the hammer to Owain and back to Brynjar, their owner giving an experimental swing of her sword before nodding. "It if gets me out of here, lead the way."

***

The destruction of Bevin's communication crystal had sent a blast of magical feedback through the connection. Galaxy reeled back in pain from the deafening screech resonating from her crystal straight into her head. Loosing a curse as she shook her head to clear away the noise, she changed the connection to Owain's crystal, her heart crawling up her throat as the sounds of fighting came through, shouts and crashes of metal on stone and flesh.

"Dang it! Dang dang dang verdammt!"

Galaxy spun to throw the useless chunk of crystal overboard, instead stabbing it into the wood deck with a scream and rushing to lean over the railing. With her gryphon eyes she could see the unicorns in the courtyard forming into even rows in the direction of the main doorway, horns glinting with the magic of charged bolts. She beheld the heavy iron doors heave out, then buckle, the volley of magic bolts glancing harmlessly off one of the doors as Brynjar used it as cover, throwing it forward to scatter the defending soldiers. A score were knocked down, the continuing bolts from those still standing their ground blocked by a shield spell from Owain, keeping the three-strong charge from faltering before it could close the distance into melee combat.

For a few brief, shining seconds, the prospects of the battle actually seemed hopeful. At least half of the unicorns that had been in the courtyard turned tail and ran from the fury of Brynjar's hammer swings, Bifrost's swift sword strokes, Owain's precise bolts; draftees from nearby Markhaven, Galaxy guessed, without a day of honest training between them. Better, the reptilian Zakarian mercenaries seemed to take this as an attack of opportunity for themselves, many turning and throwing themselves at the soldiers who moments before had been issuing them orders and weapons, many others swarming the fortress for whatever valuables might be inside. Cowardly and treacherous as that might have been to Galaxy, at least it gave the Imperials more targets.

Renewed terror as the fortress's crystal drones swarmed to its defense. The bladed pinwheels raked across the battlefield indiscriminately, beheading Zakarians and opening the backs of shrieking unicorns, one narrowly missing taking off Brynjar's left wing. Their rain of magic bolts from extended crystal spires forced Owain permanently into a defensive role, shield spell flashing in and out of life around the two gryphons as they struggled to cross the courtyard to the outer gates. Make it out the gates, make it out of the fortress's anti-teleport barriers, make it to the air-yacht and safety.

~They die,~ hissed Ashe over the sounds of fighting still echoing from the communication crystal behind them. ~Need help.~

~I know, know, I...~ Galaxy's talons dug into the railing as she leant forward, intent to dive off into the fray, but stopped. Her chest hurt, a tremor running down from the middle of her scarred back to the bottoms of her scuffed hooves as a familiar terror took hold. Breathing hitched, wings dropping uselessly, eyes wide as she stared down at a different fortress suddenly, the river gone, replaced by a giant canyon and bridge, Grimhilt's Folly looking up at her now, Lord Mordred there on the bridge, grinning madly back at her. Wailing, a harsh wailing on the wind, screams, stinging pain, a bitter taste of iron and ash and biting cold, salt, tears—

~Galaxy!~ "Galaxy!"

Rough claws grabbed her by the shoulder. She jerked back, horn lighting, shoving Ashe backward with a shield spell. She couldn't breathe, chest heaving as the cries now for help from the communication crystal bled into more voices, old voices, Ida and Sascha and Siegfried, King Erentil and Princess Gwendolyn, Captain Blackbird, the bookshop owner in Port Oil, Bevin, crashing rocks, screech of cockatrices, Spell Virus's laughter—

"Galaxy!" Ashe was there again, shrunk to almost Galaxy's size, gripping tight onto both shoulders. Galaxy shoved with another shield spell, growling as the dragon clung tight. "I... ssscared... too! Have... help! Die. Without. Without. Usss!"

"Gal, can you hear me? We need you now!"

"Bifrost, no, that's Bevin!"

"Where's Galaxy!?"

Galaxy jerked her head, shattering the communication crystal with a burst of magic. The world fell silent, heavy upon her. No distraction, no lie, only truth. "I... fear. I'm broken. I can't, I can't—"

Ashe's grip turned gentler, claws dragging up from Galaxy's shoulders to hold her head in place, soft and supportive. Eyes met, Galaxy transfixed by the fire in the dragon's eyes, fierce and unyielding. "Grimhilt... could... Galaxy... can. Galaxy... taught strength. Galaxy strong. No... fear. Friend."

"Grimhilt could... I can..." Galaxy breathed deep, the once-cold air tinged with the dragon's warmth. Galaxy felt it thaw her body, her limbs feeling her own again, tremors easing as she thought to herself, thought it over again and again, that Grimhilt had been through this and worse and kept going, that her mother had been through this and worse and kept going, that SHE could get through this and worse and keep going.

"No fear. No fear. No fear." Turning, wings flaring as she mounted the railing, Galaxy set her horn alight. The magic of the Waters of Life within her came to her call quick as a thought. Exhilarating as her first flight. "No fear."

***

Brynjar sat half-collapsed against the very door he had thrown to start their charge, talons of his right foreleg clamped against a deep gash in his side from a unicorn lucky with her horn. His other talons held tight to Owain's shoulder, the unicorn trembling beside him, glaring daggers at the Imperial soldiers forming ranks around them. Bifrost knelt just behind them on the other end of the crumpled door, sword dropped and wings at her sides, head dropping with despondence. Scattered across the courtyard lay the broken forms of the zakarians that had tried fighting as well, beaten and blasted with a special vehemence for their treachery.

As a half-conscious Bevin was led over to their small group by two soldiers, blood flowing freely from a cut across her head, a unicorn stallion in white barding decorated with gold filigree denoting rank as the fortress's commander marched forward. His black mane was matted to his dun coat with mud and blood, but despite this he carried an air of triumphant arrogance that rattled Brynjar. "I don't know what you were expecting to accomplish here, rebel scum, and I don't particularly care. You've all cost me enough soldiers for one day. Execution is in order."

"No!" Bevin, somewhat coming to, shook off her captors and staggered to stand between the stallion and the rest of them. Brynjar felt touched, despite the severity of the rest of the situation. "You don't have the authority! The fight is over, our weapons thrown down. We are prisoners, not—"

The fortress commander stepped forward, a telekinetic slap sending Bevin reeling. Owain shouted his rage, Brynjar barely holding him back as surrounding soldiers drew in tighter around them. Through it all, the commander scoffed. "Don't think a traitor like you can lecture me, Bevin. I'm aware of who you are. Traitor to the grand Avalon Empire! Alone against former comrades, former friends, former allies! You think these beasts would have stood beside you once your usefulness was spent? You think they wouldn't have thrown you to the wolves at the slightest sign it would help them!? Heathens and beasts, why!?"

Brynjar waited with bated breath. Bevin shook her head, still swaying from the blow as she lifted her head back up to the fortress commander. Then, with a whinny, she lifted her head up higher, craning her gaze up to something in the sky. Confused, Brynjar followed her gaze, eyes widening moments before the red blur sped down into the river past the fortress walls, the resulting explosion of water raining down on them all like a fine mist.

Remembering this from the last time it had happened, in Port Oil, Brynjar grabbed tight to Owain and braced himself just in time for the following burst of pressure and sound from Galaxy's passing. The sheer force sent all gathered in the courtyard staggering, several of the crystal drones smashing into the ground or surrounding walls.

"What-what in—" The fortress commander clawed back to his hooves, eyes wild and armor askew. "What in Sheol was—"

"You best find something to hold onto," said Brynjar, bracing himself against the door while drawing and holding Owain tight against his side with a wing, the raven-gryphon, Bifrost, following suit a moment later. From the corner of his eye Brynjar saw Bevin sitting down on all fours, ropes of stone rising up to bind her in place. He could feel the mounting pressure, an intensity in the air weighing heavy on the back, the head, could hear the nearby river churning. They all could. "My sister's here."

***

Galaxy rose once more into the sky, wings beating and forelegs held out to the sides, talons up. She brought the river with her. It flowed and stretched, 20 feet wide here and 40 there, thrumming with power. Her power. She was Water, fearless, her core alight with fiery ice from her heart to the tips of her wings.

Below, in the fortress courtyard, she saw unicorns in Imperial armor, surrounding her friends and family. At a shout they turned and leveled a volley of magic bolts from their horns at her, dozens of bolts, hundreds. She scoffed, breaking a sheet of water from the river to catch the barrage. The resulting steam she shunted back down, cries of shock and pain arising from the soldiers.

A high-pitched buzzing caught Galaxy's attention. She looked up, beheld two dozen crystal drones speeding her way, and with another scoff she knocked them from the skies with a water whip as thick as her body. By this point, the soldiers in the courtyard had resumed firing their magic bolts her way, joined by more soldiers on the bridge spanning the river between the two halves of the fortress. Most shot wide, the few that didn't impacting harmlessly against a shield spell she conjured around her.

Galaxy grew tired of all this, worry for her loved ones gnawing at the core of magic deep inside. With a surge of power up through her horn, she growled and hefted the river higher, smashing apart the bridge and sending stone, wood, and flailing unicorns scattering to the ground. The screams of terror rang loud as she spun in place, whipping the river into the fortress's towers next, shattering them as easily as stacks of cards. She continued her turn, roaring as she lifted the river higher, intent on slamming down into the courtyard—

"MERCY! PLEASE!" The fortress commander had fallen into a kneeling stance, shaking as he gazed up to Galaxy. The sight was enough to give her pause, allowing the stallion to continue. "Please, mercy, mercy! We yield, no more! Take the others and go, just leave the rest of my soldiers in peace!"

Galaxy slowed the beating of her wings, becoming aware enough of herself beyond the ice in her veins to feel her ragged breathing, the shaking of her talons as she magically hefted tens of thousands of pounds of water overhead for an earth-shaking hammer blow. She saw the other soldiers cowering near their leader, gazing up at her in shock and terror, weapons and helmets thrown aside in the slightest hope for leniency. She saw Bevin near them, Owain, a scarred and tortured Bifrost, Brynjar grimacing, clutching a wound in his side. Brynjar staring up at her with the same look, a look she'd seen before—

"Because growing up there were days when I, or Sascha, or Siegfried, came home bruised with hoofmarks,

with... sh-shouted words that made Mom cry when we repeated th-them... years of rocks and rotten fruit thrown at you, at us, s-su-slurs on our walls about you, returning from the market... and n-n-n-nothing Mother could go to for help without bruises for her tro... trou... so she just learned to live with it.

"But you..." He looked back at her, Galaxy marveling in horror that she could remember none of this, not until she saw the Horror Sickness in her brother's eyes. *"But you can get blood for every pain... destroy cities like an Imperial warship... and th-that terrifies me..."*

Galaxy lowered the river back into its banks, the cold power slipping away as a different ice grew in her. She hovered down into the courtyard, alighting before the far taller but infinitely cowed fortress commander, looking the stallion and his remaining band of soldiers over to gauge as best she could the honesty in their surrender. Seeing nothing immediately traitorous, Galaxy glanced at her friends and family, relieved for their relative wellbeing and lack of fear toward her now, heart aching at the state Bifrost was in, so emptier than the brave, solid raven-gryphon she remembered. And that Bifrost stood alone...

"Do you have no other prisoners?" Galaxy asked, keeping her voice as level as she turned back to the fortress commander. "Nobody else?"

Slowly, seeming hesitant to answer, the stallion shook his head. "The rest of the Gryphonbough and Gateway survivors, sent away, used up in experiments by... certain parties. Nobody..." But then he frowned, looking from Galaxy to where Owain crouched, his eyes narrowing in thought or recognition, Galaxy couldn't say. "No, there's... a prisoner in the infirmary. A unicorn, a traitor, only just kept from dying. Mordred's toy for some betrayal."

Time, the world, everything seemed to slow around Galaxy. She looked to Owain, seeing him rise on shaky knees, green glow of healing magic fading, Brynjar rising half-supporting and half-supported by him. Galaxy's tongue was dry as she turned back to the fortress commander. "This unicorn... palomino?"

A quick, jerky nod was all the answer needed. Galaxy felt her stomach drop, not looking at the sound of hooves galloping into the fortress, heavy wingbeats following.

***

The fortress infirmary stood all white. Maddeningly white. The walls were painted a plain white, as was the floor, as was the ceiling. The curtain dividers between "rooms" were plain white cloth, motionless. The crystal batteries mounted to the walls released a clear, sterile sort of light. Even the cabinets lining the walls every five feet, filled with white jars of herbs and medicines, were a dull white wood. Nothing to distract the mind from the pained, labored breathing echoing through the mostly-empty room.

Brynjar watched from the closest dividing cloth as Owain knelt beside the cot in the far corner from the entrance. The unicorn stallion left sprawled on the cot was barely recognizable as such. Coat burned away by some intense heat (lightning, Brynjar's darker thoughts told him), skin charred black, cracked and oozing. Mane and tail gone, eyes crusted shut, once-proud horn a splintery stick of charcoal that stopped halfway up. The unicorn's body shook with every labored breath, each more of a struggle than the last.

"Fa..." Owain's voice faltered, his own body shaking. "Fa... Father?"

The unicorn on the cot jerked, eyes struggling to open, head turning slowly in the direction of Owain's voice. "Mmmmy... my son?"

'Y-yes," said Owain, voice almost a whisper as he reached a hoof out to, as gently as he could touch his father's cheek. "It's me, Owain. I'm here beside you now, safe and sound. The hippogryph, and Brynjar her brother, they're safe too. We took the fortress with Bevin's help, saved the remaining pris... prisoners. We're... we're here to save you, Father."

"Sssafe..." Urien's lips trembled, cracking and bleeding as he forced a unicorn smile. His head lowered back to the cot, breathing growing somehow easier. Or no, Brynjar realized with dread. Weaker. "Safe... like I al... always wanted... I t-tried to save the pu-puh-prisoners... save just one... f-for you..."

A sound like dying fell from Owain. A hoof fumbled helplessly, trying to find a better position for the slim pillow gifted Urien. "It's okay, it's okay, just rest, please, j-just..."

But Urien wheezed, gaze drifting away, past Owain and Brynjar to somewhere else. "O... Owain?"

"Y-yes, Father?"

The smile stayed even as coughs suddenly wracked Urien's body, blood spattering the edge of the cot. The rise and fall of his side slowed. "I am so... so... proud of you, my—"

The unicorn's sides stilled completely, the infirmary going quiet, the struggles for air ended. Governor Urien of Featheren Valley and the Avalon Empire was no more.

"Fa... Father? Father, please—" Owain's voice cracked, body heaving. He lowered his head, sobbing openly as he pressed his horn lightly against his father's shoulder, as close as he seemed able to get. "Please no, no no no, it's not fair... Nnngh..." His body seized up, head raising to the ceiling. The scream that tore its way from his throat echoed raw and bloody. Broken.

Slowly, Brynjar left the curtain divider to go to Owain's side, hesitating for a second before settling beside the unicorn and draping a wing over his back. Owain turned his head and pressed against Brynjar, continuing to sob, words long-fled before the grief.

CHAPTER TWELVE

Unicorn funeral rites were deep, complex, and time-consuming, containing a summation of the deceased's achievements in life, a summation of their failures, a reciting of any and all notable historical lineage they possessed. Cocooning in thrice-blessed wrappings. Careful application of herbs and poultices for swift degradation. All culminating in setting the body off on a boat onto the ocean, returning the unicorn to the waters from whence they all, countless eons ago, rose from.

They had no time for any of this. The oceans bordering the continent of Heraldale were all days or weeks away, even by flight. The Smaragd Fluss, despite its nearness, was too busy a waterway for Urien's body to reach the ocean unhindered. Yet they could not simply leave him there, in the den of his murderers.

And so, at Bifrost's suggestion and Owain's blessing, they gave Urien of Featheren Valley a gryphon funeral. Atop the rocky, low-lying peak of Fernsicht Mountain, 30 miles southeast of the Markhaven fortress, Galaxy and Brynjar and Bifrost stacked layer upon layer of wood and brush, dried of snow and ice by Ashe's heated breath. The wood square rose five feet high, 15 feet wide, and 15 feet long, large enough to rest Urien's body on with room to spare. What flowers they could find were sprinkled across the top as a soft bedding, a glimpse of beauty in the end.

As son, Owain lifted Urien onto the pyre, shaking from the strain on his magic. Then came the tarp to cover the body, a flag of the Unicorn Empire found stored away in the air-yacht's depths. The look of revulsion from Owain at the sight of the white diamond upon a black field was all-new. Galaxy understood.

The time came when all was prepared. Their motley crew stood there upon the peak, a stiff wind at their backs and the sky overcast with coming snow, the rock around them barren save for scant patches of frosty moss and stubborn grass. At a nod from Owain, Ashe spit a stream of fire at the pyre's bottom, quickly spreading through the entire structure, Urien with it. Galaxy resisted the screaming in her head to back away from the dancing flames, though the talons digging into the rock threatened to break and the muscles keeping her wings pinned to her back felt ready to tear. Not now. Not with Owain just beside her, his fire-lit eyes now dry, the tears all cried.

Bifrost broke the silence after the first minute, voice halting from her own bodily hurts, accent almost unintelligible in the snatch of old song. "Wir stolze Menschenkinder, Sind eitel arme Sünder Und wissen gar nicht viel; Wir spinnen Luftgespinste Und suchen viele Künste Und kommen weiter von dem Ziel."

Owain said nothing, unreadable in the clash of flames and approaching gloom of evening. Bevin whinnied, tossing her mane and stomping a hoof. Galaxy and Brynjar shared a look from where they stood on opposite sides of Owain, Galaxy seeing a growing resolve in her brother's eyes to which she could only nod. Brynjar looked forward to the flames again and closed his eyes. Another moment passed with naught but the crackle of flames, the whistles and shrieks of wind through the mountain's crevices. The fire had reached Urien's body now, the wrappings disappearing in a swirl of ash and sparks.

Then Brynjar's voice, low, Galaxy's heart clenching at the feel of weeping in the song.

"I had a dream last night,

It was such a worrisome dream,

There was growing in my garden,

A rosemary tree

"A graveyard was the garden,

A flowerbed the grave

And from the green tree

The crown and flower fell.

"The blossoms I gathered

in a golden jar,

It fell out of my talons,

And smashed to pieces.

"Out of it I saw pearls trickling

And droplets rose-red
What could the dream mean?
Oh, my love, are you dead?"

Owain's head had fallen, eyes closed against a fresh wave of tears. Ashe loosed a keening sort of growl as, as if on cue, a sharp crack rang out, the middle of the pyre collapsing in and sending a thick flurry of sparks into the air. They were caught on the wind and sent streaming away, a river of dancing, blinking light disappearing into the distance. Galaxy swallowed at the sight. Gryphons, when able, burned their dead, releasing their souls back to the sky they had come from in ages past, to find their way to Sheol in peace. She did not know if the cinders meant anything with a unicorn burning, but she could hope...

The pyre was halfway-burned down when Bevin turned away, descending the mountainside toward where they had landed the air-yacht. Galaxy spared a final look to Owain before following, using her wings to keep her descent lighter and quieter as she caught up to the soldier. "It's disrespectful to leave during a funeral. Some would argue blasphemous."

"If there's anyone out there who cares," said Bevin, not slowing or looking back as she continued hopping down the rough path, "they can strike me down right now. Get your money's worth on your matchsticks."

Galaxy stumbled, cawing in outrage. She fully took flight, circling around and landing in front of Bevin, looking up at the unicorn coming to a stop on a higher outcropping. "Damn it, Bevin! Feel an ounce of grief! Can't you do that for even a day, for even one of your own!?"

". . . grief?" The mare looked back up the way they'd come then, to the figures of their companions still silhouetted by the burning pyre, then back to Galaxy. "I guess not. Haven't had anything to grieve over since I was 9 years old. Not that that's much to tell of."

Galaxy flinched. She remembered the story Bevin had told her and her companions far back in Port Oil, the story of her family being murdered by gryphons, of her being left to die and saved only by Lord Mordred. Quieted, Galaxy did not try to stop Bevin as the soldier dropped down level with her and shouldered past her toward the air-yacht waiting in a leveled dell, only turning to once more follow her. "But then you must understand a little of Owain's pain. You must remember the terror and grief, surely?"

Bevin did not stop, though she did slow as they reached the dell, allowing Galaxy to pull up beside her. "I remember... it's a blur. Stress and trauma eroding those long-past days. I remember... fire. Gryphons... a queenly figure, I think, and maybe... maybe some noise, like a wailing. A newborn's wailing."

Galaxy had watched the emotions play out through Bevin's blue eyes, so sharp and vibrant even in the growing dusk. She had seen the bitterness, the regret and yearning, and toward the end a confusion, as if the mare herself was not certain of what she was saying, or was frightened of what she was saying. It sure as Sheol frightened her.

But that could all wait until another day, when danger was not so near, when they were all fat and fresh and groomed again, and they could pick their scars apart at their leisure. Galaxy circled again to land atop the air-yacht's boarding ramp, forcing Bevin to stop again, refusing to make eye contact. "Okay then, fine. I understand, Bevin. I do. You lost everything. Then you lost it all again, lost Mordred. But that doesn't have to be the end! You can have something new! New friends, new family, new purpose! Owain's lost his family, but he still has us, and Brynjar and I'll be there for him no matter what. Let us—"

"I NEVER ASKED FOR IT!"

Galaxy stumbled back, nearly slipping off the boarding ramp's side. The shout echoed off the surrounding rocks, distorting and mocking. Bevin tossed her head, mane flying as she stomped and huffed. "I never asked for it, for this! I'm here to fight and serve, to slay Lord Mordred and avenge myself! I'm not here for rescue missions, or mourning the lost, or, or laughter beside campfires, teasing you with your brother like you people—" her voice broke, a deep lungful of air as Galaxy noticed with a horrified start tears, actual tears, glimmering in the mare's eyes. "I never asked to feel scared when I saw Brynjar take that horn to his side, and I never asked to worry how Owain might take his father's passing, and I never asked to panic when you didn't answer our calls for help, thinking drones or other air-yachts had come upon you, thinking you might be... I never asked to CARE about you stupid, stupid, STUPID people."

"I'm sure the feeling's mutual."

Bevin whinnied and whirled, spooked. Galaxy looked over her to see the others coming down the mountainside, Bifrost leading the way, helped along by Ashe shrunken down to almost gryphon-sized. Bifrost's haunted look, disbelieving, as if this might all vanish and return her to her dungeon cell at any moment, was abated somewhat by a touch of amusement at the unicorn before them all. The pyre had burned down to little more than cinders atop the peak behind them, ash indistinguishable from the fitful snow now starting to drift down.

"Caring's something that happens," continued Bifrost, pausing and sitting to catch her breath. "Whether we want it or not. So Lady Quetzal says."

A low-throated growl sounded, Bevin shooting Galaxy a glare before scrubbing at her eyes with a foreleg. Head high, as if the outburst moments earlier hadn't occurred, she lit the cherry-sized crystal batteries lining the outside of the air-yacht's railing for light before once more shouldering past Galaxy. She turned to follow, to try again—

"Gal, wait."

Galaxy stopped, turning back to the group at Brynjar's voice. As she watched, he and Owain looked to each other, a silent debate going on between them in subtle cues that Galaxy couldn't follow. Eventually Owain nodded, at which Brynjar drew away and took flight, following after Bevin onto the air-yacht. Though Galaxy could not see them from where she stood halfway down the ramp, she could still somewhat hear their voices, low and heated, but not, thankfully, violent.

Frowning at this mystery, Galaxy ignored it for more pressing matters at the moment. She fluttered down the ramp, crossing the short distance to wrap both forelimbs around Owain's neck, talons digging into his mane as she pressed the side of her head to his. The unicorn felt like a statue. "I'm sorry. I am so, so sorry. If we had gotten there sooner—if, if I'd not wasted so much time training—I-I'd trade myself for him, you know I would, I—"

"I know. I know. I know." Galaxy felt a foreleg move up and over her neck in a return of her gesture, before Owain pulled away enough to look her in the eyes. The dead, poisoning sorrow she saw there felt like a lingering stab to the heart, his voice when he spoke a flat, unliving tone. "I know. Brynjar would kill us both for entertaining that. I know... how lucky you got, back in Port Oil, thinking your family gone forever. I know. I just... need time. I can't get it talking to you."

The curt dismissal stung. Galaxy backed away, wiping her tears away with a wingtip before putting on the best reassuring smile she could manage. From there she turned, looked around at her scattered companions, saw Ashe and Bifrost some distance away, conversing in their own low tones. The two survivors, she thought in her head. For a moment, Galaxy just stood there and watched, the sight of the once-proud raven-gryphon physically painful to behold, angry red scars easy to pick out through her thinned plumage. She seemed so much smaller, and without the blue scarf, so much more vulnerable.

Eventually, Galaxy managed to approach them at a lull in conversation. They looked to her, Bifrost's eyes lighting up as she stood. "My princess, you... you came for me. You truly came for me..."

"I did, yes." Galaxy looked down, the stone providing no good answers. "I wish... I wish I had come sooner. I was too late. You were hurting while I—"

"I heard you and the unicorn," spoke Bifrost, tone unyielding despite her hurts. Her rainbow eyes grew empty, terrifyingly so to Galaxy, distant with memory. She sat, drawing in on herself with wings and forelimbs. "Listen to him. I... I would not wish what I went through on you, on anyone. The... the pain, the fresh pain every day of... hunger. Hot n-nails, iron rods beating me, a-almost drowning, couldn't breathe, a pressure in my head, demanding answers I couldn't give, answers I wanted to give, to shout, anything to stop Mordred's tortures, her humiliations, the, the—"

She choked to a stop, panting for breath, eyes clenching shut as a shudder of phantom pain tore through her. Galaxy started forward to help, stopping when Bifrost opened her eyes and smiled at her, bitter, beak cracked, Galaxy noticed for the first time. "Mordred's a Wolf-Lord, of course. Sh-shapeshifter. Being he or she or it is just a matter of which hurts y-you the mo-most. And I can't, I, I can't face that again, I can't go back, not to that, not to the fighting. I've seen too much, I can't, I just can't, please—"

Galaxy finished crossing the distance this time, reaching out to grip Bifrost's shoulder. She stopped babbling, still panting and looking ready to fly as Galaxy looked her in the eyes. "You won't. I promise. I won't let them send you anywhere you don't want to go. I promise. You've earned your peace. I promise."

"You promise... you..." Bifrost swallowed, nodding her head jerkily, limbs slowly loosening from her body. She glanced around them and then back at Galaxy, shame now appearing there for her outburst. Galaxy opened her beak, but before she could reassure the raven-gryphon that there was nothing to be ashamed of she spoke again, voice a shade firmer. "I... I can't go back, but, I can still tell you... things. Things I saw and, and heard. Especially that I saw on the battlefield. Statues..."

Galaxy jerked back, feeling struck. She looked back to see Owain at least momentarily shaken to full alertness by the comment, staring back at her with as much terror at that one word as she certainly felt. "It can't be. We trapped Spell Virus all the way back in Port Oil."

Looking back at Bifrost, Galaxy clasped her other shoulder, struggling to keep her voice low and calm when all she wanted was to shout and beg. "Tell us everything. Now."

***

Mordred paced the fortress courtyard, clenching her remaining hand, tail batting the gathering snow as she fought to keep her calm. Around her stood rows of unicorn soldiers, many bearing signs of recent wounds, all winded from their prior efforts to clean up the remains of the fortress's once-proud towers. Their eyes, all on her or Lord Thoth, psychically keeping the shivering fortress commander in place, kept the calm just out of her reach.

"So, in summation," said Mordred at last, not looking at the commander as she did, not needing to as she could smell the stench of his fear, "you allowed the hippogryph and her comrades to leave unhindered, without an alarm raised or magic bolt fired to stop them." The cold of the air stung the exposed bone and connective tendons of her face's right side, falling snow like pinpricks into her already-frayed nerves. "Like cowards."

No answer. Mordred saw Thoth frown, followed by a whinny of pain from the fortress commander. Lines of red trailed down his cheeks from his eye sockets. "M-mo-most of us were still injured, many gravely. The fortress was a ruin, our strength scattered, the hippogryph not even winded. I did wh-what I... thought... be-besssst for sss-sssoldiers under my command."

Mordred nodded, stopping her pacing while facing away from the commander, toward a group of dumbly-grinning Harmonized soldiers. She popped her neck one way and then the next as she repeated the confession over in her head, wolf ears twitching with some satisfaction at the nervous nickers from some of the surrounding soldiers. "A noble response, for sure. Allow me to tell you the far nobler report I shall deliver to Empress Nova personally. We found the fortress completely demolished, its Imperial garrison slaughtered down to the last stallion in defense of their incalculably precious prisoner."

Screams rang out through the courtyard then as Mordred spun in place, rage turning her vision red as she raised a hand crackling with lightning at the fortress commander, screaming loudest of all. Before Mordred could loose her blast, however, the stallion was flung from where he sat by Thoth's telekinesis, the sphinx barging up in front of Mordred and forcing her to draw back her attack. "Mordred, no! We can't kill our soldiers meaninglessly anymore! We don't have the numbers to get away with it!"

"HE WAS PRICELESS!" Mordred howled, turning and blasting a stable to cinders with a lightning bolt, sending those soldiers nearest it screaming away. Mordred turned back to Thoth, putting her full height to use as she loomed over the sphinx, fist and horn blazing with enough lightning to level what remained of the fortress all on her own. "Priceless! Worth a 100, 200 unicorn soldiers! We had him broken! Broken! Another session with you and we could have used him to teleport the combined fleet of the Empire straight to the Floating Mountain! Had this war won within a fortnight! NOW THAT'S ALL GONE!"

Thoth shied away from the lightning-bound fist inches from his head, eyes squinting in the light. "Be that... as it... may, we still can't... can't... FOR EMPIRE'S SAKE, MORDRED, CONTROL YOURSELF!"

Satisfied with that small play of dominance at least, Mordred backed a step away, keeping the lightning dancing between her fingers as she turned to resume pacing. If large-scale murder wasn't an option, there had to be a way to think around this, to turn this from an embarrassing defeat into some kind of advantage. Empress Nova would accept nothing less after so much failure. She'd failed to capture the hippogryph in Featheren Valley, failed to cover their tracks in Port Oil, failed to capture the hippogryph in the Elderpine Forest, failed to extract anything useful from the first Vogelstadt gryphon captured in years—

"Please," said Thoth behind her, humor returned to his voice, "continue the mental self-flagellation. Don't forget your failure to even capture again that drag... dragon..."

Mordred stopped her pacing, realizing the spark of possibility Thoth had caught. She looked at the sphinx, laughing at the dumbfounded, hungrily hopeful expression on his flat face, before turning to the fortress commander, still huddling terrified on his knees. "Tell me... the hippogryph and her companions... did they have a dragon among them?"

At first, nothing but blank incomprehension. Then the stallion's eyes widened, the soldier surging to his hooves as he clasped at the question like the final chance it was. "Y-yes! After the fighting, when they b-brought their air-yacht down to load the traitor's body onto it, I saw the p-pink dragon on it, terrified to be there!"

Mordred turned again to her fellow Lord of the Empire, finding a grin to match her own as she stalked back over to the sphinx. The falling snow didn't hurt anymore, instead almost refreshing as new ideas and possibilities sprouted to life, thoughts she was happy for once to share with any psychics present. "They still have the dragon with them."

Thoth nodded, looking struggling not to burst into laughter. "The poor, tortured dragon, scared child, wanting nothing more than a return to home and family,"

Mordred had no such compunction to keep her dignity, giggling as she knelt to eye level with Thoth and clapping her hand onto a shoulder. "We can't stop them from going—"

"—but we can take their destination from them." Thoth licked his lips, eyes alight with malice. "Beautiful."

***

Galaxy paced the dell from air-yacht's side to the trail leading back up to the peak, her tail lashing her tracks in the snow. Bifrost had finished recounting her time in captivity minutes before, and Galaxy didn't know what to say. There were so many oddities to take in, so many half-formed questions crowding to be asked. The news that the Empire's failed experiments in Port Oil had apparently succeeded elsewhere, granting them a petrification weapon, was troubling enough. But nothing else mentioned seemed to fit it. Once more, a mystery she just knew she didn't have all the pieces for.

"And you're sure it was the Elk they'd been ordered to leave alone?" she managed at last, stopping at the foot of the trail to look back at her companions near the air-yacht. Bifrost nodded and Galaxy frowned, thinking back on her last encounters with the forest-dwellers. "But that makes no sense. King Erentil seemed terrified of an Imperial attack. That's why he turned traitor in the first place. To keep that from happening." The sudden mental image of Princess Gwendolyn among a forest of stone trees, frozen in a moment of terror, made Galaxy shake her head and shudder. "No sense…"

"Maybe..." Owain paused as all present looked at him sitting against Ashe's side, cold and grief having overcome any lingering fear. "Maybe... a traditional attack wasn't what King Erentil was actually afraid of?"

"A traditional attack..." Galaxy paced closer, wings twitching, the gears grinding away in her head as she mulled the phrase over. Another phrase popped in, "Grand Harmony", bringing her up short as something she'd been taking for granted was flung in her face. "Owain... only unicorns can be Harmonized, right?"

At this question, Owain briefly bore a dangerous resemblance to a fish dragged up out of the water, eyes wide and mouth gaping open and closed, open and closed. The unicorn looked between them all, bewildered, a hoof tapping the uneven ground nervously. "I don't... no such thing as a Harmonized Elk has ever been heard of, but... I mean... they've hardly ever left the Elderpine to BE Harmonized..."

"But this is insane," said Bifrost, looking between Owain and Galaxy. She tried to smile, coming off more as a grimace. "Insane. The Empire could completely replenish their forces with a Harmonized Elk army. They would have long before now if..."

"Unless it's new..." Galaxy had started pacing again. She looked out beyond the dell, a fear growing that any moment she might see the evening sky light up with crystal drones, the dark shapes of air-yachts moving as shadows through the curtain of falling snow. They had traveled far from the Markhaven fortress, but they had been on the mountain for a while now, and the fire had been large. "Ashe mentioned... at first proper meeting, Ashe mentioned the experiments being done on her and the other captured dragons..."

With each word, the aggressive front the dragon had managed up to this point crumbled. She huffed and shuffled back, away from Galaxy's reaching talons. Her hisses and growls were a strain to filter into anything meaningful. ~No other dragonsss dead dead dead changesss failed! No ssstone ssscale head talk make changesss only fail! Not make think right! Unicornsss hurt pain burning. Ssstorm essscape! No hurt thought, no hurt!~

Galaxy looked at the dragon curled around Owain, staring back at the hippogryph with a wearied hurt that transcended language barriers. "Experiments on the mind. They couldn't get Harmonization to work on dragons, but an Elk is so much more similar to a unicorn. So much easier, I'd imagine. Four legs, hooved, herbivorous, horns composed of alicorn for channeling magic. It makes sense they'd at least try to make Harmonization work."

Bifrost groaned, dragged talons down from the top of her head to her neck. "But even if so, what can we do about it? We don't know where else these experiments were conducted, we can't possibly return to the Markhaven fortress, and Port Oil is days away, flying straight there. And to top it all, the Dragonback Mountains and safety are right there! Scant hours away, reachable before daybreak!"

Ashe perked her head up at the mention of her native mountain range, tail slapping the ground. Galaxy huffed a sigh, dragging her talons down the back of her neck, the best she could do instead of screaming at the friction between two needs. She had promised Ashe, sworn to the dragon, that she would return her home safe and sound. But she couldn't abandon the Elk, however their king had betrayed her, not if Harmonization was their potential fate.

"There is another option."

Galaxy loosed a frantic laugh of relief at the sight of Bevin standing at the top of the air-yacht's boarding ramp, looking down on them all as composed as ever. Brynjar stood a step behind her, catching Galaxy's eye and nodding to assure her that, whatever the soldier's problem had been before, it was better for the moment.

"Another way to confirm or deny everything you've been discussing," Bevin continued, "without deviating from our flight to the Dragonbacks at all. Someone who can tell us all."

A sinking suspicion arose in Galaxy. "Who?"

Bevin's gaze remained steady as she answered, sending Galaxy's stomach plummeting. "Spell Virus."

Brynjar summed it all up for them.

"Gottverdammt."

CHAPTER THIRTEEN

Time passed. The world rested beneath a pre-dawn moon, a land defined by snow and ice. The storm blown out hours before, leaving behind endless fields of stars, almost reachable in the freezing cold air. Between the sky and land, their air-yacht flew as a boat upon a placid lake, seeming slow in its smallness. Everything was cold, like ice to the core. It collected on the railings, on the ropes, on the deck where their heat did not touch it. Cold, cold, a world turned cold.

Galaxy stood at the air-yacht's bow, gaze to the straight south. Far in the distance, but yet not so far, an hour of steady flying at most, she could see the Dragonback Mountains looming into sight, a curving, jagged line of black against a world of white and grey. Bevin had insisted, demanded, that they put time and space between them and the mountain they had laid Urien to rest on before attempting their quest for answers.

"The Mind-to-Mind Spell is meant as a way to alleviate Horror Sickness and other disorders of the mind," the soldier explained, marching one end of the air-yacht to the next and back again, voice projected loud for them all to hear clear as crystal. "However, it provides a unique opportunity for our unique problem. The

hippogryph and I both briefly had Spell Virus within us, within our minds. The Mind-to-Mind Spell allows its participants to delve into their memories for healing and closure, but could also allow us to delve into Spell Virus's memories lingering somewhere within us, revealing everything he might have known of these experiments and their purpose."

"It sounds insane," Brynjar remarked. "But then again, what doesn't?"

The sleep Bevin had ordered to prepare for the spell attempt, welcome after an entire day of fighting and planning and stressing, had come quickly but briefly to Galaxy, filled with the same terrible nightmare, only now with Bifrost and Ashe among the dying. Yet even while running on only two or three hours of sleep, Galaxy did not feel tired. She felt possessed of a nervous, almost frantic energy, something that couldn't just be explained by the nearness of journey's end.

"YOU'RE GOING TO GET THEM ALL KILLED, YOU KNOW THAT, RIGHT?"

Galaxy ignored the dream voice, listening instead to the creak of the deck behind her, the shuffle of weary hooves. Owain appeared to her right, eyes to the south and just as distant. Galaxy kept her peace, dragging talons down the feathers along the back of her neck. Aside from Bifrost managing the air-yacht's controls after a brief lecturing from Bevin, she had not realized anyone else was awake.

"It's quiet up here."

Galaxy looked over at Owain, surprised by his voice. After a moment she looked ahead again, nodded. "Yeah, it is."

"Father never liked the quiet. When Mother was... there would be music in the house, always music, one of them working a cello with their magic, or there'd be singing crystals imported from the Zakarian Confederacy, or a gry... gryphon servant... after she left, there was none of that anymore. So Father, he began talking. So much talking, on and on. Acquaintances left, friends, unable to bear it. We were sent to Featheren Valley, to... to new servants and soldiers and responsibilities. Father resorted to talking to himself when he thought there was nobody to listen. I wondered... I feared he never even realized he was doing it... and I never told him, I never said anything, I never helped, I only did what everyone else did and got ANNOYED and I, I, I never..."

Owain broke off, breathing heavy. Galaxy kept her silence, watched, let him grieve how he needed to.

"He sa-said he was proud of me," Owain managed at last, blinking away tears. "I can't... how do I deal with that? I expected disappointment. I don't know what to do with pride..."

"You... accept it," said Galaxy, once it became clear the unicorn was legitimately hoping for an answer. "I know it's difficult, trust me, but accept that you are worthy of somebody's pride. Sometimes it's all you can do."

A minute of silence from the unicorn passed. Galaxy shifted where she stood, uncertain if she had helped at all or simply made things worse. But then Owain gave a short, jerky nod, head lowering onto the railing. "Thank you, Gal... I... it's hard... not blaming you for all this, when it all started with you. I'm... thank you."

Galaxy said nothing, knowing he could be right in blaming her for everything as she laid down in a similar position to him, head resting on the railing gaze turned again on the frozen, broken world below.

". . . she has the same eyes as you, you know."

Galaxy jolted in alarm, glancing at Owain for a brief second before turning her attention back to the mountains ahead instead of behind them to their fellow travelers. "Yeah, I... I know."

***

Time passed. A glow rose along the eastern horizon, dawn eager and grasping. Below them it revealed lands bereft of snow, miles of charred foothills and valleys from decades of unicorn sieges upon the dragons. The approaching sun stabbed veins of light through the heavy clouds ever-present over the Dragonbacks, smoke and ash, hot cinders, lightning. A strange, haunting contrast to the snow draped upon many of the mountains still.

Sometime, Galaxy didn't notice when, Owain left and Bevin took his place. For several minutes neither said anything, simply finding strange solace in the sight of the falling snow and ash, two opposites come together in mutual purpose, obscuring all in white and grey. Galaxy had never seen volcanic ash before and quietly marveled at it collecting on the railing in front of her, brushing it away with a wing whenever it piled too high.

"You know," Galaxy eventually said aloud, happening upon an idea. "You know, the minotaurs performed tests upon tests and found, through years of experimentation, that volcanic soil is some of the most fertile in the world. A certain richness of minerals, the right acidic balance... funny, yeah? Something that's outwardly so destructive, but so rewarding if you only look a little longer."

The nearest peaks were a scant half-mile ahead. Bevin's gaze kept on them, expression unreadable in the strange gloom. "I suppose that's the both of us in a nutshell. Such disappointing first impressions for what would eventually come. Comradery."

"Friendship," ventured Galaxy, another word almost slipping from her beak, a word she didn't dare speak, no matter her suspicions regarding the mare beside her. There were so many questions left to ask, so much about Bevin that Galaxy didn't know, so much... but so little time. No time.

Bevin snorted, shuffling on her hooves and giving her mane a nervous flick. "Just... remember, as we do this. The last time you went in search of strange knowledge, Lord Mordred almost killed you before I stepped in."

"Yes," said Galaxy, fighting to keep a smile away. "I remember Mordred saying that there we were, back together again, at last. Whatever he meant then... I'll always have you to keep me out of trouble from the start, won't I?"

If Bevin caught the point Galaxy was trying to make, she said nothing. When the unicorn turned and stalked from the bow to the center of the air-yacht, Galaxy feared she had pushed too far and made Bevin break rather than bend. But then Bevin turned to face her, head high and body squared. Her voice rang loud, rousing the attention of the others. "It is time to find out what truth Spell Virus can give us. Princess Galaxy, stand level with me. Keep eye contact."

Galaxy did as told, catching Brynjar's worried eye as she did and shooting him her best reassuring smile. Focusing again on Bevin, Galaxy almost jerked back as the taller mare bowed her head, spiral-etched horn pointing Galaxy's way. "Touch your horn to mine. Tip to tip, if you can manage it, but don't give up solid footing. Summon your magic, but don't release or cast, or even reach out until I say."

With the height difference, it took three tries for Galaxy to satisfactorily touch the tip of her horn to the tip of Bevin's. Even without reaching out, she could feel Bevin's magic through the physical connection, warm and fluid, so similar to hers, but with an additional graininess that could only be the Stone Elemental within the unicorn.

"Good," said Bevin, closing her eyes. Galaxy followed suit. "Now, focus with me. Shut out the clutter. We have time to slow, to pick and choose. Good. Think back. Remember Port Oil. Remember Spell Virus. Reach out, remember—"

"The lightning," said Galaxy.

Suddenly, with a jerk at her horn, Galaxy felt herself rush forwardflyforwardfallforwardsofarnotstoppingneverstoppingforeverandeverandflamesandlaughterandscreamsohGodsheisbleedingbleedingbleedingithurtsfatherithurts—

Hooves and talons slammed down onto another deck, wider, slick with water, Galaxy staggering into Bevin beside her as they both struggled to regain their bearings. The world rang deafening around them, Galaxy feeling a panic attack threatening to break out as lightning crashed all around them, thunder and hundreds of pounding hooves and screams. In front of them on the boat stood the Bevin of memory, eyes glowing an unnatural blue as she snarled and pulled at the Galaxy of memory clinging to the ship's mast.

"Give it to me! Give me! I hunger! Always hunger! Give me!"

"Almost there," said the real Bevin beside Galaxy, hooves tapping with nerves. "A moment more, keep your foc—"

Blue lightning flashed from Memory Bevin's mouth, just as red snapped from Memory Galaxy's horn to the crystal battery atop the mast. Again the world turned into a blur, as disorienting as the first time, worse in how this time she had to focus on it.

The imperial garrison at the center of Port Oil, tall and multi-turreted block of metal and stone—

Steel corridors, hooves clanking, black-coated unicorn stallions trotting past rows of crystal containers holding twisting Elementals—

"Progress continues as foreseen, Lord Mordred—"

Different corridor, different unicorns, rows of cages filled with blindfolded cockatrices—

A filly crying inside a burning cottage, unicorn and gryphon bodies all around her, Lord Mordred advancing—

"Wait," Galaxy found herself saying. "That was different the first—"

A cry of "Focus!" from the Bevin beside her snapped Galaxy from that thought. Around them the world shifted with a flash of gold magic, Bevin's. They saw a brown-coated unicorn stallion pacing nervously in a white-walled room, miniatures of tools Galaxy only half-recognized littering a table before him. Across the table sat Lord Mordred, a sphinx, and a gangly unicorn stallion the varied hues of a peacock.

"I need more time!" The stallion that seemingly would become Spell Virus was saying. "I need more cockatrices! We have the spell and we have the power source, but without a way to connect the two, our Empress Nova's Grand Harmonium is a foal's dream!"

A hiss from Mordred, the light on the scene turning strange. With a start, Galaxy noticed the walls seeming to slowly be consumed in fire.

"No more time—"

"One year—"

"Spring equinox. But, more cockatrices can always be arranged—"

"Galaxy," hissed Bevin, stomping at her talons with a hoof as the fire spread to the table, the three Lords of the Empire slowly consumed by it. "Galaxy, focus, damn you! Spell Virus! Cockatrices! Not this!"

Galaxy closed her eyes, shook her head, breathing growing hard as her old terror of fire hit her. "Grand Harmonium, please, please, what—"

She saw again suddenly, without consciously opening her eyes. First another white-walled room, far larger, the stallion before them drawing equations in the air with magic light. Then they stood on a beach of shattered stone, black and stabbing, waves crashing beneath a stormy sky cut through with streaks of fire, the stallion himself helping tether down a bound and blindfolded cockatrice. Then they stood among mountains, the southern ranges that bordered the queendom of Schwarz Angebot. The trees below them burned, cinders rising in the wind in great sheets. Ahead of them a vast pyramid, Hiraeth Arian, and behind that a tower, half-completed, taller than any Galaxy had seen before, sheer white and gold. Words echoed through Galaxy's head at the sight of it, the stallion's voice praising it as if it were a god. "The Grand Harmonium... peace at last..."

"I know it now, a machine," *came Bevin's voice from beside her, faltering. The fires continued to roar, growing closer toward them, strangely heatless to Galaxy.* "So much more done now than last I was here. Tuning glyphs, focusing rods, amplifier chambers, all... all to a scale I've never dreamed of. The spell range from that could be... limitless..."

341

Galaxy scoured the tower with a hungry desperation, head throbbing as clues came together and possibilities presented themselves. "Cockatrices, petrification spell too aimless, affect everything, use to draw upon something to power... power... Grand Harmonium, Harmonium... the Harmonization spell! Bevin—"

She turned to her fellow memory traveler and froze. An unaccountable dread suddenly filled her at the sight of the white-coated unicorn before her, the fire framing her from all corners, smoke and ash swirling about. The dread locked Galaxy's limbs in place, drove out a scream of terror that had Bevin prancing back in alarm. Bevin. The fire. Bevin. The fire. Bevin, fire, fire all around, heat burning, grasping choking, fire fire fire fire screams blood through the air FIRE FIRE FIRE—

"Galaxy, no! Focus! Galaxy—"

The world shattered around them. They fell, but did not fall, rising. Sound and sight rolled through them. No air, but they could breathe. No light, but they could see and feel the Fire. The pieces gathered, twisted, reformed around them. The pair found themselves side by side, standing in the corner of an old and decrepit log cabin. There were three glass windows to each wall, a large fireplace along the wall to their right, a door barred and piled high with tables as a makeshift barricade far to their left, several of the windows across from them broken. Through them could be seen trees, vast trees—

A door near the fireplace burst open, Galaxy immediately seizing up at the sight of a unicorn stallion nearly identical to the one that appeared so often in her dreams, though this one's mane and tail were a dazzling scarlet. He wore knightly armor and barding that might have been expensive and imposing, once upon a time, but by that point was nearly scrap. Blood ran from a gash across his forehead, dangerously close to blinding eyes a startling, familiar blue.

"Lancelot, wait!"

The unicorn turned and regarded the—

"Oh God," said Galaxy, gaping at the cardinal-gryphon standing there in similar armor to the unicorn. But no, she realized after a second, it wasn't Queen Grimhilt. It couldn't be Grimhilt, for this cardinal-gryphon's feathers were not the same vibrant red as Galaxy's, nor did she move at all with a queenly bearing, more alike to a common berserker.

A glance toward Bevin, however, dispelled any concern over the gryphon in Galaxy's mind. "Bevin?"

"Fa..." Bevin swallowed, looking ready to bolt out of there as she stared at the unicorn stallion in terror. "I remember now... I remember him now... father..."

"Elsa, what are you still doing here!?" The unicorn named Lancelot marched toward the gryphon. Elsa,

343

Galaxy noticing for the first time a sword with the symbol of the Knights Le Fay held in his magical grip. "Your sister and the rest are escaping to the boats as we speak, and you should be there with them. It is my duty to protect the Queen, to hold back the foe—"

"It is your duty," snarled Elsa hovering to meet his eyes, "to be there with your new wife! With your children!"

The moment froze for Galaxy at those words, echoing through her mind in an ever-increasing scream. She dared a look over at Bevin and saw her similarly frozen, a look in her eyes, almost betrayed.

A deafening bang ringing through the scene snapped Galaxy back from her daze. Looking, she saw the barricaded door shudder and crack, something massive hitting it from the other side. But this was nothing but a distraction, she almost just as quickly realized, as from her vantage point in the corner she could see gryphons in dark armor creep in through the far broken windows as Lancelot and Elsa turned toward the shaking barricade, unaware of the danger nearing from the side and behind.

"No," said Bevin suddenly, voice grown soft with a child's terror as she chanced a step forward. "No, behind you! No—"

The shout went unheeded, the events before them long past. They watched as a hummingbird-gryphon buzzed up behind Elsa, stabbing a dagger three times into her side. She screamed and wrenched away, staggering to the side as Lancelot whirled around and took the offending gryphon's head off with a single swing of his sword. But as he turned to block a blow from a bluebird-gryphon, Galaxy saw his eyes go wide with a kind of horror that could drive an immortal to death as he looked to something behind his foe. "Bevin, no!"

Galaxy followed his gaze and there she was, a unicorn filly no older than 9, standing in the doorway beside the fireplace, terror flooding her tiny features. In every way but age, she was a perfect reflection of the soldier now sobbing quietly beside Galaxy.

The moment's distraction cost the Le Fay knight dearly and immediately, the bluebird-gryphon drawing his own dagger and burying it hilt-deep into Lancelot's neck.

"NO!" Bevin fell to her knees, matching perfectly the memory of her child self. "No, Father, no!"

Falling to his own knees, Lancelot choked on the blood now gushing up his throat and out from his neck, eyes bulging, mouth a horror of red foam as the gryphon gloated over him. The gloating didn't last long, Lancelot driving his horn into the gryphon's exposed belly, sword flashing meanwhile to hack off the front left leg of a crow-gryphon coming from the right. But then he faltered. A golden eagle-gryphon bashed him to the floor with a single swing of a war hammer, another swing caving in his chest and sides to a gurgling scream of agony, a third swing toward the head—

Galaxy looked away, tear-filled eyes clenching at the sudden wet crunch that rang through the room.

"There goes the abomination's daddy, now get his brat!"

"No!"

Galaxy opened her eyes and turned back, watching with a sort of morbid wonder as the cardinal-gryphon, thought downed by the sneak attack, flew at the gaggle of gryphons stalking toward Memory Bevin. Grabbing up Lancelot's sword in her shaking talons, Elsa flew forward and opened the war hammer-swinging gryphon's throat with a single slash, blocking a sword strike from a sparrow-gryphon before reaching out and burying her talons into his chest. Her fury was terrifying, her screams for them to leave the child be near on deafening.

But fury and skill made up for little with a dagger in her side and numbers on the foes' side, and before long Elsa disappeared beneath a rain of swords, axes, and hammer strikes from half a dozen gryphons. All the while, the memory of young Bevin watched, horn flickering with magic frenzied by terror. An errant burst of telekinetic magic, a sudden cracking support pillar, a whoosh of flames from the fireplace, and then the gryphons and their surroundings were burning, the gryphons screaming, Bevin crying, the roof of the cabin looking ready to come down.

It was only when the gryphons had died or fled and Memory Bevin started staggering toward the broken body of her father that Galaxy realized there were two last elements of this scene not aligning with the memory as Bevin had passed it to—

"Bevin! BEVIN! LANCELOT! ELSA! Oh God, no!"

Galaxy turned once more to the doorway by the fireplace, dreading what she knew she'd find there. Knowing didn't lesson the blow from the sight of a regal cardinal-gryphon hovering there in the doorway, a wailing bundle of clothe held tight in her forelegs, eyes wide and full of tears as she took in the fire, Bevin, and the dead bodies littering the floor. A pillar crashed to the floor near her and she flinched, but otherwise Queen Grimhilt remained steady as she advanced into the room, the wailing from the bundle growing weaker and choking. "B-Bevin, come quickly, we need to go! Now!"

Memory Bevin remained crouched beside the crushed form of Lancelot, crying and heedless of the unnatural shadow Galaxy saw nearing her from the smashed and cleared barricades. "D-Daddy..."

"Bevin, please, we c-can't—Bevin, no!"

A piece of flaming ceiling dislodged and came crashing down toward the unaware Bevin. Right before it could crush her, however, tendrils shot forth from the open front entrance, grabbing the piece of ceiling and throwing it to the side. Grimhilt froze where she flew, no, actually hovered away a pace as a towering black unicorn strode into the flaming cabin, eyes dark with some unfamiliar emotion as he took in Lancelot's corpse. "Mordred! Get away from them!"

Grimhilt made to move forward again, stopping as Mordred ensnared Memory Bevin with his tendrils. His muzzle split into a joyless grin. "Daughter of your blood, queen, or daughter of a stranger's blood."

Galaxy felt a part of her heart shatter as she watched Grimhilt, her mother, look back and forth between the unicorn filly hanging limp in Mordred's grasp and the gasping bundle in hers for several seconds, expression turning to one of absolute agony as she slowly backed away and out of the room. "I'm sorry... I'm sorry... I'm sorry..."

"No... nooo... NO!"

With a jerk from her magic, Galaxy felt herself falling backward, the memory crumbling away. A moment of shrieking darkness all around, then she found herself and Bevin back on the air-yacht once more, both on their knees, a phantom smoke in their throats and tears in their eyes.

"YOU ABOMINATION!"

Galaxy barely cast a shield spell in time to block the silver sword lobbed straight at her head, breath catching as her eyes focused on the gleaming tip nearly skewering her. Before she could finish standing Bevin was there, neatly sidestepping the shield as she tried for another stab at Galaxy's head.

"Abomination! Freak! Useless!"

"Bevin, stop, please!" Galaxy backed away from the enraged unicorn, keeping her shield up to ward away the blinding-fast sword strikes. Spotting Brynjar and Bifrost start to fly forward to join the fight, she held the talons of her right front leg out to motion them to stay back, quickly yanking the limb back to her as Bevin tried to slice it off at the elbow. "Ack! I said stop it! I'm sorry, please—"

A bolt of magic from Bevin's horn carried enough power to send Galaxy skidding backward across the air-yacht's deck even despite the shield spell. Bevin advanced toward her, shooting a glare at Ashe to keep the dragon from trying to interfere as she went, before turning that glare at Galaxy. "All this time! All this time, I knew that gryphons had killed my father, my only family. But I never could have guessed! Never could have known! That he died because of YOU!"

Another bolt of magic sent Galaxy stumbling into the mast. She ducked beneath a swing of Bevin's sword, shoving the unicorn away with a shield spell. Now Galaxy felt her own anger rising for all they had seen, anger hot as the fires of memory. "He was my father too! I NEVER EVEN GOT TO KNOW HIM!"

All aside from the two combatants seemed to slow. "What!? Owain's voice had gone shrill as he stumbled down the ramp to the air-yacht's rear deck. "You two are—"

"No!" Bevin leaped forward, slamming her forehooves down at Galaxy's shield spell with enough force to make the hippogryph kneel. "Don't say it!" She spun and kicked out with both rear legs, Galaxy barely rolling to the side enough to avoid getting her head cracked open. "Don't even think it!" Spinning back around, Bevin lowered horn and sword and charged, forcing Galaxy to take flight. "I refuse it!"

Landing near the bow of the craft, Galaxy conjured two shield spells and twirled them like saws, rearing back and ready to charge. "Fine, then, you selfish—"

The air-yacht shuddered, tilted to the right with a terrible crack and crunch of breaking wood, all suddenly scrabbling for purchase on the deck. Moving to a hover, Galaxy saw the sudden fight had distracted them all too much, the air-yacht drifting from Owain's inattention at the controls until it began scraping across the jagged peak of a mountaintop. "Owain, bring us up, hurry! Before—"

Bevin cut her off with a whinny and charge, sword flashing. Pain flared in Galaxy's right leg as she barely flew out of the way, the silver sword leaving a shallow gash from hip to hoof. "Agh! B-Bevin, stop! Please, at least let us land first! We're going to attract—"

"RROOOOAAAAARRRRRGH!"

Galaxy dropped to the deck, shuddering to her bones, deafened to the point of physical pain. Half-blind, she felt Brynjar and Bifrost drop down near her, Owain whinnying, Ashe loosing a roar in return. Blinking, Galaxy looked up to the smoke-clouded skies, seeing darker shadows moving within them, even the smallest as large as the air-yacht. "Dragons..."

Another roar, closer, the wood of the air-yacht creaking from the sheer force. Struggling to stand fully, Galaxy saw Bevin stagger to the railing and point to something with her sword. "There! A plateau! Throw the dragon out so we can finish our real business, hippogryph!"

"For God's sake!" screamed Brynjar from beside Owain at the controls, "Bevin, this isn't the time for this!"

"You don't start with me!" screamed the soldier back, whirling to Brynjar, sword jabbing his way. "You're old enough! All this time, you—"

A horrible, violent heat sprang to life above them all. Screams rang out as a stream of fire shattered the air-yacht's sail in an instant. Splinters rained down like daggers. Galaxy recoiled in pain, her breath stolen as another stream of fire slashed across the middle of the floundering air-yacht. The blackened trench deepened, cracked, the craft snapping in two in understated suddenness.

A scream through the air, her own or someone else's. Galaxy fell, wreckage hitting from all sides, the world of blacks, greys, and burning reds tumbling around her. With one rotation, she saw a blur of brown and gold collide with something palomino and flail past a dividing peak. Another rotation, a foot from her, the gold light of the frozen teleport spell gifted to her seemingly so long ago, forgotten until now, forgotten though it could have solved so many a problem. Past it, farther away, Bifrost, eyes closed and body slack, red streaming from the back of her head.

Without pause for thought, Galaxy kicked out with a rear leg, sending the frozen spell smashing against the raven-gryphon just as the fall took them from her sight. An endless stretch of white shot through with black greeted her, a sudden crunch into something powdery, and then came darkness.

CHAPTER FOURTEEN

Cold. Galaxy felt cold. Cold, and aching, and pain. Time passed, thoughts slowly coalescing into something approaching consciousness, and then arose the peculiar sensation of being dragged by her tail across alternating patches of something bitingly cold and crunchy, and hot and pebbly. Next returned hearing, dueling voices, a steady THUMP THUMP THUMP of massive feet hitting the ground, and a sound like a bellows the size of a galleon's sails.

~Lisssten, bird wake. Make her work.~

The deep voice had barely finished growling its command before Galaxy felt whatever had been dragging her let go of her tail. Before she could summon the strength in her battered form to move, there came the terror-inducing sensation of a clawed hand wrapping clear around her middle, lifting her off her back and then roughly back down, so fast she barely got her legs under her in time to stand rather than slam belly-first into the rock. "There, hippogryph. Open eyes and start walking. Our Prime will see you."

Galaxy did as commanded, gaping at her surroundings. She stood in a broad, shallow valley within the mountains, their peaks hidden by storms loosing furious sheets of snow. Immediately in front of her towered a pair of dragons, each at least 20 feet long, not counting the tails sweeping the snow behind them. One, a male, bore scales a beautiful sapphire blue. The other, a female, scales a deep forest green. She stood bipedal, wings draped across her shoulders like a cape to shelter the limp pink form in her arms. "Ashe!"

The male huffed and spat, showing off his teeth. "Hippogryph feigns concern well, even learned dragon name. Insulting. The Prime will be displeased. Come now, before the cold proves deadly."

Galaxy could barely keep up with the dragon's speech, worn from the long day and traumatic fall, scattered thoughts still trying to make some sense of the unintended dive into hers and Bevin's shared past. Yet as the dragons turned away she managed to let out a "Wait!", flinching away as the pair turned to glare at her again. Having already opened her big, stupid beak, she swallowed and pressed on. "Please, tell me if she's okay. She was my friend. I was trying to bring her back! And the others! Did you see anyone—"

"Dragons," growled the female, scarlet eyes narrowing as she lowered her head level with Galaxy, "do not say please. Nor do we make friends with gryphon- or unicornkind. We command. And we command hippogryph now to follow us. Or else we will carry hippogryph in stomach until we reach the Prime and hope she comes back up in one piece!"

Galaxy fell in line after that, casting an anxious look about for any sign of anyone else, Brynjar or Owain, Bifrost, even Bevin. She saw nobody, nothing save some burning bits of wreckage from the destroyed air-yacht, already being covered over by the falling snow. A twinge of hurt passed reflexively through her at that sight, even as she turned away to focus on keeping up with the dragons. The air-yacht had seen them so far and through so much since Port Oil, been their home and escape. If any of them had fallen with it…

Ahead, the dragons hissed and snarled to each other in a dialect Galaxy couldn't follow, their tails lashing and the male's wings twitching. Past them Galaxy saw a cave yawning open in the mountainside, 80 feet tall and 40 wide. It was noticeable from the black rock it'd been carved from through a steady orange glow coming from within. illuminating nearby rocks and puddles of melted snow. As they drew closer a wave of heat hit her face-on. Volcanoes, she thought to herself, slowing for but a moment before a snap of the female's jaws had her speed back up. Volcanoes and dragons.

They entered the cave without fanfare, though as Galaxy looked back to the sound of stone on stone she saw the entranced covered by a great slab of runed rock, the dragon pushing it into place more scars than scales. But then the path began a downward turn and the dragon and entrance both were lost to Galaxy's sight.

Down, down, downward they trekked, the path crumbling, charred stone that cracked and pricked at Galaxy's hooves. The two dragons said little as they led her down, though Galaxy knew this didn't mean they were inattentive or uncaring of her presence, their dragging tails kept just to her left and right to block easy escape. Galaxy took this in stride, forcing herself to remember as the minutes dragged on that the dragons, for all their savagery, were still allies of gryphonkind against the Unicorn Empire, bound as such by the Prime Dragon Kur's forced oath of peace upon the spear Gungnir. And surely, if the Elk had learned of her and her exploits, the dragons here had as well?

But then, she had to remind herself, King Erentil had betrayed her to the Empire, and he too was supposedly ally and friend to Vogelstadt...

A sudden blast of heat from her right snapped Galaxy from her thoughts. The cave wall there had opened up, revealing a cavern large enough to hold a whole fleet of air-yachts. She saw smaller dragons of various colors and kinds moving among pools of magma 10 to 20 feet across, each pool ringed by amber-colored crystals. Within the magma, Galaxy could see black eggs resting, some shifting around from inner movements. It was difficult to tell from such distances, but she estimated each egg to be at least the size of her head.

"Nursery," spoke the male ahead of her. "One of hundreds throughout mountains. Work hard to replenish numbers. Magma rich and nourishing, perfect heat for growing eggs."

Galaxy nodded, turning forward again as the wall returned, cutting off sight of the cavern. Gradually, the path levelled off. They must have been closer to the base of the mountains than the peaks by that point, and though the roof was high for the dragon inhabitants, still she felt the weight of those mountains pressing down on her. Even more, the deeper in they went, the harder it would be for her to find the rest of her companions again. Thinking back on the attack on the air-yacht, she thought she could recall Brynjar reaching Owain while they were still falling, a good sign, the golden eagle-gryphon more than strong enough to carry the unicorn and fly. Bifrost, she hoped had been teleported away to safety when she hit the frozen spell into her. Bevin, however…

The dragons halted. Galaxy stopped as well, eeping as the female dropped Ashe to the cavern floor without warning. Her spirits lifted as she saw the pink dragon lift her head up and look around warily, awake but seeming still dazed from the crash and fall. ~Ashe!~

Ashe whipped her head around to Galaxy and let out a happy hiss, hurriedly hopping to her feet and scurrying over to the hippogryph. Galaxy laughed, giddy for at least one friend being alright, rearing back to hug Ashe's neck as the dragon leaned in to nuzzle the back of Galaxy's neck and upper back with her chin. A clearing throat made Galaxy look up to see the female dragon looking between them, scarlet eyes narrow once more. "You speak dragonic, hippogryph? Why keep silent?"

"It never came up," said Galaxy, dropping out of the embrace to stand her ground before the two dragons. Ashe sidling beside her bolstered her courage. "I heard you two speaking Common first, so I didn't see a need. Is this a problem?"

The male huffed in what might have been amusement, before shouldering the female to turn back ahead and starting forward again. "Maybe. Come."

"Not sure what I expected," mumbled Galaxy as she started after them, repeating herself in dragonic for Ashe's benefit as the pink dragon fell in beside her. Ashe loosed a huffing dragon laugh, but otherwise kept quiet.

Looking ahead, the walls grew more even, transitioning from a smoothed cavern to a true hall, grand in scale and polish. They began to pass other dragons through connecting halls, some as large or larger than the pair leading them on, others nearly as small as Galaxy. They looked upon her in open surprise and wonder, and to Galaxy's relief little wariness or disgust. Amusingly, or perhaps heartbreakingly, Ashe looked about them with an almost equal amount of open wonder, joy in every tremor of her body as she shouted a greeting to every dragon to passing by. Galaxy kept an eye on this, smiling despite her own repressed terror for her other friends and family. Whatever was lost, they had done it, the quest complete, the innocent dragon child returned safe to her home and people.

~Hail Claw, hail Cinder!~ shouted a stick-horned noodle of a dragon meeting them at a hallway junction and falling in with the small group. Galaxy barely kept from gaping at the serpentine dragon, brass-scaled and utterly wingless, coiling through the air above them without aid. ~You bring sssecret lovechild to public at lassst, I sssee? And ssstranger, too!~

~Sssilence, Ryu,~ hissed the female, Galaxy not certain if she was Claw or Cinder. ~Sssurvivorsss of downed ssship. Take to Prime Dragon. Ssspread word.~

The humor bled away from the dragon Ryu's features. He gave a nod before, quick as he'd come, he sped away down another hallway, heedless of other dragons having to duck and swerve out of his way.

Galaxy had little time to ponder this before they passed through an intricately carved doorway as large as the cave entrance that had started the long trek. Beyond it Galaxy stopped, the urge to gape finally satisfied. The cavern they stood in easily rivaled the open spaces of Hollereich she, Brynjar, and Owain had escaped Featheren Valley through, the distance stretching for miles ahead of them, the walls continuing on and on to their sides.

Yet, size was the only real similarity to that subterranean city, empty and swollen with shadows. Pools of magma dotted the area, while braziers large enough to house an air-yacht blazed with fire atop plateaus dug into the walls. Above, meanwhile, so high above that Galaxy was not certain she saw right at first, the cavern opened up to the outside world, the lightning of the Dragonbacks' eternal storms adding their own distant light onto the scene.

A lake dominated the center of what she now recognized with a measure of terror as a volcanic crater. The water sat unnaturally dark for all the countless light sources around it, smooth as a mirror yet reflecting nothing across its mile-wide surface.

At a gently growled word from the male dragon, Ashe motioned for Galaxy to rejoin them at the volcano lake's shore. Galaxy did so, craning her neck to meet the eyes of the greater female. ~What now?~

"Now," she answered, tail slapping the ground behind her, Galaxy recognizing the subtle beat after a moment as it was joined by the distant thump of wings, "we wait. And for all our sakes, speak Common. Your Dragonic is abysmal."

"Wait on—" Galaxy began, stopping as she noticed a dragon, purple-scaled and twin-headed, perch upon one of the plateaus lining the inner walls of the crater. And then another, silver-scaled and wingless, coiling near a magma pool. And then another, and a fourth, Galaxy swiftly losing track of the countless colors and shapes coming to line the crater. "Oh," she commented, little solace arising from Ashe's joyous countenance. "Wait on this."

***

On one side, Bevin felt uncomfortably hot, even burning. On the other, cold, freezing. She opened her eyes and found herself sprawled on her right side mere feet from a snow-swept cliff edge, her belly collecting wind-driven snow and her back dangerously near to the burning ruins of half an air-yacht. After a further moment she closed her eyes and flopped her head back down to the rock surface, further finding that she just didn't care.

All these years, some semblance of the rage that had driven her for so long spoke out, all these years of not knowing, not remembering, only to have it all brought crashing back on accident, a stupid hippogryph's weak will and weaker sense.

Half-sister, spoke the crumbling remnants of Bevin's sorrow for a family lost so long ago she had been unable to even remember their faces. A half-sister right under her nose, her father (Lancelot, Sir Lancelot, greatest of the Knights Le Fay, impossible) having child with Queen Grimhilt of all creatures. A gryphon!

A gryphon, her rage echoed. Sick. Sick, disgusting, abhorrent—

"I don't care," croaked Bevin, silencing both sides. She didn't care. She didn't. She couldn't deal with it and didn't want to. There, abandoned in the snow, she cursed the night Lord Mordred had taken her in. Cursed Princess Galaxy for ever saving her life that day in Port Oil.

"She's your sister. You always wanted one of those. The other soldiers never completed you."

Bevin lifted her head up, neck muscles straining in the cold, banged her head down against the stone. Rest, please. Let her die there in the cold.

Snorting, Owain chanced eyes with Brynjar for a moment. "Next you'll be telling me that stews and soups work best when containing water."

The first laugh broke from Galaxy's beak like a cross between a belch and a hiccup, and from there, it was impossible to stop. Brynjar slumped onto his belly beside her, one fist beating the ground with his full-bodied guffaws. Ashe, though probably unable to follow a lick of the conversation, let out a snarling sort of chuckle that made Galaxy laugh all the harder. It was a good laugh, the kind that worked its way up from the gut, teetering just on the right edge of breathless. Owain shook where he stood, adding his own whinnying laugh to the mix.

"They're her family. Your family. You always wanted one of those."

Bevin opened her eyes again, stared out into the darkness past the cliff edge. Out there in the dark of night and snowstorm, she could hear dragons roaring. Let her die, she thought. She was tired and needed rest. Let her shed her soldier's needs and soldier's will and just die.

"Noticed isn't the right word," interrupted Bevin from her place by the fire as Galaxy tried relating the day's events to the others in the group. "This sad sack of bruises and exhaustion tripped on a root, rolled down a hill, and fell literally beak-first into a bush of the berries. It was the funniest thing I've ever seen in my life."

"Not bad," said Brynjar once he'd finished slapping Owain's back to help dislodge the chunk of potato he had started choking on in the middle of a laughing fit. "But I've seen better. Somedays I don't know how Gal survived long enough to bother you unicorns."

"Ohhh no," said Galaxy from across the fire, heaving herself up into something approaching a respectable sitting position. "You are not bonding over tales of my most embarrassing moments. That's just sick."

"I concur," said Owain, immediately gaining Bevin's interest with his tone of mischief. "And besides, is it even

really possible to embarrass someone whose go-to insult is calling your face a freak?"

An unbidden laugh forced its way from Bevin's muzzle at the memory. She huffed, shaking her head, blinking to rid herself of the tears welling in her eyes. She didn't want this. Please, she didn't want—

SKREEEEEEEEEE!

Bevin jerked where she lay, head snapping up to the storm around her. That had been sharper than a dragon's roar, shriller, talons upon glass mixed with a banshee's wail. "A wyvern... a wyvern's shriek..."

Her body moved on its own, standing and shaking away the snow collected upon it. Bevin ripped a burning plank of wood from the wreckage to light her way through the storm, casting her gaze around her for a long minute before spying a distant, deeper darkness that might have been a cave entrance. Ignoring the sharp pain in her left foreleg's knee, she began marching toward the cave, the Soldier mentally preparing herself for whatever fight would lead her to her sister's side.

***

It was difficult to say how long it took for the volcano crater's walls to finish filling, the thousands and tens of thousands of dragons moving among themselves, their gossiping voices mixing to an overwhelming background roar. At some point the male dragon had left to join them at Galaxy's desperate urging to seek any word on the others that had been on the air-yacht with her, leaving only her, Ashe, and the green female, who Galaxy had learned was named Cinder, there beside the volcanic lake.

Galaxy just began to wonder if their time might be better spent searching for her companions or Ashe's family when the entire host fell silent with such a resounding quickness that Galaxy nearly took flight in alarm. Looking, she saw that Ashe too seemed unnerved, glancing about and trilling a question to Cinder that went unanswered, their guide's gaze on the placid lake.

There came a tremor, pebbles dancing among their feet. The water rippled. Galaxy's breath caught as the lake surface bulged a foot, five feet, ten feet. The surface tension broke, drenching those gathered at lake's edge. Galaxy backed up as she blinked the water from her eyes. Her jaw dropped as she watched yard after yard of black-scaled dragon rise up from the volcano lake's depths. More erupted from the water and she realized she'd only been seeing the neck of the hidden titan. Hands the size of air-yachts dug into the stone to further haul the dragon up, each finger tipped by a claw bigger than Galaxy's own body.

A ROAR, like a tornado touching down, resounded through the cavernous volcano crater as wings hundreds of feet broad spread from the dragon's back,

Galaxy's only warning before the wall of displaced air sent her, Ashe, and Cinder tumbling, cries of similar distress rising from the dragons along the walls. Galaxy just managed to get her talons into the stone after a few yards, further anchoring herself and Ashe to the ground with magic. Her heart hammered as she forced herself to look up, neck aching to reach the head looking down at them, reptilian smile showing off every one of those cedar-sized teeth, eyes burning sunfire-white. Even half-submerged still, the dragon before them towered well over a hundred feet tall. Only one dragon in all the world was so overbearingly large, so powerful just in presence alone.

"P-Prime Dragon…"

"Kur," spoke the titan before Galaxy, not aloud but in the heads and minds of all present. She suspected that if he even tried to actually speak with his mouth, even the barest whisper would shatter her eardrums. The thought-voice was high and regal, weighted with centuries of weariness. "I am Kur. Prime Dragon. You are stranger, hippogryph. Explain yourself now, who you are, how you came to be here, why you travel with a dragon. Tell all truth, or burn."

Galaxy had expected the dragons to know something of her, as the Elk had. Caught off-guard, she worked her beak for a moment as she stared around to the vast gathering. "I don't... So many of your host are so far away. My voice wouldn't reach—"

"They will hear as I hear," said Kur, a huff of breath from his distant nostrils like fire on Galaxy's back. "Now speak, or burn."

~Go on,~ whispered Ashe to Galaxy's left, prodding her with a wingtip. ~Tell asss Kur sssaysss, fassst. My family waitsss for me.~

Once again, a feeling of familiarity with the scene came to Galaxy, her talons tightening and heart aching for Brynjar and Owain, missing where they had stood beside her with King Erentil. Though she knew they could probably take care of themselves, and she still had Ashe there with her, something felt wrong in continuing without those who had been with her from the start. "I am... I am Princess Galaxy of Featheren Valley, daughter of the late Queen Grimhilt of Schwarz Angebot and... and Sir Lancelot of the Knights Le Fay..."

She didn't know what all the dragons around her knew, so Galaxy told all as clear as she understood it. She told of Queen Grimhilt's last stand in the Elderpine Forest, and Galaxy's being given to the loyal Sir Ida to raise. She told of Owain and the cockatrices in the Rotwald, of Urien's weakness and mad Lord Mordred's destruction of her home. She told of that terrifying flight through Hollereich, of the horrors of Spell Virus in Port Oil. She told of saving Princess Gwendolyn, of meeting

King Erentil, of the Waters of Life and the Elk King's betrayal. She told of the promise to return Ashe safely to her home and people, waylaid only briefly by the mission to rescue Bifrost. Galaxy told all, save the dive into her shared past with Bevin, the sister she had never guessed at. That moment, she knew, was a private matter.

By the time Galaxy finished her recounting, her throat felt dry and raw, body shaking from the exhaustion of standing. All around the dragon host murmured, too low and distant for her to make out, while Kur remained high and resolute. For an unknown period, Galaxy and Ashe stood there, waiting for something to happen, before another deep huff from the Prime Dragon signaled displeasure. "I remember receiving word of the raid, years ago. A whole mountain to the north, laid bare. Its elders killed, its eggs and young seized. What few members of the clan that had been away dashed themselves upon the rocks in anguish, or else led despairing attacks upon the Empire that saw them paralyzed by Quetzal's forced Oath of Pacifism and killed."

Galaxy's hopes fell at Kur's words. Beside her, Ashe physically faltered, becoming as small as Galaxy. ~Family... dead? All dead?~

Kur nodded. Ashe huffed, shook her head, gritted teeth dancing with flames as she stomped and clawed at the ground. ~No! No no no! NO!~

"I'm afraid yes, actually."

The volcanic crater, at first loud with the whispers and lashing tails of dragons, fell into crushing silence. Galaxy froze with a wing halfway out to Ashe, turning instead to that strange yet familiar voice. Lord Mordred strode toward them across the crater floor, dark robes and cloak blending against the backdrop, yellow eyes glowing and a mane of hair cascading down her back. Her face seemed fully healed from Bevin's attack, the lost right arm replaced by a metal construct that twitched with the hiss and crackle of lightning.

~YOU!~ Ashe snarled as she spun to face the Wolf-Lord, spurring a torrent of growls from the dragon horde all around. ~YOU!~ "YOU!" ~Tormentor! Killer! Enssslaver! I kill you!~

~Ashe, hold!~ Galaxy chivvied up beside the spitting and snarling dragon, eyes kept on the deadly lightning dancing across the Wolf-Lord's artificial hand as she shouldered her friend back. By instinct she raised a shield spell between them and her long foe, ready at any moment to cast another to match any attack.

Yet Lord Mordred, angling her approach, cleanly ignored both of them. Galaxy turned to keeping a shielded watch on her as the Wolf-Lord instead came to a stop a respectful number of yards from Kur. Keeping her head up and arms straight out to the sides, Mordred bowed low, the only break in the feigned solemnity her wagging tail. "My masterful Prime Dragon, most glorious and godly, reign your excited children in. Do they truly think that I, alone and vulnerable to the slightest fire breath, would waltz straight into the heart of dragon country, alone and unarmed, seeking war? That's something I would expect from the dumb, warmongering gryphons, not wise and splendid dragons."

Galaxy gagged on those honey-laced words, knowing full well the Wolf-Lord's true, vicious nature. Yet the sounds around them did slowly die down, Ashe alone remaining ready to attack Mordred at the slightest provocation. Above them all Kur rumbled, a single claw tapping the cavern floor once. "Speak, Mordred, last Wolf-Lord of Heraldale, traitor and kinslayer, thief and worshipper of war."

A chuckle, unamused, escaped Mordred. She stood back to her full height, glancing back at Galaxy once with a fang-filled smile before sweeping her gaze grandly over the gathered dragon horde. "I am many things, oh mighty Kur, but a kinslayer is not one of them. As for war, though, I suppose I do worship it, when it is just, when it is deserved. And that is why I stand before you all today." She turned back to Kur. "I have come, with

Empress Nova's blessing, to present to you and your people... an immediate ending of hostilities between dragonkind and the Unicorn Empire."

Silence. Galaxy stood, feeling as if the ground had been swept from her feet, one wrong move away from bursting out into laughter. Beside her Ashe had stilled, lower jaw slack and wings boneless. Even Kur high above seemed, for several seconds, at a complete loss for words. "After decades of bloodshed, you would surrender to us now? When the hippogryph brings word of your ultimate weapon of Harmony?"

Mordred recovered gamely enough in Galaxy's eyes, shooting only a quick look of surprise her way before snapping back to all charms and smiles. "My Prime Dragon, if you will allow me a moment... I am a Wolf-Lord. The last in these lands, as you said. I know what it means to be the victim of genocide. To be... helpless, against foes hungering for your destruction. That... is NOT what the Empire wants with the dragons. Always and ever you have been only an obstacle to be overcome, an unwitting shield between us and our true enemy, the enemy of both unicorns and dragons... Lady Quetzal and her gryphons."

Roars echoed throughout the cavernous crater from dragons all around, shocking Galaxy with their utter loathing. Looking around at the dragons bashing the stone with fists and tails, heads thrown back to loose flame to the sky, she hurried to stand equal with Mordred. "No, she lies! That is all she does or has ever done! The Empire wants only total control of Heraldale! We gryphons fight for freedom, Lady Quetzal's Floating Mountain a symbol of hope and peace—"

More roars from the surrounding dragons, jeers and cries of outrage mixed in now. Mordred chuckled, giving her a look of amusement that sent Galaxy's blood roiling before looking back up to Kur. "The hippogryph speaks with either blindness or cruel indifference, my Prime Dragon. But we both know the truth. Yes, the Unicorn Empire seeks to expand to all corners of Heraldale. But what does the Lady Quetzal do? Decades of her people suffering at the Empire's hooves, whole nations falling, and what does she do but hide behind your vaunted mountains, letting YOUR people bear the brunt of our attacks year after year! She does nothing to stop the war, nothing to bring about the peace she allegedly cherishes so! In that way, at least, even ignorant little Princess Galaxy here is her better."

"That's not... You, you're taking everything out of cont—"

"Well I say no more!" continued Mordred. A small but rising chorus of approving roars answered her. "The Empire is done fighting a pointless, aimless stalemate, wasting endless resources and lives! At the prompting of all Lords of the Empire, Empress Nova declares through me an end of all hostilities between our people! Quetzal's forced oath of peace upon you keeps dragonkind from ever striking in force against unicorn- or gryphonkind again, but it does not bind you here to fight Quetzal's defensive war for her! Leave, as I wish I could! Leave your ancient tormentors to destroy each other on their own! To the southeast, the Wolf-Lords make their living anew in a vast archipelago, mountainous and ancient. Join them."

Another round of roars, greater than the last. Insides bubbling with a hot, gritty rage, Galaxy struggled not to attack the grinning Wolf-Lord. Forcing herself to turn back to Kur, she rose in a hover to make herself more prominent. "My Prime Dragon, I implore you, don't listen to this monster beside me. She is a murderer and a liar, representing all the worst of the Avalon Empire. Whatever good she offers, there are 10 unseen hurts waiting behind it. The Empire wants to control the world! They weren't content with their own islands, or with Schwarz Angebot, or the Gryphonbough Forest. You must know that, even if they conquer all the rest of Heraldale, from the Zakarian Plains to Lady Quetzal's Floating Mountain itself, they won't be content! Sooner or later they will come for you and the Wolf-Lords, no matter how far you flee!"

"Don't be absurd," spoke Mordred from below Galaxy. "I am a Wolf-Lord, however long I've been abandoned here, however long I served in a unicorn's guise. How could I ever betray my own people like that?"

To that, Galaxy failed to keep in her hard, bitter laugh as she turned and hovered down to eye level with the Wolf-Lord, imagining pecking those yellow orbs from their sockets. "The same way you betrayed the Knights Le Fay, you rotten mongrel! The same way you betrayed friends and allies, betrayed my mother! You're a beast, serving only your own self-interest! Monster, scavenger, tormentor, fiend, born trait—"

"ENOUGH."

The single word from Kur dropped Galaxy to the ground, wings freezing to her back and ground shaking beneath her talons and hooves. Chest burning for breath beneath that unyielding pressure, she staggered, nearly fell, catching on Ashe's side as the dragon came to assist her. Before them both, Mordred loomed, seeming unaffected save the sudden disappearance of her smile. "Ah. A battle of reputation, then. I was waiting for that legendary temper of yours, hippogryph. So like your mother."

To Kur, Mordred raised his gaze, the bone-grey horn sprouting from the Wolf-Lord's head taking on a white glow Galaxy had never seen before. "But how else might she take after the late Queen Grimhilt? Grimhilt, who stood by and did nothing as the Empire's former Lord of War cleansed the north of dragons. Oh, the rivers, the lakes, the oceans of blood on her talons for just a few more years of peace. Do you expect the child to be any better?"

"Silence," said Galaxy, the words falling dead from her beak as she hovered there and stared at Mordred. Somewhere inside she knew she should have put more emotion into the demand, but something stopped her.

Mordred ignored her. "Because of course, we all know the stories. The legends. The nobility of the hippogryph. The unbridled goodness of them, the simple decency and dignity. Heroes all, acting only for the good of others. Oh, what lies we tell our children."

The barest twitch of Kur's spread wings quieted his host's renewed murmurs, barely noticeable past the strange cold invading Galaxy. The Prime Dragon had focused all his attention on Mordred now, claws tapping the cavern floor. "Reveal your truth, Wolf-Lord. This meeting grows long and my patience thin."

"But of course, my Prime Dragon." The white magic lifted from Mordred's horn, rising and spreading, forming what Galaxy could only call a mirror of magic, angled for her and Kur to see into at once, and through Kur, the rest of the dragons. "Only, remember. Memories, shown straight from the mind as so, can't be altered or edited in any fashion, for good... or ill."

An image appeared in the magic, the burst of forest-greens and earthy-browns and pure white of snow almost blinding after the continuous gloom and darkness of the volcanic crater. It took a moment for her to recognize the air-yacht sitting in the forest clearing, so long ago their time in the Elderpine Forest seemed. An ache of longing hit her at the sight of Brynjar, Owain, and Princess Gwendolyn atop the air-yacht, all three in deep conversation.

The sound of paws shuffling through the snow and underbrush echoed from the memory as Mordred's past self crept closer to the edge of the clearing. The voices of those on the air-yacht followed.

"And there are no other places you could take her? Gateway perhaps, or Wedjet?"

Brynjar lifted his wings in a shrug. "Owain and Gal say the Dragonbacks are only place in Heraldale dragons live. Best chance of finding any family left. Besides, as I keep telling Owain, taking lost, hurt dragon back home will be great for Gal's friendship with dragons."

Gwen frowned, visibly put off by the reasoning. "That seems a cold-hearted way to treat the situation."

"Pragmatic," called Owain from the controls. "The word you're looking for is pragmatic. Not that Galaxy cares."

"It doesn't matter if she cares or not," said Brynjar, returning most of his focus again to the supplies. "As far as anyone else should know, it's her kindness, plain and simple."

The memory faded, the magic retreating back into Mordred's horn. A tomb's silence followed, thick with the seething fury of the entire gathered dragon host. Galaxy stared at where the memory had played out, the words repeating in her head, heavy as a guillotine blade. Her brother couldn't have...

Ashe pulled away on unsteady legs, eyes filling with tears. ~Friend, you CAN'T—~ Her voice cracked, wings flaring to propel her away as Galaxy tried to follow. ~You jussst USSSE me?! My falssse friend!~

~No!~ Galaxy followed after the backing-away Ashe, trying to formulate a response that could fix all this, failing to tear her breaking thoughts from her own sense of betrayal at her brother's words. If he and Owain were only there with her, they could salvage this, could find a solution together like they always had. ~I didn't know! I promissse, friend, pleassse, I beg—~

The silence broke, roars and the crack of tails on stone ringing from. Pillars of fire breath scorched through the air to splatter between the pair. Galaxy reared back, a screaming as she backpedaled. Then Mordred was there, forcing Galaxy to continue her backward retreat with a whip of lightning flaring from her pointer and middle finger. Brighter than the flames outlining her black figure, the lightning hissed and spat through the air like a snake, cracking the stone at Galaxy's talons with a fury matched by the glare of

Mordred's yellow eyes. "Dragons do not plead and beg, wretched little mutt! They are proud and powerful, worthy of so much more glory than the SCRAPS your Prime Gryphon has forced upon them! So like your mother, begging others to be her shield, stealing my knight-brother from me, weak and cowardly—"

There was no rational thought to what came next, no reason or planning. Galaxy stood there, Mordred's claims washing over her. Galaxy rammed the Wolf-Lord, vision red behind the shield spell forming without command around her. She rammed and kept going. She slammed them both into the cavern wall, kept going, shattering stone and scattering dragons. She screamed, throat tearing, beak bloodening, every wingbeat driving them on, scars on back burning, shield spell between her and Wolf-Lord and stone spattered with blood and flesh.

Rock gave way to sky, dark and lightning-wracked. Galaxy dropped the shield, kept going, drove her horn into Mordred's chest—

—pain, an alarming crack as her horn skidded off a steel cuirass beneath Mordred's robe. Galaxy jerked back, talons reaching up to grip her throbbing head. "Augh!" Yet even so, through tears of pain she watched with satisfaction as Mordred fell away from her toward the mountains below them, the Wolf-Lord looking up at her with an expression of terror. But then the terror disappeared. The back of Mordred's robes bulged, tore, great black wings spreading to catch her just above the mountainside.

Galaxy gaped at the changeling powers of a Wolf-Lord on full display. A flap of wings and Mordred was there before her. Galaxy cast a shield, just managing to catch a metal backhand before it broke her beak. Mordred's flesh hand jabbed forward. Lightning broke Galaxy's shield, scorched her chest black as she was driven back. Mordred charged again. Galaxy batted her away with another shield spell, caught her on another angled to slash across her cuirass with the thin edge. She cast a third and Mordred raised her metal arm, a glow there in the palm—

The shield spell warped, scattered. Galaxy pulled back from a charge, watching wide-eyed as a rod grew from the palm of the metal arm, the same strange white. The rod grew, thinned, flattening at the end into a gleaming blade. "Lunar steel..."

"Lunar steel," Mordred agreed, catching the 7-feet-long spear by the middle once it had finished revealing itself and giving it a twirl. Her eyes remained on Galaxy the entire time, smoldering with a cold hate. "Your father had a spear much like this of the metal. And your mother, a pair of wing-blades. Incredible powers, if forged right..."

The spear flew at Galaxy fast as a crossbow bolt. Galaxy cast a shield spell, hurriedly flew upward out of the weapon's way as the shield once more warped and scattered at the spear's approach. Before she could dive down to attack the now-disarmed Mordred, the Wolf-Lord jerked her metal arm back. The spear reappeared in her grip with a crack of displaced air, stopping Galaxy in place with the bladed end pointed her way. "Incredible powers. It will be a joy avenging myself with them."

Now Mordred flew at Galaxy, forcing her backward, further into the sky and away from the mountains ranged below them. Snow and ash flurried past them, stinging the eyes and choking the breath. Lightning flashed and BOOMED all around, Mordred's and the storm's. Stabs and swipes of the spear came just as fast, its reach longer than Galaxy's horn, its metal stronger than her talons could break. Soon she struggled for breath and space, brain scattered, every thought and stratagem hindered by flashes of pain as Mordred began scoring blows. A shallow cut across her side. A barest stab into a thigh. A crack of the spear's flat end against her beak, scattering stars and blood before her eyes. All the while the Wolf-Lord spoke, words a spell of despair all their own.

"What was your plan here, hippogryph? What did you think would happen? That you'd make up for centuries of unwitting servitude with one act of basic decency? Show the world that you're one of the Good Ones? Fly into Vogelstadt a hero, praise heaped upon you? Lead their armies in a final, pitched battle against the Avalon Empire in a desperate bid to save the world!? Faith, useless faith in a Prime Gryphon who's sat back and done NOTHING to halt the Empire's atrocities! Desperately chasing after the memory of a woman who FAILED!"

"Quiet!" Galaxy stilled her wings and dropped like a rock for distance, flaring out again as Mordred kept the distance. "Don't you dare talk about my mother that way! You have no right—"

Lightning, straight for her head. Galaxy spun around it, sweeping up over Mordred, chased by the Wolf-Lord's words. "You can't silence the truth, hippogryph! She failed, her nation falling, the war continuing, achieving nothing but leaving a whole world's hopes on her own daughter! With her last breath, she doomed you to pain and failure!"

More lightning. Galaxy reflected it off a shield spell, a second shield spell angling to reflect the bolt back at Mordred. The Wolf-Lord caught it with a thrust of her spear, spinning to cast it down at the Dragonbacks below. She paused, muzzle splitting wide. "Oh, that, that's beautiful."

Against her better judgment, Galaxy looked. She immediately wished she hadn't. Far below, among the peaks of the Dragonback Mountains, a migration had begun. Dragons rose from the central volcano's crater, thousands of them, tens of thousands. Hundreds more rose from other caves scattered through the mountain range, summoned by a deep, melodious roar carried on the wind. The rivulets joined together eastward, a sweeping sea of red and green and bronze scales, more colors than Galaxy could count, led in the distance by the titanic form of Kur, Prime Dragon, known also as Snarl.

"They're... they're leaving. They're all leaving."

"Of course they are. Why would they stay?"

Galaxy said nothing, could say nothing, remained watching the exodus below them. The full magnitude of her failure hit her all at once, talons gripping her chest from a pain so much deeper than the still-smoldering scorches from Mordred's lightning. Brynjar was gone. Owain was gone. Bevin was gone. The dragons were leaving, her own ignorance of the hearts of her family robbing Vogelstadt of its greatest defense. Bifrost was gone, having never been told of the superweapon Galaxy and Bevin had discovered delving into Spell Virus's memories. So much. Gone. On her shoulders.

"I know, I know. It hurts to have such a bright, brilliant hope, only for the world around you to come up... short."

A low, painful sob tore through Galaxy's body. She felt like she was drowning, half-blinded, barely staying aloft.

"It's like I've always tried to tell you, hippogryph." Galaxy felt Mordred draw close, a hiss in the air. "The world's angry. Mean, so mean. No heroes, no saints. Your father learned this in a pool of his own blood, surrounded by gryphons. Your mother learned this drowning in her blood, dead by her true love's own people! Trust and faith in others besides yourself and your own kind will leave you with nothing! And you, hippogryph, have NOTHING!"

SCHLUNK.

"AAAUUGH!" Galaxy spasmed from a pain worse than any before. She looked down, uncomprehending, beheld Mordred's spear buried deep into the socket connecting her left front leg to its shoulder. Surrounding feathers turned a deeper red. The Wolf-Lord's smile gleamed in the storm.

Then, a blinding flash, a deafening KRAKA-BOOM of thunder, a moment's blazing pain, a following vacant numbness. Galaxy fell, saw Mordred above, something twitching and bleeding red grasped in her flesh hand.

The darkness rose from all sides. Closing her eyes, Galaxy gave into it.

Then, oblivion.

EPILOGUE

One hoof, then the next, then the next, then the next, that was the way, that was all she had to do, just keep moving her hooves, just keep moving.

The wind howled, stinging, ash choking. Bevin kept it behind her, shallow breaths all she could manage. All around, a barren, mountainous wasteland shrouded in a haze of ash, each hoofstep kicking up more. The snow was left long behind, hours or days or years behind. Her belly ached. Her parched mouth and throat begged for water's relief. Her legs trembled, gave out, precious minutes wasted finding the strength to stand back up and keep going. Upon Bevin's back, Galaxy rested with a mountain's weight, more dead than alive.

One more hoofstep, just one more. Bevin had found the hippogryph the same time she had found the last sign of water, floating at the center of a volcano lake, unmoving, barely breathing, her left side a horror show, death perhaps preferable. Wasted time, trying to wake her. Wasted time, mourning her. Wasted time, debating whether to mercy kill. Couldn't. Bevin had grown weak, soft, couldn't bring herself to do it. Wasted strength, deciding they should die together out there, lost in the mountains.

Another step. Another. She just needed to take another. Time grew meaningless. Bevin could not keep track of night or day. Yet however tired she grew, she could not stop to rest, a terror of waking to find Galaxy not breathing driving her on more fiercely than the wind ever could. And oh, how the wind blew, beating upon every part of her back that Galaxy's limp form did not shield, scouring the pelt of her legs and exposed neck with grit. Bevin could not imagine the state the hippogryph was in.

Then, without warning, almost without notice beneath the growing fatigue, the wind stopped. Bevin stumbled to a halt, swaying, nearly falling. She felt Galaxy start to slip off her back and summoned her meager dregs of remaining magic to keep the hippogryph steady. She looked around them for the first time in ages, feeling the ash and dirt caked to her body, and saw they had entered a deep valley or gulch of some sort, narrow where they stood before widening ahead. The ground sloped downward beneath her hooves. The air felt cold, a stifling chill, but clear and free once more.

Ahead, beyond the confines of the valley, Bevin could dimly make out figures in a pre-dawn gloom, just discern the beat of feathered wings. She tried to start walking again, only to find she had lain down, legs folded and numb beneath her. The world disappeared, returned, her eyes growing heavy. She tried to stand, but could not. She tried to call out to the distant figures, but nothing left her throat but a dry, heaving cough.

Galaxy slipped from her back, hitting the ground with an ugly sound and remaining there, Bevin unable to tell if the hippogryph's chest still moved. Tears welled up in her eyes and she closed them, head falling to the ground. Again, she heard the sound of beating wings, closer now, what might have been voices. She slept.

~~Galaxy and friends will return.~~

Harmony is coming.

Brian McNatt lives in humble and comfy Chickasha, Oklahoma, his life kept magical by seven rambunctious Corgis. He has self-published one stand-alone Western/Samurai/Fantasy novella, *Estranged*, as well as his Fantasy Heraldale Universe series, all available on Amazon. He has also had short works published in multiple magazines.

You can find him on Facebook and Twitter, where he is always happy to discuss the finer points of Fantasy and Sci-Fi with fellow fans.

Made in United States
Orlando, FL
08 April 2022